POISON IN THE TEA

FIONA'S STORY

A ROSEMARY MOUNTAIN MYSTERY
BOOK FOUR

NICOLE GARDNER

For the peacemakers.

For my ancestors, Irish and English alike.

And for my Nonnie, whose door was always open to her neighbors, who planted extra greens in her garden to share with the poor, and whose faith was the purest expression of fearless love that I've ever seen. I miss you every day.

READER NOTE

Half of this book takes place in Rosemary Mountain, but the other half tells the story of Fiona's life in Northern Ireland and the events that led to her move to the United States. Fiona is fictional, but what she experienced isn't. It's a story shared by a very real group of people during a period of history called the Troubles.

Because of this, there is more heaviness in this story than there was in the trilogy. It is a story of war—war is never pretty, and it felt disrespectful to overly sanitize the experiences of real people who suffered.

Thanks to the internet, we have a wealth of video footage, photographs, and accounts from people who lived through the Troubles. I've tried to honor their voices by telling an honest historical story, balanced with the cozy world of Rosemary Mountain that we all love.

For additional details regarding content, please see: https://nicolegardnerbooks.com/pittcg/

I hope this note doesn't discourage you from reading the book, as the things mentioned here are only part of the story. Beyond that, I believe it's important to read difficult stories and learn from them—that's an entire conversation in itself. Still, I felt a responsibility to address the fact that this novel contains some heavier elements than the others. I hope you love it anyway.

Also... It's still a Nicole Gardner book. I may break your heart, but I promise I'll put it back together before it's all said and done. I hope you'll trust me and come along for the ride.

1

HERBS AND OMENS

Fiona

Spring 1969
Glenarm, Northern Ireland

A soft breeze rustled my skirt as I gazed at the hawthorn tree in front of me. I pulled a pinch of dried tobacco from my pocket and placed it near the roots as an offering, quietly asking permission to harvest some of the fragrant blossoms for medicine. This was the way Mamó, my grandmother, had taught me, and the way that hers had taught her. You never took a plant without asking. They were as alive as we were, and it had to be their choice.

Nor would it do to take something that belonged to the *sídhe*, the wee folk, as hawthorn trees often did. Wild hawthorns that grew up on their own in the middle of a field were always suspect, as were ones marked by stone. I wouldn't dare approach a hawthorn that had a ring of rocks around the trunk. Those trees were where the faeries gathered after dark to make their music and dance. Mamó had warned me to never even walk within sight of one at night, as the faeries were known to abduct anyone they took a fancy to.

If you wronged the fae or offended them, they might use their magic to get revenge. My cousin, Huey, had once carelessly broken a branch from a hawthorn tree known to belong to the faeries. The next morning, a large branch was found right on the front window of his car, having smashed it to pieces. There wasn't a tree nearby for it to have fallen from. Those who didn't believe the old stories thought it must have been a prank by some lad who wanted to get back at him for something. But the rest of us knew the truth. It was because he'd offended the fae, breaking what was theirs without thought and not even trying to make amends. Of course they'd break something of his in return. Huey should have expected it.

The particular tree I stood in front of didn't have a ring of stone around the bottom, nor had it grown up mysteriously on its own. It had been planted by Mamó herself from a cutting she'd been gifted from another tree—one that *had* belonged to the *sídhe*, if you believed her. She claimed to have a good relationship with them, as they respected her for the care and honor she gave to the plants she worked with. They'd wanted her to have a hawthorn that belonged to her for her medicine making, so she said.

For years, we'd harvested the flowers and berries for teas and tinctures and had never had a problem with the fae over it. But I still always asked first. I asked every plant, but...I took extra care with this one, just in case a fae who didn't know of Mamó's arrangement ever decided to make the tree its home.

As I stood before the tree, my heart felt the plant singin' "yes" to me, and my senses felt no hint of warning. So I said a little blessing and began to clip flowers here and there. I was always careful not to take too much. Only what I needed, and never enough to hurt a plant. This, too, was teaching from Mamó. "Only a wee haircut," she'd say as she showed me how to do it.

Quiet footsteps came up behind me as I dropped the flowers into the leather bag I wore across my body. I smiled, knowing exactly who they belonged to. I could feel it every time he came near, like my heart recognized the beat of his quicker than my eyes could catch up.

"Fiona, my sweet." His low voice danced like music. Ian, my handsome husband, with his dark hair, sparkling green eyes, and strong hands that felt like magic on my skin. Two months married and I could still hardly believe how happy he made me.

He came up behind me and put those magic hands on my hips. I twisted around, wrapping my arms around his neck so I could kiss him. His lips tasted like the sea, from the saltwater that always sprayed him when he was out on his fishing boat. I closed my eyes, lingering in the kiss as he pulled me tight against him.

"What are ya doing here?" I asked when we finally broke apart, knowing my face was lit up with delight. He wasn't due home until tomorrow.

"I couldn't stand being away from ya any longer," he said, his lips brushing against my ear and sending shivers up my spine. "Come home with me."

"I can't. Not yet. I haven't gathered all I need. I promised to get the herbs drying before Mamó gets back," I murmured, hardly able to form a coherent sentence as his rough fingers traced up and down my spine and his lips found the bare skin at the crook of my neck.

"Then be with me here," he said, pulling back to cup my face in his hands. There was a twinkle in his eyes and a grin on his face that was half dare.

"Here?" I gasped.

"We're married. 'Tisn't wrong." He nuzzled my neck again, and I felt all my defenses fading.

"Well..." I looked around. There was no one else in sight, and wasn't it true that I rarely came across another soul out here? Mamó was in Belfast for the day, taking medicine to the families in one of the slums. She wouldn't be back for hours yet, and my sister, Annie, was still in school.

"Come, Fiona," Ian whispered, tucking the strands of hair that had come loose from my braid behind my ear. "My beautiful Celtic princess, with hair of pure gold and eyes that shine brighter than sapphires. Come lie with me underneath the trees, in the green, green grass, as the wind whispers through the fields and serenades us with a song. A song that honors the love between us, the love of a husband and wife, bound for all time like the sea and the shore." He threaded his fingers through mine, his green eyes holding my gaze.

My pulse raced and my skin tingled with anticipation. "Alright," I whispered back, giving him a shy smile. The man always knew just what to say to turn me into putty in his hands.

He grinned and lowered me to the ground, kissing me again as his hand slipped beneath my skirt, lightly skimming up my thigh. Any thoughts of propriety went straight out of my head as his calloused fingers explored freely. Within minutes, he had me completely undressed, bare beneath the clear spring sky. The wrongness of it gave me a thrill, even as everything in my soul told me that it wasn't wrong at all—that this was how it always should be. Me and him, making love against the background of green and blue, of earth and sea, of soft grass and the gentle mist that rolled down from the hills.

It was perfect.

Afterwards, we fell asleep in the grass, intertwined in each other's arms, kept warm from each other and from the rare sunshine that blessed the day. I felt more content than I'd felt in my whole life.

But after a time, I awoke, feeling a chill creep across my body. The clouds had come, darkening the sky. I pulled Ian's arms more tightly around me, then sat up, my heart pounding.

"What is it, my love?" he asked drowsily, trying to pull me back to him.

"Nothing," I said, praying for it to be true.

But it wasn't nothing. Though it had been faint—so faint as to second-guess myself—I'd heard a wailing cry in the distance.

The *bean sídhe*. The banshee.

An omen of death.

2

THE DREAM

Daphne

Rosemary Mountain, Tennessee
Present

My tight leather boots feel unsteady on the flagstone pavement in the dark alley. My hands grip the straps of the heavy bag slung over my shoulder, pulling it tighter to my body as if that can somehow keep me safe here in the heart of danger. No matter how many deep breaths I take, my heart pounds in fear, even as it throbs with grief. How can a heart keep beating after it's been shattered?

I should be dead.

Maybe I am. Maybe this is purgatory. Maybe that's why everything is so dark, so empty.

There are gunshots in the distance, but I barely notice them. You get used to things like that. It's strange how it happens, really. How something that was once so shocking can become so part of the tapestry of your life that you become numb to it.

I'm not used to this though—the darkness. It's dangerous enough to walk these streets during the daytime. At night?

It's a death wish.

A woman like me shouldn't be in these dark alleyways where the air feels heavy with rage and paranoia. Where it's impossible to tell friend from foe. Where even your friends might turn out to be your worst nightmare.

Except...I'm someone's worst nightmare now. So maybe this is exactly where I belong.

A door creaks open, and my heart nearly stops. The woman stares at me with malice on her face.

I wonder if she's as afraid of me as I am of her.

I give her a feeble smile, then divert my eyes, trying to show her I'm no threat. But I watch her in my peripheral vision. She closes the door slowly, and I let out a breath, my shoulders sagging in relief.

But my belly cramps with fear when I reach my destination—the door I must knock on in order to leave behind the danger surrounding me on all sides.

Out of the frying pan and into the fire.

I have no choice. Not really. There's only one shot at safety now.

No choice, I tell myself over and over as I stand before the door with a clenched fist held frozen in midair, refusing to obey my order to knock.

No choice, my mind says.

But my soul knows the truth.

There's always a choice, and the one I made will cost me everything.

My head hangs. A single tear falls down my cheek as I finally bring my fist to the heavy door. And then I know I'm not dead—yet—because my broken heart shatters all over again.

I jerked awake, sitting up in bed with a loud gasp. My heart thundered as my eyes darted around the room, taking in my surroundings.

No alleyway. No wooden door.

I was safe and warm in my own bed, with my husband, Emerson, sleeping beside me. The sight of his bare shoulders and strong arms began to ease my racing heart. He was here, and I was safe.

It was just a bad dream.

I took deep breaths, trying to fight off the darkness that lingered.

Emerson stirred at my side. "Is everything okay?" he mumbled, reaching for my hand.

"Everything's fine. I had a nightmare," I answered, interlacing my fingers in his.

But as I said the words, I realized I didn't really believe them. The dream had been so vivid that my body believed I was in danger. My heart pounded so hard I could feel it in my ears. The grief was so overwhelming that it threatened to swallow me whole. Even now, it held a grip on me that wouldn't fully let go. When I closed my eyes, the images returned, even with Emerson's hand reminding me of where I was.

A sinking feeling came over me. It had been a long time since I'd had a dream that felt this way. I'd been born with the second sight, a gift passed down from my mother, but it seemed to come and go, showing up only when danger was near. There had been no danger, no threats, for over a year now.

If this dream was the sight returning... The thought made me shudder.

Emerson pulled me to him. "You're okay," he assured me as he stroked his hand down my back. "I've got you."

I sank into his comfort, but I couldn't relax. Not with those images and feelings playing on repeat.

"I'm just going to check on the baby," I said, slipping out of his arms and sliding my legs over the edge of the bed. I grabbed the heavy robe I'd left flung over the chair in the corner and pulled it on over my fleece pajamas, seeking warmth and comfort.

The effort was futile. The house was chilly, but the cold that crept through my veins was from something else entirely.

"Want me to come with you?" He sat up, studying me with his brow furrowed like he knew I wasn't telling him everything.

"No." I waved him back, attempting a smile. "Go back to sleep. You have to work tomorrow. I'm sure I'll be fine after I check on Ellie. If I'm not ready to sleep after that, I'll make a cup of chamomile tea and curl up with a book."

"You're sure you're okay?" Doubt was evident in his voice.

"I'm sure," I said, taking a deep breath and forcing my body to relax so that he wouldn't worry.

"Alright. Love you." He gave me a sleepy smile.

My heart swam with love for him. Nothing in the dream had been about Emerson specifically, but after the soul-crushing grief I'd felt during it, I was so grateful he was here. Grateful that we'd found each other, that he was mine, and that we'd survived the darkness that had threatened to rip us apart. Grateful for every moment of this life we'd created together.

I leaned over the bed and placed a soft kiss on his lips. "Love you, too."

He cupped the back of my head and deepened the kiss. My blood turned warm, erasing the icy chill I'd been unable to shake. I almost climbed back into bed just to lose myself in his warmth, but my heart still hammered a warning that something wasn't right.

So I broke away.

Emerson grinned. "If your goal was to get me back to sleep, you shouldn't have kissed me like that."

"It was supposed to just be a peck. You're the one who turned it into more," I teased as I headed toward the door, clinging to the banter like it was a weapon that would chase away the dark. From the moment we'd met, Emerson had felt like safety—a light in the dark, an anchor in a raging sea, warmth on the coldest night.

But the feeling of safety and warmth disappeared the moment I padded out of our room with Thor, our German Shepherd, following behind. He stared up at me like he knew something was wrong, and unlike Emerson, it would take more than a kiss to reassure him otherwise. I shut the door behind the old dog's tail, then crossed the hallway to Ellie's room.

When I cracked the door to her nursery and saw her sleeping peacefully on her new toddler bed, I sighed in relief. Her chest rose and fell in the slow rhythm of deep sleep, as moonlight shone on her sweet face. Although she didn't look very sweet at the moment, I had to admit. Her red hair was a mess of tangled curls, half of which were plastered to her cheeks and her forehead by sweat, and she had chocolate smeared below her pouty bottom lip. My lips twisted as I wondered where she was hiding the candy she wasn't supposed to eat after we brushed her teeth at night—and who she'd sweet-talked into giving it to her, since I'd started hiding it all in a top cabinet.

The terrible twos had hit us like a whirlwind, turning my precious angel into a sassy toddler who I feared was more stubborn than I was.

It hit me that she was creeping up to the same age I'd been when my mother had died in this very house. I leaned my head against the doorframe, pondering. Maybe that was the fear and grief I'd been feeling—a reminder of what I'd lost, and fear of history repeating itself.

We're safe, I reminded myself. The monster who'd taken my mother was gone and would never touch Ellie's life.

It was just a bad dream.

I gently closed her door and made my way downstairs to the kitchen, knowing I couldn't sleep. I put on the teakettle, then pulled out an old mason jar and unscrewed the lid, breathing in the sweet floral scents of chamomile and lavender. Fiona, my next-door neighbor and honorary grandmother, had grown and harvested them herself, blending them into my favorite relaxation tea.

Fiona. The nightmare rushed back at the thought of her. I gripped the counter and closed my eyes, fighting off the wave of grief and fear that flooded me again.

The shattered heart wasn't mine. It was *hers.* The truth of it slammed into me with undeniable force.

It was her feet on the pavement.

Her fist refusing to knock on the door.

Her intense fear and overwhelming grief.

Something is wrong.

I forced myself to move, turning off the teakettle as I glanced at the clock. Only eight minutes until five. It was nearly time for her to get up anyway. With a feeling like this, I'd break down her door to check on her regardless of the time, but at least if I was overreacting, she wouldn't gripe too much about me disturbing her beauty sleep.

I traded my robe for the olive-green jacket that hung by my back door, then shoved my feet into the rubber boots I kept there.

"Come on," I said quietly, motioning for Thor. "Let's go for a walk. We need to check on Fiona."

He followed me out the door, staying right by my side as we headed toward the forest trail that cut from Fiona's house to mine. I carried a flashlight but barely needed it. The full moon was bright, and I knew this path by heart, having walked it nearly every day for the last couple of years. The trail wound through the hemlock, oak, and spruce trees that covered the mountain until it opened up at the back edge of Fiona's garden. Thor and I let ourselves in through her garden gate, my heart hammering at the sight of her dark house. Yes, it was early. But Fiona was always up by five, and she seemed to have a sixth sense about me coming. It was rare for me to walk up to a closed door; she was normally already waiting with a big grin on her face.

I glanced up at the sky. Her chimney was cold, without the smoke that normally rose from it each morning. I picked up my pace, jogging past the chicken coop and raised beds to Fiona's back porch.

"Wait here," I told Thor.

He sat, his eyes full of reproach, as if he thought I should allow him to go first. I scratched him on the head, then pulled my keys out of my pocket and unlocked the door to the house.

"Fiona?" I called softly as I slipped off my boots, leaving them on the screened porch with Thor. The house was cold and dark. I flicked on the kitchen light and frowned. There were dirty dishes in the sink and a half-eaten sandwich left on the wooden table

Fiona Flanagan would never willingly leave her kitchen in such a state.

Panicked, I went from room to room, calling her name louder.

No answer.

When I finally got to her bedroom, I flipped on the lights.

The bed was empty. The quilts and pillows remained in place as if she hadn't slept there at all.

Fiona was gone.

Back at home, I paced the floors with my hands on my stomach, sick with anxiety. We'd almost lost Fiona to a heart attack a couple of years back. This felt even worse somehow.

Emerson stopped me, pulling me into his arms. "We'll find her," he said, burying his face in my hair. "I promise."

I closed my eyes, sinking into the softness of the worn-out white T-shirt he'd thrown on. Everything about him was so familiar—the feel of his strong arms around me, the soft scent of sandalwood and cedar soap that clung to him, the reverberations in his chest as his deep voice comforted me. He was an anchor in the storm, the one I always held on to.

But Fiona was my anchor too. She was the person who had helped me understand the second sight, the person who'd told me about the mother I'd lost too young to even remember. She'd saved my life more than once—both literally and metaphorically. And now she was missing, and my world felt as shattered as her heart had in that dream.

"Her truck was still there," I said, the words muffled on his chest.

"I know." He stroked my back, offering comfort. "But this *is* Fiona we're talking about. She might have gone for a walk last night and decided to sleep outside somewhere on the mountain. You know how she is."

"I know exactly how she is," I said, pulling back so he could see the stubborn look on my face. "And she wouldn't have done that without cleaning up her dinner first. You know how tidy she keeps her home. Something *made* her leave."

He pulled me to the couch, keeping my hands in his. "I hate to say it, but this could be age-related. Have you noticed any signs of dementia creeping in? Any forgetfulness or wandering off on her own at all?"

"No." I glared at him. I couldn't believe he would even suggest such a thing. "She's as sharp as a tack and healthier than women half her age. You know that."

"I know," he admitted. "But sometimes it can come on suddenly. You have to admit it's a possibility. You have to prepare yourself, babe. She's not going to live forever."

Thankfully, his phone vibrated before I could answer. I was certain my reply wouldn't have been very nice.

"It's Greg," he said, his face flashing with relief. Sheriff Greg Morrison was his best friend—and now officially part of our family, having married my stepmom, Janet. Greg had been our first call, but it had gone to voicemail, and he'd texted saying he'd have to call us back.

I waited impatiently, nervously rubbing my thumbs together as Emerson started to explain the situation to him. His face grew serious when Greg cut him off, saying something I couldn't hear that made Emerson grow quiet for several minutes.

"I see," he said finally, his brow deeply furrowed. "But how— okay. I understand. We'll be right there."

He hung up the phone and gave me a look that was unreadable.

"Have they found Fiona? Is she okay?" My heart was in my throat, as a thousand fears played in my mind.

"She's... Dammit, Daphne, she's at the county jail. They brought her in for questioning last night." He ran his hand through his thick brown hair, then scrubbed a hand over his weary face.

My head jerked back. "Brought her in for questioning? And they kept her *all night*?" Oh, Greg was going to hear about this. "What on earth are they questioning her about?"

Emerson looked me in the eye, putting his hand over mine. "I'm not sure how to tell you this."

My heart felt like it was going to stop. "Just say it."

"Fiona has been accused of murder."

3
RARE OPPORTUNITIES

FIONA

Summer 1969

Glenarm

"Feels like rain," Mamó commented as we worked together to plant some herb seeds for an autumn harvest. She deftly moved down the rows, using her finger to poke precise holes into the dark soil, while I followed behind and dropped in our seeds one by one. I was a bit slower than her—always, but especially today, as I found myself daydreaming of my Ian and the seeds we were planting in our own life.

"Rain? In the north of Ireland?" I laughed, shaking my head as I winked at her. "Surely not."

"You know what they say," she said, tossing her long white braid behind her back.

"Course I do. If in the sky you see cliffs and towers, it won't be long before there is a shower." I repeated the words I'd heard no less than a thousand times before.

"Cliffs and towers so we have, but it's not just them today," she grumbled. "My wee knee is acting up, so it is, making me almost as slow as *you.*"

Ah. So she'd noticed how distracted I was. But I didn't want to talk about that, so I kept the focus on her. "And I suppose you haven't done a thing about it, have you now?" I chided her. "Always taking care of everyone else and not bothering to keep yourself in fighting shape, so."

She sighed, but the look she gave me let me know I was right. "There's always so much to be done, dear one. So many people are suffering. It's hard to take a moment for myself."

"Then let me take care of ya," I said, my heart swelling with love for the grandmother who'd raised me and my wee sister, taking us on after my young mother had passed. "I'll make you a poultice, so I will, and we'll see if we can't get your knee feeling right as rain."

"Perhaps you should aim for as right as sunshine today," she said, giving me a playful smile across the garden bed that stretched between us.

"Can't do it," I said with a laugh, smacking my gardening gloves onto my thighs. "Sunshine's the oddity here, so it is. So if you're wanting me to fix you up like normal, then we'll have to shoot for the rain."

"Fine, fine," she muttered, though there was a smile in her eyes. "Is the poultice becoming your favorite treatment, then? You've suggested it half a dozen times lately."

"No," I said, shaking my head. "I prefer teas myself, but you can't ignore how effective a well-made poultice can be, especially when it comes to achy joints."

"That you can't," she agreed. "Though a tea can be just as effective if you get the blend right and use it consistently."

"I don't yet have your skill at creating tea blends," I admitted. "Feels like I'm guessing. I don't know how you're able to just look at someone and know what they need, know just how to put it together so that it does what it needs to do and also tastes fine enough for them to want to drink it."

"It's a gift," she said, her face turning solemn. "One I don't take for granted."

"Aye, you're a right *bean feasa*, so you are," I said, only partly teasing. A *bean feasa* was a wise woman, a woman of knowing who had been entrusted with healing powers.

Her lips twitched. "Oh, go on with ya."

"I only hope I'm able to do the same someday," I said, meaning it. I'd seen how many people she'd been able to help.

It *was* a gift—a needed one. One that had helped put *me* back together after the accident that had claimed my wee mother. I'd been thirteen at the time, an age when I so desperately needed a mother's love. Though, I suppose, we all need that at every age. But at thirteen, the loss had threatened to swallow me whole. I couldn't let myself fall apart though—Da already had, drinking himself into oblivion every day to drown out his grief. Annie needed me to be strong.

Then Mamó had arrived, bag in hand, having left her home in County Cork to come care for us all. She had the same soft accent my mother had, a voice that sounded like music compared to the clipped Ulster tones of the people in our village. She sounded like home, like love, and her medicine had helped heal my hurting heart in more ways than one.

I wanted to be just like her someday.

"You'll have the gift too," she said softly. "I've seen it."

Her words sent a thrill down my spine, but the troubled look on her face tempered it.

"Every gift comes with a responsibility to use it well," she said, her sharp eyes honing in on mine in a way that made me feel as if she could see right through me. "You must remember that, child."

"Of course." But I couldn't understand her words, unless she meant that I needed to stay dedicated to the study, the practice, the way she did and put the needs of others above my own. That I needed to keep my head out of the clouds and plant the seeds in the soil instead of dreaming away the day.

Whatever troubled her vanished as her face brightened with a smile. "Your young man is here," she said, throwing me a wink.

I spun around, but no one was there. At least, not yet. Seconds later, Ian came around the back of the house and opened the garden gate, striding right toward us.

How does she do that? Another one of her gifts, I supposed. I could always sense him when he was close, but only him—she seemed to sense everyone who arrived before they even set foot on the property. I shot her a knowing smile, but she just winked again and went back to making rows in the soil.

I stood and brushed the dirt off my slacks as Ian reached me. He grabbed me around the waist and spun me around, then planted a kiss on my lips, right in front of Mamó.

"Hello, my love," he said, setting me down again with a grin. But he kept his arms around me, pulling me tightly to him. "Put on your prettiest dress, because we're going out to celebrate tonight!"

My heart leaped. "You got it?"

He nodded, his eyes lit up with pride. "I got it, so I did."

This time, I was the one grabbing his face for a kiss, not caring who was around to see.

"What's the craic?" Mamó asked, looking up at us with a cautious smile.

Ian turned to face her, slipping one arm around my shoulders. "You'll be happy to know we'll be getting out of your hair, so we will, moving into a place of our own. You're looking at the winner of a Dunwoody Scholarship. I'll be studying civil engineering at Queen's Belfast."

My chest was bursting with pride for him. His posture and tone told me how desperately he wanted her approval, as well as mine.

She gave him a kind smile."What a fine thing, Ian. I'm proud of ya, so I am."

But I could see the shadows in her eyes and wondered at them.

The tension in Ian's back eased. "Thank you, Mamó."

"So you'll be moving to Belfast, then?" she asked, those shadows growing darker.

"Aye, at the end of summer." He turned toward me, excited. "How soon can ya be ready? I want to take ya somewhere special for dinner and tell ya all about it."

"I just need to finish the planting. Then I'm going to make a poultice for Mamó's knee. Give me an hour."

"Oh, go on," Mamó said, waving us off. "The rain is coming. We'll do the rest of the planting tomorrow. It's a fine achievement indeed, and your young man wants to celebrate. Don't worry about me." Sure enough, the rain began to fall like mist before she finished her sentence.

"But your knee," I protested.

She shook her head, rising from the ground. "'Tis barely a twinge now, so it is. Nothing a cup of tea won't cure me of."

The raindrops became heavier, and all three of us grabbed the gardening supplies and made a run for the house. When we got everything carried inside, Ian gave me a quick peck, then headed to the outbuilding that had been converted to a wee cottage for us so he could change.

But I stayed with Mamó, concerned about the troubled look she still hadn't been able to shake.

"What is it?" I asked her. "Is your knee bothering ya more than you're willing to admit?"

"No, Fiona," she said quietly. "It's not my knee."

"What is it, then?"

She swallowed hard. "I suppose I'm just a wee mite overprotective is all. But I don't like to think of ya in Belfast."

I gave her a smile. "Is that what it is? It's only for a time, Mamó. Ian loves the village as much as I do. We'll come back as often as we can, maybe every weekend. And I'm sure we'll plant our roots here when he's finished with his schooling."

"Aye, I hope ya do." She sighed. "The city is a hard place, child. I fear the trials you and your young man might face there."

"Everyone has trials. Isn't that what you've always told me?"

"Aye," she muttered. "Perhaps I tell you too much. But there are many different trials. Some are worse than others." She gave me a serious look. "It's not the same in Belfast as it is here, child. It won't be easy for the two of yous there, being Catholics."

I patted her hand. "We've grown up being the minority our whole lives. We know the rules aren't fair. But things are changing."

"Aye, they are. But not the way you think, I'm afraid." She looked weary.

"Have a little faith," I said, giving her a smile.

"I fear for you, so I do. I can't help it."

I wrapped my arms around her and planted a kiss on her snowy white hair. "We'll be fine, so we will. It's only a hop and a skip away, now, isn't it? I'll be back to visit so much that you won't even know we've gone. Now, let me make ya that poultice before we leave. Ian's dinner can wait long enough for that. I see how you're still favoring that knee," I said, shaking my finger at her.

"You're a good child," she said, relenting. "Oh, I love you so, Fiona."

"Everything's going to be okay," I said brightly as I started making preparations for the cabbage leaf poultice I'd put on her knee. "It's a good start for us. A university degree, can you imagine?"

"Will you continue your own studies?" Her voice sounded weary.

"Of course," I said, reassuring her. I used a rolling pin to bruise the cabbage leaves and make them floppy enough to mold to her knee. "I'll have time to read the herbals you gave me, and I'm sure there's loads of people there who could use my help."

"You're right about that," she said, mulling it over. "I'll admit I was shocked when I went with the priest this last spring to take medicine to the families in the slums. There are so many who have so little, living in the worst conditions you can imagine."

"Exactly. I doubt I'll have a place to grow herbs, but I can take dried ones with me and make teas for people there. It will be good practice for me and a blessing to them as well."

"Aye, it would."

"See?" I turned to her, giving her a bright smile. "Ian wouldn't have gotten the Dunwoody Scholarship if this wasn't meant to be. It's a gift to us all."

"Maybe you're right," she said, patting my hand.

"Of course I'm right," I said, chiding her. "Don't go breaking your shin on a stool that isn't in your way."

She rolled her eyes but gave me a grin.

I gave her a nudge to pull her skirt up a bit, then began to wrap her knee with the cabbage leaves, letting my mind drift to Belfast.

It was exciting, so it was. I knew I'd never be one for the city long term, but living there while Ian attended Queen's felt like an adventure. It was something new that would expand my wee world and hopefully help me feel more like a married woman than a child.

I fixed the poultice, then stood, proud of my work.

"Feels better already," Mamó bragged. "You're a natural, so you are. Keep tending your studies and you'll be a *bean feasa* in your own right before you know it."

But I barely heard the words. Despite the confidence I'd shown while I was reassuring her, part of me suddenly felt terrified to leave her protection.

All I could hear in my head was the echoing cry of the banshee.

4
THE JAIL

Daphne

Rosemary Mountain

Present

I stared out of the passenger's window in shock as Emerson drove down Lonely Oak Road, the twisty mountain lane we lived at the very top of. Ellie jabbered in the back, in a pleasant mood despite being woken early and bundled up for a drive.

Even now, despite the difficult new stage we were navigating as she asserted her strong will and desire for independence, she really was the best. My eyes watered as I thought about how much of that I owed to Fiona. Despite never having had children herself, as a life-long midwife and herbalist, she was an expert at all things babies. She'd held my hand every step of the way and had an answer for every one of my parenting questions.

Fiona was a fierce, feisty woman. She was stubborn and funny, and she could drink me under the table. But she was also the most gentle soul I'd ever known. She was compassionate, patient, and full of wisdom.

How could anyone accuse *her* of murder? It was ridiculous.

Emerson reached for my hand as we pulled onto the highway at the bottom of the mountain. "Everything is going to be okay. We'll get it figured out."

"I cannot believe Greg arrested her," I said, fuming.

"I never said arrested. He brought her in for questioning. There's a difference."

I glared at him. "Legally, maybe, but it's still traumatic. And he kept her there *all night*? Why would he do that unless he actually thinks she might be guilty?" The thought of it made me furious. "He *knows* her."

Emerson chuckled. "Yeah, he does. Maybe that's the point."

"*Excuse me?*" Okay, I was officially mad at Emerson too.

He shot me a look. "I know you adore Fiona. I do too. But do you know *why* I adore her?"

"Because she's wonderful? Because she's loving, generous, and kind to everyone she meets? Because she wouldn't hurt a fly?"

He snorted and shook his head. "No, and now you're trying to paint a picture of her that isn't even true."

"Fiona *is* wonderful," I protested.

"Yes, she is," he agreed. "But she's not a saint, and she's certainly not a pacifist. Frankly, that's *why* I adore her. When your life was in danger, she came running with a loaded shotgun. We both know she wouldn't have hesitated to take that shot if she'd needed to."

He wasn't wrong.

"That doesn't make her a killer," I grumbled.

"We don't know what happened. Greg said she had been accused of murder. If she killed someone, it was probably either an accident or self-defense," he said, trying to soothe me. "In either case, I'm sure she'll be cleared and everything will be fine. But Greg has to follow procedure. You know that."

"I can still be mad about it."

Emerson squeezed my knee and gave me a grin. "Let's find out what he has to say before you get too mad."

I crossed my arms and refused to agree.

When we reached the building that housed the county jail and the sheriff's department, I asked Emerson if he would get Ellie out of her car seat. While he did, I stormed in and marched straight to Greg's office.

I barged in without knocking. "Where is she?" I demanded.

Greg stood behind his desk with his hands lifted in his standard calm-down gesture. "Take a breath, Daphne. Get yourself together."

"You *arrested Fiona*. Does Mom know?" I asked, crossing my arms and tapping my foot. I had no doubt she was going to be as pissed off at him as I was. Fiona had changed Mom's life too.

That's what Fiona did. She always seemed to recognize a broken heart, and she knew exactly what to say to help you figure things out, just like she knew exactly what herbal tea you needed to help heal and put yourself back together. She'd done it for me, for Emerson, for Mom, and for countless others.

She deserved a medal—not a jail cell.

"Whoa," Greg said, his tone sharpening. "She hasn't been arrested."

"Semantics." I waved him off. "You might as well have arrested her. She's been here *all night*."

His nostrils flared. "No, it's not semantics. And yes, she has been here all night—by her own choice. We told her she could leave hours ago, but she wouldn't. So I know you're upset, but you need to calm down and stop acting like I'm the enemy here. I think I've earned more than that."

I swallowed hard. He was right, but it felt so hard to see past the protective rage that had roared up in me. I knew exactly what Fiona would say about that—that it was the Irish in me, my heritage from my biological mother. Even though she'd died when I was too young to remember, according to Fiona, I was just like her. She'd given me more than the gift of the second sight. I'd inherited her red hair, her green eyes, her stubborn spirit, and her Irish temper.

A temper I was having a hard time controlling right now.

It hit me that I was acting exactly like Ellie on the days when parenting her made me want to pull my hair out. It seemed that I'd passed on more than my red hair and my green eyes to my daughter, and I couldn't exactly expect my two-year-old to control her temper if I wasn't able to control mine.

I took a long breath, squeezing my eyes shut and trying to block out the floodgate of emotions that had raged since the nightmare that had awoken me. I pictured myself in my little herb garden with the sun shining down on me and my hands in the soil. Grounding, Fiona called it—connecting to that calm earth energy even when you couldn't be there physically.

It helped. Just like everything else she had taught me.

"I'm sorry," I said, finally opening my eyes and giving him an apologetic look. "I'm just... I'm falling apart here. She's family, and she's protected me so many times. I just want to protect her too." Tears sprang to my eyes. With the anger fading, all I felt was grief and fear.

"I know," he said, giving me a nod that let me know the apology was accepted. His voice was gruff when he spoke again. "I'm not having an easy time with this one, either. She's become family to me too. Believe it or not, I don't want her here any more than you do."

I studied his face. There was exhaustion there, along with regret. I'd seen that look before, and seeing it again made the last of my anger die.

He wasn't the enemy. Greg was a good sheriff and a great man. He was the love of Mom's life, a fact that made me incredibly happy, even though I had loved my dad dearly. My dad had never stopped loving the mother I'd lost so young, and his marriage to Janet hadn't been fair to either of them. She was blissfully happy with Greg, and we'd created this awesome little family here in

Rosemary Mountain, despite a complete lack of biological relationships.

Fiona was part of that—maybe even the reason for it. I believed Greg when he said that he wanted her home as much as I did.

His words from before struck me. "What do you mean she refused to leave? I don't understand."

"Sit," he said, gesturing at the chair in front of his desk. "I'll explain everything to you."

I didn't move. "I need to see her."

"I know," he repeated gently. "I'll take you to her after I fill you in. I'm hoping that you can talk some sense into her and that you'll be able to take her home for me. But there are some things you need to know first."

I relented and took the chair in front of his desk just as Emerson and Ellie appeared in the doorway.

"Sorry," Emerson said, giving Greg a smirk. "I should have realized she was going to ambush you when she asked me to get Ellie. Then Sanderson caught us in the hallway. She didn't pull a Fiona and slap you, did she?"

Greg snorted. "No, but she wanted to."

I rolled my eyes. "Yeah, yeah. Can we get back to the situation at hand?"

Greg hesitated. "Maybe Ellie shouldn't hear this," he said, raising his eyebrows.

My shoulders sank. He was probably right, but I needed Emerson here by my side for whatever it was that was so terrible Greg couldn't say it in front of our daughter.

Like he could read my mind, Greg reached for the phone. "I'll have Jackson entertain her for a few minutes."

"Jackson's here?" I asked, sitting up straighter.

Greg nodded and made the call, smoothly catching Ellie in his free hand when she dove across the desk for him.

Jackson, Greg's righthand man, was practically a brother to me—more of that honorary family we'd all created on the mountain. He and his wife, Allison, were two of our closest friends. But Jackson was also the department's lead homicide detective, and there was only one reason for him to be here this early in the morning.

My stomach cramped with fear as I realized they were taking this very seriously. Arrested or not, there was a real homicide case—and Fiona was at the very center of it.

5

BELFAST BEGINNINGS

Fiona

Fall 1969

Belfast, Northern Ireland

"Fiona!" Ian's rich voice called out over the crowd as I stepped off the train in downtown Belfast.

My face broke into a wide smile when I spotted his wave. I ran to him, wrapping my arms around his neck as he swung me around.

"I missed you so," I said, feeling like my heart might explode. We'd only been separated a few days, just long enough for him to get us set up in an apartment here in the city, but it might as well have been a year.

"I missed you too," he said, his eyes full of warmth and love. He grabbed my bag and took my hand in his as he led me away from the crowd at the station.

"Have we a far walk?" I asked, though it didn't matter if we did— I was just happy to be back together again.

"About fifteen minutes." There was a bit of tension underneath his words.

"What is it?"

He shook his head, forcing a smile. "Nothing. I suppose I just feel a bit out of my element here, is all."

"Has it been a rough time?"

"Not rough. Just different than I was expecting, I guess. I don't think city life is for me." He chuckled, but the strain remained.

"Nor me," I agreed, feeling a bit shocked by the whole thing now that I had eyes for more than just Ian. It was overwhelming, so it was. The bustle of people, smoke from trains and cigarettes, constant noise... There was something to catch your attention coming from every direction, and I felt like my head wanted to spin right around trying to keep up.

If Ian hadn't kept tugging me forward, I might have gotten lost in all of it, but he kept striding ahead with a hurry in his step he'd never had in the village. I could feel the tension in his hand, could feel how anxious he was to get out of this area.

I didn't need to ask him why.

I clung to his hand, my eyes darting from side to side as I took it all in. There were police in dark helmets on every corner, it seemed, watching every move we made with suspicious eyes. I counted nearly a dozen Union Jack flags on the first block. It was shocking, so it was. Back in the village, I was only used to seeing the Union Jack flown on the Queen's birthday or when the Orange men would march in July. But here, it felt different, like the flags were on display to send a message—a message that felt like a warning somehow.

My mouth dropped open at a giant mural of King William III on a white horse. Then it dropped again when we passed by a wall of graffiti covered in Catholic slurs.

No, I didn't have to ask Ian why he wanted to walk so quickly out of this area. I knew.

We weren't welcome here.

I gripped his hand harder. He gave me a tight smile but said nothing. We simply kept walking.

The city changed with every step. It was subtle at first, a slow decline in the maintenance of the sidewalks and buildings, windows boarded up, and an increasing amount of graffiti. Then we turned a corner and I gasped at the sight of British soldiers ahead. They stood in front of concrete barriers and barbed wire, rifles in hand. I shrank back, my steps slowing.

"It's alright," Ian murmured, giving me a kind smile. "They're here as a neutral party, trying to keep everyone safe."

I swallowed hard and nodded, trusting him. He gently pulled me along.

One of the soldiers stepped forward, eyeing the bag in Ian's hand. "Where are you heading?" His voice was gruff but not unkind.

"Falls," Ian said, his voice steady. "I just picked my wife up from the train station."

The soldier looked us over carefully. "Is that right?" he asked, directing it toward me.

I nodded. "Yes, sir."

The look on his face was grim, but he waved us through.

Past the checkpoint, the changes I'd noticed before came so quickly it seemed I was in a different city—no, a different *country*—altogether. There were no Union Jacks here—only the tricolor flag of Ireland flew in this part of Belfast. The Virgin Mary kept watch over gardens and windows, and King William was nowhere to be found.

I felt Ian relax, and I tried to do the same, but something still didn't feel quite right. There were no police officers here, but I still felt under surveillance somehow. Every person we passed watched us with narrowed eyes.

We were outsiders, and something in my soul told me that was dangerous.

"That's our place," Ian said, pointing at the stark gray tower up ahead. He glanced at me. "I know it's not exactly what we imagined. I'd hoped to find us a place closer to the university. But we're lucky to have been offered this, so we are. It's supposed to be the best of modern living."

I stared at the gray building, thinking that it looked more like a prison than what I'd imagined when I daydreamed of a chic flat in the city. But I forced a smile onto my face. "Aye, modern living. And it's a place of our own, isn't it?"

He nodded and gave me a grateful look. "Come on. Not much farther. Almost home."

I held the smile on my face as we walked the last bit of the way, but behind it was a deep discomfort. I wasn't sure what I'd expected, but it wasn't this. The area felt like a war zone, and not just because of the soldiers we'd had to pass. The sidewalks were crumbling. The telephone booth on the corner looked like a bomb had gone off in it. Signs of poverty were everywhere.

I wasn't afraid of being poor—it's all I'd ever known. That was life for a Catholic in Northern Ireland. All the best jobs and housing went to the Protestants. But this... This was something different. It was a fiercer, harder kind of poverty than I'd ever seen up close. It was one thing to be poor when you had the wealth of a garden and the sea, of friends and neighbors who were willing to share your burdens. It was another thing altogether here in a sea of concrete, where every face looked hard and suspicious. I couldn't shake away the fear that was coursing through me.

When we got to the tower, Ian dropped my hand so we could climb the concrete stairs one by one.

"We're on the third floor," he told me over his shoulder as I followed behind.

"Well, that should give us a bit of exercise, anyway," I said, my cheeks hurting from the fake smile I wouldn't drop.

The stairwell led to a shared balcony that was busy with other people: children chasing a ball, women chatting over the laundry, old men talking in hushed tones. They watched me and Ian with the same guarded expressions I'd seen on everyone else. There wasn't a friendly face to be found among them.

I tried to make eye contact and smile, tried to form some kind of connection between us and these people who would be my new neighbors. But it changed nothing. The only thing that seemed to make a difference was when one of the men recognized Ian and gave him a nod, then whispered to the people around him something that made them relax.

Ian seemed oblivious to it all—or at least pretended to be—but nerves of his own flashed in his eyes when we reached our doorway. He stopped and turned, worry on his face.

"It isn't much," he said, his voice full of regret that nearly broke my heart in two. "There weren't many options, and I was limited by the grant."

"I'm sure it's wonderful," I said, putting a hand on his chest in reassurance. "We both knew the student life would be a poor one. The sacrifice will be worth it."

My words and my smile gave him what he needed, even if my heart wasn't entirely sure they were true. I felt a wave of homesickness that I knew wasn't quite fair. Ian was my home now—where he went, so would I. As long as we were together, that's all that really mattered.

I repeated the words in my head, even as my feet longed to take off running all the way back to the village, where I might be able to breathe again, surrounded by the trees and rocks that felt like home. Where the people always had a smile for me, unlike the wary eyes that watched me now.

Ian opened the door and set my bag inside, then surprised me by picking me up into his arms.

"What are you doing?" I said, laughing as I wrapped my arms around his neck. I caught two women watching us. They smiled at me for the first time, amused by his little display.

It eased some of the worry in my heart and made me glad he had done it.

"Carrying my bride across the threshold, you silly goose." He nuzzled his nose into my neck, then walked into our flat, gently set my feet on the cheap carpet, and closed the door behind us.

I sighed in relief, glad to be outside the view of all those watchful eyes. We were really here, in a home of our own, the first one that was all ours. I'd been perfectly content in the little cottage, but it felt good to be on our own two feet, paying our own way.

Our very own flat in Belfast. It was hard to believe. I slowly turned, taking it all in.

"I told you it's not much," Ian said, wincing.

And he was right—it wasn't. In fact, it was even smaller than our wee cottage back home. The kitchen was tiny, with only a few mismatched cupboards, a sink, and a small gas cooker. The wallpaper was peeling, and the place smelled of dampness. The furniture he'd gotten from the Catholic charity—a small table with two mismatched chairs, a green couch, and one side table with a lamp—had seen better days.

But it was all ours, and I knew that meant as much to him as it did to me.

I threw my arms around his neck again and kissed him. "It's perfect," I whispered, glad to see the relief in his eyes.

"Really?" The dimples in his cheeks made me want to kiss him again.

"It needs a good scrubbing, that's all. That and a few things to make it feel like home. Once I get my hands on it, it will be right cozy, so it will."

He grinned. "I'm sure you'll find a way to turn it into a fine palace. Come, let me show you the bedroom."

"Getting ideas already, are ya?" I wiggled my eyebrows at him.

"Maybe, but not the kind you're thinking." He slipped his hand over mine and tugged me toward the back, motioning toward a doorway on the left. "That's the bathroom."

I poked my head inside. It was tiny, but it had an actual bathtub, which was more than I had been expecting. A pleasant surprise indeed.

"And here's the bedroom," he said, opening the final door to reveal a decent-sized room with a double bed and a small sitting chair. "It's only one. I'd hoped we could swing a two-bedroom, but..."

"That will come in time," I said, patting his chest. "And we only need the one for now anyway."

"Yes, but it's right spacious, isn't it? Big enough so we could put a crib in here if we needed." His eyes were hopeful.

I nodded, smiling. "Yes, big enough for that. If we needed it."

His gaze held mine, but a knock on our front door interrupted us. He frowned. "Let me see who it is."

When he opened the door to a stranger, the tension within me rose again. The man's body language was tense, and his eyes shifted around the room like he was checking the place out.

"Hello," Ian greeted him. "What can we do for you?"

"I heard you've moved into the building?" The man's voice was gruff.

"We have," Ian confirmed. "Come say hello, Fiona." He gestured for me to join him.

Something about the man made me want to shrink and hide. I put my hands behind my back, grasping my palms together to hide my nervousness.

You're being silly, acting like a wee child instead of the married woman you are. Mamó would be ashamed of you, so she would, for not being hospitable to a new neighbor.

Somehow, I made my legs propel me forward. When I reached the doorway, I forced myself to outstretch my hand and gave the man a friendly smile when he clasped it.

"Hello," I said. "Do you live here too?"

"I do," he said, eyeing me. "What are your names?"

Ian put an arm around my shoulder. "Ian and Fiona Ó Flannagáin." He squeezed my arm in what felt like a warning.

The man relaxed. "Ó Flannagáin you say? I knew some Ó Flannagáins once. Good people." He grasped Ian's hand in a firm handshake. "I'm Fergus O'Reilly. Welcome to the building."

"Thank you," Ian said, pumping his hand. "We're glad to be here."

"We all look out for each other here," Fergus said. "I'll let the others know I've met ya, that you're alright. If ya need anything, let us know. And if ya see any trouble, do the same."

There was something underneath his words that felt like a warning.

"I will," Ian promised.

Fergus nodded and turned on his heels, leaving.

When the door closed behind him, I gave Ian a perplexed look. "What was—"

He put his finger to his mouth, warning me not to say anything.

6

THE CASE

DAPHNE

Rosemary Mountain

Present

When he came into the room, Jackson gave me an apologetic smile before turning his attention to Ellie. Her eyes lit up, and she started cooing his name and clapping her hands the moment she saw him. She adored her Uncle Jackson.

Greg stood from behind the desk with Ellie in his arms. When Jackson walked over and stuck his hands out, she dove for him and planted a sloppy wet kiss on his cheek.

"Hey, girl," he said, grinning. "I missed you too. Want to see if the vending machine has anything good today?"

Ellie's face brightened even more. "Chocolate?"

"Sure, we can get some chocolate. If it's okay with your mom, that is." He shot me a guilty look, like he realized he should have asked first.

"It's fine," I said, waving him off. It seemed silly to worry about something like her sugar-to-vegetable ratio at a time like this. I gave him a grateful smile. "Thanks for entertaining her for a bit."

"No problem." He put a reassuring hand on my shoulder. "We'll get this figured out, okay?"

But the cautious look in his eyes didn't reassure me at all.

After Jackson took Ellie out, Greg lost the smile he'd maintained while his granddaughter was in the room.

"How bad is it?" Emerson asked.

"Pretty bad." Greg placed his hands flat on the desk in front of him like he was bracing himself. "I'm going to speak openly, trusting that you both know whatever is said in this office stays here." He gave me a sharp look.

"Agreed," I said, nodding.

"Alright then." He took a deep breath. "One of Fiona's clients died two nights ago. A Ms. Alva Jean."

"I know her," I said, taken aback. "She wasn't just a client. They're good friends—have been for years. Alva is a master gardener, and they love visiting with each other. Or...loved," I said, realizing those days would be over.

Fiona had to be heartbroken. Alva had been such a good friend to her. Sure, they squabbled over gardening techniques, and there was a friendly rivalry between them every year at the state fair. But I knew that Fiona genuinely liked the woman. *I* genuinely liked Alva. She was a vibrant, wonderful person.

I shook my head, saddened by the news. "I can't believe it. What happened?"

Greg's face was grim. "We don't have toxicology back yet, but witness statements and the manner of death suggest that she was poisoned."

"Poisoned?" My head jerked back. I'd been so surprised by the news about Alva that, for a moment, I'd actually forgotten that Fiona had been accused of murder. "And they think *Fiona* did it?"

"Alva's nephew has suggested it," Greg said carefully. "She died after drinking a cup of the herbal tea blend Fiona delivered to her that morning. When he got there that night, her body was on the floor in front of her sitting chair. The teacup was on the floor beside her."

"Okay, but why are you jumping to *poison*?" I asked, confused. "Alva was almost Fiona's age. I know she was in fairly good shape, but she still could have had a stroke or a heart attack. Fiona's incredibly active and she had one."

Greg shifted like he was uncomfortable. "She could have had something like that, yes. But we don't think so."

I stared at him. There was something he wasn't telling us.

Emerson clearly thought so too. "Do you mind telling us *why* you're jumping straight to murder?"

Greg sighed and rubbed the back of his neck. "Look, medicine isn't my field, and I hate to jump to conclusions before we have an autopsy report. But I've seen a lot of deaths from natural causes and none of them looked like this. What happened was violent. There were signs of a struggle."

"A struggle?" I felt even more confused.

He nodded. "Two of her teeth were broken and her shoulder was dislocated," he explained. "She'd vomited all over herself. Her tongue was nearly bit in half, and the side table beside her chair had been kicked over."

I raised my hands. "Okay, that sounds like homicide, alright, but not poisoning. I'm confused. Do you think someone sedated her, then beat her to death?"

But Emerson let out a breath and sank back, defeated. "No," he said, shaking his head. "They think she was having seizures."

Greg nodded. "*Violent* seizures."

I still wasn't getting it. "Okay, but that brings us back to death by natural causes. Seizures would suggest an underlying medical problem, right? Fiona gave Alva herbal tea. I don't think herbal tea typically causes seizures."

"Some can," Emerson said, rubbing his chin as his mind whirred. "I read an article recently about a man who developed grand mal seizures after taking camphor. Ginkgo biloba is frequently taken as a supplement, even though it has been shown to increase seizure activity in rats. Do we know what Fiona was treating Alva for? And do we know if she was taking additional supplements that Fiona wasn't aware of? Maybe it was an accidental overdose of herbs that can trigger seizure activity in someone who was already prone to them."

An accidental overdose. Of course. It had to be. If there was some reason they were sure Fiona's tea had contributed to Alva's death, then it had to have been an accident.

Fiona had dedicated her entire life to herbal medicine and midwifery. She'd been trained in Ireland by her grandmother, but she stayed up to date on all the current research. I'd seen her notes and had watched her prepare teas and tinctures for clients. She was careful and cautious, and she measured everything. She wrote out strict instructions and took the time to show her clients exactly how to prepare and measure their tea.

Alva had to have been taking something else Fiona didn't know about. There was no other explanation.

"That was my first thought," Greg confirmed, nodding. "And that's what I told the nephew who alerted us to Fiona's potential involvement. Even he agreed that made more sense than a deliberate poisoning."

I relaxed—slightly. "So he brought her to your attention, but he's not convinced she intentionally murdered Alva."

Greg shook his head. "No. He's not convinced it was her."

But his tone wasn't reassuring.

"I'm surprised he assumed it was Fiona's tea in the first place," Emerson said, shaking his head. "Maybe Alva deliberately overdosed on pills and washed them down with a cup of tea. Or maybe it was something else altogether. That's a big accusation to make without any evidence."

Greg sighed. "You're one hundred percent right. For what it's worth, I think he panicked. He walked in on a disturbing scene, the teacup was beside her body, the jar of dried tea was on the kitchen counter, and he jumped to conclusions."

"So if we aren't even sure this is a murder, then why was Fiona brought in for questioning?" I asked, feeling more confused by the minute.

But Greg ignored my question.

"There's no motive that I can see," he said, throwing his hands up. "Fiona and Alva were friends, and Fiona's been successfully treating her for years. There's no indication that they'd had a falling out. Even if they had, Fiona's not the kind of person to kill someone over something petty. She'd pull the trigger to protect her family, but I can't see her committing premeditated murder to settle a score."

"Sounds like you need to look at the nephew," I pointed out. "He may be framing Fiona."

Greg smirked. "Tell me something I don't know. But the timeline backs him up. Fiona, by her own admission, delivered tea at nine o'clock that morning and spent an hour visiting with Alva. The nephew, Erick, works twelve-hour shifts at the hospital. He clocked in at seven, two hours before Fiona delivered the tea, and didn't get off work until that evening. When he swung by Alva's house on his way home, she was already dead. The medical examiner puts the time of death between noon and two."

"Still, there are a million different things that could have killed her," Emerson said. "It wasn't necessarily Fiona's tea."

"I agree with you," Greg said. "We'll have to wait and see what toxicology says, but I'll tell you both, I'm hoping there's another explanation that doesn't involve Fiona at all. Because if toxicology says Alva was poisoned, well, Fiona's going to be in some serious trouble."

"Even if it was a mistake or some kind of accident?" I asked, swallowing hard. "I mean, what if it wasn't Fiona's fault at all? What if Alva didn't follow directions and took too much on her own or, like Emerson said, took supplements with it that she hadn't disclosed to Fiona?"

Greg eyed me, drumming his fingers on the table. "Best-case scenario, if Fiona isn't at fault at all—meaning the tea was a safe herbal tea and she gave appropriate, clear directions that her client disregarded—she might walk away with a slap on the wrist. But the family could file a wrongful death lawsuit. They could accuse her of practicing medicine without a license. And if she can't prove she gave appropriate, clear directions, or if it turns out she put the wrong herbs in the tea, we'll be looking at criminally negligent homicide or even reckless homicide."

My stomach sank. "For an accident? After everything Fiona's done to help people?"

Greg glanced at Emerson before settling his gaze on me. "Daphne, there was a time when you were thinking about using your, um, *gifts* in an investigative capacity. I know you decided against that after Ellie came along. I respect that. But this is Fiona, and I need your help."

Emerson leaned forward, half blocking my body with his own. "Wait a second. What are you saying?"

Greg glanced at him again, but there was no apology in his eyes. He turned back to me. "Daphne, I'd like to bring you on as a consultant."

I sat back, shocked. "Wait. You're asking me to investigate? *Officially?*"

He nodded. "Officially. You'll be a paid consultant with access to the crime scene and the case files. You'll report to me and Jackson and assist us however we need on the case—but you absolutely will *not* do anything behind our backs. Understood?"

I rolled my eyes. "So this is more about *containing* me than it is about getting my help?"

He shook his head. "Not entirely. We both know you're going to investigate regardless of whether or not I make it official. Making you legit gives me the added benefit of knowing what you're up to and being able to put some boundaries on it. But beyond that, I genuinely want your help with this one. "

"Isn't having Daphne on Fiona's case a pretty significant conflict of interest?" Emerson asked, his eyebrows raised.

"It is," Greg admitted. "I'm crossing some major lines here, and we're going to have to tread *very* carefully in case this ends up in court. *I* probably shouldn't even be on this case. Neither should Jackson, to be honest. All three of us are biased as hell when it comes to Fiona, and the most ethical thing to do would be to turn this over to state."

I studied him. "Then why aren't you?"

He leaned back, settling heavily into his chair. "Because my wife and my daughter-in-law will never forgive me if I don't do everything within my power to keep Fiona Flanagan out of jail. And if I turn it over to state, that's exactly where Fiona's going."

"You don't know that," Emerson interjected.

"Oh, yes, I do," Greg said, staring him down.

"Why?" I asked, feeling almost dizzy with foreboding. I could feel the thread of what had gone unsaid weaving through the room. Whatever it was, it was the reason Greg was desperate, the reason he was crossing lines.

It was also the reason I would agree to be a consultant and do whatever he wanted me to do even though I'd promised myself I'd never investigate again.

Greg took a deep breath. "Because Fiona confessed."

7
WE'RE IRISH, OF COURSE

FIONA

Fall 1969

Belfast

Ian motioned for me to follow him to our bedroom. Only there did he finally speak, and he kept his voice lowered when he did.

"Sorry," he said, sitting down on the bed and scrubbing his face wearily. "The walls are paper thin, and I didn't want him hearing you question me about the name."

I put my hands on my hips. "What on earth is going on here?"

I wanted answers about all of it—the soldiers, the stark difference between our neighborhood and the other part of Belfast, the suspicious gazes of the people here, and the way Ian had presented us to Fergus. My head was swimming.

There'd been some segregation in the village, aye, but nothing like this. I felt like I was in a foreign land, and I didn't know how to make sense of it. I was overwhelmed and scared, and I just wanted to go home.

It wasn't fair, but I also felt a bit of resentment toward Ian for bringing us here. It shamed me, so it did. I should have been nothing but proud of my husband for winning a scholarship and creating such an opportunity for us. But here, in this harsh world of concrete and barbed wire, it didn't seem quite worth it. I'd have rather been poor in our village by the sea than have a grand home in this angry city.

My heart softened at the look on Ian's face. His shoulders slumped, and he looked so tired that I couldn't find it in me to be angry anymore. I sat down beside him and rubbed his shoulders.

"Is it as bad as all that?" I murmured, leaning my body against his for comfort.

He nodded, slipping his hand onto my knee and rubbing it like you'd rub a penny for good luck. "They warned me that Belfast is different than what we're used to," he said carefully.

"Aye," I said, resting my head on his shoulder.

"Ya know, in the village, the old men gripe about the Prods in power. Jobs are scarce, and we Catholics always get the last of the lot. But when it comes down to it, nobody cares that much where their neighbor goes to church. We're all poor people from the bog, trying to make the best of it. But it's not like that here. Here, it matters. It's segregated, like. More than churches and schools, I mean."

"I saw that on the walk over." My mind flashed to the way the flags had changed colors. Even without the checkpoint, it had been clear there were two very different Belfasts—one where we belonged and one where we didn't.

He squeezed my knee. "Tensions are high right now. The people who live here have had a rough time of it, so they have. They're cautious about outsiders."

"That was obvious enough," I retorted.

"They have good reason to be," he said, a twinge of reproach in his voice. "You saw the news about the riots here in August."

"Aye." I'd seen the news—and tried to forget it, especially when it had made Mamó so worried that she'd actually suggested Ian give up his opportunity, telling us it was too dangerous to go to Belfast.

"But that's over now," I said, unsure whether I was trying to reassure him or myself.

"So it is," he agreed. "And I hope we see nothing like that again. But you have to understand what these people went through. It was so much worse than what we'd heard back in the village, ya know. Catholics were told they could only live in certain neighborhoods. Hundreds of homes were burned to the ground just to force them out. People were shot, Fiona, and not just by rioters, but by the RUC."

My jaw dropped again. It was no secret that the Royal Ulster Constabulary, Northern Ireland's police, only enforced laws *against* Catholics and never in defense of us. But surely I'd misunderstood what he was saying. "The RUC was shooting innocent people?"

He nodded. "Aye. They fired a machine gun straight into apartment buildings. A young Catholic boy was killed in his own bed."

I covered my mouth with my hand. "That's horrible."

Sorrow painted his features. He squeezed my knee again. "That's why the British troops are here. Trying to stabilize things, keep the peace. A neutral party, like. We can't trust the RUC. They're happy to shoot Catholics for no reason."

I shuddered. "There were so many of them at the train station. They stared at us in a way that made chills run down my spine."

He nodded, grim. "I haven't had any trouble personally, but the evidence of it is all around, and I've heard plenty of stories in my few days here. It's all anyone's talking about at the pubs."

I bit my lip. "Do you think it's a bad idea for us to be here? Mamó told me she was worried. She warned me that life here would be harder for us. I think maybe we underestimated how much."

His shoulders slumped again. I could see how torn he felt between wanting to earn his degree to build a better life for us and wanting out of here as much as I did. I felt so guilty about how badly I hoped he would tell me Mamó was right and that we should give up the whole idea.

But he didn't.

He straightened and gave me a reassuring smile. "Now that the soldiers are taking over, we should be safe. Falls Road is a Catholic neighborhood. The people here take care of each other. They'll watch over you while I'm at school, and you'll have no trouble. That's one benefit of being here instead of in a flat down by Queen's, where you don't know who your neighbors are or how strongly they feel about things."

My heart sank. I knew that Ian felt reassured about me being here alone in a Catholic neighborhood, but when I thought of Fergus's face, I felt unnerved. There was a hardness to him that I'd only seen in some of the oldest men in our village, men who'd fought in the war.

I knew some of the things they'd done. They were heroes to those of us who wanted a free and united Ireland, sure, but I'd always felt a little scared of them.

"Why did you tell Fergus our name was Ó Flannagáin?" I asked. Ó Flannagáin was the older, Irish spelling of our last name, but Ian's family had used the Anglicized "Flanagan" as long as I'd known them.

"To let them know we're Catholic," he explained.

I shot him a skeptical look. "And Flanagan wasn't good enough for that? Every Flanagan I've ever known has been a Catholic."

A guilty expression crossed his face. "Yes, but using the old spelling lets them know we're also Irish."

"Well, of course we're Irish," I said, laughing.

"Exactly," he said, a wry smile painting his features with more tension than humor. "We're Irish. We don't fly the Union Jack."

I swallowed hard, understanding him. "I see. So when you say you were letting them know we're Irish, what you really mean is—"

"I'm letting them know we're Republicans," he said, squeezing my knee again. "Did you not notice the street signs as we were walking, once we got past the checkpoint? How they'd painted over the

English names and gone back to the Irish ones? How proudly they fly the tricolor flag?"

I sighed heavily, letting it all sink in. He was right, of course. The difference between the two Belfasts went far deeper than religion. It wasn't just Prods versus Catholics. It was Unionists who supported British rule versus Republicans who wanted our northern counties to be free and united with the rest of Ireland.

Ian aligning us with the nationalists made me uneasy, though I couldn't exactly tell why. Nearly all the Catholics in our village were Republicans, and I agreed with their desire for freedom. Supporting the crown was unthinkable when the Brits treated Catholics like second-class citizens in our own land, refusing to give us a voice.

But Mamó had always discouraged that kind of us-versus-them thinking, saying it never led anywhere good. Besides, the laws might have been unfair, but everyone in the village was poor, not just Catholics. We all ate from the same sea and grew our food on the same land. We suffered together and celebrated together, even if we went to different churches. I'd never *felt* like a second-class citizen, even if the government considered me one, and I'd had just as many Protestant friends as Catholic ones.

But things were different in Belfast, I reminded myself. Even Mamó had said so.

"I understand now," I said, though part of me knew I didn't really. "They need to know we're on their side, so you were letting them know without coming out and saying it, so."

"Exactly." He let out a relieved sigh. "You know, when I got here and saw what was happening, I almost told you not to come. I understand if you want to go back home while I get my degree, but I think things are going to be okay."

I took the hope that sprang up at his statement and squashed it, locking it down tight so that I couldn't feel it. He needed me here—he was doing all of this for us, and I couldn't ask him to face it alone just because I was scared like a wee child.

"I don't want to go back home," I said, putting my hands on his face. "*You* are my home, Ian."

"And you are my world," he said, caressing my hand, then bringing it to his lips for a kiss. His eyes brightened. "I think things are changing, Fi. People are standing up for equality, and not just here. There's a whole civil rights movement happening in the United States. Young people like us are ready to make the world a better place for everyone."

I squeezed his hand. "You sound hopeful."

"I am." His smile faded. "It's hard, you know, wanting to provide for a family and struggling to find work because of who you are."

"You're providing just fine, Mr. Winner of the Dunwoody," I teased. "And you never had trouble finding work in the village, either."

"We've got good prospects, so we do. But I've a new friend here who told me the shipyards in Belfast are ninety-five percent Protestant now. They keep letting the Catholics go. He's not sure what he's going to do."

"That's terrible," I murmured.

Anger flashed in his eyes. "Aye, it is. The Prods keep making it so Catholics can't work, then complaining about them being on the dole. We can't win. But as I said, things are changing." His tone brightened. "I think there's hope for the world yet."

Hope. It was a lovely word.

A lovely, empty word that wouldn't save us from the fire that was coming.

8

THE CONFESSION

Daphne

Rosemary Mountain
Present

I blinked twice, certain I'd heard Greg wrong. "What did you just say?"

He grimaced. "Fiona confessed. She said she's guilty and that she'll waive her right to a lawyer and sign whatever confession she needs to sign, so long as we give her twenty-four hours to move her chickens over to your coop and say goodbye to Ellie."

Time seemed to stop, and my body felt frozen in place. A thousand thoughts raced through my mind, fighting for attention, but they were overshadowed by an overwhelming sense of grief.

Fiona isn't fighting.

Fiona Flanagan, the strongest, feistiest woman I'd ever known—the woman who'd convinced me not to give up so many times before—wasn't fighting this accusation. It didn't make sense. Either she was protecting someone else or...

Or she was actually guilty.

And I had absolutely no idea what to do with that.

Emerson looked at me, his eyes revealing shock that mirrored my own. I gripped his hand but was unable to say anything over the lump in my throat.

Fiona had been accused of murder ... and she had confessed.

Nothing in the world made sense anymore.

Greg cleared his throat. "Daphne, I'm sure I don't have to tell you that I'm walking a fine line here. I have a dead body, an accused suspect with the means to do it, and a confession. No motive—even Fiona seemed stumped when I asked her *why* she did it. She said the why of it wasn't any of my business."

A little smile broke through my sadness. It was exactly the kind of thing Fiona would say.

"But otherwise," Greg continued, "it's a slam dunk as far as investigations go. I'm a damn fool for holding back on this."

"She confessed," I said slowly, catching up to where he was. "But that doesn't change things for you. You still don't actually think she did it. Deep down, you really do believe she's innocent." The thought gave me fresh hope.

"I do." He sighed, scrubbing his hand over his face. "I don't know if I've grown too soft or what, but I just can't believe she's actually guilty. Something about it doesn't feel right. I *know* she's not telling me the whole story. I'm hoping she'll tell you."

"I hope so too." I'd trusted Fiona with all of my secrets. I had to hope she'd trust me with hers.

Emerson interjected. "You're still sending Fiona home even though she confessed? Can you do that?"

Greg nodded. "I can. I'm allowed to use some discretion here and I'm doing what I think is right. My gut says she'd be giving us a false confession, so I'm trying to avoid that by sending her home pending toxicology results—and by praying we get a miracle in the meantime."

"Thank you," I whispered.

He gave me a tight smile. "I need you to understand we don't have much more wiggle room here, especially when it comes to you being a consultant. You have to be completely honest with me, even if you don't like the answers you find."

"I will. I promise." I owed him that much.

He took a deep breath. "Good. We've got one shot to figure out what's really going on. I hope we're right and that she's innocent. But if we're wrong and the evidence points toward her involvement, I'll have to put aside my feelings—and yours—and ask an outside agency to step in and take over the investigation as a neutral third party. Because let's be honest, neither you nor I is neutral as far as Fiona goes."

"No, we're not," I agreed, shaking my head. The fact that Greg wasn't neutral, either, made me love him even more. I felt guilty for the anger I'd felt toward him earlier. He'd already earned my trust more than once. I should have trusted him with this too.

"Talk to her," he urged. "Get her to tell you what's going on. And, you know, do your other thing." He shifted in his seat, his expression turning awkward. Even though he'd seen my gift of the second sight help solve a case before, he still wasn't entirely comfortable with it and didn't like talking about it.

I understood, as I wasn't entirely comfortable with it myself.

He stood. "I'll draw up paperwork today, making your position official. After you get Fiona settled at home, either Jackson or I will make arrangements to take you over to the crime scene so you can... You know."

"Do my thing?" I filled in, fighting a smile.

"Exactly." He took a deep breath. "You ready for this?"

"Yes." I'd been dying to see Fiona since the moment we got here.

But the look on his face made me worried that I had no idea what I was about to walk into.

Greg led us down the hallway to the interview rooms, stopping at the one-way mirror where we could see Fiona sitting alone at a table. Her white hair was stringy and unbrushed instead of woven into the neat braid she usually wore. Her posture was slumped and defeated, and her hands shook slightly as she twisted them together in her lap.

I wanted to burst into tears at the sight of her like that.

Emerson's face was lined with worry. "She looks terrible. Has she slept at all? Had food or water?"

Greg shook his head. "We've offered her all three, but she refused. She said she's waiting until she gets an official agreement to her terms."

"The twenty-four-hour thing?" I asked.

He nodded, confirming.

"Why haven't you given it to her?" Emerson asked.

"Because I don't want to make an official agreement that involves her confessing," Greg said as if it were obvious. "I gave her my word that she would get the time she wanted and more. Good grief, toxicology won't even be back that soon. But she wanted it in writing, and I'm not having her sign something like that—yet."

"You're trying to protect her," I said, putting a comforting hand on his shoulder. "Thank you."

"I hope you're thanking me when all this is over," he said, shaking his head. "Because we're all going to be in a world of trouble if she really is guilty."

"She's not," I said even though part of me was starting to worry.

When I tried to imagine a scenario where Fiona was falsely accused, I imagined her getting so spitting mad that she was ready to raise hell over the whole thing. I'd never seen Fiona cave like this. She'd completely crumbled. Nothing about it made sense.

There was more to this story. That's the only thing I knew for sure.

"Go talk some sense into her," Greg urged, motioning toward the doorway.

I gave him an uncertain nod, then walked around the corner to face the woman I barely recognized.

Her head jerked up when I opened the door. When she saw me, her eyes narrowed. "What are you doing here?"

"I'm here to take you home," I said smoothly. "Greg said you needed a ride."

"Has he decided to give me my twenty-four hours?"

"Yeah," I said, deciding to go with it. "We need to get the chickens moved over, right?"

"Right." Her eyes narrowed again. "Where's my agreement? I said I wanted it in writing."

"Sorry." I shrugged. "Greg explained they can't do that. But don't worry. Emerson and I made him promise you'd have at least the twenty-four hours you requested."

She gave me a suspicious look, but when I didn't change my expression, her chest heaved with relief. "Well, I'd prefer to have it in writing, but I guess I'll have to take him at his word. He'd lie to me, but he wouldn't cross a promise to *you.* Janet would make him pay for that until the end of time."

I couldn't help but laugh. "You're probably right, although you don't know her very well if you think she wouldn't make him pay for breaking a promise to you too."

Her expression turned mournful. "I'm real sorry to have to burden you with the chickens, but you're the only one I trust to take care of them. It may take a few days to get them integrated into your flock, but they'll learn to get along. It will all be okay." She seemed to be reassuring herself as much as she was me.

"I'm sure it will be fine," I said. "But do you not think you're getting ahead of yourself?"

"What do you mean?" Those sharp blue eyes of hers narrowed again.

I took the seat across from her, feeling more than a little awkward knowing that Emerson and Greg were watching. "I mean, we don't even know what happened yet. This could all be nothing."

"Alva Jean is dead. That's what happened," Fiona said, her voice level.

"Right, but that doesn't mean you're going to be arrested. She could have died of natural causes, or —"

"She was poisoned," Fiona said calmly. "By the tea I made her."

I shook my head. "You don't know that. It could have been a heart attack or a stroke or something completely different. Just because her nephew was concerned about the herbal medicine she was taking doesn't mean that's what killed her. And even if it was the tea, it could have been an accident. Maybe she was taking something you didn't know about or had an allergic reaction that you could never have seen coming. You're not a murderer, Fiona."

"A *poisoner.*" Fiona leaned across the table, her eyes darker than I'd ever seen them. She jabbed a finger at me. "I'm a *poisoner.* I've already told them I did it. You're just too stubborn to believe it. You think you know me better than that, don't you? You think, 'Oh, sweet Fiona wouldn't do that.' But you're wrong, because I would, and I did." She sat back with her arms crossed, daring me to contradict her.

Her sharp tongue felt like a slap across the face, leaving me speechless.

But as I studied the angry eyes across from me, I saw that underneath the anger was grief that rolled like a raging river. I knew she was only lashing out because of it.

"You're right. I am stubborn," I said quietly. "But I *do* know you. You fought for me. You believed I was innocent when everyone else thought I was a murderer. You believed I was sane when everyone else thought I was crazy. And you showed up for me every time my life was in danger, refusing to let me go down alone. So if you think for one moment that I'm not going to do the exact same thing for you, then *you're* the one who doesn't know *me.*" I stood, straightening my shoulders. "Get up. I'm taking you home."

Her eyes flickered with what looked like hope. But it snuffed out just as quickly.

"I don't deserve to go home," she said quietly.

Greg appeared behind me. "Deserve it or not, I need this room," he said, using the no-nonsense tone that we both knew would work best for her right now.

"You can't just let a dangerous criminal like me loose without something on paper," she argued, shaking her finger at him.

"Why not?" He shrugged. "Other agencies do it all the time. I'm sending you home with a warning: Don't leave town. Keep yourself available for questioning. But I'm not taking your confession until I know we're dealing with an actual murder. I'm entirely too busy to file unnecessary paperwork."

She opened her mouth like she was going to argue again, then snapped it shut. The fire came back into her eyes, and she stood, lifting her chin like a queen. "Fine. I'll go home and settle my affairs. But I'll also help speed things along for you. Toxicology goes faster if you know what to look for, right?"

"Right," Greg said slowly.

A satisfied look settled onto her face. "Then tell your coroner to look for evidence that Alva was poisoned with water hemlock. Cicutoxin—that's what they're looking for. We'll see if *that's* enough for you to believe I'm guilty."

She picked her purse up off the table and put it on her shoulder, then walked out of the room as Greg and I stared at each other with our mouths hanging open.

9
BOMBS IN BELFAST

FIONA

Fall 1969

Belfast

My heart fluttered with excitement as I put the finishing touches on the dinner I'd prepared to celebrate Ian's first day at Queen's. I'd never been one to want that kind of education, but I knew he did, and I couldn't wait to hear all about it. My Ian, the first of our families to go to university. I was so proud of him I felt my wee heart might burst with pride.

When the doorknob turned, I whirled around and yanked off the apron that covered my outfit. I'd dressed just for him in the plaid mini-skirt that showed off my long legs and the turtleneck sweater that almost made it look like I had a bit of a chest. It was the most modern outfit I owned, and I hoped it made me look as fashionable as the girls at Queen's.

Ian's face broke into a wide smile when he saw me, but there was a weariness in his eyes that I wasn't expecting.

"What's wrong?" I asked.

"Nothin'," he said, dropping his bag by the door so that he could pull me into an embrace. "Not now, anyway. I'm as right as rain now that I have ya in my arms."

"Something happened," I said, studying his eyes.

He shook his head. "No, nothin' happened, Fiona. It was just a long day, so it was."

I put my hands on his firm chest and reveled in it. He had the mind of a genius, but he'd built his body as a fisherman. Seemed I'd won the lottery when it came to husbands, getting the best of both worlds—the brain and the brawn together in one perfect body. On top of it all, he had the sweetest soul I'd ever known.

I still didn't know how someone like me could have been so lucky as to catch the eye of Ian Flanagan, the heartbreaker of our village who could have had any girl he wanted there but who had only ever had eyes for me.

"Are ya tired of books and lectures already?" I teased.

"Never," he said, kissing my forehead. "The books and lectures were the second-best part of my day."

"And the first?" I asked, trailing my fingers up his neck and massaging the back of his head. There was already tension there, knots that spoke of a harder day than he was letting on.

"This." His lips found mine in a slow, luxurious kiss that was familiar and strange at the same time. He no longer tasted of the sea, and it made me feel as if I were in uncharted waters so to speak.

I felt his body relax as we held each other. It was pure medicine, so it was, having the kind of love we shared.

"Are ya hungry?" I whispered the question against his lips.

"Starved. There wasn't time for lunch, not with trying to find my way around."

"Come, then." I slipped away from his hold and grabbed his hand, dragging him to the tiny table and two chairs tucked in a corner that we laughingly referred to as the dining room. I gently pushed him into his chair and grabbed his bowl, taking it to the stove so I could ladle up his dinner.

His eyes lit up when I put the dish in front of him. "Beef and Guinness stew?"

"Your favorite," I said, giving him a quick kiss on the head before grabbing a bowl for myself.

"Aye, but I wasn't expecting anything so grand. You must have been slaving over the stove for hours."

"It's not every day a girl's husband starts university." I sat down across from him and tucked a napkin into my lap. "Now tell me all about it. I want to hear every detail."

A guarded look crossed his face. "Are ya sure?"

"Of course I'm sure. We've always told each other everything." My worry returned.

He took a bite of his stew, quiet for a moment. "I don't know how to get used to this. It's a strange thing, living here."

"Aye, it is," I agreed. I'd been nervous all day here in the flat without Ian. There was too much noise and nowhere to go to escape it.

"My walk to the bus stop took me right past blackened buildings that still reek of smoke from the bombings. You hear of things like that on the news, but it's different seeing it up close."

"Not just seeing it. *Living* in it," I pointed out.

"Exactly." He shook his head, a strange mix of shock and anger coating his features. "Then I had some trouble at the checkpoints. The soldier didn't want to let me pass. I had to show my papers and prove I was a student."

"Whatever for?" I sat back, stunned.

"Because I'm a young man and I was carrying a bag outside of a Catholic neighborhood. They searched it. Dumped my notebooks right out on the ground, so they did."

A shocked laugh slipped out. "Searched your bag? Like you might have been a bomber or something?" It was so unbelievable that it was almost funny. My Ian, with his poet's soul, being searched on his way to university? I couldn't even picture it.

"Aye." He shrugged, trying to make light of it. But it was clear the indignation of it all had shaken him to his core. "Anyway, that was the start of it. The rest of the day was mostly just overwhelming, trying to figure out where to go and what to do." He looked down. "I don't fit in there, Fiona."

I reached across the table and squeezed his hand. "Course you do. You're a Queen's student, same as the rest of them. You've earned your place."

He shook his head. "It's going to be harder than I expected. I'm starting to think this was a mistake."

"What do you mean by harder? The coursework?"

"No," he said quietly. "I mean… I don't think we're Catholic enough to be living in this neighborhood. But I think I might be too Catholic for Queen's."

"Too Catholic?" I frowned.

"Too Catholic, too poor, too rural." His face turned dark. "I don't dress the way they do. It marks me right away, along with the calluses on my hands. And the moment I say a word, they know I'm not from Belfast." He dug into his stew with so much force that it splattered out on the table.

I picked up my napkin and wiped up the mess, giving him a gentle smile at his look of apology. "Aren't there students from all over, though?"

He nodded. "Aye. But some people don't seem to want there to be. They seem to think that, because I'm from the country, I can't possibly understand the material. That I'm not smart enough."

"Well, you'll show them soon enough, won't ya? You're the smartest man I've ever known."

He needed the praise, but it was true. He'd been born for more than fishing. His mind was brilliant, and he loved to study.

His shoulders relaxed. "You're too good to me, Fiona. I love you. I'm sorry for complaining and ruining such a good meal."

"Don't be sorry, and you haven't ruined anything at all. I wanted to know everything, didn't I?"

"Aye, so ya did."

"So what else?"

He groaned. "Another student called me a bogman."

I snorted. "And so ya are, but you're the bogman that will beat him in exams, aren't ya?"

"Aye." He grinned. "I think I just might."

"First days are hard," I said, reaching across the tiny table to squeeze his hand. "But now you know what you're doing. You'll feel more prepared tomorrow."

He finished the last of his stew. "Aye, I will. Besides, for the most part, everyone's nice enough. It's only a few bad apples. I shouldn't let them spoil it for me."

"That's the spirit," I said, smiling. "You'll win them over, and if ya don't, they're not worth your time anyway."

He grinned. "Ya know, I was feeling poorly about it, but with your magic stew in my belly, I feel just strong enough to face the world again."

I rolled my eyes. "Yes, I'm sure enough that it's my stew doing it."

He gave me a wink. "Come on now. We both know ya put a few extra herbs in there to give me a boost, now, didn't ya? Fess up. What was it? A bit of thyme to ward off negative energy? A bit of rosemary for protection? Maybe even a four-leaf clover or two for good luck?"

I blushed. "Don't be daft. It's just stew. There's nothing magic about it," I said, waving him off.

His eyes sparkled across the table. "Fiona, my love, *everything's* magic with you."

That first week in Belfast seemed to stretch out into a month. It was lonely being in the flat all day by myself, but the city was so over-whelming that I didn't quite feel safe venturing out too far on my own. I walked down to the shops every morning to pick up ingredients for dinner, but otherwise I stayed put, scrubbing the flat and making plans to turn it into a cozy home. I studied the herbal books Mamó had tucked into my bag and took careful notes on the plants I'd not used yet.

Mostly, I counted down the hours until Ian would come home and I could feast on his stories about the people he'd met and the things he was studying.

My heart was lonely, so it was. I said a few hellos to the other women in the flats, and they were polite enough in responding. But they didn't invite me to join their conversation or linger with them in the hallways. They seemed to look at me like I was a wee babe, too young to have anything to add to their circle.

Maybe they were right. I was a young girl from a fishing village with no children of my own. When I'd pass by them, they were always talking about either their children or the political situation in Belfast. I didn't have anything to say about either.

When Saturday rolled around, I was almost giddy at the idea of spending the whole day with my Ian. I had a long list of things I wanted to do and places I wanted to go.

But we'd only just started when the world turned to madness.

We were walking to the shops when the first explosion happened. All I heard was glass breaking at first, followed by a loud boom as the petrol bomb exploded. Then I felt the heat on my face as the building in front of us caught fire.

I froze. My mind wouldn't even work.

Ian grabbed my hand. "Run, Fiona!" he yelled, half dragging me away.

My feet obeyed even though my mind couldn't catch up.

Another shattering of glass.

Another boom.

Another building going up in flames faster than I ever would have imagined possible.

Screams of pain. The wretched smell of smoke and burning flesh.

My feet kept moving, one after the other, but I felt like I was in quicksand. Like I'd never be fast enough.

Then we were turning, running down a brick alleyway. I didn't know where we were going, just that Ian was trying to get us as far away from all of it as quickly as possible. I clung to his hand for dear life.

When he finally stopped running, I gasped for breath, clutching my side.

"Are ya okay, Fi?" He grabbed my shoulders, looking me over like he was afraid I'd been blown to pieces.

"I'm fine," I gasped. "You?"

"Aye, I'm grand." He took a deep breath and looked around, then yelled out toward a man who was running in the same direction from which we'd just come. "What's going on? What happened?"

The man shook his head in disgust, then spat on the ground. "There was a Loyalist rally today. After it finished, some of them decided to start throwing petrol bombs over the barricades into the neighborhood."

"Over the barricades?" Ian looked confused. "Are they mad? The barricades are manned by British soldiers. You'd have to have a death wish to do something like that."

"Yeah, well, maybe not. Those soldiers aren't doing a damn thing," the man said, spitting again. "What good are their rifles if they won't raise one to defend us? They're no better than the RUC."

Ian and I looked at each other, the shock on his face mirroring what I felt in my own soul.

"I thought... I thought they would protect us," Ian stammered. "I mean, that's why they're here, isn't it?"

The man snorted. "You're a baby, so ya are. Not from here, are ya?"

We shook our heads.

"Well, you're here now, and you're going to learn a thing or two about how the world works," he said, a grim look on his face. "The soldiers aren't going to save us. I've said it once, and I'll say it again.

We'll have to save ourselves." He gave Ian a dark look, then took off again down the next alleyway.

We stood in stunned silence until the sound of another distant explosion shocked us out of it.

Ian grabbed me and pulled me to his chest. "I'm so sorry, Fiona."

"It's not your fault," I said, clinging to him.

"I shouldn't have brought ya here. I shouldn't—"

"Stop," I said. "Please. I don't want to talk about it."

Ian nodded, his brow knit in concern.

I didn't know what he thought exactly, if he thought I blamed him or that I was angry. I wasn't. Not at all.

I just couldn't talk about any of it—not what had just happened, or the soldiers, or what might happen in the future. None of it. Because while Ian and that other man might have been ready to process things and make a plan, I wasn't. I couldn't think straight. Not when my mind was still stuck, caught in a loop I didn't know how to escape.

Glass.

Boom.

Flames.

Glass.

Boom.

Flames.

Glass.

Boom.

Flames.

10

THE SIGHT

Daphne

Rosemary Mountain

Present

In Emerson's truck, Fiona acted as if nothing out of the ordinary were happening at all. She played with Ellie, telling stories that made them both giggle. If I kept my eyes on the road, I found nothing in her voice to suggest she was emotional about the accusation against her—or what she'd confessed to doing—at all.

But every time I turned to look at her, I was struck by how frail and sad she looked. She was putting on a good show for Ellie, protecting my daughter. But she couldn't fool me.

Fiona was a wreck.

When we pulled into her driveway, she jumped out of the truck and headed toward the door without inviting us to join her.

I glanced at Emerson. "I need to make sure she's okay."

"Agreed." He sighed. "I don't like this at all."

"Me either."

He drummed his thumb on the steering wheel. "I'll take Ellie home. Fiona's not going to open up around her. Call me if you need me to come pick you up later."

I gave him a soft smile. "I'll be fine. Thanks for being everything that you are."

"What do you mean by that?" His mouth turned up in a smile.

"You're my rock," I said. "I don't know what I'd do without you."

"You'd be just fine. But..."

"Yes?"

He reached over and took my hand, his eyes turning serious. "I understand why you've agreed to help with this investigation, and I know you might not be able to tell me everything since you're doing it officially. But please don't cut me out this time. I almost lost you once. I can't..." He trailed off, his eyes saying the words he couldn't.

"I won't," I promised. Unlike the last time we'd found ourselves in a situation like this, I meant it. He had almost lost me, and I'd almost lost the chance to build this beautiful family we'd made together. I wouldn't risk anything like that again.

"Okay." He gave me a nod. "Good luck in there."

"Thanks." I groaned and took a deep breath, steeling myself. "She's a stubborn woman."

"So are you," he said with a wink. "I'm sure you'll be able to handle her."

"I know you're in there," I called after knocking for the second time on Fiona's closed door. "I just dropped you off, remember? You can't pretend you're not home."

I heard her muttering underneath her breath inside.

"I have a key," I said loudly, reminding her. "I can just come in if I want."

The door flew open, and Fiona scowled at me. "Girl, I've been up all night, and I want to go to sleep. Can't you take a hint?"

"Give me five minutes. Please."

She rolled her eyes but moved aside and let me come in.

It was a victory. The only problem was that I had no idea what to say to her now that I'd won the chance.

She closed the door and turned to face me with her arms crossed. "Well?" She tapped her foot impatiently. "You said five minutes and the clock's ticking."

"Fiona, please tell me the truth," I begged. "Come on. You can't honestly expect me to believe that you murdered your friend. What in the world is going on?"

She set her lips in a firm line and refused to say anything.

"Are you covering for someone? That's it, right? You're taking the fall to protect someone else?"

Nothing.

I shook my head in frustration. "Fiona, do you realize that if you're right and she died of whatever that toxin was—"

"Cicutoxin," she said, interrupting.

"Okay, cicutoxin." I threw my hands in the air. "If you're right and that's what killed her, you telling them that makes you look guilty. You're going to go to jail unless you tell me who you're trying to protect."

She shot a single eyebrow up as high as it would go. "Now you sound just like Greg did earlier. But I've already told you the truth. I'm not covering for anybody. I'm a poisoner—you just don't want to accept it."

"I don't believe you."

She sighed. "That sounds like a *you* problem. Now, if you'll kindly step aside, I'd like to get some sleep. Today might be the last time I get to sleep in my own bed, and I'd like to make the most of it. I'll be by later to start transitioning the chickens to your coop."

She pushed past me, walked to her bedroom, and slammed the door shut.

I stared at the closed door in shock and confusion. Maybe she was right about me not wanting to accept it, but it didn't make any sense. I'd known Fiona for years now, and while she was feisty and opinionated, she wasn't hateful, and she certainly wasn't violent. She didn't even use regular mousetraps. She would only catch and release, gently returning the mice to the woods with a square of cheese to fill their bellies when she dropped them off.

A gentle soul like that would never commit murder. She had to be lying to protect someone else.

I repeated it like a mantra, even as doubt struck my heart like a venomous snake. Fiona was gentle, but she also believed in justice. It was as hard to imagine her lying to protect a murderer as it was to imagine her committing one herself.

I walked to her kitchen to clean up the mess she'd left the night before. When I picked up her plate, I was shocked by an unexpected vision, the first in nearly two years.

Fiona was sitting at the table eating when she heard a knock on the door. She got up, humming a little tune, and opened it. She greeted Greg with a big smile—a smile he didn't return. She welcomed him in and asked what was wrong.

He said he needed to ask her some questions about a suspicious death.

She asked him who'd died.

When he said it was Alva Jean, Fiona grabbed onto the back of her couch for support and covered her mouth with her hand. Tears pricked her eyes as she asked how it had happened.

Greg hesitated, then told her it was possible that Alva had been poisoned.

Fiona's face changed completely. The grief and the shock were still there, but they were overshadowed by pure horror.

"Poison?" she asked shakily.

Greg nodded. "I'm sorry about this, Fiona, but we know she was drinking one of your herbal teas before she died, and some questions were raised about that. We just need to ask you some questions to rule you out as a suspect. Do you have a few minutes to chat?"

Fiona's eyes grew hazy, like she was only half hearing him. But when he finished speaking, she cleared her throat and straightened, standing tall. "*I think we'd better go on down to the station and do things proper like.*"

Greg frowned. "*It doesn't have to be as serious as all that, Fiona.*"

"*Oh yes, it does,*" *she said. She walked out the door, leaving him staring at her, confused.*

I sank into the kitchen chair, letting out a breath as I tried to recover from the most detailed, intense vision I'd ever had. It was astonishing for the sight to return so powerfully after lying dormant for so long. But I was glad it had, because what I'd just seen confirmed what my heart already knew.

There was absolutely no way Fiona had intentionally poisoned her friend.

Fiona Flanagan wore her heart on her sleeve and was completely unable to hide her emotions. I could read her like a book. She'd been devastated by the news. But more importantly, she'd been shocked —she'd had no idea that Alva was dead before Greg told her.

But the horror on her face when she heard that Alva had been drinking her tea bothered me. Was it possible that Fiona suspected she'd accidentally poisoned her? That maybe Emerson was right and she was starting to have some cognitive decline and was scared she'd miscalculated something?

I didn't know what was going on, but I knew two things for sure.

One, that Fiona hadn't committed murder.

Two, that Fiona seemed to believe she had.

11
PRETENDING

Fiona
Fall 1969
Belfast

The rioting went on all weekend, but we stayed in our flat and tried to pretend like it wasn't happening. We played cards to keep ourselves distracted. While Ian studied, I made meals out of whatever scraps we had left so that we didn't have to go out shopping again. I prayed silently for the families whose homes had been burned and for the loved ones of anyone who'd died. And I prayed for our own building to be protected, selfish of a prayer as that might have been. We held each other tightly through the nights, like we were afraid it might be the last time.

But we didn't voice our fears.

We tried not to talk about it at all.

When Monday came around and Ian had to go back to class, I forced myself to make my normal outing to the shops. Made myself walk normally, eyes ahead, instead of gaping at the fresh destruction all around me.

The streets were quiet and empty, save for the people who were out trying to clean up the mess.

I kept my chin up, pretending like it was completely normal that buildings I'd walked past a few days ago were now burned-out hulls of emptiness. I pretended like my mind was focused on my shopping list instead of replaying the horrors of that day.

I pretended I wasn't scared.

Ian came home that evening and told me that hundreds more soldiers were being brought in to protect the neighborhoods and that the government had promised to make things better.

We both pretended that those promises actually meant something.

It's funny how quickly something that was once unfathomable can become your norm. That first weekend in Belfast was shocking. Terrifying. Life-altering in the worst way.

But we didn't leave.

I thought about that so many times in the months and years that followed, about how different things would have been if we had just packed up and gone back home to the village. No one would have blamed us. We'd been right in the middle of a bombing. We'd been there when our neighborhood was attacked, when buildings exploded and flesh burned and screams tore through the air. Belfast had gone mad. But instead of packing our bags and leaving, we stayed.

I think that was the maddest thing of all.

Looking back, it seems clear that we should have given up the scholarship and gone home. I've asked myself a thousand times why I couldn't see it then. How could my vision have been so weak?

Love's a funny thing. I loved my Ian with all my heart. Because I loved him, I thought the most important thing was for me to support his dreams. Ian had been given an opportunity no one else in our families had ever had. How could I possibly ask him to give that up?

It was unthinkable—more unthinkable than living in a war zone, apparently.

All I knew was that my job as his wife was to support him. To follow where he would lead. To endure it all as his helpmeet. That's what I'd been taught.

I've learned since then that love should always be honest.

One of the hardest burdens I've had to bear is knowing that, if I'd just asked him to give it up, he would have. He'd have done it in a heartbeat for me. We could have gone back to our wee cottage and made a dozen babies and my whole life would have turned out different.

I was trying to be a good wife. But if I could do it all over again, I'd have been selfish. I'd have told him just how scared I was and how much I wanted to go home.

Because now I know that, deep down, he was scared, too. But he wasn't honest, either. He didn't want to be weak or disappoint me. He didn't want to throw away the opportunity he had to make me proud and to be a good provider.

We were both playing our roles.

When Christmastime came, we retraced the journey we'd made when I first arrived, heading back to the train station so that we could go home for a visit. I was a bundle of nerves when we set out, fear and excitement mixed together.

Ian said not to bring a bag, that we'd just make do with whatever we'd left there in our cottage, so as not to face trouble at the checkpoints. Tensions were still high, and we didn't want any attention. It was strange, having to think about those things, and yet I didn't bat an eye. You learned to do whatever you needed to do to keep safe. And though I wanted to bring gifts to my family, in the end, it didn't really matter. All I really cared about was getting out of Belfast.

I didn't relax until we were off the train and on the bus that would take us the rest of the way into the village. My heart soared when the soft curves of the seaside came into view.

The sea was as blue as ever, and the countryside felt like pure magic compared to the grimy slums in the city. The sight of it made my soul come alive again. It was like I could finally breathe for the first time in weeks. I clasped my hands together like I was saying a prayer. Maybe I was. It was a prayer without words but full of more gratitude than my heart could hold.

Ian slipped his arm around me. "The bus won't go faster, no matter how hard you squeeze your hands together," he murmured into my ear, a tinge of amusement in his voice.

"Want to bet?" I laughed, shooting him a wink.

He shook his head. "Not me, no, sir. I'd never bet against Fiona Flanagan." He whispered into my ear, sending a thrill of pleasure down my spine. "She's a *bean feasa*, don't ya know."

I slapped his knee, though my lips twitched in a grin. "Don't go cursing me with old age before my time. I'm no such thing. I'm still a wee young soul with a lifetime of learning ahead of me."

"Aye, but you're the best healer the flats have ever had, at least according to Fergus O'Reilly." Ian's face turned solemn.

"Fergus? What did he tell ya?" My brow crinkled in confusion.

"He told me his wife, Peggy, was ill last week and that ya saw her walking through the hallway looking like death warmed over. Said ya helped her get inside her flat, then brought her some tea that stopped her fever right away and had her back on her feet in no time. Told me to tell ya he's right grateful and that they're happy to have us living there, so they are."

My heart warmed. "It was nothing. The sad woman looked like she was going to faint straightaway. Had a touch of the flu, so she did, and was burning up with fever. All I gave her was some of my cold tea to help break it and get her immune system working again."

"Well, he's forever in your favor," Ian said, giving me an admiring smile. "Thinks ya saved her life, so he does."

"It was a small thing," I murmured.

"Not small to them."

I settled in against his warm body as the bus drove the last few miles home, trying hard to be patient. But patience went out the window the moment the bus stopped. I practically danced down the aisle, and nearly wept when my feet hit the ground.

Home. The village was home in a way I knew Belfast never would be. I wanted to sing and weep and dance at the pure poetry of the place. I marveled at how fresh the air was, without even a tinge of the smoke that haunted us in the Falls, and at how relaxed and happy the children looked playing compared to the ones in our apartment building who'd faced bombs and bullets.

It was a different world here, and so help me, I didn't know how I was going to find the strength to get back on that bus when we had to return for Ian's second term.

Thoughts of Belfast disappeared completely when Mamó and Annie came into view. I ran into Mamó's arms, then kissed my sister with tears streaming down my face. We walked back to the house together, all talking at once, wanting to catch up and share the craic.

For a little while, everything was right in the world again. Belfast felt like nothing but a bad dream. We were safe, we were happy, and we were together in the sweetest place on earth, ready to celebrate Christmas together as a family.

If I had known that it was the last time life would ever be like that, I would never have returned to Belfast. I would have begged Ian to leave it all behind, to get his job back as a fisherman and be content with our small, happy life.

But I didn't know.

I didn't know the Troubles were about to change us forever.

I didn't know it was the last Christmas we'd all be together.

12

THE CRIME SCENE

DAPHNE

Rosemary Mountain
Present

A few hours later, Greg picked me up.

When I climbed into his truck, I gave him a grin. "Have you told Mom you hired me yet?"

"No," he admitted, looking guilty. "Have you?"

"Nope. I can't decide if it's better that she hears it from you or me."

"Me either," he said, scratching behind his ear. "But I was kind of hoping you'd tell her. Then I'd tell her as soon as I get home, apologizing profusely for not being able to call earlier to give her a heads-up."

I laughed. "So you want me to deal with the fallout, but you don't want her to know that you planned it that way. Got it."

He grinned. "We're probably worried over nothing. Right?"

"Right," I said, assuring him. Although I really wasn't sure.

Mom had been incredibly supportive of my efforts to solve my biological mother's murder a few years ago—well, once she'd realized I was going to do it whether she liked it or not. But I'd almost died during that final investigation, and my injuries had put me in a wheelchair temporarily. It had taken nearly a full year of physical therapy to be able to walk without a noticeable limp. After all of that, the idea of my investigating again terrified her.

It hadn't terrified me, strangely enough—until I had Ellie, that is. I'd planned on becoming a private investigator right up until the day I gave birth. Having a child had changed everything. It was too big a risk. I'd lost my own mother so young. The thought of Ellie growing up without knowing my love had been enough to bring me to tears. So I had put aside my plans, and when my gift of the second sight seemed to fade away, I was kind of ... glad. Without it, I didn't have to feel guilty for not using it.

But I was grateful it had returned if it meant I could keep Fiona out of prison. I was also grateful that I was working with Greg and Jackson, who I knew would keep me safe. No more running off into danger or investigating things on my own. Those days were over.

"You're awfully quiet over there," Greg commented.

"Just thinking about things." I filled him in on the dream I'd had and the vision at Fiona's.

He shook his head. "Damn, that's spooky. Not sure I'll ever get used to that. What you saw is pretty much exactly how it happened. And I agree with you—I thought she looked shocked by the news too."

"I don't know why she thinks she's guilty," I said, chewing on my thumbnail. "That's the strangest part."

"Yep. It's very strange." He pulled into the driveway of Alva Jean's impressive house, where Jackson's truck was already in the driveway. "Have you been here before?"

"Once," I said, nodding. "I came with Fiona to a garden tea party Alva hosted. She was a nice lady."

"She was. A little eccentric, but I guess we all are in our own way." He threw the truck into park but motioned for me to stay put. "I've never worked with a, um, psychic before. You know, other than with you the last time around."

"I'm not exactly a psychic," I said, wincing. That word still made me super uncomfortable. "My family has always called it the second sight."

He grinned. "Okay, but psychic is a hell of a lot easier to say than 'someone with the second sight.'"

"True," I admitted.

"Anyway, what I was trying to say is that I don't really know if there's a certain way we should do this, especially if we're talking about a potential court case. Hell, I don't know how psychic testimony holds up in court, period, and then we're adding on the fact that you're personal friends with the suspect. My guess is that we can't use anything you see as evidence at all."

"That won't matter if I can point you in the right direction so you can get real evidence," I said.

"Exactly. Just in case we *can* use anything you get, I want to send you in cold. I'll brief you on more details after you've been in there, but I'd like for you to do your thing without knowing more than you already do first."

"Got it." I put my hand on the door handle, then hesitated and turned back to him. "Greg, I have to tell you I don't always get anything. This is the first time I've had anything at all like this since I gave birth to Ellie. It's not exactly something I can control."

An understanding look crossed his face. "No one's expecting miracles, Daphne. You're here. You showed up. That's all that matters. If you get something, awesome. If you don't, you don't. No one can blame you for that. But I figure it's worth a shot."

I took a deep breath. "Okay. Then let's do this."

We got out of the truck and walked up to the front door, passing Alva's impressive front gardens on the way. The woman was a genius with flowers, and even though it was autumn and long past when I'd expect to see them, she somehow still had gorgeous fall blooms lining her curved walkway. The stately steps to her front porch were decorated with whiskey barrels full of mums and Cinderella pumpkins. I stopped in my tracks at the sight of them.

"What is it?" Greg asked.

"I think Fiona grew these," I said. "She had a big plot of them in her garden this year. She said when we carve Jack-o-lanterns next week that she wants to paint one of these like a carriage for Ellie's dolls."

But if Fiona was in jail, we wouldn't be carving pumpkins together this year. The thought made me so sad I wanted to cry right there on Alva's porch steps.

Greg put his hand on my shoulder and squeezed. "Don't give up yet," he said.

I nodded, swallowing over the lump in my throat.

Jackson opened the front door. He was wearing gloves on his hands and had blue booties over his shoes. He held out sets of each for me and Greg.

I stared at them. "We don't even know that this was a murder," I said, devastated.

"We have an accusation and a confession," Greg said under his breath. "However unofficial it may be. We're already crossing other lines. We've got to do everything we can by the book."

"I understand," I said, even though I hated it.

I wanted so badly to be able to prove that this was an accident and there was no murder at all, much less one committed by Fiona.

I slid the booties over my real boots and pulled on the gloves. "This may affect my ability," I admitted. "I usually get the most when I touch something."

"Do your best," Greg said.

Jackson held his hand up. "Before you go in, Daphne, you should know that it's not pretty."

"I've seen crime scenes before," I reminded him. "I was the victim in one of them, remember?"

He grinned. "Fair enough. We'll follow behind you. You can

touch things if you need to, as long as you keep your gloves on. We've already photographed the place thoroughly."

"Okay." I braced myself and walked inside, with Greg and Jackson on my heels.

Alva's foyer was as much of a statement as her front yard. The woman had an eye for design that even I envied. Muted aqua walls met white wainscoting and rich espresso hardwood floors. A chandelier hung from the ceiling above a round marble table with a driftwood base. A single white orchid sat on the table in a ceramic pot that matched the aqua on the walls. Beyond the table was a gorgeous cascade staircase.

I ran my fingertips over the table as I walked past it, then turned to the dining room on my left. It was as stylish as the entryway, with an impressive table and a modern chandelier. Everything was elegant and beachy at the same time, managing to look both expensive and comfortable.

But as much as the artist in me wanted to take my time soaking in the details that had changed since I'd last been here, I had work to do, and nothing in the dining room seemed to be triggering anything helpful.

I turned to Jackson. "Where was she found?"

"The sitting room," he said, pointing behind himself with his thumb. "In front of the fireplace."

I took a deep breath and headed there next.

The sitting room had a cozier feel than the breezy entryway, and I could tell that it was where Alva spent most of her time. It was a room designed for comfort, with plush leather recliners in front of an electric fireplace that had a large TV mounted above it. One of the chairs was obviously more well-used than the other, and beside it sat a magazine rack full of fashion magazines and romance novels.

Directly in front of the chair were blood stains on the rug.

It wasn't the first time I'd seen blood stains. I'd had to cover them up in my own house. But the sight of them jarred me more than I'd expected, taking me right back to the danger I'd experienced before.

"You okay?" Greg asked, shooting me a look of concern.

"I'm good," I reassured him. "There's just … more than I was expecting."

"The tongue has a lot of blood vessels," Jackson said, wincing.

"Apparently so." I looked away and focused on the chair, putting my hands on it.

Nothing.

I bit my lip and moved to the table that sat between the chairs where the teacup would have been, touching it and closing my eyes in hopes of a vision.

Still nothing.

Dread filled my soul when I realized I was going to have to put my hands down on the ground where she'd died. That was something I really didn't want to see.

But Fiona's life was in the balance. So I sucked it up and knelt down, placing my hands near the bloodstains on the rug.

I felt the energy immediately. *Panic. Confusion. Pain.*

My impulse was to jerk my hands away and block it out, but I overrode it, forcing myself to stay open to the horrid sensations.

Then I began to see flashes of what had happened.

Convulsions. Pain. Attempting to cry out for help but being unable to.

When it finally ended, Greg and Jackson were hovering over me with terrified looks on their faces. I pushed myself off the floor and stepped back, shaking.

"You were right about seizures," I said, trembling. "And … she didn't die right away. She felt the pain. She tried to call for—" I cut off, covering my mouth with my forearm as I ran for the bathroom so that I could throw up.

13
HAWTHORN AND
HEARTBREAK

FIONA

December 1969

Glenarm

I could feel Mamó's sharp eyes watching me as I peeled potatoes. Every time I looked up, her eyes darted away.

After the fifth time, I couldn't take it anymore. "What is it?" I asked, laughing. "Why are ya staring at me so?"

But there was no laughter in her voice when she answered. "I'm sorry, Fiona. I'm just worried about ya is all."

I leaned over and kissed her on the cheek. "And why are ya worried? I'm here, aren't I?"

"Aye, ya are. But you and Ian both look like you've seen hardship the past few months."

I started to deny it, but I'd never been able to lie to Mamó.

"You're not wrong," I admitted, keeping my gaze on the potato in my hand. "It's been a challenge, so it has."

I wasn't sure how much Mamó knew about how bad things had

become in Belfast. It wasn't as if we'd been blind to the tension between the Loyalists and the Republicans. But I would never have believed how bad things really were if I hadn't seen it with my own eyes, and she'd never been one to pay much attention to the news, saying she preferred to give her attention to the ground underneath her feet instead of worrying about things she couldn't change. But people in the village had to be talking about the riots, and I knew at least some of the news had to have trickled Mamó's way.

I just didn't know how much, and I didn't want to be the one to reveal anything she didn't already know.

"Tell me about where you're living there," she said, an odd sharpness to her voice. "Is it by the university?"

"No," I said, still keeping my eyes focused on the potatoes as I took my frustration out on them, barely missing my own finger as I yanked the knife with too much force. "Ian couldn't get us an apartment by Queen's. He found us a place in a neighborhood a couple of miles away, on Falls Road."

She took a sharp inhale. "Fiona, no."

I looked up and met her gaze. Her eyes revealed that she knew more about what was happening than I'd hoped.

"Yes," I said quietly.

"The bombings..." Her voice fell apart.

"Aye, but we're okay." I gave her my most convincing smile. "The worst of it was before we got there. There was one rough weekend, but..." My voice broke, and I stopped trying to pretend to be optimistic.

As much as I wanted to play it down so she wouldn't worry, the truth was that I still had nightmares about the sound of breaking glass and the heat on my face as the building went up in flames. About the screams and the horrid smell of burning flesh, a smell I hoped never to experience again in my whole life.

Mamó put her hand on mine. "Leave the potatoes for the moment," she said kindly. "Tell me all of it. You're carrying troubles, trying to be strong, but it's eating away at ya. Ya need to get it off your chest, girl."

I nodded, pulling my apron up to wipe my teary eyes, before sitting beside her on the kitchen bench. With nothing else to focus on, the memories came back and I shuddered.

"We were walking to the shops to buy bread."

It was the first time I'd spoken aloud of it since that day. It was like an unwritten rule between me and Ian that we wouldn't talk about it. But I told Mamó the whole story, even the parts that felt like sandpaper on my throat. She listened, saying nothing, while I got it all out.

When I was finished, she held me, and she didn't act like the women in that apartment building. She didn't make me feel like I was a wee child for reacting so.

I hadn't known how much I needed someone to understand how badly it had shaken me and not judge me for it.

"I was afraid something like that was going to happen," she admitted. "When I went to Belfast this spring, the city felt like a stick of dynamite just waiting to blow." Her eyes darkened. "Felt too much like Cork did before the war. I felt sick when yous told me about your big plans."

"I know," I said, remembering. "I told ya everything would be alright, but I was wrong."

She stroked her hand down my back, soothing me without a word.

I looked up at her. "Why do they hate us so?"

Her face clouded with sadness. "Because they've been taught to fear us. They see us as a threat to their way of life."

"But why? I don't understand."

She sighed. "I'm glad ya don't. I wish I didn't. But these lads stirrin' up trouble... Their grandfathers fought to stay British, just like my brother fought to be free. The treaty was supposed to bring peace, but now the Prods fear that Catholics will take the north of Ireland from them too. Fear is a powerful thing. When people are afraid, it's far too easy to see the other side as an enemy instead of as a fellow human. Plant the seed of fear and you'll grow a vine of hatred."

"Maybe this will be the end of it," I said, trying to be hopeful. "Maybe they just needed to get it out of their system and things will settle down. There are more soldiers there now. Trying to keep things peaceful, like. They were already there beforehand, but the government sent a lot more after that weekend and promised to do a better job of protecting the Catholic neighborhoods."

Mamó's face showed her doubt. "Is it working?"

No. I let out a long breath. "I've seen no trouble personally since they came," I said carefully.

"Well, that's a mercy, anyway. But there will always be those who are looking to stir things up again on both sides. Remember that. Once a mob starts, common sense goes out the window." She gave me a piercing look, like it was important for me to understand.

"I will," I promised.

"Remember who you are. No matter what comes." She touched her finger to my heart.

"I will," I said again, not fully understanding her words.

"Good. Now, are you having nightmares about what happened?"

"I am," I admitted, turning red.

She shook her head. "There's nothing to be ashamed of, Fiona. It's only natural for a person to react that way when something so horrible has happened. It's war and bombing that's not natural. Don't be ashamed that your mind and heart struggle with it—it's the ones who think so little of human life that they throw bombs who should be ashamed."

I nodded, grateful for her understanding.

"Your heart needs healing." She got a sad, worried look on her face. "And that's nothing to be ashamed of, either. They say all great healers must first go through their own healing before they can really begin to help anyone else."

I looked at her as if seeing her for the first time. "Did you? I mean, did ya have to go through something...?" It hit me how little we'd spoken of her life before she came to live with us.

She nodded slowly. "Aye."

"Will ya tell me?"

She looked away, quiet for so long that I thought she wasn't going to say anything else, before finally speaking. "Ya know I grew up in County Cork. It's where I was born and where I thought I'd spend the whole of my life. My mother was only blessed with two children, me and my older brother, Patrick. He was a good brother, so he was. Funny, kind, and protective."

Her gaze fell to her fingers, where she twisted the hem of her apron. "I was just a teenager when the War of Independence broke out. Patrick and my father both joined the IRA, fighting for our freedom. I wanted to help too. I did what I could, using my herbal skills to help bandage wounded lads, and even helped hide a few in our family home. Sometimes I helped move packages or get information to the spy network. The Brits didn't look too closely at us lasses, so we were able to do more than the lads could."

"You were a brave woman," I said softly.

She gave me a smile. "There were many brave women who helped. I'm not sure we would have won the war otherwise. We all wanted to build a better Ireland."

"And ya did," I said, encouraging her. "You won the war and freed Ireland—most of it, anyway—from British rule."

But her face darkened, and she let out a heavy sigh. "Aye. When the news of the truce reached us, we were so hopeful. But there's always a price to pay in war, and I didn't know then how steep a price it would be. War had hardened Patrick. He said the treaty wasn't enough, that half a republic wasn't a republic at all."

She gazed off into the distance, seeing memories from long ago. "Most of Cork agreed with my brother and didn't want to accept the treaty. But my father agreed with Michael Collins that the treaty was the right step toward freedom and peace. So the men who'd just fought together for our freedom turned against each other.

Brother against brother—or in my case, my brother against my father."

I stayed quiet, not knowing what to say. We'd never spoken of the war like this.

She bit her lip. "Patrick's side had the most men. But the Free Staters had the backing of the British, along with their weapons. They moved quickly and took Cork. The things I saw..." She squeezed her eyes shut, shaking her head. "It was brutal. We'd already lost so many of our own in the first war, but we kept killing each other in the second."

Mamó grew quiet for a moment. The air felt heavy with grief. When she spoke again, her voice was broken. "My father survived the fighting, but Patrick was wounded. He came to me, knowing I could tend him and help hide him until he'd healed. I did, of course. I didn't realize the danger it put me in, but I don't think it would have mattered anyway. He was my brother. I'd do anything for him. But I made a mistake."

"What mistake?" I asked in a whisper, terrified of what her answer would be.

Pain washed over her face. "I told my mother. I never thought..." Her voice broke. She shook her head, clearing her throat.

When she spoke again, her voice was brisk, like she was trying to get the words out as quickly as possible, trying to separate herself from the emotions. "My mother told my father that Patrick was alive and okay. She, like me, was just trying to pass on good news of her family. But my father's loyalty wasn't to us anymore. He was only loyal to his cause. He followed me when I went to take supplies to Patrick and betrayed him."

"He betrayed his own son?" I was shocked beyond belief.

"Aye." She nodded. "Patrick was executed by some of the same men he'd fought beside. There was no mercy." The grief on her face was as strong as if it had just happened.

"I'm so sorry." It wasn't enough, but I didn't know what else to say.

She swallowed hard. "So am I. The war ended, the truce held, and we had our freedom. But our family was never the same again, and in the end, the war didn't make much difference. The problems we'd had before didn't go away. Our government was Irish, but it was just as corrupt as when it was British, and our people still suffered from poverty and injustice. Did you know that they airbrushed the faces of women who'd served in the army out of the photographs and refused to pay them the military pensions they were owed?"

My jaw dropped. "That's terrible."

"Aye." She sighed. "It doesn't matter what face the powerful have; power corrupts British and Irish alike. And violence never solves anything, not truly."

"How did your heart heal from all of that?" I asked softly.

"It wasn't easy," she admitted. "I'd seen things that gave me nightmares, and I grieved the loss of Patrick. I was wracked with guilt, knowing that if I hadn't told my mother he was safe, he wouldn't have been betrayed. My father didn't want to speak of him. Neither did my mother, though for different reasons. And I couldn't talk to anyone else about him because he was considered a terrorist. I was expected to pretend like everything was fine, that I was glad he'd been executed, even though my heart felt ripped to shreds. So I started going on walks in places where I knew I wouldn't see another soul. It was the only way I felt any sort of peace. And one day, I came upon the hawthorn tree." She smiled, remembering.

"*The* hawthorn tree?"

"Aye, the one from which I got the cutting that now grows in our very yard." Her gaze turned wistful. "It was a beautiful tree, all lit up in the sunlight and covered in flowers. If I'd been thinking straight, I wouldn't have approached it at all, knowing the legends about the faeries. But I wasn't thinking straight. Or maybe I was and I had a death wish. I don't know." She chuckled.

"Did the faeries whisk you away to another world and teach you all their healing secrets?" I teased.

She shook her head, a playful grin sneaking onto her face and making her look ten years younger. "No, they didn't. But I sat down beside that tree, and I swear it spoke to my heart. I poured out all my troubles to it. The tree felt like a friend somehow, a safe friend that I could tell my story to. I spoke to it about my brother, my guilt, my torn loyalties, and the atrocities I'd witnessed. In telling my story, it started losing some of the power it held over me."

She took a deep breath. "At the time, I thought I was going half crazy. I didn't understand the medicine that the hawthorn tree held. But it spoke to me anyway. It told me to take some flowers and make myself a tea and to come visit it every day. So I did. Every day, I grew a little bit more whole, and I finally forgave myself for what I'd done to Patrick."

"Hawthorn for the heart," I said, repeating what she'd told me a thousand times before, even though she'd never told me her personal experience with it.

Hawthorn was good heart medicine, the first we turned to for anyone who was having cardiac difficulties. But it was good for the emotional heart too, so she always said. It was the tea she always made for someone who was grieving.

"Aye." She nodded, taking a deep breath. "Hawthorn for the heart. There's no way to really explain it, Fiona, but that tree helped me put my shattered heart back together, piece by piece. Years later, when your ma died and my heart shattered again, I went straight to the tree. I told it goodbye, saying I had to come take care of yous girls. The tree told me to take a piece of it with me so I could keep sharing its medicine with those who needed it. So I did."

"So it wasn't the faeries after all?" I asked.

She shrugged. "Who's to say? Maybe it was the tree itself talking, maybe it was the faeries who guarded it. Maybe it was the Good Lord speaking through a hawthorn the way He spoke through the burning bush to Moses, although it seems a wee bit presumptuous to think He'd take the time to deal with my little problems personally when the whole world was needing attention.

"But it doesn't really matter, does it? I gave up trying to understand how the world works a long time ago. We can worry our human brains to pieces trying to figure everything out, or we can settle into the mystery and simply say thank you for the gifts we're given. I find that's a whole lot better for the soul."

"*You're* good for my soul—and my heart," I said, smiling in a way that felt more real than it had in a long time.

"You're good for mine too," she said, her eyes twinkling. She patted my hand. "Now, let's leave the potatoes and make you some tea."

We made the tea together while she gave me a verbal lesson on all the many medicinal uses of hawthorn. I took the lesson to heart.

But years later, after I'd done something truly unspeakable, I realized I'd missed what she was trying to tell me all along.

14
THE SUSPECTS

Daphne
Rosemary Mountain
Present

When I returned to the crime scene, Jackson and Greg were gracious enough not to mention my vomiting. Greg offered to end things for the day if I wanted, but I told him no way.

I had two motivations now. I wanted to prove that Fiona was innocent, but I also wanted to take down Alva's killer.

She hadn't deserved to die like that.

So I refocused. I wasn't quite ready to face the spot where Alva had died again, so we went to the kitchen. When I didn't feel anything in there or the formal living room, Greg suggested we go upstairs.

"Again, I want you to go through each room cold," he said. "Then we'll fill you in on what we know so far."

I agreed and headed up the impressive staircase to the upstairs bedrooms.

The first room we came to was a guest room. I expected to feel nothing when I walked inside, but I was surprised to pick up on some residual energy. The look on my face must have alerted Greg, because he stepped forward and asked what I was getting.

"I don't know exactly," I said, frowning, "But the energy in here is different than the rest of Alva's house. It's colder somehow—and I don't mean temperature-wise."

Alva's home felt warm and friendly. Inviting. But this room … didn't.

I walked around, letting my hands run along various surfaces, hoping to get something. But I didn't see or feel anything other than the cold energy.

"Do we know who has stayed here recently?" I asked.

Greg and Jackson exchanged glances.

"We do," Jackson confirmed. "Alva's nephew, Erick, has been staying here off and on. He said he was worried about her."

"Is this the same nephew who brought up Fiona's name?" I asked, my eyebrows raised.

"It is," Greg confirmed.

"Why was he worried about Alva?"

But Greg shook his head. "Not until you're done."

"Okay," I said, letting out a breath. "Let's move on, then."

The next room was another sitting room. I smiled the moment I walked in. It was a happy-feeling room, another place where I could tell Alva had enjoyed spending time. The foyer downstairs had been subtly themed to the seaside, but this room had nothing subtle about it. It was like walking into a beach resort, with billowing curtains, chaise lounges, driftwood tables, and a seascape mural that took up an entire wall.

"Wow," I said, dumbstruck. "This is amazing."

A quick look around told me that this was where Alva had done her design work. The wall across from the mural was lined with shelves of gardening and design books, and a sketching table sat beside the picture windows. The sketchpad on it had a half-finished garden design with symbols and a key that explained which plant each symbol stood for.

"Was she still working?" I asked, looking up.

Jackson nodded. "Yeah. From what we understand, her retirement only lasted about six months until she got bored and started taking on jobs again."

"She loved what she did." I could feel it in my bones.

"Getting anything else?" Greg asked.

"Other than envy?" I joked. "No. The energy in here is warm and happy again, unlike the last room. But I'm not really..."

I trailed off as a framed newspaper clipping on the bookshelf caught my eye. I walked over and picked it up, feeling the squeeze of heartbreak.

The photo in the clipping showed Alva and Fiona with their arms around each other, sharing a ribbon for first place in a regional gardening competition. They were both grinning from ear to ear.

Beside it sat another framed photograph—another one of Fiona and Alva, I realized with a start. This one was much older. Fiona couldn't have been more than thirty-five years old, maybe even younger. They were both holding up turnips, posing the way men do with their fish. Fiona was making a silly face, while Alva pretended her turnip was six inches bigger than it actually was.

It made my heart hurt for Fiona. I hadn't realized that she and Alva had been friends for as long as they had been—longer than I'd even been alive. No wonder Fiona was devastated by her death.

Jackson moved to my side. "Getting anything off those?"

"No," I said, putting the photographs back. "Let's move on."

I felt too sad to stay in this beautiful room any longer.

The next room was another interesting one. It was clearly lived in, but it didn't belong to Alva. Greg and Jackson waited patiently while I explored it.

I turned around and gave them a perplexed look. "This room

feels different too. It's lived in, but it feels very neutral. I don't know how to explain it, but I don't get a sense of personality in here. The clothes tell me it's occupied by a young woman, but... There are no photographs, nothing personal, and no real emotions that I'm picking up on. I don't know if that means anything, but that's all I have."

They exchanged looks again.

"This room is occupied by a full-time housekeeper," Jackson explained. He looked at his notes. "Name is Megan Keller. She moved in with Alva about six months ago."

I frowned. "Six months is a decent amount of time. It's strange that there's *nothing* personal, isn't it?"

"You tell me," Greg said, his face flickering with amusement. "What else are you getting?"

I took my time, touching multiple things in the room, but came up empty.

"Nothing," I said, shrugging. "All I get is the *lack* of energy. That may be a me thing—it's not like I pick up energy constantly. But I've felt it in the other rooms, so... I don't know. It's weird that this room feels so blank, especially knowing she's lived here for six months."

"Noted," Jackson said. He and Greg exchanged glances again, making me wonder what else they hadn't told me.

The final room upstairs was Alva's bedroom. The moment I walked in, I was hit with a strong energy I didn't particularly want to feel— or describe to my father-in-law.

"Did Alva have a boyfriend?" I asked, unable to keep my face from flushing red.

"Yes," Jackson answered, grinning. "Why?"

"Nothing," I said, shaking my head. "I just get the sense they were ... having fun. A *lot* of fun."

Greg leaned against the dresser, chuckling. "Good for Alva."

"Finish reading the room. Then I'll fill you in," Jackson said, his lips twitching like he was holding back a laugh.

I tried to read the room, but that was all I could feel. I didn't even want to touch anything because I did *not* want to risk a vision of two seventy-year-olds having quite that much ... fun.

When we stepped out of the room, Jackson explained. "According to the nephew, Alva got this new boyfriend a couple of months back. Erick and his wife were already concerned that the housekeeper was taking advantage of Alva's generosity. They got doubly concerned when she started dating this new guy"—he checked his notes— "Neal Anderson."

"Why were they so concerned?" I asked as we started heading down the stairs. "I get the feeling she was pretty happy."

Greg smirked.

"Honestly? I think that's *why* they were concerned. The nephew rubs me the wrong way," Jackson admitted. "My take? He was more worried about Alva's money than about her. He mentioned con artists multiple times, like he thought the housekeeper or the boyfriend was trying to con Alva out of her money."

"*Her* money or *his* inheritance?" I asked, raising my eyebrows.

"Exactly," Jackson confirmed. "Erick and his wife both work decent jobs, but they don't have the kind of money Alva has, and they have an eighteen-year-old son starting college this fall. Alva didn't have any children, so I think Erick assumes she'll pass every-thing to him. Any new attachments would be a threat to that."

"Hmmm." The theory made sense, especially with the coldness I had felt in the bedroom where he stayed. There hadn't been any sense of love in there.

We walked back into the sitting room where Alva had died and I was hit with sadness again. I took a deep breath, knowing I'd have to go into that scene and try to see the truth at least one more time.

I dreaded it.

"I went through every cabinet and every drawer looking for supplements or potential medicines that would interact with Fiona's tea," Jackson said. "I didn't find anything that raised red flags for me, but I made a list and sent it to the medical examiner. Her assistant said she'll review it this morning and call me. In the meantime, take a look at these." He pulled a stack of photographs out of the notebook he was carrying and handed them to me.

I flipped through them, feeling sick. Each one was of something I'd seen during my vision, and it brought me right back to those horrible moments Alva had endured.

The spilled teacup on the floor.

Alva's body, her arm at an odd angle from her shoulder.

Foam and blood on her mouth.

The table on its side.

Books and magazines scattered across the floor from when her feet had likely kicked the magazine rack.

Something wasn't right, I realized. The table was upright again, and the books and magazines had been put back on the rack. Jackson had photographed the scene, but he wouldn't have moved things without cause.

I looked up from the photos and frowned. "Who cleaned up the mess?"

"Erick," Jackson said, his lips tight. "I took those photos the morning after Alva died, right after he told us his concerns. When I arrived this morning, he was here. Said he was starting the cleanup. I had to remind him that he's the one who suggested this was a crime and that he'd just contaminated an active crime scene."

"A *potential* crime scene," Greg corrected.

But his optimism didn't make me feel better. My hopes of this having been an accidental overdose had dwindled significantly.

I mulled it over. "If he came back to clean up, he could have taken evidence. Supplements, medicine bottles... Anything that would have pointed toward something other than Fiona's tea."

Jackson nodded. "Absolutely. Of course, he could have taken evidence before he even called us, and his fingerprints and DNA would have already been all over the scene anyway since he's the one who found her. Still, I don't like it, and I got the feeling he wasn't telling me the whole truth about why he was here."

Greg's jaw tightened. "We need to keep an eye on him."

"Agreed," Jackson said.

I flipped to the final photographs: the jar of tea Fiona had brought over, bearing one of Fiona's handwritten labels. The back of the jar with Fiona's neatly printed instructions and ingredients list. A strainer in the sink with what certainly looked to be the same herbs that were in the jar.

My stomach sank.

I handed the photographs back to Jackson and walked over to the chairs again, feeling like an invisible magnet was tugging me there. But instead of touching Alva's, I sat down in the one beside hers— and had another vision.

It was morning. Fiona was sitting in this very seat, flipping through a gardening magazine. Alva came in, carrying a tray with snacks and a tea set.

Fiona snagged some cheese and crackers, poured a cup of tea, and laughed when she took a sip. "You're serving your medicine as tea for company?"

Alva smiled and poured a cup for herself. "Why not? It tastes better than anything at the store, and you said the herbs in it wouldn't hurt anyone."

"They won't, and they'll give everyone some much-needed vitamins and minerals. But I think you'll find that not everyone shares your preference for the taste of horehound, stinging nettles, and clover," Fiona said, winking. "Most people around here want their tea black, iced, and sugary sweet, thank you very much."

Alva laughed. "You're right about that." She took a sip, then put her cup down and reached for some grapes. "Before you leave, remind me to show you my desert rose. It's having its second blooming!"

Fiona choked. "Are we talking about a plant or your desert rose? Because there's some lines I won't cross even for a friend like you." She made a face.

Alva blinked twice, then died laughing. "It's a succulent, you silly woman. Although..."

"Stop!" Fiona held her hand up.

The vision faded. When it was over, tears streamed down my cheeks.

"What is it?" Greg asked.

"There's no way Fiona killed her," I said. "They adored each other. Besides, when Fiona delivered the tea that morning, Alva made a pot and served it while Fiona was still here. Fiona drank it. She wouldn't have done that if it had poison in it."

Greg's shoulders relaxed. "That tells us what we've suspected all along. Fiona's not being honest with us. I just don't know why."

"I don't, either," I admitted. "But it wasn't Fiona's tea."

Jackson snapped his notebook shut. "The testing should prove that, then," he said with a satisfied look. "When the results come back, Fiona will be cleared."

His phone rang. He checked the caller ID. "This is the ME calling me back about the supplements. Excuse me." He held up a finger as he answered it and walked out of the room.

"Maybe we'll get good news and she'll have identified something Alva was taking that might have caused this," Greg said, rocking back onto his heels. "I'll have Jackson take a look at Alva's gardening supplies, too, in case there are chemicals in them that could have caused a reaction like that. We'll figure it out. I'm just glad to know you saw Fiona drinking the tea. The results will clear her, and we can focus on finding out what really happened."

"Yeah," I agreed, although I didn't share the relief he clearly felt. I knew that Fiona hadn't done it, but it still bothered me that she'd confessed.

We were missing something. I just didn't know what. But whatever it was, Fiona was connected to it somehow, and I wouldn't feel true relief until we knew the whole story.

Jackson walked back into the room. His face was pale. "We might have a problem."

Greg's eyes turned sharp. "What do you mean?"

"No red flags on the supplements or medications, although we'll send them for testing to make sure they really are what they're supposed to be. But I also gave them a heads-up to consider cicutoxin poisoning since Fiona said that's what we're looking for."

"And?" My heart hammered as I waited for him to answer, even though I knew what he was going to say.

His face was grave. "The ME said cicutoxin poisoning fits perfectly with the manner of death. It's rare. She's only seen it once before, in a victim who was foraging for food and thought it was a wild carrot. But … it fits. Toxicology will take time, but they'll be able to test the tea more quickly. She's willing to bet money the results will be positive."

Greg groaned and turned away, pacing the front of the room.

I sank back into the chair, confused and utterly distressed.

Fiona hadn't killed Alva. I believed that with all of my heart.

But how had she known what the poison was if she hadn't given it to Alva herself?

I'd seen her drink the tea. But what if she had given Alva "clean" tea, knowing that Alva would serve it to her, and then put the water hemlock in the jar before she left?

I could not imagine Fiona committing murder. But she'd confessed, and she'd known exactly what poison had killed Alva. How was that possible?

I was starting to wonder if Fiona was right and I just wasn't willing to face the truth about who she was and what she was capable of.

15
IRA RUMORS

FIONA

Spring 1970
Belfast

Christmastime was over all too soon. I said goodbye to Mamó and Annie with a heavy heart. But the time with them had renewed my spirit, and I had high hopes that the new year would bring peace to Belfast.

In the weeks that followed, it seemed that most of the fighting was between the Loyalists and the soldiers, which gave me a stronger confidence that things really would get better. The way I saw it, if the Prods were throwing bombs at British soldiers, then the soldiers would naturally be more inclined to help protect us Catholics. After all, we were being bombed by the same people. There was nothing better to unite two forces than sharing a common enemy. Surely nothing like what had happened last September would happen again.

I repeated this hope to Ian, who agreed with me—at first, anyway. But as the weeks went on, his attitude started to change.

As we became more accepted in Falls Road, he started talking more with the men who'd been here longer than us. They didn't share my hope in the soldiers. They'd lost all hope in the government a long time ago.

I soon started worrying that Ian was losing hope too. Not just from hearing their stories, but from the little things he was experiencing every day. It was bad enough for me in our neighborhood. With the barricades being guarded more, I felt at least a little bit safe there, despite the trouble we'd seen. The soldiers never gave me any trouble, and their presence gave me a sense of reassurance even though I lived with a constant underlying fear that what had happened the weekend of the bombings would happen again.

But it was much worse for Ian.

He had to pass through the checkpoints every day just to get to school, and he was doing so as a Catholic man carrying a bag. The soldiers would dump his bag out on the ground, not caring what happened to his books. He had to show his papers repeatedly, even though he'd proven time and again that he was a student. And that wasn't even the worst part of his daily journey.

He crossed enemy territory every day, walking down streets filled with the very people who'd thrown those bombs, people who seemed to resent his very existence for no reason other than the fact that he was Catholic. They hurled slurs at him, threatened him. I knew he never really felt safe until he got to campus, and even there, he still felt like he had to watch his back.

He had friends, though, in the neighborhood and at Queen's. Most students were willing to leave their politics at the door, and many of them were sympathetic to the plight of Catholics in Belfast. They were eager to join the movement for equality. He found a community there, and I was glad for it, even if I hadn't quite found one of my own.

He started bringing two of his new friends around, Seamus Doyle and Kieran O'Connor. Kieran was a stonemason. I never really figured out how he and Ian had become friends, because Kieran didn't go to Queen's and he didn't live in Falls. But Seamus had grown up in Falls and was a fellow Catholic attending QUB on scholarship. They'd meet at the apartment, saying it was to study, but it never took long for their conversation to turn to the Troubles.

One spring evening, Seamus came over uninvited, throwing our door open without even knocking. He came in with a silly grin on his face and tossed Ian a beer. Kieran followed behind him wordlessly, giving Ian a nod of greeting before turning his dark eyes in my direction. I quickly looked away, unsettled by his intensity.

"Drink up, lads. We're celebrating," Seamus said before plopping down on our saggy sofa. He sprawled his arms out over the back of it like he owned the place, leaving no place for Kieran to sit.

Ian returned Seamus's grin, taking his place in the green fabric chair I'd found at the secondhand shop that week. "Should I ask what we're celebrating or just be grateful for the free drink?"

Seamus's eyes flicked toward me, where I stood drying dishes in the kitchen. I gave him a nod and a little smile. It was the best I could do. Seamus was alright. He didn't unnerve me the way Kieran did, but I resented his constant intrusion into our lives. I wanted to be glad Ian had such a good friend at the university, but it seemed like Seamus was taking up more and more of his time and I was getting less and less of it. Without any real friends of my own in the city, I was feeling more than a little lonely, and I missed the quiet nights Ian and I used to share just the two of us.

Seamus turned back to Ian. "The rumors are true," he said, grinning again.

Ian smiled, though his was more guarded. "Are they now? Ya know for certain?"

Seamus nodded, then drained his beer and smacked the bottle down onto our coffee table with so much force I winced across the room. "Aye. Fergus confirmed it."

"What are we talking about?" I asked from the kitchen, sticking the last dry plate into the cabinet. I put away my dish towel and walked the few steps into the living room, taking a seat on Ian's knee since Seamus was taking up the entire couch.

Kieran had taken one of our kitchen chairs, his tall frame looking like a giant at a doll's table. The second chair was still empty, but it was far too close to him for comfort.

The three men looked at each other. I got the feeling they'd rather not tell me at all. It caused a flash of anger to rise up in me, so it did. After all, Ian and I were man and wife, and we'd always told each other everything.

"Come on now," I prodded, giving Ian an annoyed look. "What's the craic?"

Ian slipped his arm around my waist. "There have been rumors about a new approach to things. That we're taking matters into our own hands."

Kieran's eyebrows rose. He shot Ian a look of disapproval, but he kept his mouth shut.

"What do you mean?" I asked. Ian's words made my stomach twist like knotted ropes.

"This isn't well known yet," Ian said, keeping his voice low. "But Fergus says there was a split in the IRA."

"The IRA?" I looked at him, dumbfounded. The Irish Republican Army, as far as I knew, was just a bunch of old men with antique guns who liked to get together on weekends to play at "war drills" south of the border.

Seamus scoffed. "They should be renamed the 'I Ran Aways' after what happened last fall."

"What do you mean?" I was still lost.

"People weren't just upset at the soldiers for not protecting us," Ian explained. "In the old days, the IRA fought to protect their people. They were heroes. Freedom fighters. But they were as useless as the British when our neighborhood was attacked."

"But they're not a real army anymore," I protested.

"What if they could be though?" Seamus leaned forward, his eyes flickering with a sharpness I'd never noticed before. "That's what we're saying. There's a new group, a split-off. The Provisional IRA. They want to push the soldiers out of our area and take over defense."

I stared at him, stunned. "I'm not sure that's something to be excited about."

"They have to do something," Ian said, surprised by my tone. "You've seen what's happening. Are we supposed to just sit here defenseless while Prods throw bombs into our houses, killing children in their sleep? While the RUC and the British soldiers and even the IRA do nothing?"

"Of course not." I didn't know how to express what I was feeling —I wasn't even sure myself. What Ian and Seamus were saying was right. If the government wouldn't protect the people, it only made sense for the people to protect themselves.

But I had a terrible feeling I couldn't explain. I couldn't help thinking about Mamó's words to me, about how there would always be people wanting to stir up trouble on both sides.

The people here had a right to be afraid, and of course, they had a right to defend themselves. But I'd also seen anger in their eyes. I'd heard them talk about the other side with as much venom as that side directed toward us. I had a sick feeling that all of this was just going to make things worse.

I didn't say that though. After all, I didn't know anything, really. It wasn't my neighborhood. It wasn't my fight. Seamus and so many of the others had been there their whole lives. They knew Belfast and the ins and outs of how things worked there better than I ever could. Surely they knew what was best, more so than a young girl who couldn't even figure out why she felt the way she did about it.

"Are you alright?" Ian asked, his eyes crinkling in concern. "You look pale. White as a ghost."

I forced a smile. "I've a headache is all. I think I'll make myself a cup of tea and tuck in early since you have friends to keep ya company."

Seamus visibly relaxed. "Aye, that's a good idea. Always best to sleep off a headache, so I say. Besides, we lads have important matters to discuss."

But they didn't discuss them in front of me. They turned their talk to school and the exams they had coming up while I put on the teakettle and chose the herbs I wanted for the headache that didn't exist. When my tea was ready, I slipped off to the bedroom, leaving the door cracked so I could hear their conversation. But when I left the room, their voices dropped low.

I knew they weren't talking about exams anymore.

I let the tea go cold while I cried silently into my pillow, feeling as though I'd somehow lost a battle I hadn't even known I'd been fighting.

16

THE NEPHEW AND HIS WIFE

Daphne

Rosemary Mountain
Present

The three of us met back at the office, where Jackson and I started doing our own research into water hemlock. My stomach sank with every note we made.

It was the most poisonous plant in North America, responsible for the violent deaths of humans and livestock. Not only did water hemlock cause seizures, convulsions, and rapid death, it grew wild in Tennessee—and had a sweet taste that could easily be disguised in herbal tea.

Jackson closed his laptop and settled back into his chair. "This looks really bad."

I blew out a breath. "Yeah. It does."

It looked *very* bad. Water hemlock fit our victim's manner of death, Fiona had mentioned it by name, and it was easily accessible to an herbalist with decades of experience in foraging wild plants.

Even if she hadn't confessed, Fiona would be the number-one suspect.

Jackson sighed. "You know her better than I do, but I would never have pegged Fiona as being capable of something like this."

"She's not," I insisted, fighting against the doubt that kept trying to creep into my heart. "There has to be something else going on."

"I want to believe that," he said earnestly. "But I've been working in law enforcement for a long time, and the reality is that sometimes people do things that we would never expect of them."

"I know, but—"

I was cut off by Jackson's hand, held up in warning. I turned to look where his gaze was pointed and saw a wiry man making a beeline for us. Strolling behind him was a woman with an amused smile on her face.

"That's the nephew, Erick, and his wife, Regina," Jackson explained quickly. He muttered a warning under his breath as he rose to greet them. "Let me handle the talking."

I stood, happy that my only job was to observe. I had a feeling Jackson was about to get chewed out about something.

"I was told that you released Fiona Flanagan," Erick announced as he reached us. He was probably in his late forties or early fifties. Small, with an even smaller mouth that pursed into an odd circle when he spoke. He wore round glasses and was going bald but hadn't accepted it yet, if the thin strands of hair carefully brushed over his dome were any indication.

"She was never under arrest," Jackson answered easily, clearly used to dealing with difficult people in his job. "We asked her some questions, she cooperated with open and honest answers, and we instructed her to stay in the area in case we need to talk to her further."

"But she murdered my aunt!" The man's face turned bright red.

Jackson held his hand up. "We're taking your concerns very seriously, Mr. Jean. We've spoken with the county medical examiner, who has authorized a forensic autopsy. Your aunt's body is being transferred to the regional forensic center in Johnson City, and they'll run a full toxicology panel. But until they tell us otherwise, this isn't a homicide case."

The woman reached the man's side, giving me a cool look. She was probably younger than him but somehow managed to look older thanks to false lashes, bleached hair, and lips injected with so much filler that I had a hard time not staring at them. She crossed her arms and put the amused smile back on her face.

"I'm sorry about Erick," she said, though I didn't sense any genuine remorse. "He loved his Aunt Alva dearly, and he just wants to make sure justice is served."

"Trust me, that's what we want too," Jackson said confidently.

"See?" She turned to her husband and smiled at him. "We're all on the same team, *remember*?"

He took a breath. "Yes, of course." He adjusted his glasses and turned back to Jackson. "I apologize for being rude. This has been a very trying time."

"Of course. I understand," Jackson said.

The wife spoke again. "And who is your new secretary?" Her eyebrows shot up as she turned her gaze back on me.

"This is Daphne Sullivan. She's a consultant for our department. We've brought her on as an extra resource to make sure your Aunt Alva gets the attention she deserves," Jackson answered.

I had to give it to him. He'd gotten really good at this part of the job, and he'd always been a great detective. Greg was lucky to have him heading up the investigative division, and I was proud of Jackson's advancement. He was like a brother to me, and I loved watching him shine in his element.

"I thought so," the wife said slowly. "Daphne Sullivan. Local psychic, right? Interesting choice for a consultant."

I tensed. After my disastrous first few weeks in Rosemary Mountain, I'd only shared my sight with my most trusted friends. But there had always been rumors, just like there had been whispers about my mother and her sight.

Apparently, those rumors had reached Regina Jean, and it made me deeply uncomfortable.

Erick's eyes widened. "A psychic? Seriously?" His fingers trembled slightly as he adjusted his glasses again.

Jackson's fingers pressed into the desk in front of him, the only sign that he was struggling for control. "You wanted every resource, right? Daphne has been an integral part of solving several high-profile cases. We're all lucky she was available—and willing—to lend her assistance to this one."

"Lucky indeed," Regina said with a coy smile. "Especially lucky for Fiona Flanagan, who happens to be Daphne's dear friend."

Erick's eyes somehow widened even more, making me worried they were going to pop right out of his skull. He eyed me nervously. "Now, to be clear, I'm not convinced that Fiona did it. And if she did, it might have been an accident. I mean, these things happen, right? A wrong ingredient, perhaps?"

Regina squeezed his arm in a clear signal to stop talking.

"I assure you we're looking into every possibility," Jackson said. He turned to Regina. "And anyone who works for this department, even as a consultant, is dedicated to justice—even if that means we have to face hard truths about the ones we love. Ms. Sullivan and I both have personal experience with that."

I only noticed the tiny tic in his jaw because I knew him so well.

Regina raised her hands in defense. "Oh, of course, I certainly never meant to question *you*. We know you turned on your own father."

Jackson's fingertips went pure white.

I spoke up, defying his order to let him do the talking. "I'm curious what motive you think Fiona Flanagan might have had? We haven't been able to come up with one." I gave them a perplexed look.

Jackson, instead of being angry, shot me a grateful look for changing the subject. I knew he hated it when people brought up his father, and I didn't want him to have to respond with kindness to Regina's callous remark.

The amused smile never left her face. "Oh, I think she might have one, but we won't know for sure until Alva's will is read. What I *will* say is that I don't think either of you knows Fiona as well as you think you do. She has a long history of … trouble. I hate to point fingers, but if it does turn out that Alva was murdered, I think there are a couple of other suspects you need to look at as well."

"Oh?" Jackson asked, recovered from his momentary anger. He grabbed a notepad and a pen. "I'll be happy to look into them—*if* Alva's death is declared a homicide, which I must remind you, we're still a long way away from."

Regina took a deep breath as if he'd finally flustered her. "The housemaid," she finally announced. "I suspect she was stealing jewelry from Alva. Several prized pieces went missing recently."

"How do you know that?" I asked.

"Because I asked to borrow them and Alva couldn't find them," Regina answered, speaking to me as if I were a five-year-old. "Beyond that, I suspect that the housemaid was trying to weasel herself into Alva's will. Alva always was a sucker for a sob story."

"We'll make note of that," Jackson promised.

"And Alva's new boyfriend!" Erick pointed out. He glanced at me but seemed to have finally recovered from the revelation of my "psychic" abilities.

"Yes," Regina added. "We've had concerns about him. He was apparently quite attractive and … energetic. And we suspect he was trying to con Alva out of her money."

"Yes, Sheriff Morrison told me you had mentioned that," Jackson said tightly. I could see he was losing patience, though I admired him for keeping it for so long.

"That's a strange theory though," I said, butting in again. "If he were a con artist trying to get her money, why would he kill her *now*? Don't they usually try to marry their victims first so that they have legal rights to the money?"

Erick's face turned ashen. "That's right," he admitted to Regina. "That wouldn't make sense."

"Unless he found out she'd already added him to her will," Regina pointed out. "Or unless Alva caught onto his con and threatened to tell the police. That's a motive for murder."

Erick turned back to us, bold again. "Exactly. That's motive."

"We'll look into it," Jackson promised. "For now, do your best to focus on grieving. We'll be in touch if there are any developments."

Satisfied, Erick shook Jackson's hand, threw me an awkward look, and exited as quickly as he'd walked in. Regina lingered a moment longer, attempting to freeze us with her cold smile, before trailing after him like she had all the time in the world.

When they were finally gone, Jackson sank into his chair and blew out a breath. "They're a piece of work."

"You are not wrong," I agreed, taking the seat we'd dragged over so that I could look at his computer while we researched.

He turned to me. "What did you think? Did you get anything?"

I shook my head. "Nothing definitive. Although I thought it was strange that you said Erick's the one who has been staying in that guest room, because it's Regina's cold energy I felt there."

"*That's* interesting," he said, jotting it down quickly. "Anything else?"

"They're obsessed with Alva's will," I said flatly.

"Bingo." He cocked a finger gun my way. "We know Erick has an alibi for Alva's time of death, although I think there's at least a chance it could have been faked. But I'd like to know where Regina was that afternoon."

"Why didn't you ask?"

He shrugged. "We still aren't dealing with a homicide—officially. For now, I want them to think I'm on their side. She'd only be a flight risk if she thought I was onto her. The will is too enticing for them to leave."

"Good point." I fidgeted with one of the ink pens on the desk. "So what now? It seems like it's kind of a waiting game until we hear from toxicology."

Jackson shook his head. "Who knows how long it will take to get those results? It could be weeks—and frankly, I hope it is. We'll have to turn this over to state if toxicology comes back positive for cicutoxin. There's no way we can keep the case in-house with a conflict of interest like that. This is our only chance to figure out the truth and prove that Fiona's innocent—if she is."

My heart sank. "She is. She has to be."

"I hope you're right, but I'll admit I'm starting to have some doubts."

I was too. But unlike him, I wasn't ready to admit it.

I straightened, putting on a confident face. "There's no way. Even if Alva died of water hemlock poisoning, I still don't think Fiona did it. She's got to be covering for someone else."

He eyed me, drumming his fingers on the desk. "Alright. Then we need to figure out who really killed Alva—and who Fiona would care enough about to sacrifice herself for."

17
UNANSWERED PRAYERS

FIONA

Summer 1970

Belfast

Ian promised me that we would spend the summer in the village. He'd have nearly three months off, and I was aching to spend them in our wee cottage by the sea, surrounded by people we loved. But as the time grew closer, he started acting strangely and hinting that it might be better for us to stay in Belfast. I thought he was joking at first. Better to stay in Belfast? In what world could it possibly be better for us to stay in a city so close to exploding in rage that I thanked God every night for helping us survive another day?

But I began to realize Ian wasn't joking at all, that he was trying to get me used to the idea. I didn't know which made me angrier, that he actually wanted to spend our summer in the grimy slums of Belfast or that he was trying to manipulate me into it rather than coming right out and saying so.

Finally, on a blessed evening where Seamus wasn't gracing us with his presence, I confronted Ian about it.

"Please tell me you're not seriously thinking it would be better for us to stay in Belfast over the summer when you promised me we'd spend it in the village." I stood over his chair with my hands on my hips, giving him my sternest look.

His lips twitched in a grin. His hands came to my waist and tried to pull me to him, but I resisted, staying firm.

"Ah, Fiona, don't be getting mad at me now. I'm just trying to be practical. We can't sublet the flat, but we'll have to keep paying rent on it anyway. Seamus says he can get me a job in the shipyards over the summer. It'll be extra money in our pockets to help tide us over."

My fists clenched. "You'll make just as much on the fishing boats, I'm sure. And we may have to pay for the flat, but we don't have to live here. It's not as if we'll have to pay rent to live in our cottage, and food will be cheaper anyhow with the garden and fresh fish available to us."

He gave me a sober smile. "I suppose you're right about that. But Seamus—"

"Seamus nothing," I said, glaring at him. "Seamus isn't your wife, now, is he?"

Ian chuckled. "You're right again. All I was trying to say is that I promised Seamus to help him out with something next week when my exams are finished. I gave my word, Fiona. Can we at least wait until after that?"

"How long will it take?"

"A few days," he said, shrugging. "A week tops. We could leave for the village the first weekend of July."

"No later?" I wagged a finger at him.

"No later." He smiled at me with his boyish dimples and sparkling green eyes.

I felt my anger melting away and let him pull me into his lap, curling up against his hard chest. The troubles all seemed to fade when I was in his arms.

"Alright," I said, relenting. "The first weekend of July. But I'm warning you now, Ian *Ó Flannagáin*, that come the second week of July, I'm getting on the train and leaving the city with or without you." I put enough steel into my voice to make him believe I meant it, even though I wasn't at all certain I had it in me to leave him behind.

He nuzzled my neck, chuckling again. "Then I'll make sure the job is finished well before then, because I couldn't stand a single night without ya, my love."

I circled July fourth on the calendar and began counting down the days until I could kiss the ground in our village. But it didn't come fast enough. One week before we were to leave, the Orange Order went marching throughout the city, threatening to burn Catholics out of their homes.

Once again, the British soldiers did nothing to protect us.

What started as a march turned into riots all over Belfast. Then someone fired a shot and the riots became an all-out war. The "Battle of St. Matthews," they later called it, named after the church where men from the IRA set up with sniper rifles to defend against the incursion.

Everyone argued back and forth over who had started the gun battle, but there was no real argument about who won it. The victory, such as it was, belonged to us. Miraculously, only six people were killed.

Five of them were Protestants, shot by the IRA.

Clearly, it was self-defense. But the next day, over five hundred Catholic workers lost their jobs at the shipyards, dismissed by Protestant employers who wouldn't let the victory go unpunished. I grieved for those families, people who were already struggling so financially. Selfishly, I was relieved, thinking there was no way Ian would change his mind and want to stay in Belfast after that. After all, there was no chance of his getting a job at the shipyard anymore. We'd have to go home for him to find work.

Six more days. It was my constant prayer. *Just let us get through the next six days so that we can go home to our families.*

It was the first of many prayers to go unanswered.

I hummed to myself as I put the teakettle on the stove, glancing at the calendar on the wall to reassure myself again that tomorrow was the day. Just one more night; then I could say goodbye to concrete, soldiers, and fear. Ian was finishing up his favor to Seamus. He'd be home for dinner soon. We'd finish packing, curl up in each other's arms, and leave first thing in the morning.

When the kettle whistled, I poured the hot water over my chamomile, lemon balm, and skullcap blend. Normally, I saved chamomile for bedtime, but the excitement of going home had kept me buzzing with energy all day. I'd put the boost to good use, cleaning the flat from top to bottom, but now that the work was done, the extra energy made me feel nervous. At least, I hoped that's what was causing my anxiety.

Something felt off.

Don't go breaking your shin on a stool that isn't in the way, I reminded myself. There was no reason to worry. It was just nervous energy and excitement.

I glanced at the clock. There was no need to start dinner before Ian got home since we were only eating cold sandwiches. Maybe there was something else I could clean, some corner that hadn't been scrubbed yet.

It was probably silly to give the flat a full scrub-down before we left, seeing as how the dust bunnies would likely move in while we were gone anyway. But I liked the idea of leaving it spotless so that we'd return to a clean home when we came back in September.

My stomach clenched the moment I thought about returning. Part of me hoped that Ian would be so happy back in the village that he'd decide he didn't want a university degree after all. I shook myself, knowing I shouldn't think like that. This was his dream.

Besides, three months was a long time—maybe long enough to change things so that, when we did return, it was to a safer, happier city. The riots couldn't last forever.

I'd just taken my first sip of tea when there was a timid knock on my door. When I opened it, Peggy, Fergus's wife, was standing there with a look of fear on her face.

"Peggy, what's the matter? Come inside," I said, opening the door wider for her.

She shook her head quickly. "I can't. There's no time. I'm only here to tell you the army is on Balkan street."

When I stared at her blankly, she shook her head in frustration. "They're doing a raid," she said pointedly, like I'd know what she meant. "If you've anything to hide, hide it now. Pass it down the chain if you have to. Then stay inside, love. Lock your doors. Fergus is with the lads."

She squeezed my hand, giving me a sympathetic look, then hurried down the hallway.

I stood frozen in the doorway, trying to process her words. As I did, I realized why something felt off.

There were no children playing on the balconies, no sounds of laughter anywhere. All the doors were shut tightly, and everything was strangely quiet. Other than Peggy, the only people I saw moving around were a few men carrying odd packages wrapped in old coats. Something told me not to make eye contact with them, so I ducked my head, pretending not to notice.

But my head jerked up when I heard a burst of gunfire in the distance. It was followed by another burst.

Then another.

Peggy was five doors down now. I looked her way, my mouth open in shock. She met my eyes and gave me a sad smile.

"Go inside, love," she called, giving me a nod. "Stay away from the windows."

I backed inside, closed my door, and slid to the ground.

I knew in my soul that we weren't going to make it home after all.

18

THE HOUSEMAID

Daphne

Rosemary Mountain

Present

Jackson knocked on the door of the motel room Alva's housemaid, Megan, was staying in temporarily.

I tried not to think about my own motel stay in Rosemary Mountain and the crazy chain of events it had started. That was then; this was now. I was safe.

Megan, a young woman with pale skin and frizzy red hair, cracked the door open just enough to see. Her worried face flashed with relief when she saw Jackson.

"Can I go back home now?" she asked, hopeful.

"Not yet," Jackson answered. "I'm sorry. This is Daphne Sullivan, by the way. She's a consultant who works with me. Do you have a minute to answer a few of our questions?"

"Sure." She glanced behind her. "There's nowhere to sit in here, though, except the bed."

"There's a picnic table out back," I offered. "Has a great view of the mountains."

"Alright." She grabbed her key card and shoved it into the pocket of her navy sweatshirt, then motioned for us to lead the way.

When we sat down at the table, Jackson apologized again for displacing her from her home and reassured her that he was working as fast as he could to release it.

"Do you really think Ms. Alva was killed?" Megan asked, picking at her fingernail. Her chapped lips trembled, and she blinked quickly.

"I'm not sure," Jackson said carefully. "It might have been an accident. Regardless, there is good reason to believe that Alva died after ingesting a toxic substance."

I noted that he'd deliberately avoided the word poison.

Her eyebrows pinched together. "Toxic substance? Like ... chemicals?"

"Maybe," Jackson answered casually. "She was a gardener. I'm sure she dealt with a lot of pesticides and herbicides. She might even have dealt with some toxic plants. It could even be as simple as her mixing too many supplements. You lived with her. What can you tell us about the day she died?"

Megan relaxed slightly. "Not much. Saturdays are my day off, so I left early that morning—around eight, I think? I knew Ms. Fiona was coming over. She comes most Saturdays. Ms. Alva had plans to spend the day working on a new garden design for a home in Morehead City."

"Morehead City?" I asked. "Where is that?"

She glanced my way. "North Carolina. It's a beach town there."

"Why was she working so far away?" Jackson asked, frowning. "That's gotta be a long drive."

"It's about seven hours," Megan said. "But her boyfriend lives there, so she's been going over for one week each month. It's easier for her to travel to him because he still works full-time and she can work anywhere. Anyway, on her last trip, Ms. Alva visited a nursery there and started talking plants with someone, and next thing you know, they'd hired her to design their landscaping."

"How often does her boyfriend visit her?" Jackson asked.

Megan thought back, biting her lip. "Not often. Only a couple of weekends that I can remember."

"Regina and Erick mentioned concerns about him possibly conning Alva to get her money," I said. "Do you think they're right to be concerned?"

She gave me a strange look, then busted out laughing. "No way. Mr. Anderson is even richer than she was."

"Sometimes con men will pretend to have money," Jackson pointed out.

But Megan shook her head, clearly thinking the idea was ludicrous. "He's not pretending. He owns a fancy marina where rich people keep their yachts and tourists pay for chartered deep-sea fishing tours."

She pulled her phone out of her pocket and showed us a picture of a beaming Alva wearing a bikini on a yacht. The man with his arm around her had a deep tan, a charming lop-sided smile, and a toned body despite his gray hair and wrinkles.

"Wow," I commented. "I'm not sure whether I'm more impressed with the boat or with Alva. Holy cow. How old was she?"

"Sixty-six," Megan said, putting the phone back into her pocket. "She's *amazing*. She's like this ... super-cool career woman who does pilates every day, but who also knows how to be like the grandmother you never had." She dropped her chin as a tear slid down her cheek.

"You really loved her," I said, giving her a sympathetic smile.

She nodded. "I did. She meant the world to me. This job changed my life."

"Just a couple more questions," Jackson said, frowning. "How serious were Alva and this Mr. Anderson?"

"Pretty serious, I think," Megan admitted. "Ms. Alva was talking about selling her house and moving to Morehead City. She loved the beach, and she always sort of sparkled when she got back from visiting him."

"How long have you been living with Alva?"

"About a year now," she said.

"Is this the first time she's gotten serious about a man?" Jackson asked.

Megan nodded. "Since I've worked for her, yes. They met about ... three months ago, I think? Maybe four? Before that, I don't remember her dating anyone."

"Do Erick and Regina know that she was thinking about selling her house and moving there?" I asked, realizing where Jackson was going with his line of questioning.

"Yeah. Ms. Alva told them a couple of weeks ago." Megan made a face. "They didn't take it very well. That's when Erick and Regina started randomly spending nights at Ms. Alva's house." She rolled her eyes.

"When you say they didn't take it well..." Jackson left the question open-ended.

Megan sighed. "They told her she was crazy. That she was an elderly lady who was probably being taken advantage of. Erick also gave her a sob story about how he and Regina had always dreamed of living in her house as grandparents, so that their kids and grand-kids would have a big place to celebrate the holidays together."

"What did Alva say to that?" I asked.

Megan snorted. "She told them she didn't know why when they'd never spent any holidays there before. She tried to blow them off, but Erick kept pushing. I think half of why she was excited to move to Morehead was to get away from them."

Jackson and I exchanged looks.

"Regina said that you've been stealing jewelry from Alva," Jackson stated, giving Megan a hard look.

Her face went slack with shock. "*What*?"

"Have you?"

Anger flared in her eyes. "Of course not! I would never steal from

Ms. Alva. I'd be homeless if not for her. She took me in and gave me a job when I had nowhere else to turn. Ms. Alva was probably hiding her jewelry from Regina because she didn't want that nasty woman getting her filthy hands on it."

"We're not accusing you," I said, trying to soothe her.

Megan relaxed—slightly.

"I can tell you loved Ms. Alva a lot," I said, hoping it would get us back on track.

She let out a deep breath. "She was like family."

"What are you going to do now?" I asked. "I mean, where are you going to live? Do you have any savings?"

Her eyes flicked from mine to Jackson's and back again. She cleared her throat. "Well, I guess you're going to find this out anyway, so there's no point in hiding it. Ms. Alva put me in her will."

Jackson sat up straighter. "She did?"

Megan nodded. "She left me the house, most of the furnishings, and a fund to take care of it. Nobody else knows. She did it after I'd been living with her for a few months. Said she'd rather it go to me, someone who was working so hard to take care of it and could genuinely use it, than give it to her greedy nephew."

"Wow," I said, taken aback. "That's very generous."

"That was Ms. Alva." She softened momentarily, then straightened again. "So please tell me as soon as I can go home. It's *my* home now, not Erick and Regina's, and I need to make sure they don't try to take it over."

"We'll let you know," Jackson said, his eyes narrowing. "Uh, Megan, I have to ask. Where did you go the day Alva died?"

She froze, turning pale. "I went shopping. In Asheville."

"Alone?"

"Yes." She fidgeted with the cuff on her sleeve.

"Do you have a way to prove it? Receipts?"

Her cheeks flushed. "Um, maybe. I'll have to look."

"Credit card statements would help," Jackson suggested.

"Ms. Alva tipped me in cash," she said, her cheeks now flaming. "I ... didn't use a card."

"Hmm." Jackson gave her a serious look as he stood. "We'll be in touch. Don't leave town, okay?"

Her eyes went wide.

She stayed at the picnic table, picking at the skin on her thumb while we walked away.

19

FALLS CURFEW

FIONA

July 1970

Belfast

The clock was no longer my friend.

Every minute felt like an hour.

"Fergus was with the lads." Did she mean Fergus was with Ian and Seamus?

The thought was terrifying.

My entire body was tense with fear that came from all directions. Fear of the gunfire I could hear even with my door closed. Fear of not knowing where Ian was or if he was safe. Fear of the raids—what did that even mean? The soldiers were a neutral party. Why was Peggy acting like they were an enemy? Who were they raiding and why?

Below all of that was the deepest fear of all. I didn't fully trust Fergus, and Peggy's words terrified me.

What favor was Ian doing for Seamus anyway?

Why would Peggy think we had something to hide from the soldiers?

Another minute crept by.

I heard the sound of running on the balcony and a man's voice shouting. I strained to hear what he was saying, but I didn't have to —he banged on my door and hollered through it.

"The army is in the Falls! Stay inside! Doors locked!"

Fresh fear coursed through me. I double-checked the lock, then turned out the lights. I curled up in Ian's chair and wrapped a blanket around my shoulders, wishing it was his arms instead.

Then I waited—and prayed.

It felt like centuries passed before the next fist pounded on my door. I clutched my blanket and cowered, not knowing what to expect next.

But Ian's voice came through this time. "Let me in!"

I threw off the blanket and ran to the door, unlocking the deadbolt and yanking it open. Ian rushed inside. His hair was disheveled, and his eyes were wild.

"Where were you? Are you okay?" I cried, scanning him for injury. There was no sign of blood or burns, but their absence wasn't enough to assure me he was alright.

He slammed the door shut and locked it, then rushed to me, pulling me into his arms. "I'm sorry, Fiona," he choked out. "I'm so sorry."

I pulled out of his grip, needing to see his face. "Tell me what is going on."

The devastation on his face broke my heart.

He touched my cheek with his thumb. "The fighting's started up again, only this time, it's between the IRA and the soldiers. They've turned against us."

I gasped. "What?"

His face flashed with anger. "They did nothing to protect the Catholics last week when the Orange Order invaded our neighborhoods, but apparently, they don't want us to be able to defend ourselves, either. They're searching homes for weapons. Taking them. Disarming us all so that the next time the Loyalists want to burn down our homes, we'll have no way to stop them."

I gaped at him, shocked both by what he was saying and by the unfamiliar anger on his face. "Surely you heard wrong," I began, shaking my head. "The army is here as a neutral party; they're supposed to protect..."

But I couldn't even finish the sentence. They *hadn't* protected us. I'd heard the stories after the attacks, stories of soldiers standing aside and letting the Loyalists waltz right through with their bombs and their guns and their murderous hatred.

Even I couldn't pretend they were neutral anymore.

"I didn't hear wrong," he said, his face turning hard. "I saw it with my own eyes."

I started to ask him more, but someone pounded on our door.

"It's Fergus," the man hollered.

Ian flipped the lock and opened the door for him.

Fergus stood with Seamus and Kieran. All three of them wore the same anger and outrage that Ian did.

"How bad is it?" Ian asked sharply.

"Bad," Fergus said, shaking his head in disgust. "They're using the gas now." He glanced at me, a mix of respect and pity in his eyes. "I figure we'll be needing your healing services after this is over. For now, make sure you have wet cloth ready."

"Wet cloth?" I looked at him in confusion.

"For the gas," he said gently. "It's drifting this way already."

"Did you get the—" Ian didn't finish his sentence, giving Fergus a pointed look instead.

"Aye," Fergus said, nodding. He gestured toward Kieran. "They're in the right hands now."

"Do you need me for anything?" Ian asked.

My heart stabbed with betrayal that he would even think about leaving me during all of this. When Fergus shook his head, I let out a breath, my shoulders sagging in relief.

"No," Fergus said, his face grim. "Stay with your woman. You can't trust the Brit bastards with her. They've hurt our women before. I'm going to protect my wife too. Kieran and Seamus will take care of things."

Ian's fists clenched. He nodded sharply.

Kieran started to say something to Ian, but his words were drowned out by the whirring of helicopter blades. A man's voice came through a loudspeaker as the helicopter passed over the building:

"This area is now under an indefinite curfew. Stay indoors. Anyone found outside will be arrested."

We all looked at each other in shock. Kieran's face contorted with rage. He and Seamus exchanged glances, then darted off toward the stairwell.

Fergus spit. "Unbelievable." He gave Ian a final stare. "Protect your woman. Get inside. And no matter what happens, don't say a fucking word."

Ian nodded, then grabbed my hand and pulled me back as he slammed the door shut and locked it. "Imperialist pigs, thinking they can put us under a curfew," he said, disbelief in his voice. "First, they take our weapons. Now, they're locking us in our own homes? Those bastards think they own us."

I stared at him, my jaw on the ground. I'd never heard my Ian speak in such a way. But then again, we'd never faced anything like this before.

He paced the floor, muttering to himself about politics and the rule of law.

But while he was thinking about the big picture, my mind shifted to more practical matters.

The loudspeaker had said this was indefinite. We'd eaten up all of our food, save the makings for one small, cold sandwich each tonight, thinking we would be leaving in the morning.

I felt numb as I went to the kitchen and pulled out two dish towels to wet in case Fergus was right about the gas. The calendar on the wall caught my eye, mocking me.

Only one more night, I'd thought.

I'd wanted to escape Belfast. But there was no escape. I should have known better than to hope for it.

The curfew destroyed any hope I had left. It was all gone, not a single crumb left to hold on to. All that remained was Ian's anger and my quiet acceptance. This was our life now.

It's strange how quickly hope can disappear. How one event can break someone and turn them into someone else. Except it's never just one event. There's always a trail leading up to it.

When hopes are dashed time and time again, hope becomes a danger, not a friend. Better to simply accept what you can't change than deal with the utter disappointment of unanswered prayers and broken dreams.

I was eerily calm.

But what I didn't know was that it was the kind of calm that comes before the storm.

20

THE BOYFRIEND

Daphne

Rosemary Mountain

Present

When Jackson and I hopped into his truck, I shook my head, shocked.

"She has a legitimate motive," I said, feeling excited that we'd identified someone of interest other than Fiona.

"She does," Jackson agreed. "Erick and Regina do too. They all wanted the house. If Alva was thinking about selling it to move closer to a boyfriend…"

"One of them might have killed her before she could."

"Exactly." He let out a breath. "Erick and Regina supposedly didn't know about the will. So they're still in this. But Megan panicked over the alibi. I don't think she was expecting me to ask her about that."

"No." I mulled it over. "Which, honestly, makes her seem less likely to me. If she planned this out, don't you think she would have practiced an alibi? Or made sure she at least had one?"

"You'd think," Jackson agreed. "But what if she didn't plan it out? What if it's something she did on the spur of the moment? Maybe she went out that morning, came back, and interrupted Alva while Alva was working in her studio. Alva tells her she's decided for sure to list the house and is going to call a realtor. Megan goes downstairs, panics, and puts something in the tea. Since nobody knew Alva had left the house to her, she didn't worry about being looked at as a suspect."

"It totally could have happened that way," I agreed. "And honestly? I can't see Fiona lying to cover for Erick or Regina. But a down-on-her-luck girl that Alva had taken in? That's totally the kind of thing Fiona would do—if she wasn't angry at Megan for killing her friend, that is."

Jackson mulled it over. "I wonder if there are any cleaning supplies that ingesting would mimic the same symptoms of water hemlock. I'm not real familiar with poisons."

"She wouldn't have had to use cleaning chemicals," I pointed out. "Megan lived with a master gardener for a year. I'm sure she helped Alva in the garden some if she was getting paid a full-time salary and being given a place to live. Alva might have pointed the plant out on her property and told her to avoid it."

"That's a great point," Jackson agreed. "Maybe we should go back to the house and look around, see if there's any water hemlock growing on Alva's land. If there is, we can check for signs of recent disturbance, see if it looks like some of it was dug up recently."

"Awesome," I said, feeling cheerful. "I'll pull up pictures of it so we know what it looks like."

But when Jackson pulled into Alva's long driveway, we saw a Range Rover parked out front and a man standing on the porch, staring at the crime scene tape.

"I think that's Mr. Anderson," I said, recognizing the gray hair, tanned arms, and toned build.

"I think you're right."

Jackson pulled his truck up behind the Range Rover and parked. We got out and walked up to Mr. Anderson, who turned around to face us. His mouth hung open in shock.

"Mr. Anderson?" Jackson asked, walking up and flashing his badge.

The man nodded. "Yes. I—what's happened? Is Alva okay?" His voice cracked.

Jackson shook his head. "I'm sorry to have to tell you this, but Ms. Jean was found deceased Saturday evening."

The man's face crumpled. "Oh, God, no." He covered his face with his hand as his shoulders shook.

"I'm so sorry," I said, feeling sick. How could Jackson and Greg do this kind of thing regularly? Telling someone that a loved one had died had to be the worst thing in the world.

The man dropped his hand and looked at me, tears shining in his eyes. "What happened? She was supposed to come to my place last night, but she never showed. I tried calling... When she never answered, I got so worried I drove straight here today. But I never... Please. What happened?"

"We're not entirely sure yet," Jackson answered. "It appears she ingested a toxic substance. We're working to figure out if it was an accident or if it was intentional."

"Intentional?" The man blanched. "You mean ... suicide? Alva? There's no way."

Jackson shook his head. "No, not suicide. Murder."

"Murder?" Mr. Anderson's expression changed to horror. "*Alva?*"

"Possibly. I'm afraid I can't let you inside, but I'd appreciate it if you could give us a few minutes of your time. We think we may have identified a person of interest, and you might be able to help us out by answering a few questions."

His brow furrowed. "Well, of course. Anything I can do to help."

"Great." Jackson pulled a card out of his pocket. "Meet us down at my office. The address is on there."

"I'll follow you," Mr. Anderson said. He started to step off the porch, then turned, looking again at the crime scene tape with sorrow in his eyes. He swallowed hard before shaking himself and walking to his vehicle.

When we arrived, Jackson led the way to an interview room. "Sorry for the formality," he said. "But there's nowhere else here that's really private."

"It's fine," Mr. Anderson said absentmindedly. He was glancing around with a strange look on his face.

"Are you alright?" I asked.

"Yes, thank you. I've just never been in a place like this before," he said. "It's different than what you see on TV."

"It is," I agreed, remembering how awkward I'd felt the first time I'd been in this building.

"Right here," Jackson said, opening the door and gesturing for us to go inside.

The man paused, looking at the table with that strange look on his face, then took a seat. "This is all a bit surreal," he admitted. "I keep thinking this must be a bad dream."

"That's understandable," I said, giving him a sympathetic look. "I'm Daphne, by the way. I'm a consultant working with the sheriff's office."

"Lovely to meet you," he said, reaching across the table to shake my hand.

"I adore your accent," I said, finding him to be incredibly charming. He was wealthy, handsome, in great shape, and a total gentleman. No wonder Alva had been smitten with him.

He grinned at me. "That's kind of you. I've worked hard to tame it over the years, as not everyone finds the Kiwi accent easy to understand, and I'm required to do a lot of talking with my job."

"You own a marina, Mr. Anderson?" Jackson said.

Mr. Anderson looked at him with surprise. "That's right. And you can call me Neal. Should I be worried that you've looked into my background?"

Jackson gave him an easy smile. "Not at all. We were talking to Megan Keller earlier, Ms. Jean's housemaid, and she mentioned it."

Mr. Anderson relaxed. "Ah, Megan's a sweet girl. She takes good care of my Alva. Or did." His face crumpled again.

"Megan mentioned that Alva was thinking of selling her house and moving to Morehead," Jackson said, letting the statement sound like a question.

Surprise flashed on Mr. Anderson's face. "Did she really? She hadn't mentioned that to me. But that's lovely to know. I would have enjoyed that very much."

"She didn't tell you?" I asked.

"No, I'm afraid not. I'm a little surprised, to be honest." His brow furrowed. "Don't get me wrong; I was crazy about Alva. She's the most fun woman I've met in decades. But at our ages, I guess I thought we were both pretty set in our ways. We both had established lives, homes, and careers we loved. I thought we were happy with the way things were."

"Alva's family seemed concerned about your relationship. Can you tell us why they would have reservations about it?" Jackson asked.

Mr. Anderson laughed. "I suppose you're talking about Erick and Regina."

"Have you met them?" I asked.

"No. Nor did I want to. Alva wasn't particularly fond of them." He shook his head, annoyed. "Erick was the only son of Alva's brother. Shawn, I think was his name. Something like that, anyway. He was killed at a fairly young age, and Alva helped out his widow financially. Paid for Erick's school, things like that. Instead of being grateful, Erick seemed to think of her as his personal bank."

"That's terrible."

"It is," he agreed, frowning. "Alva and I got along beautifully. If they were concerned about our relationship, I can only imagine it's because they worried it threatened their inheritance."

"Were they right about that?" Jackson asked.

Mr. Anderson shot him another annoyed look. "Why would it have? I have my own money, and after going through one expensive divorce, I know better than to mix my finances with someone else—even someone as lovely as Alva. And what she decides—decided—to do about her estate is, frankly, none of my business."

"Did you have any concerns about Megan taking advantage of Alva?" I asked, curious.

He looked surprised by the question. "Megan? No, I can't say that I did. I didn't know her well personally—she tended to stay out of the way if I was visiting. But Alva only said good things about her. I think they doted on each other, actually. Alva preferred her company over Erick's, certainly."

"Is there anyone else you can think of that might have had reason to want to harm Alva?" Jackson asked.

Mr. Anderson thought for a moment. "No. But I really didn't know any of Alva's friends here. Maybe an unhappy business client? But that's impossible," he said, shaking his head. "She was wonderful at her job."

"Of course I have to ask: Where were you this past Saturday, between the hours of nine a.m. and seven p.m.?"

"Me?" Mr. Anderson looked stunned. "Well, working, of course."

"On Saturday?" I asked.

He looked at me like I was stupid. "I own a marina. Weekends are our busiest time. That's why Alva usually tried to come up on Sunday evenings—because I could take Monday off to be with her."

"And I'm sure you can verify that," Jackson said, his tone reassuring.

"Of course." Mr. Anderson pulled out his wallet and tossed a business card onto the table. "That's my place. My assistant can vouch for me. And if that's not enough, I'm sure any of the clients who were there that day will. As I said, Saturdays are quite busy. I probably spoke with twenty or thirty people over the course of the day."

"I appreciate it," Jackson said, grabbing the card. "I'm afraid I can't let you into Alva's house."

"That's alright," Mr. Anderson said. "I think I'll head home anyway. Maybe the drive will help me process what happened. I still can't believe it."

I reached across the table and patted his arm, feeling terrible for the man. "It will feel surreal for a while. I know from experience. Be gentle with yourself and give yourself time to come to terms with it."

He winced. "I just wish I didn't have to. Tell me—or maybe I don't want to know. Did she suffer?" His eyes were full of pain.

"No," I said, giving him the only thing I could—a lie. "She passed quickly."

His chest heaved with relief. "I'm grateful for that."

Jackson gave me an understanding look as we ushered Mr. Anderson out of the room and to the hallway that would lead to his car. The man walked away, looking strangely lost.

Jackson put a hand on my shoulder. "You're doing great."

"This is hard," I admitted. "I don't know how you guys do this all the time."

"We do it because the victims deserve it," he said.

"Yes." I took a deep breath. "And Fiona does too."

"Come on," Jackson said. "We'll wait for him to leave. Then we'll head back out to Alva's and look for that water hemlock. Then we'll find out if Erick's alibi could have been faked—and if Regina has one at all."

"Sounds like a plan."

21

SURVIVAL

Fiona

July 1970

Belfast

British soldiers broke down the door to our flat shortly after midnight.

I must have been afraid, but I don't remember feeling fear. I only remember Ian's anger and my numb acceptance.

I envied his anger, in a way. Anger was proof you were alive, proof you still cared. Whatever had broken in me earlier that night had broken my will to fight. It wasn't like me, but then again, when nothing is normal, it's hard to say what the real you is. Maybe that broken shell of a woman *was* the real me, and the version I'd always been before was the pretense.

I didn't know. I didn't know anything anymore. I was observing but not feeling, like I was in some sort of hazy dream that couldn't really be happening. But it was.

Three soldiers pushed their way into our flat, brandishing their rifles like they were just waiting for an excuse to shoot. The one in front, a man with cold eyes and a jagged scar beside his mouth, barked out orders for our place to be searched.

The two younger men started going through our things with no care at all, tossing our cushions off the couch, pulling our books off the shelf, and flipping through the pages only to throw them onto the floor.

The older soldier kept his gun pointed at us. Hatred glittered in his eyes, and I cowered at the sight of it.

But Ian didn't cower. He stared back, his proud chin lifted in defiance.

"If you have any weapons hidden in here, we'll find them," the soldier threatened. "Better to tell us now."

One of the younger soldiers dropped my rosary onto the ground and crushed it beneath his boot. A sob escaped before I could stop it. The rosary was a family heirloom, one of the few things I owned that had belonged to my mother, and it cracked my heart in two to see it destroyed like that.

"We've no weapons and nothing to hide," Ian snapped. "You've got no right to destroy our home, our things like this."

As quick as lightning, the soldier flipped his rifle around and slammed the butt of it into Ian's skull. Ian sank to the floor, dazed, as blood dripped from the wound to his head.

I ran to him and threw myself onto the floor, cradling his head in my lap. My eyes welled up with tears, but I refused to let them fall.

He was alive. Breathing but unconscious. I said a silent prayer of thanks for the strong pulse underneath my fingertips.

Something shifted inside me. The pieces of my broken, numb heart seemed to melt back together somehow, but not the way it had been before. It was like it formed into something new. A fire rose up inside me, burning away the numb acceptance.

I would be strong for Ian. I would fight for him.

I glared at the soldier who'd hit him, refusing to show fear. One side of his mouth turned up in a twisted smile, and my heart stammered as I realized the danger I faced.

Three against one. Three male soldiers and one young woman who couldn't possibly defend herself against them. My blood ran cold as I thought of the stories I'd heard of what British soldiers had done to Irish women during the War of Independence.

I let the fire inside me build, let it turn my blood to iron as I made myself a vow: They would not break me.

The soldier with the scar took a step forward, his twisted smile growing wider as his eyes raked down my body. "Get up," he commanded coldly, pointing his rifle at Ian's head even though the words were addressed to me.

But he jerked the rifle away at the sound of heavy footsteps racing down the hallway. Another soldier poked his head inside our shattered door. When he saw Ian on the ground, his expression grew concerned.

"Everything alright in there?" he asked, glancing at me before turning his attention to the man who'd held us at gunpoint.

"This one got aggressive," the soldier with the scar said. "Tried to attack me. I had to defend myself."

I gaped at his lie.

The newcomer's eyebrows furrowed. He looked from the soldier to me, and his eyes seemed to hold a question in them.

I gave him a subtle shake of my head, hoping he understood.

The hard set of his mouth told me he did.

"I'm surprised to hear that," he said reproachfully. "I know that one. He's a student at Queen's, studies with my brother there. I've met him a few times when I've snuck away for lunch with my brother, and he's never given me any reason to think he's a problem."

The soldier with the scar turned red-faced and spat on my carpet. "You mean to tell me your brother eats with the Fenians?"

The newcomer's eyes narrowed. "They're not all bad. You can't judge an entire group of people based on what a few have done to us."

"I don't trust any of them. They're animals, the whole lot of them."

I winced at the pure vitriol in his words.

The newcomer opened his mouth to respond but clamped it shut again when the other two soldiers emerged from my bedroom, looking disappointed.

"The place is clear," the one in front announced.

"Perfect timing," the newcomer said, giving them a nod. "We have a situation developing and we need reinforcements. All three of you are needed down on the street."

"Let the other two come with you, and I'll keep searching the flats by myself," the soldier with the scar said, standing his ground. His knuckles turned white as they tightened on his rifle. "If we give them an opening, they'll just hide whatever they have stashed here and move it to the flats we've already searched. We can't leave the building unmanned."

The newcomer shook his head. "If you have a problem with it, you'll need to take it up with the Major. These are his orders. All three of you need to come with me."

The soldier with the scar let out a growl, then turned and glared at me with a look that said he'd find his way back at the first opportunity.

I glared back, refusing to shrink underneath his gaze. Ian's blood coated my fingers, hot and sticky. I let it fuel the anger inside me that was burning like a wildfire.

The three soldiers traipsed out, leaving my home in ruins. When the one with the scar disappeared, I let out a breath, trembling. He might return, but I'd won the battle for now.

The newcomer waited until they were halfway down the hall before speaking to me in a low voice, his face apologetic. "I'm sorry for what happened to Ian. He's a good chap. If you have anything to put in front of your door, do it."

"To keep soldiers out?" I asked breathlessly.

He shook his head, his face turning dark. "Furniture won't keep them out. But they're using the gas more heavily than they should. Try to keep it out of your apartment. Use wet rags with water and vinegar if you can't." He glanced down at Ian again, sorrow coating his features.

"Thank you, Mr.—I don't even know your name."

He smiled, bowing his head. "Lieutenant Montgomery, at your service."

"Lieutenant Montgomery." I tried to smile back. "I'm Fiona. Thank you. Really. I think you may have saved my life tonight."

The sorrow on his face returned. "Don't judge us all on the actions of a few. Stay safe, Fiona. Tell Ian hello from me when he wakes up." He gave me a sharp nod, then turned on his heel and headed down the hallway.

The new fire inside me fueled me to action. I grabbed one of the cushions that had been tossed onto the floor and gently moved Ian's head onto it so that I could get up. Then I went to the kitchen and retrieved a jar of dried yarrow, a bowl of water, a mortar and pestle, and clean rags.

Kneeling beside Ian, I cleaned his wound with fresh water, wincing at how wide it was—and at how much blood ran out from it. I shook some of my dried yarrow into the mortar, ground it up into a powder, rinsed the wound one more time, and then packed it with the dried herb.

When the bleeding stopped, I took my first full breath.

With one emergency taken care of, I moved to the next: blocking our door. The sight of it made the anger rise again in me. The cheap lock would have given way easily with a kick; there had been no reason other than cruelty to break the door the way they had.

I closed it as best as I could. The top part was mostly intact, but the latch wouldn't hold, and there was a gaping hole underneath the doorknob where the soldier with the scar had kicked it repeatedly. I shoved our couch up against it to hold it in place, then stuffed the visible holes with wet dishcloths.

I stepped back, looking at my work proudly.

But it wasn't enough.

Nothing I did that night was enough.

22

THE POISON

Daphne
Rosemary Mountain
Present

Ellie shoved a doll into my arms. "You hold," she commanded.

I mindlessly began to rock the doll, ignoring the mild pain of my spine hitting the hard wall each time I went back. Physically, I was sitting on the floor in Ellie's room, but mentally, I was a thousand miles away.

Ellie got right in front of me and put her hands on her hips, frowning. "Mama sad?"

I stopped rocking, jolted into the present. "Yes, baby," I said softly, reaching out to tuck one of her curls behind her ear. "Mama is sad."

Days had passed without any real progress on the case. When we hadn't found a trace of water hemlock on Alva's property, Jackson had sent me home, saying he'd call when they needed me again. I knew they were still working on checking alibis and digging into our suspect list, but they weren't ready to bring me in on that part of the investigation. My job was to help put them on the right track, but I wouldn't be a reliable witness in court. Until they called me in to help, my only hope was getting Fiona to tell me why she'd confessed.

But Fiona was barely speaking to me, and every hour that passed felt like we were ticking one step closer to having her taken away from us. I felt helpless and frustrated.

Ellie studied me; then her face brightened. She held up a finger like she'd had a realization. "Mama needs chocolate."

I smiled despite myself. "I don't think chocolate can fix this, sweetie."

She ignored me and ran to her toy box, casting a nervous glance my way before reaching in and pulling out a candy bar. She brought it over and offered it to me with a sweet smile.

My eyebrows shot to the roof. My daughter had her own secret stash of chocolate. *Interesting.* I had to wonder who'd provided her with it since this particular brand wasn't one that I bought.

"Thank you," I said, my lips twitching. "Who gave you this?"

Her face went innocent, and she shrugged. Then she grabbed the baby out of my arms and took it over to her doll bed.

Very coy, I thought, fighting a laugh. It was annoying how alike we were.

I shrugged and bit into the candy bar, deciding to let the whole thing go. I had bigger things to worry about.

A fact that was reinforced when my phone rang and I saw Greg's name on the caller ID.

"Hello?" I answered, feeling a sudden rush of anxiety.

"Daphne, we have some news. Can you come down here?"

"Emerson's at work," I replied. "I have Ellie."

"Drop her at the store with Janet," he said. "It's important."

My heart thudded in my chest. "Got it. I'll be there as fast as I can."

I wrapped up the rest of the chocolate bar, suddenly unable to stomach it. Ellie watched me from her tiny rocking chair with a serious look on her face.

I took a deep breath, forcing a smile. "That was Papa Greg. He needs me to help him at work for a little bit. Would you like to go hang out with GiGi and Willa at the store?"

Ellie brightened and clapped her hands.

At least one of us was still easy to cheer up.

I dropped Ellie off with Mom and Willa at the boutique Mom owned. Both women looked worried but did a great job of trying to hide it from my daughter. Not that they really needed to try hard—she was so distracted by the new display of handbags that she only gave them quick kisses before toddling off to take a look.

"She's already into fashion," Mom said proudly, watching Ellie ooh and ahh over a jeweled clutch.

"How could she not be when you spoil her with a new dress every week?" I teased.

"Oh, let me have my fun." Mom reluctantly peeled her eyes away from our girl and gave me a worried look. "Any news?"

"No. Greg didn't say why he needed me. But I feel sick about it." I put a hand over my stomach like it could somehow make me feel better.

"Me too," she admitted. "I don't know details—just enough for him to explain why he hired you. But I'm worried because *he's* worried. He told me he's sure it's all a big misunderstanding, but if that's true, then why is he a wreck over it? He's barely sleeping."

"Same." I sighed. "But try not to worry. We know she's innocent, and we'll figure out a way to prove it."

She squeezed my arm. "I believe in you both. But you don't have to prove she's innocent. It just takes reasonable doubt. There has to be plenty of that, right? I mean, this is Fiona."

"Right," I said, nodding.

I couldn't tell her that reasonable doubt wouldn't apply in a case where Fiona pled guilty.

Greg was on the phone when I arrived. He waved me in anyway. I took one of the chairs across from his desk while he wrapped up, feeling my anxiety grow by the minute at his clipped tone and short answers. When he hung up, he scrubbed a hand over his weary face.

"If you have bad news, let's get this over with quickly," I said, too anxious for small talk.

He nodded. "Fair enough. The initial autopsy report is back. Cause of death is pending full toxicology reports, but it looks like she died of cardiac arrest, which the ME said fits with the possibility of cicutoxin poisoning. Testing for that takes weeks, but the standard tox screens are back and are negative."

"Okay..."

He gave me a hard stare. "You know what's crazy? Alva had a documented seizure a couple of years ago after a bad respiratory infection. Fiona brought this tea to her because Alva had recently gotten over pneumonia. If Fiona hadn't confessed and told us what to look for, odds are this would have been written off as death by natural causes. Infection, followed by seizure, then a cardiac event. With a documented history of this exact thing, there was no reason to assume murder."

I sank back in my chair. "If Fiona hadn't confessed, there would be no murder investigation," I repeated slowly. "We thought she confessed to protect someone else, but what if she confessed to get us to investigate?"

"It doesn't add up," Greg said. "Fiona knows that if she asked me to look into it, I would. It's the son who brought up the whole poisoning thing. And I have a hard time believing she'd confess to protect him."

"Agreed." I shook my head. "I am so confused."

"Me too. But before we get any further, there's more."

"More?"

The hard look returned to his face. "The forensic team sent a sample of the dried tea to a private lab with quick turnaround. They were able to confirm the presence of *Cicuta*—that's water hemlock—via plant DNA."

I wanted to puke.

"The ME says we might not find it in the victim," Greg went on. "It degrades quickly after death. But the fact that it matches up with the way Alva died and with Fiona's confession..."

"This is really, really bad." I couldn't believe it. "But if what you're telling me is true, to me it just lends more evidence to Fiona's innocence. She would have gotten away with this—and you know she knows enough about plants to know that. So why would she tell us and point you in a direction nobody would have looked if she hadn't said anything? What killer in their right mind does that?"

Greg shrugged. "Some people need to confess. They can't deal with it being on their conscience."

"No." I put my hands to my head, shaking it. "This doesn't feel right."

"I know it doesn't. But, Daphne, it gets even worse."

I gave him an exasperated look. "How can it possibly get worse than this?"

He slid the notes he'd been taking during his phone call across the desk. "Because Fiona's in the will. Megan Keller gets the house and a small fund for taxes and maintenance. Fiona gets everything else—stocks, bonds, cash, jewelry... If she wasn't going to jail, she'd be a wealthy woman."

I stared at the words in front of me in shock.

Alva had died exactly the way Fiona said she had.

And now, Fiona had a legitimate motive.

23
SEPARATED

FIONA

July 1970
Belfast

I was dying.

Slowly. Painfully. Burned alive, tied to a pyre that smoldered but refused to go up in flames.

The smoke choked me. I fought for each labored breath, but every lungful of air came at a cost. The breaths kept me alive, but they felt like broken glass scraping across the surface of my lungs.

Then I felt the water on my face and realized I'd been wrong all along. I wasn't burning—I was drowning. Every breath I took was actually killing me, filling my lungs with fluid that burned like fire.

"Fiona, my love, wake up!" Ian's voice, urgent and pleading, broke through the haze, waking me from my nightmare.

I wasn't drowning—I'd been asleep. But when I sat up, dizzy and confused, gulping for air that wouldn't come in a flat that reeked of gas, I knew I'd only moved from one nightmare to another.

He dipped a fresh rag into water and vinegar, then gave it to me. I covered my mouth and my nose with it, grateful for the small relief it offered. Ian watched me with worried eyes.

"What's happening?" I asked, my voice muffled through the rag. It was a stupid question. The soldier had warned me about the gas, but for some reason, I needed to hear it from Ian.

He pulled his own rag away from his face. "One of the gas canisters hit the balcony outside. Being that close, it drifted right in through the vents and our shoddy windows." He coughed, then covered his face again.

I stretched my fingers toward him, needing to feel him and see that he was real. "You're awake."

He nodded. "Thanks to you."

"All I did was stop the bleeding."

"And likely saved my life." He dropped the rag again, and for a moment, I saw a glimpse of the boy I'd married. The one with the boyish grin, the dimples, and the innocent eyes that hadn't suffered the horrors of Belfast.

I wanted to weep for that boy I'd lost—and for the girl inside me who'd died last night, only to be reborn different. The one whose gentle heart had been broken and forged back together again through fire instead of through proper mending.

I knew I'd never be the same again.

"I think the gas is dissipating," he said cautiously before coughing again.

I let my rag drop and took in a deep gulp of oxygen, grateful that it didn't burn quite as badly as before. But the air still stank of the foul gas, and my eyes and my lungs hurt too badly for me to get my hopes up.

Not that I would have anyway. My new heart didn't know how to hope anymore.

Things went on that way all through the night and into Saturday. On Saturday afternoon, they announced a one-hour break in the curfew for those who needed to buy groceries. We grabbed money and clean rags soaked with water and vinegar, and then we rushed out, hoping to get food. But the lines to the local shops went all the way down the block, and before we made it inside, people started coming out empty-handed.

Fergus's wife, Peggy, spotted us in line as she was leaving. She stopped to check on us, anger flaring when she saw Ian's wound.

"I see you two had a rough night of it. They kept their hands off us, so they did, but they stole my pearl necklace and busted out our window. We had a terrible time with the gas, especially young Michael." Tears pricked her eyes. "He's been coughing something terrible. And now we can't even get food because the soldiers took it all! Clara said they were coming in, buying up food and cigarettes most of the night until their commander put a stop to it. What are they trying to do, starve us to death?"

She spat the words in anger, but her eyes betrayed her fear. For the first time, I was glad Ian and I hadn't yet been blessed with a little one. I couldn't imagine watching my child suffer through this, knowing I couldn't do anything to help them.

"This can't go on, can it?" Fresh fear crept down my spine. "Surely they won't keep us locked up until we starve."

"Has anyone tried to leave?" Ian gave her a look that told me he was asking something I didn't fully understand.

She held his gaze. "The lads who needed to get through did so."

His face remained neutral, but his shoulders dropped an inch in relief. "And is Fergus alright?"

"Aye, he's grand. He's sitting with Michael. We thought it better that I go out and do the shopping instead of him." Another meaningful look.

Ian nodded. "Is there any way for the rest of us to get out?"

She shrugged. "I'm sure there's a way, but I don't know it, and

Fergus doesn't, either. They've barricaded us in, and they're not showing any mercy. Our sources say there's three thousand soldiers surrounding us."

My jaw dropped. "*Three thousand?*"

"Aye." She shook her head. "Three thousand men here with weapons and tanks. They ran over Charles O'Neill. Just ran him down in the street, they did. They've shot others, busted heads with rifles. They've stolen from us and beaten us. They won't be content until we're all dead."

She shot a dirty look at the soldier who stood in the street near us.

His eyes narrowed, then shifted to Ian—the only one he seemed to think might be a threat. "Move on now. This isn't a social hour," he snarled. His hand hovered over the baton hanging from his belt.

Ian squeezed my elbow. "If there's nothing left for us to buy, we should go home," he said quietly.

"That's a good idea," I agreed.

Saturday turned into Sunday. Our bellies ached from hunger, our lungs burned, and our eyes stung from the constant assault of gas. I did my best to help it all with herbs, using mullein to soothe our lungs and nettle tea to give us some vitamins and energy. I passed tea to the neighbors as well, as we all got brave enough to slip out of our flats and into each other's homes, sharing what we could. I tended to Michael, saving most of the mullein for steams to soothe his fragile lungs, and was grateful to see that it eased his constant cough and helped him breathe.

A group of us made up our minds to break the curfew and walk together to the church to attend mass, an act of righteous defiance that we agreed was worth the risk. We were driven back to our building with rubber bullets and fresh gas and rifle butts that split the skulls of more of our men.

I soon ran out of mullein, yarrow, and nettles.

Then, on Sunday afternoon, our salvation appeared. Three thousand women and children, an unexpected army matching the size of the one that held us captive, marched from Andersontown carrying food and medical supplies. The British soldiers weren't expecting them and couldn't hold them back. The women forced their way right through the barriers, bringing relief and liberation with them.

And just like that, the curfew was lifted.

A few days later, Ian and I walked to the train station. The air still reeked of lingering gas, and bullet casings littered the streets and sidewalks. Nothing felt normal yet.

I wasn't sure it ever would.

For the first time, I felt genuine fear when we passed through the checkpoints, wondering if the soldiers were going to beat Ian again simply for being a Catholic man. My anxious eyes darted to every face, fearing I'd see the soldier with the scar who haunted my nightmares. But we made it through unscathed, and I breathed a sigh of relief when we made it to the stand to buy our tickets home.

The relief was short lived though. Ian took my shoulders and turned me to face him.

"I'm not going with ya," he said sorrowfully.

"What do you mean you're not going with me?" I glared at him. "Don't tell me you're going to stay here."

"I am." He nodded.

I wanted to scream and cry and stomp my foot like a wee child. But I only let one word pass my lips. "Why?"

He glanced around to make sure no one was listening to us. "We're in a war, Fiona. Ya know that. I can't go home and pretend that it's not happening, not while our friends are being starved, beaten, and gassed. I have to help."

If there hadn't been two soldiers standing nearby, I might have caused a scene. I wanted to shout a thousand hurtful things at him. It felt like he was choosing our new friends over me, *Belfast* over me. What was happening here was horrible, yes. But we had a life somewhere else, a home somewhere else. *Family* somewhere else.

We could leave this place together and not look back.

"I am not okay with this," I said under my breath, my voice breaking on the final word.

"It's only for a few weeks," he said, soothing. "I'll come in August."

"Then I'll wait—"

"No." He shook his head, the tight set of his jaw letting me know he wasn't interested in negotiation. "It's too dangerous here. Go home. Be with your sister and Mamó. Restock your herbs, because God knows we'll need them. I'll be there in August. Then we can make a plan for the future together, alright?"

"Do I have a choice?" My voice was broken with betrayal.

"As if I could ever force ya to do anything." His eyes softened. "Please, Fiona. I need to know you're safe."

"And what about me? Do I not get to sleep well at night knowing *you're* safe?" I couldn't hold back the tears any longer.

"I've the luck of the Irish and the love of Fiona Flanagan, a *bean feasa*." He looked at me tenderly. "I'll be grand. I just have to do something to help."

I swallowed hard. I kissed his cheek, then hugged him tightly and whispered into his ear, where the soldiers couldn't hear. "Please promise me you'll be safe. That you won't do anything that puts you into danger. I couldn't bear it."

He pulled back so he could look me in the eyes. "Aye, I promise." He touched my cheek, then ran his fingers through my hair. "I love you, Fiona. You're my world. I'm only staying because I want to make it better for you. I'll be safe, and I'll be home in August. You have my word."

"I love you too," I whispered.

The train whistle covered the sound of my sobs. Ian pushed me forward, then stood on the track and waved goodbye as I climbed on board and took my seat. I stared at him through the window, twisting my neck to keep him in sight until we'd gone so far I couldn't see him anymore.

He'd promised he wouldn't put himself in danger.

I think we both knew he'd just told me a lie.

24

THE SEARCH

Daphne
Rosemary Mountain
Present

Greg took a deep breath. "Look, at this point, I've got to start treating Fiona like a legitimate suspect. I need to call in TBI for assistance, if nothing else, and I need to get a search warrant for her house. You're not to breathe a word of that to anyone, got it?"

"I understand." I swallowed hard.

"But I'd like your opinion," he said, softening. "Which do you think would be easier for Fiona: me and Jackson executing the warrant or strangers from TBI?"

"You and Jackson," I said, not even needing to think about it.

He looked surprised. "Really? I was thinking it would be the other way around, that it might feel less violating if it's strangers than if it's her friends."

I shook my head. "As someone who's been through it... It should be you and Jackson. She trusts you. Plus, you care about her, so you'll be careful with her things. A search feels violating, no matter who does it. But it will be easier on her if it's you." I blinked back tears. "This is awful."

"I know." Greg looked as miserable as I felt.

"What can I do in the meantime? Can you think of anything that might help?" I wanted to cry.

"Still no luck getting Fiona to talk to you?"

"No." My utter failure was depressing.

He sighed. "Well, you can't try now. It would be irresponsible for me to let you talk to her before we get to her house and search, even though I know you won't give her a heads-up. But we don't need anything else that could bite us in the butt at court."

He put his hands behind his head, leaning back in his chair as he thought for a moment. "Follow up with Jackson. He's writing up the warrant as we speak. See if he's had any brilliant ideas."

"Alright." I stood and started to walk out, but then I stopped and turned back to him. "Thanks. No matter how this turns out... Thanks for trying so hard." He would never know how much it meant to me that he had fought for Fiona as long as he had.

"Chin up. We're not giving up yet."

I nodded but felt too deflated to agree.

A few hours later, I stood behind Greg and Jackson, feeling like a traitor as they knocked on Fiona's door. It still felt odd to stand and wait for her. She used to always be waiting for me with her door wide open.

Things had changed, and I still didn't understand why.

We heard her muttering as she unlocked her deadbolt—another change. She opened the door and gave us all a suspicious look.

"I suppose you're here to search my home," she said stiffly.

"That's right." Greg nodded. "I have the warrant—"

"No need," she said, cutting him off. "Do what you're going to do. Though I'll warn you right now, you won't find any water hemlock on the property. I'm not an *eejit* who keeps poison around the house. I don't even let that stuff grow on my land." She scowled.

Greg chuckled. "Then why were you an *eejit* who confessed to a crime you didn't commit?"

Her eyes went wide with surprise. "Oh, you think you know everything, don't ya now?"

"We know you didn't do it," I said quietly. "I wish you'd tell us why you're pretending you did."

She looked away, guilt painting her features. But when Greg and Jackson began their search, she shuddered and her eyes filled with tears.

"I can't watch this," she said, her voice cracking with emotion. "Not again. It's all too much."

She covered her face with her hands and ran out the door.

"Fiona, wait!" I cried, following after her.

She didn't respond. Her shoulders were slumped, and her arms wrapped around herself as she strode quickly away from the house, around to the back, and up into the woods.

I followed behind her as she climbed, winding through trees, pushing back branches until she reached a clearing. When she got there, she fell to her knees and wept, her sobs mixed with guttural groans and anguish.

Nothing had ever frightened me more. Fiona and I had faced death together twice, and both times she'd done so with a brave face and a steady countenance. But now... Now she wept like everything within her had shattered to pieces.

I knelt beside her on the damp grass, placing my hand on her back so she'd know I was there. But I was at a loss for words.

When her tears stopped, she lifted her head, wiping her face on the sleeve of her rust-colored cardigan. "I'm sorry you had to see me like that. I thought I could handle it all better than I am."

"Handle what? Fiona, please. You have to talk to me." I grabbed her shoulders, desperate. "Whatever is going on, we'll fix it. But you have to tell me the truth."

"Girl, the truth is that the ghosts from my past have come back to haunt me," she said gloomily. "I suppose it happens to us all eventually. I'm alright now." She patted my hand. "I'm ready to pay for my crimes. It was just a moment of weakness."

"But that's just it. You didn't commit a crime, Fiona. I went to Alva's house. I put my hands on the ground where she died, on the chair where you sat when you had tea with her that morning."

Fiona's head jerked back, stunned. "Why would you do that?"

"Because it's my job," I said calmly. "Greg hired me. I'm a consultant, just like my mother was."

Her hands trembled. "Then you know," she said, her voice strangely garbled.

"That you're innocent? Yes. I know. I know you drank that tea with Alva that morning and that you were just fine. I also know that you loved your friend dearly and that you would have never hurt her. So why don't you start telling me the truth?"

"Oh, Daphne. The truth is a complicated thing."

"Really?" I gave her a skeptical look. "It seems simple enough to me. You didn't kill Alva. Either you lied to cover for the person who did or you lied to get Greg to investigate instead of writing it off as an accidental death. But either way, you don't deserve to go to prison for something you didn't do."

Her gaze was pained. "But you're wrong. It's not either of those things. It's not as simple as you think. It's anything but."

I took her weathered hands in mine. "No matter how complicated it is, we'll figure it out. I just need you to tell me the truth. You asked me to trust you once. Won't you trust me?"

"Of course I trust you," she said, the agony on her face briefly changing to irritation.

"Then tell me what's going on."

She looked up, her gaze distant. Haunted.

I didn't think she was going to answer me, but she finally nodded.

"Alright," she said softly. "I'll tell you the whole story. You deserve to know the truth about who I am. But not here. When they're finished, help me put my house back together. I'll make a pot of tea"—she cut herself off, shaking her head with a strange look on her face—"or maybe we skip the tea tonight, considering. We'll have some whiskey instead, and I'll tell you the whole, complicated truth. But you have to promise me something."

"What's that?"

She looked into my eyes, sad. "When you realize I'm guilty, you can't stop me from facing the punishment I deserve."

I stared at her, confused. She hadn't poisoned Alva, so how could she be guilty?

"You have to promise," she repeated firmly.

"Alright," I agreed. "If you tell me the whole story and it turns out you're guilty, I'll stand aside."

"Thank you," she said, relieved. She turned away, gazing again at the trees in front of her. "It's a relief in some ways."

"What is?" I asked, helping her to her feet.

She looked serene in a way she hadn't before. She patted my hand and smiled. "It will be a relief for someone to finally know the truth about who I am."

The words scared me even more than her tears had.

25
THE STORY

Daphne

Rosemary Mountain

Present

Fiona sighed heavily. Her shoulders slumped as she stared into the flames dancing in her hearth. She took a slow sip of the whiskey she'd poured herself after we put her house back together. Greg and Jackson had taken extreme care with their search, care that I knew had significantly extended the time it took them to complete it. Even so, it had taken two hours of cleaning before Fiona felt like things were right again and reluctantly agreed to keep her end of the bargain.

She'd insisted we invite Emerson to join us, saying that he should hear it too. That she needed another witness. So I texted Mom, asking if she could take Ellie home with her for a sleepover.

We waited for Emerson to get off work and join us. Of course, he had to have dinner, Fiona insisted. No man should have to listen to a terrible tale on an empty stomach. So we ate, washed the dishes, built a fire, and poured the whiskey.

Half an hour later, she still hadn't said a word.

"Fiona," I said, letting a hint of warning into my tone. It was the same one I used with Ellie when she wasn't listening. Emerson recognized it and coughed to cover up a chuckle.

Fiona sighed. "I don't want to tell this story," she said softly. "It's not a happy one."

"I know." I lifted my glass to my lips, letting the smooth Irish whiskey warm me from the inside out. Part of me didn't want to hear the story any more than she wanted to tell it. I was terrified that she seemed convinced the truth would only hasten her conviction—a conviction for a crime I still desperately wanted to believe she hadn't committed.

I had no idea what was going on, but whatever it was had defeated Fiona's spirit, something that killed me to see. While I watched her fade, my heart felt like it would break in two.

I'd lost my mother so young that I couldn't even remember her. Then I'd lost my father.

I couldn't lose Fiona too.

Her hands, weathered but strong, shook as she lifted the whiskey glass to her chapped lips.

"Alright," she said, her Irish brogue thickening. "But don't say I didn't warn ya. The two of yous might not think so highly of old Fiona when you've heard the truth of what I've done."

I shook my head. "There's nothing you could tell me that would ever make me think less of you."

She tilted her head, clearly skeptical, but seemed too weary to argue the point. "We'll have to go back to the beginning," she said, never taking her eyes off the flames.

"To when you met Alva?"

She shook her head. "No. To Ireland."

"Ireland?" My eyebrows knit in confusion.

I glanced at Emerson. The look on his face told me he was as lost as I was.

But Fiona nodded, a look of steel coming into her eyes. "Aye. Northern Ireland. The place where I was born—and where everything changed." She reached for the bottle of whiskey and splashed another ounce into her glass. "I was born in Ulster. My family lived in Glenarm Village. It was less than forty miles from Belfast, but it might as well have been another world."

Her eyes grew dreamy. "Oh, but you'd love Ireland, Daphne. Rolling green hills, rocky cliffsides that drop straight into the sea. Castle ruins and stones. We didn't have much, but we had that, and that was enough."

"It sounds beautiful," I said, smiling at the wistful look in her eyes.

"It was." She took a sharp inhale. "And it was peaceful, like. We didn't have the problems Belfast had. In the village, people didn't care so much whether you went to Mass or worshiped with the Presbyterians. There were those who were loyal to the crown and those who wanted to break free from British rule and have a united Ireland, but the divide between us didn't feel all that important, at least not to a young girl who grew up with friends on both sides. The laws weren't fair, and there were tensions now and then. But it wasn't Belfast."

Her eyes went hazy again, but this time, they were marked with grief.

"I met my Ian there in the village," she said softly.

"Ian?" I asked.

She nodded. "My husband."

I blinked. I'd never heard her mention a husband before. "I'm so sorry. What happened?"

She ignored the question, needing to tell her story her own way. "He was a fisherman. He belonged to the sea. I can still picture him smiling and waving from his boat as it came into dock. He'd tie off, grinning the whole time, then jump over the side and run to me, picking me up off my feet as he swung me around. And when he kissed me, it tasted of salt and air and the magic of the ocean."

"He sounds wonderful."

The sides of her mouth lifted in a happy smile of remembrance. "Oh, but it was a love story for the ages. He whisked me off my feet, that one did. Sometimes... Sometimes I like to imagine we're still there." The smile faded, and she closed her eyes tightly, her face marked with pain. "That we'd stayed in our peaceful little town, turned off the television, and ignored everything happening in the world. If we had, I think we'd be there still. Walking down to the sea together, warming each other underneath the quilt each night." Her shoulders slumped as tears streamed down her cheeks.

"I'm sorry," I said, barely able to get the words out over the lump in my throat. Fiona had told me little about her life in Northern Ireland. I'd never seen her grieve like this, and it broke something inside me.

She wiped the tears away, though she couldn't erase the grief that shone through her eyes. "If there's one thing I could teach you, one lesson to give you, it's this: A single choice can change everything."

Then she began telling us the story of her life in Ireland, beginning with the day she'd heard the cry of the banshee. She told us about moving to Belfast with Ian, the trouble they'd faced there, and how he'd sent her back to the village alone to keep her safe.

Then she told us the story of what happened when she returned.

26

FIONA RETURNS

FIONA

Fall 1970
Belfast

The week after I left, there was another bombing in Belfast, only this time, Catholics weren't the victims. This one was set by the Provisional IRA. They bombed a bank in downtown Belfast, injuring thirty-one people.

The soldiers started using rubber bullets instead of just the gas.

The death toll started rising.

We didn't have a phone at the house, nor did Ian have one at the flat. But he'd slipped a note into my bag with directions for how I could get in touch with him. Every Tuesday evening, I'd walk to one of the phones in town and call him at a number that I later found out belonged to Kieran. The calls were my lifeline. Every day that passed without speaking to him, I'd grow more anxious, wondering if he was okay. But then I'd hear his voice on the phone, and for a little while, my heart would settle.

Then we'd hang up and the cycle would start all over again.

All through July, Ian repeated the promise that he'd be home in August. When August arrived, he said it would be just another week or two, but he didn't come home then, either. Then September came, and soon it was time for him to start back at Queen's, and there wasn't time for him to come home at all.

I knew I had a choice to make, even though he never said so. I could either stay in the village I loved and wait for him or pack my things and return to Belfast—whether he liked it or not.

I missed him terribly. Every morning when I woke up without him beside me in our bed, I felt a terrible ache in my heart. I loved Mamó and Annie, but things weren't the same as before I'd gotten married. It felt like part of me was missing now. I went about my life just like I always had, but there was no joy like there'd been before. I couldn't focus on anything, for worrying about Ian and wondering if he was safe.

The village I'd loved wasn't the same, either. The Troubles had changed it. It was still a far cry from Belfast. There weren't riots or bombings, but there were subtle shifts. I wondered sometimes if they'd always been there and I'd just not paid attention to them before. But after I'd lived in Belfast, something as small as hearing men whistling Loyalist tunes or seeing a man wearing an orange shirt would make my breath catch.

There were signs of trouble from our side too. After Mass, you'd see pairs of young men talking quietly in the shadows outside the building. There were whispers everywhere—whispers and fear. People started looking at each other with that same suspicious look they had in the Falls.

I wasn't the only one who saw it. Mamó did too, and she begged me not to return to Belfast. She started talking about us all moving to County Cork, where we'd be safe and far from the Troubles. Every week, before I was to call Ian, she urged me to tell him to rethink what he was doing and come home.

I didn't.

Truth be told, I was confused about my own feelings. There was still unease there, the same I'd felt the night Seamus told Ian that the rumors were true. Bombing the bank was a far cry from defending our neighborhoods, and it bothered me, though I tried to ignore it.

After all, they'd attacked us first, and they had no intention of stopping. Catholic homes continued to be bombed and burned to the ground. Innocent people were being kidnapped and murdered. There were regular shootings at businesses and bars.

How could it be right to just sit back and take it until they'd gotten their way and killed us all? Ian had stayed to fight for safety and freedom. I was proud of that, despite the unease that lingered in my soul. Any time my conscience tried to protest, I'd close my eyes and remember what it was like the night of curfew, when the soldier had beaten Ian and threatened me. I'd let that fire inside me grow until it pushed away anything else.

So Mamó gave up, seeing me become more stubborn every time she tried to talk to me. But she held firm on her stance, saying she'd pray daily for peace and freedom, but she wouldn't bless another bullet.

I knew she'd feel differently if the army broke down the door to our cottage or gassed the streets of our village.

Even in peaceful Glenarm, trouble began looking more and more likely. The army started making appearances, setting up checkpoints on the coastal road and making their presence known in ways we couldn't help but take as a threat. The rifles they carried told us the truth of why they were there, no matter what their words said.

Glenarm didn't feel truly safe anymore, and some of our friends began leaving it, moving to smaller villages where Catholics were the majority. Those who could moved south to the Republic, leaving Northern Ireland behind altogether, the way Mamó suggested.

If Glenarm wasn't safe anymore, then what was the point of *me* staying there? I felt like I was going to go crazy being separated from my Ian. At least if I went back, I'd know every night that he was safe instead of having to wait for the Tuesday call. Whatever he had to face, we'd face it together.

So I made up my mind. One September morning, without telling anyone, I packed my bag and slipped away, taking the bus to the closest train station that would get me back to Belfast—back to the heart of the danger.

I paced the floor of our tiny flat, biting my fingernails as I waited for Ian to come home. On the train ride over, I'd imagined a romantic reunion, one where he'd sweep me into his arms and be so grateful I'd come back to him.

But now, with dread growing inside my belly, I feared he'd be angry at me. I knew I'd taken a risk coming back, but even the walk from the station to Falls Road had felt more dangerous than it had a few months ago. Ian might be furious that I'd done it on my own.

I felt like I was going to vomit when the doorknob finally twisted and the door swung open, revealing the worn-out tweed pants and brown leather shoes I hadn't seen in what felt like a lifetime.

Ian blinked like he was confused, then dropped his bag and ran to me, sweeping me into his arms just like I'd imagined.

"What are ya doing here?" He was shocked but not angry.

"I missed ya too much," I said, the words coming out in a sob. I wrapped my arms around his neck and kissed him with tears streaming down my cheeks.

Everything was right in the world again. Sure, there was a war going on right outside our door. But we were together, and that's all that seemed to matter.

"Oh, Fiona, my love, I missed you too." He held me like he was never going to let go. But when he finally did, I saw the worry in his eyes. "Ya shouldn't be here. It's too dangerous."

"Then you shouldn't be here, either."

"Sometimes I think you're right," he admitted. A strange look of regret flitted across his face before he blinked it away. He sniffed the air. "Do I smell—"

"Guinness stew," I said, smiling through the tears. "I thought it was only fitting. Now, sit down and I'll bring you a bowl."

I asked him no questions about what he'd done that summer. I didn't want to know.

We were together. Nothing else mattered.

I repeated the words in my head until I nearly believed them.

That fall, the violence only escalated, but I became used to it somehow. It became normal to go through checkpoints, to have your bags searched before you went inside a store. Normal to hear about a bomb exploding in a shop and wounding people you knew. Normal to see soldiers chasing lads through the streets—and normal to help the lads hide, if you could.

You lived knowing every day might be your last, and somehow, you were okay with it. The bombings and murders didn't shock or terrify me the way they once had, and the sight of blood no longer made me squeamish. Fergus would bring by some injured lad at least twice a month, and I tended their wounds with the detachment of a doctor who'd spent a lifetime in the surgery.

I don't think it's right, exactly, to become numb to things like that. But many of us did. I think we might have gone mad if we hadn't.

Although, as the weeks went on, I started realizing that many of us *had* gone mad. The new IRA called themselves an army, but they acted more like gangsters. Even with the new fire I had inside me, it became hard to pretend that their actions were noble, hard to romanticize the lads as freedom fighters when they threw petrol bombs into Protestant neighborhoods, seeking revenge instead of simply protecting our people. I tried to tell myself it was justified, but Mamó's words wouldn't completely fade. They lived in my heart, working as a medicine to keep it from hardening completely, softening me even when I didn't want them to.

As my unease grew, the anger I saw in the people in Falls Road began to scare me. Even Ian's anger scared me, if I'm being honest. The night of the curfew had changed him, too. I could see how his own heart had been cracked and mended differently, forged in fire the way I'd felt that night—only his hadn't softened since. He hadn't had time in the village with Mamó; he didn't have her words working slowly to prick his conscience. Here, surrounded by angry voices and facing daily threats I couldn't imagine, his heart had grown so hard it was hard to recognize him.

Every now and then, I'd catch glimpses of the man I'd married. I lived for those moments. But more than that, I saw the person he'd become, someone who was bitter about the injustice of it all.

The more my heart longed for peace, the more his longed for vengeance. The divide between us started slowly unweaving the love we'd shared, and sometimes, it felt like I was married to a stranger.

During the day, he continued his studies at Queen's. Then he'd come home and have dinner with me, and we'd pretend like everything was normal, even though we couldn't talk openly anymore. Conversation felt like walking through a field of landmines.

At least two nights a week, one of the lads would come rapping on our door, and Ian would give me an apologetic smile before telling me not to wait up. He'd leave and be gone for hours.

I didn't ask any questions.

I didn't want the answers.

When December rolled around, I didn't bother asking him to go back to the village for Christmas. I knew he wouldn't leave the fight.

I also knew I couldn't go alone—because I wouldn't have the strength to come back to him again.

27

INTERNMENT

FIONA

August 1971
Belfast

I woke to the low rumble of engines outside. Ian tensed beside me, then jumped out of bed and grabbed his pants, yanking them on.

"What's going on?" I mumbled, sitting up and wiping the sleep from my eyes.

"Don't know," he said, his voice low as he pushed the curtain back an inch so he could get a look out the window. He jumped back as headlights swept across, brightening our room through the fabric.

Seconds later, footsteps thudded heavily from the stairwell.

"Get dressed," Ian hissed, grabbing the clothes I'd abandoned the night before and throwing them my way. He yanked his boots on, then reached for a shirt.

The noises grew: muffled voices, the thud of boots, fists pounding on doorways.

A loud wail of grief.

My heart raced. I pulled my shirt over my head, then pulled on my jeans. My fingers fumbled as I tried to button them, my hands trembling from fear.

Someone banged on our door. "Open up!"

Ian shot me a warning look, then walked out of our room toward the front. Before he reached it, I heard the too-familiar sound of splintering wood as they broke down our door.

"Can I help you?" Ian asked, his voice a picture of confusion and respect, without a trace of the anger I knew he held inside.

"You're coming with us." The voice was gruff. Demanding.

"But I've done nothing wrong," Ian protested, though he kept his voice respectful.

I heard a thud, followed by his grunt of pain, and I covered my mouth with my hand to keep from crying out.

Footsteps came my way. The bedroom light flooded on. "Out," said the gruff voice. He motioned with his head, keeping his rifle pointed at me.

Unlike Ian, I didn't protest. I put my hands in the air and walked as meekly as I could into the living room, where Ian was on his knees, his hands behind his head as a soldier pointed a rifle at his temple.

Ian shot me a warning look. *Don't fight back. Don't say anything.*

I blinked slowly instead of nodding, letting him know I understood.

One of the soldiers shoved me to my knees while two more ransacked our house the same way they had on the night of the curfew.

Dishes shattered.

Another wailing cry came from a nearby flat.

Feathers fluttered through the air when a soldier brought my pillow into the living room and stabbed his knife into it right in front of my face, then shook the feathers loose.

Ian and I stayed quiet.

"There's nothing here," one of them finally said, his disappointment evident.

"We're taking him anyway," the gruff soldier said. "They'll sort things out downtown."

They yanked Ian to his feet and shuffled out without so much as another glance at me.

I wanted to ask where they were taking him, but I didn't.

I told myself it was because I'd just promised Ian I'd stay quiet. But I knew it was at least partly because I was afraid of the answer.

Numb. That's what I felt when I closed our busted door and sat down on the couch, listening to the same scene play out over and over again as the soldiers made their way through our building. New sounds were added—the crack of gunfire and the metallic clang of metal, like someone was beating on the metal bins in the courtyard.

But it was like I was in a fog, far away from all of it. I stared at the calendar that hung on the wall across from me in the same place where the one from last year had mocked me during the curfew.

I felt nothing.

I wanted to pray, but I couldn't find the words.

When the yelling stopped and the heavy footsteps had all retreated, I stood and opened my door. The air was tinged with sweat and the foul smell of CS gas. Dozens of doors hung broken on their hinges. The concrete was splattered with fresh blood. Children cried inconsolably, clinging to the metal bars of the balcony, while their mothers tried comforting them with swollen, red eyes of their own.

There wasn't a single man to be seen.

Without even thinking, my feet turned toward Peggy's flat, knowing she'd have the answers.

Her door and her windows were all shattered. Beyond it, I could see her kneeling on the floor, holding Michael as he cried and coughed. Her older daughter, Louise, stood behind them, chewing her nails and trying not to cry. Benny, the middle boy, sat on the couch with his head hung. Unlike Louise, he didn't try to stop the tears that were streaming down his cheeks.

It felt wrong to intrude. I stopped, thinking that I should turn around and go home.

But Peggy looked up and waved me in. "So they took Ian too?"

I nodded. "What—"

It was all I could get out before my voice broke.

She sniffed hard, then stood and squared her shoulders. "I guess there's no sense in trying to hide it from the children. Lord knows they've seen more in their lifetimes than anyone should. They've rounded up all the men here. Maybe some sort of collective punishment? Only God knows."

"Will we—" *Will we see them again?* I glanced at the kids, afraid to finish the question.

Afraid of the answer.

Peggy's eyes softened, as if she could read my mind. "I don't know. But I have connections who might know more. I'll find out what I can and let you know when I do."

I nodded, biting my lip. "I-I don't know what to do."

The tears I'd been holding back fell in a cascade. As the grief washed over me, I realized the numbness had been a gift. Feeling nothing was better than feeling like this—terrified for Ian's life and helpless to do anything about it.

We had no power. Not really.

I made up my mind in that instant that if God gave my Ian back to me, I'd do everything I could to convince him to leave Belfast for good.

28

EVENING INTRUDER

Fiona

August 1971

Belfast

No one knew when our men would be coming home.

And it wasn't just *our* men. The raids hadn't been limited to our neighborhood. It had been a widespread operation, and it was still ongoing. Internment without trial. They'd decided to lock up any men even suspected of being associated with the IRA—indefinitely.

My heart sank when Peggy gave me the news. Her eyes were red-rimmed and haunted with shadows.

"How can they do that?" I cried. "It isn't right."

"Nothing they do is right," she spat, her face hardening. "It's exactly the sort of thing they'd do. But don't worry, they weren't able to get everyone."

"What do you mean?"

"We spread the alarm right quick. Some of the lads were able to go into hiding. We'll not be left entirely defenseless, and you best believe we'll show the Brit bastards that in the coming weeks." Her tired eyes flashed with steel.

I stared at her, not knowing what to say. It all felt so hopeless. If they could lock people in prison without a trial, how could we possibly fight back?

Fighting back hadn't gotten us anywhere. Things were worse now than they had been before.

Her eyes narrowed at my silence. "Don't you want us to repay them for what they've done?"

"Of course," I murmured. But my heart wasn't in it, and her cold stare told me she knew it.

"Word is that some of the men are being moved to the cages," she continued, watching me for a reaction. "And some of them are being tortured."

My heart stopped. "Tortured?"

She nodded grimly. "That's what those bastards like to do, thinking they'll get information. But they don't know our men, now, do they? Our men will die before turning tout."

I nodded numbly.

She continued with her spiel, but I couldn't stay to listen. I covered my mouth with my hand and ran to the bathroom, where I vomited until there was nothing left in me. The thought of Ian being tortured... I couldn't bear it. I felt like my soul was being ripped in two.

Peggy appeared in the doorway, giving me a softer look. "Ah, of course you're worried about your man, but it's alright. He and Fergus are together. They'll take care of each other."

I grabbed a rag and wet it, wiping my face as I sank to the floor. She stared at me expectantly, so I nodded and gave her a weak smile, as if her words had comforted me. "What about Seamus and Kieran? I suppose they got them as well."

She shook her head. "Seamus slipped out and hid before they got to his flat. Took a risk, he did, but he made it. He's with Kieran now, making plans. They didn't hit Kieran's neighborhood. Not yet, anyway."

"Good," I said weakly, though my head was spinning with fear and exhaustion. "I think I need to lie down."

"Of course you do," she said kindly, reaching out a hand to me. "I'll just tuck you into bed and slip on out while you sleep. It's a hard time for all of us. We only have each other now."

I took her hand and let her lead me. On the outside, I was calm, but everything within me was screaming that this was all wrong.

The unmistakable sound of my door creaking open woke me the next morning. I sat up in bed, my heart pounding out of my chest.

Had the soldiers come back?

Footsteps walked toward the bedroom.

My hands shook. I looked around, trying to figure out a weapon. All I had that might work was the lamp. I reached for it just as the door to my room flew open.

"It's alright, Fiona, my love. It's only me." Ian's voice was weak, and he sagged against the doorframe.

I scrambled out of bed and ran to him, flicking on the light so I could look him over. His lip was split, and his eye was swollen shut. Purple bruises marred his face, and his cheek was covered in dried, cracked blood. His shoulders sagged and his breathing was ragged, but he was alive and he was here. I threw my arms around him and sobbed onto his shoulder.

"Help me to the bed," he said softly. He wrapped one arm around me. The other he kept close to his ribs.

"Are you alright?" I asked, growing more alarmed by the second. I helped him sit on the edge of the bed, then dropped to the floor to pull off his worn boots.

"Just a few bruises," he said, giving me a tight smile.

"I didn't know when I'd see you again," I said, unable to stop the tears. "Peggy said that you'd been interned without a trial—that all the men were."

"Many of them were, aye," he said, nodding. "But they questioned us all and gave us a chance to say our piece. I told them I was a student at Queen's and showed them the paperwork I keep in my pocket. Thank God Lieutenant Montgomery was there."

"The man who saved me the night of curfew?" I cocked my head, surprised.

"Aye. I've stayed close to his brother for this very reason. Montgomery vouched for me, and since I didn't have a record and only moved here for school, they decided I wasn't a threat and let me go."

I was grateful. So, so grateful. Even if part of me knew they were wrong.

"And Fergus?" I asked carefully.

Ian shook his head. "Fergus has known ties to the IRA. He's been sent to the cages."

"Did they not question your involvement with Fergus?"

"They did," he confirmed. "But I explained that when we moved to the building, I'd been warned that this was a Republican spot and that, for my own safety, I needed to act sympathetic to the people who lived here. Told them that Fergus came over right away, questioning us like, and that he made my young wife nervous. Said that we learned quickly to play nice, but that's as far as our connection goes."

"You lied," I whispered.

He gave me a sad smile. "Now tell me, Fiona, what part of that was a lie?"

I sat back on my heels, thinking it over. "None of it," I admitted. "Except the part about your connection going no further."

Ian shrugged. "Ah, well, I couldn't exactly tell them I agree with Fergus, now, could I? If I did, I'd be locked up in the cages with him, and then I'd be of no use to anyone."

"I'm glad you're not. So glad." I put my hands on his knees and looked up at him earnestly. "Ian, we can't stay here. Ya know that, right? We need to leave. Forget about the Dunwoody. There will be more chances for you to go to school when all of this is over. Let's get out of Belfast and go back to the village where we belong."

He gave me a shocked look. "I cannot abandon the lads now. Look how few of them are left! Do ya expect me to walk away and leave our friends defenseless when they've just lost the people who were protecting them?"

"Protecting them?" Anger rose within me. "Is that what you're doing?"

"Of course it is." The shock on his face remained.

"Is it *protecting* us when the IRA bombs public places, knowing Catholics are likely to be hurt right alongside the Protestants? Is it *protecting* us when they shoot out the kneecaps of any Catholic they think is informing on them?"

"Fiona—"

I shook my head, cutting him off. "Do you really not see how the IRA has taken things too far? It was honorable when you wanted to defend the innocent, but that's not what you're doing anymore. Ya have to see that."

"It's a war, Fiona." His face hardened.

I let out a choked laugh. "Aye. A war with no plans for peace. And you're so deep in it that you'd choose it over me, over us. How can you have more loyalty to them than to our marriage? What exactly is it that you do for the IRA, Ian?"

"Don't ask me to answer that. You know I can't."

"We promised never to keep secrets from one another." My voice came out in a sob. I stared at the man in front of me, trying to find the boy I'd married.

I wasn't sure there was anything left of him.

He wrapped his hands around my arms, grasping me so I couldn't run away. "Fiona, don't ya understand? I keep secrets from you only to keep ya safe. Look at what the soldiers did to me. Do ya think they'd spare you if they thought for a moment you had information that could help them win this war?"

"I don't know what to believe anymore," I said, pulling away from his grasp.

I had Ian home, but I still felt like I'd lost everything.

<h1 style="text-align:center">29
TELLING IAN</h1>

Fiona

December 1971

Belfast

We didn't speak of that night again, but I saw signs that my words had gotten through somehow. Ian became quiet, contemplative. He still disappeared some nights, but the lads didn't come for him quite as often. His focus seemed to shift back to the degree he'd nearly abandoned, and we found a fragile sort of peace between us. It wasn't the love we'd shared before, but I started seeing glimmers of hope that we'd find our way back there.

It helped that the others weren't demanding his attention anymore, which gave us more time alone together to start rebuilding. His return had set us apart in the eyes of our neighbors—and not in a good way. Overnight, things had gone back to feeling the way they had when we'd first moved in. People watched us with suspicious eyes and whispered about us after we passed. Even Peggy grew cold, questioning me thoroughly on how he had gotten them to release him, angry that Fergus hadn't been able to manage the same. While she seemed to accept that his student ID gave him a credibility that worked in his favor, she maintained a coolness that surprised and hurt me.

I tried to give her grace, knowing that my husband was back and hers wasn't. If I were in her shoes, I'd struggle, knowing that I was likely going to spend months or even years raising my children alone. So I kept reaching out, stopping by, and trying to be a friend in any way that I could. But she put up a wall between us and seemed unwilling to fully let it down.

My feelings toward the IRA continued to become more negative. They set off a whole series of bombs in Belfast, and even bombed the Tower of London. Innocent women and children died in those explosions. No matter how strongly I felt about the oppression Catholics had experienced, I hated that Ian was involved with a group that was doing the exact same thing.

We didn't speak of it. I think we both knew that if we did, it would end in an argument and I might leave for good.

Truthfully, I thought about leaving every single day.

But I was still desperate to leave with Ian by my side. I loved my husband. Every night, when I said my prayers, I prayed desperately for him to agree to leave all of this behind and come home with me to the village.

For it was certain I would be going home sooner or later.

When the dark, cold of December set in, I realized an astonishing truth: Ian and I were going to have a baby—and I sure as hell wasn't going to do it in Belfast.

I straightened the napkins and lit the wee candles I'd bought, fussing over everything to make sure it was exactly right. Ian was due home any minute, and I'd finally worked up the nerve to tell him about our baby.

I knew when he heard the news, he'd realize what we needed to do. My heart soared at the thought of finally going home, of having this baby near Mamó and Annie and finding a way to put the horrors of Belfast behind us for good.

My heart quickened when I heard Ian's whistling coming from the hall outside our door. I stood up straight, biting my top lip to keep from grinning.

When he opened the door, his face lit up. "What's all this? Candles? And you in your prettiest dress?"

I beamed. "I thought we deserved a special dinner, that's all."

He came inside and dropped his messenger bag, then tossed a newspaper onto his armchair. I went to him and wrapped my arms around his neck.

He slipped his arms around my waist and kissed me softly. "I'm the luckiest man alive."

"Why do you say that?" I asked, teasing. It was fun to flirt with him again. I'd known in my soul it was the right day to talk to him, and I rejoiced at seeing my lighthearted husband return.

"Because I'm married to Fiona Flanagan, that's why," he said, nuzzling my nose. "Dinner smells amazing."

"It's just shepherd's pie." I took a deep breath. "I have something to tell you."

"Oh?" He cocked his head.

I bit my lip again, then smiled. "Ian, we're going to have a baby."

His face went slack, then his eyes lit with excitement. "Do ya mean it?"

I nodded shyly.

He whooped out loud and picked me up, whirling me around. "Oh, Fiona, it's the best day of my life! A baby. I cannot believe it. After all this time, I was starting to worry it wouldn't happen for us."

"Well, it has," I said, grinning.

He put me back down and gazed at me tenderly. "How long until we meet the little one?"

"Not until August. It's early yet. I'm only five weeks along."

"A summer baby." He grinned in wonder. "I cannot wait to see if it's a wee boy or a wee girl."

"I know." I couldn't stop smiling. "It's all I can daydream about."

His mind shifted into practical mode. "We'll have to get a crib. I'll see what I can find at the charity store. I suppose we'll just tuck it into our room for now, but maybe by this time next year we can start looking for a larger flat."

"Ian."

"Yes, my love?" He grinned at me.

"Ian, I want to go home."

He frowned. "What do you mean?"

"I mean, I don't want to have this baby in Belfast. I don't want to raise it in Falls Road." My face fell. "Surely you don't want that, either. After everything we've been through here, do ya honestly want to raise a child in this?"

"Well, no," he admitted. He ran a hand through his hair, frustrated. "But us leaving doesn't change things for anyone else, and maybe my staying can." He started pacing.

I took his wrists into my hands, stopping him. "Haven't ya done enough? I know you want to help, but it's not just our lives anymore. It's our child. We cannot raise an innocent child in a world like this, not when we have a safe, loving, stable place just waiting for us."

"I know. It's just—"

"And it's wrong," I interrupted him, unable to stop now that I'd started. "All this fighting and killing is wrong. I don't know what you're doing for the IRA, but I've seen the news. Women and children have died." I put his hand over my belly. "It's as wrong when their children die as it is ours. Do you not know that, Ian?"

"Aye, Fiona, I agree with you," he said softly. His deep eyes looked sorrowfully into mine as his fingers tucked a loose tendril behind my ear. "I don't like everything they're doing. To be honest with you, I've struggled with it, especially lately. But I also know that nothing will change if we don't fight back, and sometimes a man has to fight for what he believes in. It's a war. There are always casualties in a war. Can *you* not understand *that*?"

"Aye. I understand. But I cannot accept it," I said firmly. "We hated them for what they did. If we do the same, we're no better."

He sighed, but the corner of his mouth turned up in a slight smile. "You're a better soul than I am."

I shook my head. "You're a good man, Ian. You're brave and strong. You fight for what you believe in. But can ya honestly tell me you still believe in what they're doing? So much so that you'd risk everything to stand beside them? Because you're not just risking your life—you're risking mine. *Ours*." I looked down, touching the slight swell of my stomach that held a promise of so much more.

"It's not as easy to walk away as you think."

I looked back up at him. "Because you still believe in it?"

"No." He shook his head. "Because they don't take kindly to people who walk away." He said the words lightly, but the threat of them sent a chill up my spine.

"What do you mean?"

"Don't worry about it. I will protect you both, my love. I promise you that." He gripped my face, his eyes growing sad. "Have I ever given ya reason to doubt me?"

Yes. But the truth would only wound, so I gave him a lie.

"No, Ian, you haven't." I put my hand over his, clinging to him.

"Then do not doubt me now. I love you, Fiona." He sank into his armchair and slipped his hands around my waist, pulling me to him so he could rest his cheek against our child. "I'll find a way. I don't know how yet, but I will. Just give me some time. I promise you, our baby will not grow up in Belfast."

"I love you too," I whispered as I caressed his hair.

"Come, now." He dropped his hands from my waist and looked up, giving me a bright smile. "Let us eat and not worry about tomorrow."

But worrying about tomorrow was all I could do.

30
MISSING PIECES

FIONA

December 1971

Belfast

The bitter cold went straight through my coat as I walked to the shop on the corner. I rubbed my hands together and blew on them to keep them warm, keeping my pace brisker than I preferred. At some point, I'd developed the habit of walking slowly through the city so that I could keep my eyes open and scan for signs of trouble. But today, I was too cold for that.

My nerves didn't help. They sent a chill through me even indoors. Ever since Ian and I had begun making plans to leave, I felt nervous all the time. I couldn't explain it. But until we set foot in the village, I knew I wouldn't feel safe.

To be honest, I wasn't sure I'd even feel safe then. After living in fear for so long, it seemed etched into my bones. Would there ever be a time when I wouldn't wake in the night with my heart pounding, listening for the sound of soldiers' boots in the stairwells? Would I ever walk into a store without wondering if this was the time a bomb was going to explode and take me out with it?

Would I ever have neighbors I truly trusted? People that I didn't feel like I had to watch every word, every expression around for fear of them thinking I was disloyal and turning on me?

Safety seemed like nothing more than a pipe dream.

When I reached the shop, I handed over my purse to be searched, dancing from foot to foot to stay warm. When the soldier begrudgingly handed it back to me, I ducked inside, sighing at the warmth that wrapped around me.

A warmth that was replaced with a deep chill when Keiran's dark eyes locked onto mine.

The man made me uncomfortable. I knew he had to be deep inside the IRA because even Fergus seemed to look to him for direction. Was he the one who had made the decision to bomb innocents at the shops in Belfast's town center? I wouldn't doubt it. The quiet types were always the most dangerous.

He weaved past the bins and came my way, towering over me in a way that seemed to block out all the light. His hair was as dark as his eyes, and the black wool coat he wore made him look villainous. Kieran didn't try to blend in with the others. It was like he knew he was dangerous enough to not have to.

"Fiona," he said in greeting, giving me a little nod. "Ian told us your news. Congratulations." His face remained flat, without a trace of warmth on it.

"Thank you," I said, tightening my hand on the strap of my purse. "It's a blessing, so it is."

"We'll miss the both of yous," he said, still with a shocking lack of emotion.

"Aye, we'll miss all our friends here so," I lied.

"But Ian's right. Best not to raise a child here if ya can help it." His face darkened, the first sign of feeling I'd seen.

"Aye," I said weakly. "I think it's safest for the baby if we go back home."

He took a sharp breath, then clamped his lips as he let it out. His eyebrows furrowed. "Well. Take care, then."

He turned to leave, then abruptly turned around and gave me a piercing look. "If I can ever do anything for ya, all ya have to do is ask. Here's my card." He pulled a card out of his pocket, scrawled something onto it, and shoved it into my hand.

With that, he tucked his hat back onto his head and pushed his way out the door, snarling at the soldier who stood guard.

I stuck the card into my pocket and stared at his figure as he walked away.

I couldn't wait to get out of this city.

That night, I sat on the couch, fiddling with my thumbs as I watched the clock tick slowly. The cold sandwiches I'd set out for our dinner remained uneaten on their plates.

Ian was an hour late.

It was the final day of classes for the term. Our bags were packed, ready for us to head to the train station tomorrow. We'd be going home—not just for Christmas, but for good.

I'd never have to worry like this again, I promised myself. It was a promise that I repeated to myself every time the clock ticked forward, showing that another minute had passed with no sign of my husband.

The minutes turned into hours, and I found myself pacing our little living room, biting my fingernails to the quick. Something had to have happened.

I threw the sandwiches away.

When four hours had passed, I couldn't take it anymore. I grabbed my coat and threw it on over my clothes. Then I walked down to Peggy's apartment and knocked rapidly.

She opened the door in her housecoat. Her red hair was in curlers, and the flat was quiet with Michael already tucked into bed.

"Fiona, what on earth is it?" She grabbed my arm and pulled me inside. The concern on her face seemed to erase the coldness she'd held toward me for months now.

"Ian didn't come home tonight," I said, fighting back a sob. "It's his final day of classes, and he should have been home hours ago. Something must have happened."

"Sit down," she said, gesturing me toward the couch that was as threadbare as the one in my flat.

"I can't," I said, shaking my head. "I can't sit. I need to go look for him."

"You can't go out by yourself at night," she said, scolding. "Are you daft?"

"I have to find him!"

"He probably just got a drink with the lads," she said, soothing. "You said it's the final night of classes, didn't ya? They probably stopped off at a pub for a wee pint to celebrate. And ya know how one pint turns into two, and then before ya know it, they're three sheets to the wind."

I took a breath. Ian wasn't usually the type to go for drinks with his fellow students, but she was right—with this being the final night of classes, he might have decided to make an exception.

She smiled, seeing that she was getting through to me. "See? That's probably all it is. No need to worry yourself silly over it. You can give him grief for not letting you know ahead of time when he gets home. Now, go on with ya. Get yourself to bed and get some sleep. All this worrying is no good for the baby."

I startled. "How did you—"

She waved me off. "I've had four kids of me own. I know a woman who's carrying when I see her. Now, go on and get yourself to bed."

She gently pushed me out the door. I went back to my flat and tried to take her advice, but I tossed and turned all night.

Ian's side of the bed remained empty.

When morning came, I dressed and packed the last of our things. Then I sat on the couch, paralyzed.

I knew that something was wrong. Ian hadn't just gone out with the lads from school. If he had, he'd have come home already, offering me an apology paired with the boyish smile I could never resist.

It wasn't like him to keep me worrying. I knew that something terrible had to have happened to detain him. A list of imaginary horrors played like a movie in my mind.

Maybe he'd been arrested again, only this time they'd shipped him off to the cages with Fergus.

Maybe he'd gone for one quick drink at a Catholic pub and one of the Loyalist groups had bombed them.

Maybe he'd been attacked on his walk home, beaten and stabbed like so many others.

Maybe he'd looked the wrong way at a soldier and had been shot to death in the streets.

Maybe the IRA had asked him to help with one last job and it had gone terribly wrong.

Maybe he'd been helping set a bomb and it had exploded, killing him instead.

The list of terrible things that could have happened to him was nearly endless. Worse, they weren't just figments of my imagination. These were the kinds of things that happened in Belfast every day.

These were the reasons I was so desperate to leave.

But I couldn't leave now. I couldn't do anything until I knew where Ian was and what had happened to him.

With an endless list of possibilities, I didn't even know where to start.

31
SEARCHING

Fiona

December 1971

Belfast

Two days passed before I even thought about the card Kieran had shoved into my hand the day Ian disappeared. Two days with no sign of Ian, no assurance that he'd been seen by anyone.

Peggy had quickly grown tired of me asking if she'd heard anything and snapped that maybe now I understood what the rest of the women were going through, those whose husbands hadn't been released the day internment began.

Her words felt like a slap across the face. I stopped asking her for help.

On the second day, I'd gotten brave enough to ask one of the soldiers in our neighborhood if he could help find my husband. The man laughed and said he had better things to do, that if one of the filthy Fenians was missing, it only made his job easier.

I thought about Kieran's card after that. Kieran though… He made me nervous. There was something about him that was different than the others. He was quiet. Always watching. It was unnerving.

I knew I'd rather ask Seamus, but I didn't have any way of contacting him other than Kieran, and I hadn't seen him in the flats in months.

Instead, I braved the streets of Belfast, walking all the way to Queen's by myself. I could almost hear Ian scolding me for taking the risk, but I was willing to do anything to find him—I'd even brave Kieran, if it came to that.

When I made it past the barricades and the buildings scarred by bombs, the city changed. The area around Queen's was nothing like the Falls, or even Belfast's city center. If those places felt like two different cities, the area around the campus felt like a third. There were hardly any soldiers to be seen. The air wasn't heavy with the smells of petrol and burning gas. Instead, I caught a whiff of freshly ground coffee as two relaxed young women opened the door to an adorable café. They went inside, laughing at a shared joke, and didn't even have to have their purses searched at the entrance.

Tears sprang to my eyes at the sheer peace of the area.

It was like a completely different world from where we'd lived the last two years. It made me at least partly understand why Ian hadn't been nearly as desperate to leave as I'd been. Half of his time in Belfast had been spent here, in a landscape that was everything I'd ever dreamed the city would be.

Everything would have been different if we had been able to get housing here instead of the Falls.

I was grateful he'd had this experience, but I was jealous that I hadn't, and I felt resentful that I'd been trapped in the Falls while this existed so close by. The ugly feelings shamed me. It was wrong to feel such things, especially with Ian missing. He'd done his best to provide and to set things up for us.

If—no, when—I find him, I'll give him a whole day of respite before insisting that I'm in charge of choosing any future housing.

The thought cheered me enough to give me a fresh spark of energy. I popped into the café, trying not to feel embarrassed about how out of fashion my clothes were compared to the chic girls who had come in before me in their bright miniskirts and patterned tights. I splurged on a cup of coffee and a pastry, spending precious shillings on them, before asking everyone there if they knew Ian or had seen him.

When all of their answers were no, I finished my coffee and kept going, marching into every pub and restaurant in the area, showing them Ian's picture and asking for help.

All I got for my trouble were looks of pity and a big fat blister on my heel.

The next day, I went in search of Lieutenant Montgomery, thinking he was a kind man who might be willing to help. At first, no one would even help me find *him*, but I finally came across a friendly young face who was a Catholic himself, despite wearing the uniform. He wanted to help but told me Lieutenant Montgomery had just been transferred out of Belfast.

My shoulders fell.

Concern crossed the young man's face. "I'm sorry, love. I can try to get you an address if you need to write to him." His eyes darted to my stomach, as if he guessed my secret reason for wanting to find the lieutenant.

I didn't bother telling him he had it all wrong.

I shook my head. "No. If he's gone, he won't be any help to me anyway."

"Is there something I can help you with?" He had such a gentle, eager look on his face that my heart soared for a moment. Maybe it didn't matter that I couldn't find Lieutenant Montgomery.

"My husband's gone missing," I said, choking on the words. "Lieutenant Montgomery knew him and was kind to us, so I was hoping he might help me find him."

The man's face fell. "Ah, I'm sorry to hear that. I don't know if I can help, but if you'll give me your information, I'll try."

I gave him my name and my address, and he promised to swing by my flat the next day to let me know what he found out.

But he didn't. When two more days passed without news, I finally pulled out Kieran's card—and realized I should have looked at it the day he'd given it to me.

I sat on my couch, staring at the card in my hands as I fought off the nausea that threatened to overwhelm me.

On the back of the card, Kieran had scrawled a note.

Tell Ian it's a trap. Leave tonight.

I willed the words to make sense, knowing they wouldn't—not until I spoke with Kieran, anyway.

He knew something. Had known it before it happened and had tried to warn us. Surely that meant I could trust him.

My racing heart didn't agree with that logic, but in the end, I didn't have a choice. He was the only one who might know what had happened to Ian. I had to go to him whether I liked it or not.

I threw on my coat and headed out the door before I could change my mind.

Kieran's neighborhood felt even rougher than the Falls. The buildings were crumbling and cramped. The brick two-room terraces looked like they might collapse if a hard enough gust of wind came through. Some of them still had outside toilets. The tight alleyways made me claustrophobic, and although I was close to the city center, I felt completely cut off from Belfast. But unlike the safe bubble near the campus, this place made me want to run straight back to Falls Road.

The little boys who played ball in the street fell silent, staring as I approached. Up ahead, I saw older boys pelt a soldier with rocks until he turned his rifle butt on them and drove them off. A haggard woman watched me with cold appraisal as she tossed dirty dish-water into the street.

This neighborhood didn't smell of freshly ground coffee. It smelled of garbage and rot.

I kept walking, forcing myself forward. *Kieran has answers.*

It was the only thing that kept me going when I saw three grown men attack the soldier who'd fought off the boys. Even with his rifle, he didn't stand a chance.

I kept my head down and tried to block out the sounds of his screams as they beat him.

Then I tried to block out the silence that fell when his screams stopped.

One more turn, one more tight alley, then I was at the address Kieran had given me. *You can turn around and go home.* My whole body shook with fear.

But I forced myself to knock on the door anyway. And when my legs tried to turn me around and run away, I forced them to stay put.

The door swung open, but it was Seamus who stood behind it. My shoulders sagged with relief.

"Fiona," he said, brightening. "We thought you'd be tucked away in Glenarm by now. Come on in, lass. Kieran, be a better host to her than you've been to me and get her something to drink, won't ya?"

Kieran's dark eyes met mine. His face was unmoving. "Water or whiskey?"

"Nothing, thanks," I said weakly.

"Oh, come on, now," Seamus said, guiding me inside. "Did you take a taxi or walk all this way?"

"I walked. I've no shillings to spare for a taxi."

He frowned. "That's a risk, considering. Get her some water, Kieran."

When Kieran disappeared, Seamus rolled his eyes. "He's daft, that one. Doesn't understand that some of us are actually human. Have a sit-down. To what do we owe the pleasure?" He perched on a stool, giving me a stupid grin as I gingerly sat in an armchair with a ripped seat.

"I-I've come because Ian is missing," I said.

No matter how many times I spoke the words, they didn't get easier.

Seamus's expression grew concerned. "Missing? What's the story?"

"Thursday was his last day of classes. He was supposed to come home, and we were going to have dinner together, then leave for the village the next morning. He never made it." I swallowed hard.

Kieran came in and shoved a glass of water into my hand, giving me a piercing look. He held a bottle of whiskey in his other hand and wiggled it as if to say it was there if I changed my mind. He plopped down onto the couch that sat between me and Seamus, throwing his arms over the back of it like Seamus always did at my place.

"Thursday, you say?" Seamus's eyes had gone big. He glanced at Kieran as if in question. Kieran just shrugged.

"What is it?" I sat forward, holding the water in my hands but not drinking it.

Seamus dropped his gaze. "There was an incident on Thursday evening. Some of the lads were involved in an operation down in the city center, only they got caught by soldiers. We think some tout tipped off the army about what was going down. They walked right into a trap."

My heart squeezed. *A trap.* Just like Kieran had said. And if Kieran knew about it, that meant...

Kieran was the tout.

My mind swirled, trying to process it all. Kieran would get his kneecaps shot out if anyone knew he'd tipped off the soldiers. He'd taken a huge risk by trying to warn Ian in advance, knowing that either of us could have reported it to the others.

I owed him one. So I locked that information away for later and pretended I didn't know, bringing the conversation back to Ian.

"Was Ian one of them? Do ya think he's been arrested?"

Seamus exchanged glances with Kieran, then looked back at me. "Most of them were arrested, aye. I think one of them got away. But things got ugly with one of the soldiers, and one of the men was shot and killed."

No. It felt like all of the air had been sucked out of the room.

Not Ian. Please, not Ian.

"Ian told me he was coming straight home," I cried when I could finally speak. "What makes you think he was even there?"

"I don't know for sure that he was," Seamus admitted. "I'm just saying the timing and all. I was down south, but when I got back, I heard they called some extra lads in at the last minute to help. If you want, I can try to find out if he was there and get the names of those who were arrested. Maybe he's in the cages."

Kieran leaned forward and poured a shot of whiskey into a dirty glass that sat on the coffee table between us all. He downed it in a single swallow, then slammed the glass down, his jaw tight.

"He's not in the cages," Kieran said.

Seamus gaped at him.

I scooted forward. "Please. Tell me what you know."

Something in Kieran's eyes softened before the hard mask descended again.

"I'm sorry," he said, staring at the table. "Ian was shot. He's dead."

The words were a bullet to my heart. I fell onto the ground as if I were the one who'd been shot, crying out in agony, with heartbreak that I thought might kill me.

Ian is dead.

Those three words crowded out every other thought. I don't even remember how the lads got me back home and tucked into bed.

It wasn't until later, when I was alone in the dark of my room, that it hit me what a cruel joke the timing was. Just when I'd thought we were going to escape the horrors of Belfast for good, it had stolen our last chance at a future together. The years Ian had given to the cause hadn't been enough for greedy Belfast, with its endless thirst for blood. No, Belfast wouldn't let him go.

I'd fought so hard for my marriage, staying in Belfast until we could leave together.

But I'd be going back to Glenarm alone after all.

32
RAGING WATERS

FIONA
January 1972
Glenarm

A cruel wind blew in from the sea, whipping my hair behind me and forcing me to squeeze my eyes shut. I pulled my sweater tighter, hugging my arms around myself as I braced against the coming storm.

With my eyes closed, I thought of a painting I'd once seen where a woman stood on the cliffs, her eyes scanning the horizon as she waited for her love to return to her. The painting was called "The Widow Waits." It felt like a cruel joke that the viewer understood that her husband was dead, but she didn't.

It was a crueler joke still that I was now that widow, coming every day to the edge of the land and looking out to the sea while my heart grieved the one I loved. It made me realize the woman in that painting had probably known the truth all along. That she came to the cliffs every day, not because she had any real hope of seeing her love again, but because this was the only place *to* come. She had no graveside to visit, no final resting place to honor and mourn. She came to the sea because the ocean was a vessel of salty tears, the only one large enough to possibly contain the grief of a soul whose very mate had been ripped from her without warning.

They shot Ian in the streets like a dog.

My imagination haunted me with new horrors every day. Images of him lying there, alone and bleeding, suffering. His heart breaking as he thought of the baby he'd never hold, the new life we'd been so close to starting.

Images of the soldiers who mocked him, beat him, and offered him no aid.

The rage welled up inside me, and I opened my mouth, screaming my fury into the heavens. But the sound of it was lost in the storm, dwarfed by forces so much larger than I would ever be.

The tide churned. Dark waves, nearly as black as night, capped with fierce white foam, surged against the rocky shoreline. The sky swirled with threatening clouds. Lightning flashed in the distance.

It was dangerous to be out here, in a storm like this. Still, I stood defiant, angry in a way I'd never known possible before I'd learned how Ian died.

My anger wasn't just about his unfair death, though that was bad enough. But when the papers wrote about the killing, they hadn't even bothered to find out his name. To them, he was only an "IRA terrorist shot by soldiers during a thwarted bombing."

A *terrorist.* That's how they painted my Ian. Ian, with the soul of a poet. Ian, the man who'd gone to Belfast with high hopes and a desire to make his family proud by earning an education. Ian, the man who'd stayed to help the neighbors, who were being unfairly oppressed, because he couldn't bear the idea of shutting his eyes to their suffering like the rest of the world had.

Ian, the man who'd been searched daily, called names, and treated like a second-class citizen. Who'd had his home broken into twice, his house ransacked. Who'd been beaten by soldiers and arrested without cause.

I spat on the ground. He wasn't the terrorist. He was a freedom fighter. The people who'd tormented and oppressed the Catholics in Belfast were the real terrorists, and I hoped to God that somehow those people would someday pay.

I screamed into the wind again as thunder shook the ground underneath my feet.

It was wrong. All of it.

I hadn't even been able to bury him yet. The army had taken his body away, supposedly for an autopsy and inquest. The priest in Belfast warned me that it could be weeks or months before they released him—if they ever did. When soldiers killed someone in a way that reflected badly on the British government, the bodies were often "lost" in the system to cover up the truth.

So I'd come home without him, only to be slapped in the face with the news that Annie had fallen head over heels for a lad named Edward—a lad who happened to be a British soldier.

I'd left Belfast to get away from the enemy, but they were here, too, and my sister had invited one of them into her heart and actually expected me to be okay with it. As if I'd ever be able to look at a soldier and not see the ones who'd hurt my Ian over and over again.

The betrayal of it all made me scream into the wind once more.

I ducked underneath the roof of the back porch and pulled off my wellies with wet fingers that were half frozen. I'd lingered at the rocky shore too long, unable to leave even when the cold rains began pelting my face.

I squeezed the water out of my hair, my teeth chattering so hard I feared they might break. Inside the house, I heard Mamó and Annie chatting about dinner. Even without a mirror, I knew the scowl on my face was as dark as the stormy sky above me. I tried hard to keep my anger hidden at home, releasing it only on my daily walks to the sea. But some days were easier than others.

Annie's man was due to come for dinner tonight. I hadn't met him yet, and I didn't want to, but Mamó had suggested that it might be helpful for me to see that not all British soldiers were terrible people. She happened to think highly of Annie's lad, and she thought I would too.

Clearly, she didn't understand what we had suffered in Belfast.

Mamó grieved for Ian, but though she didn't voice it, I could tell by the things she didn't say that she put a good part of the blame for his death squarely on his shoulders. After all, he'd chosen to get involved in the IRA. No matter what injustices had happened in Belfast, she couldn't condone the IRA's actions.

I suspected she was also angry that he'd knowingly endangered me for so long, only agreeing to leave when there was a baby on the way. There was part of me that was angry about that too. But I kept that part buried deep underneath the rage I felt toward the government and the army.

My anger at Ian hurt too badly to face.

"You're back!" Mamó said brightly, opening the screen door. "I thought I heard something moving about out here. Look at you. You're soaked through to the bone. You'll catch your death."

"I'm fine," I said stubbornly, though I couldn't stop the shivers that wracked my body.

"Stop being stubborn. It's not good for the baby. Come in and get dried off. I'll make you a cup of tea."

"I don't want tea."

"You'll have it anyway." She gave me a look that said she wasn't to be argued with.

I rolled my eyes and followed her inside, then headed upstairs to change. My things had been put here in the main house, in my old room. I wasn't entirely sure how to feel about that. On one hand, it was strange to be a grown woman back underneath Mamó's roof after years of independence. But on the other hand, I knew if I slept in the bed I'd shared with Ian in our wee cottage, I'd do nothing but weep all night. I hadn't faced it or the memories it held yet. The idea of opening that door felt like jumping off the cliffs into the swirling sea below. I knew I wasn't strong enough to face those waters without drowning.

I suspected Mamó knew it too, though she didn't say so. She simply said it would be good for me to be in the main house during the pregnancy, and I went along with it. It made Ian's death feel less real, somehow, to sleep here where I'd never shared a bed with him. Like my whole life with him had been nothing but a dream that turned into a nightmare.

When I was in dry clothes, I headed downstairs, pausing mid-flight in confusion when I saw who was in the sitting room.

Mamó rose. "You have a visitor," she told me stiffly before excusing herself.

"Seamus, what are you doing here?" My hand gripped the stair rail.

He stood, holding his cap in his hand. "I've news for ya, so I have."

I hurried down the rest of the steps and joined him, motioning for him to sit, then took the rocking chair Mamó had vacated.

"What is it?" I leaned forward, my heart thumping wildly in my chest.

He twisted his cap. "We discovered who killed Ian. It was a Lieutenant named Montgomery. I know that doesn't do anything to bring him back, but I thought you'd like to know."

I sat back, shocked. "No." I shook my head quickly. "You must be mistaken."

"Does the name mean something to ya?" He gave me a funny look.

"He... His brother went to school with Ian." I swallowed hard. "He helped me once, during the curfew. When a soldier was about to... He saved me."

Seamus's eyebrows knit together in confusion. "Well, that's an odd thing, isn't it? Someone who knew Ian shooting him like that?"

"I can't believe—unless..."

"Unless what?"

"He vouched for Ian," I said. "When internment started. He's the reason Ian got to come home. If he saw Ian in a compromising situation"—I couldn't bring myself to admit out loud that Ian was helping plant a bomb—"then he may have taken it personally."

Seamus sat back, looking stunned. "So that's why the bastard shot him. I couldn't figure out why Ian. Out of all of them, Ian was the least likely to put up any resistance."

Hot tears sprang to my eyes. "It must have been revenge. That's the only thing that makes sense."

He leaned forward again. "It also makes sense now why they haven't released the body. The bastard probably shot him at point-blank range—or did worse to him first."

I couldn't answer him. I put my hand over my mouth, afraid I was going to be sick.

Seamus gave me a concerned look and cleared his throat. "Ah, well, I'm sorry. I also came to give ya this." He fished something out of his pocket and handed it to me. It was a stack of bills, enough to buy groceries for six months or more.

I looked at the money, confused. "I don't understand."

"We have some money coming in from donations." His voice dropped. "Me and the lads thought we'd like to give some of it to you to help out, ya know, in memory of Ian. We like to take care of our own."

"I can't—"

He flashed me a grin. "Of course you can. Better it go to you and the baby than to paying my tab at the pub, eh?" He stood. "Take care of yourself, Fiona. And remember, you're still family to us. We'll never forget how many lads you tended, stitching 'em up and helping us all survive. I stuck a card with my number in there. Got me a real phone now and everything. Ya need anything, we're here."

I threw my arms around his neck, feeling guilty for every terrible thing I'd ever thought about him. "Thanks," I said, my throat tight.

He stuck his cap on and shot me another flashy grin before heading back out into the rain.

I headed to the kitchen shortly before Annie's lad was to arrive, grateful to see that Annie was busy getting herself ready for the night. It would be easier to be nice if I didn't have to face her quite yet.

Knowing who had shot Ian and why made more of a difference than Seamus could know. It was no longer a faceless British soldier —it was a face I knew, and I knew the reason he'd done it. It didn't take away any of my anger, but it made me think there might be a day when I could accept that not all of them were the same. Maybe Mamó was right and Annie's lad was a good man, the kind of man who would have helped Ian had he been there.

I dreaded it with all my heart, but I knew I had to give him a chance. It wasn't right to blame him for something Lieutenant Montgomery had done.

Mamó hummed to herself as she stirred each pot on the stove in turn, then opened the oven to check the dish inside.

I clasped my hands behind my back and cleared my throat. "I thought I'd offer to help," I said meekly.

She turned and gave me a bright smile. "Does that mean you've decided to join us tonight?"

I nodded.

Her eyes softened. "Well, maybe your visitor did you some good after all. You can set the table, so you can."

"Alright," I said, returning her smile with one that, for the first time in weeks, felt like it might have a bit of truth behind it. It wasn't a smile of happiness, exactly. There was no joy in my heart yet. It was more like a smile of hope that happiness might still exist, that maybe

I wouldn't spend the rest of my life screaming into the wind and feeling nothing but rage and emptiness.

I pulled four plates from the cabinet, then went to the silverware drawer.

Mamó called from over her shoulder. "Grab a corkscrew and put out the wineglasses. Lieutenant Montgomery always brings a bottle with him."

My hand froze in midair. Blood rushed to my ears. It felt as if I were free-falling, like I'd somehow slipped off the side of a cliff and was hurtling toward the black surface of the raging sea. I had to have heard her wrong. Annie had been dating Edward for months, they said. Lieutenant Montgomery had been in Belfast until Ian's death. There had to be a mistake.

"What did you say?" I asked shakily, turning slowly to face her.

"The wineglasses." She shot me a concerned look. "He always brings a bottle with him."

"Not that part. His name."

"Lieutenant Montgomery," she said slowly. "Oh, I suppose Annie calls him Edward to you."

I dropped the silverware back into the drawer and clutched my stomach. I couldn't breathe. The walls were closing in, and all I could hear was the roaring in my ears.

She moved toward me, grabbing me by the shoulder. Her mouth moved, and I knew she was asking if I was okay. But it was like she was in a different world than I was, too hazy and far away to reach me. Too quiet for me to hear over the roar. I grasped at the countertop and felt my way along it, out of her grip, until I made it to the back door.

"Fiona!" Her voice cut through the fog.

I ignored it and ran out into the rain.

I didn't stop running until I reached the sea.

33
FLICKERING FIRELIGHT

FIONA

January 1972

Glenarm

When I returned to the house, my voice was hoarse, my frail body weary, and I shook uncontrollably from the cold. Mamó was pacing the kitchen, waiting for me. When she heard me on the porch, she ran out, grabbing me and pulling me inside before I even had time to take off my shoes.

She wrapped her arms around me, pressing my head to her shoulder. "Oh, my sweet girl. I've been so worried. What on earth got into you?"

"He killed Ian," I whispered, my voice raw.

Mamó pulled back and gave me a piercing look. "What?"

"Lieutenant Montgomery. He's the man who shot Ian." My voice broke on his name, and I crumbled, sobbing.

Mamó got me to the bench at the kitchen table and rubbed my back aggressively, trying to warm me through my wet clothes.

"There has to be a mistake," she said. "Maybe it's a different Lieutenant Montgomery."

"Maybe," I said, but the words were hollow. It was him. I could feel it.

She was quiet for a moment. When she finally spoke, her words were brisk. "We'll deal with that later. Right now, we've got to get you dry—again—and warm. I know you're grieving. I know you're suffering with a pain so fierce you feel like it's shattered your whole world and that nothing else is ever going to matter again." She gripped my face in her hands. "But, Fiona, ya can't keep doing this. If ya won't take care of yourself for your own sake, take care of yourself for your wee child. For *Ian's* babe. If nothing else, hold on to that."

I swallowed hard and nodded. It was enough to make her eyes flash with relief.

But all I felt was the overwhelming emptiness that came every time I'd exhausted the rage.

I didn't intend on facing the man I hated so soon. But Annie had left the sitting room door open, and when Mamó ushered me out of the kitchen toward the stairs, they saw us. Lieutenant Montgomery jumped up, his hat in his hands the same way Seamus had held his earlier that day. His eyes were riddled with worry.

"Mrs. Flanagan," he said, bowing his head. "Annie told me about your loss. I'm so terribly sorry."

I just stared at him. Mamó tugged at my elbow, trying to pull me away, but I kept my feet planted the same way I had when I stood on the rocks during the storm.

"I was surprised," he said awkwardly. "I didn't think he…"

"You didn't think he was in the IRA," I said calmly, though my voice still sounded strange and hoarse.

He frowned and nodded. "He seemed different than that lot. I know it's wrong to speak ill of the dead, but I'll admit I'm disappointed. I'm sure you are as well. I thought he was better than that."

My nostrils flared. Mamó squeezed my trembling hand in warning.

"Ian was a good man," I said, my weak voice shaking with anger.

"Exactly." He shook his head, like the thought genuinely grieved him. "I believe he was. It makes you wonder, doesn't it, how they got him to turn? How could a good man take up with a lot like that? A lot that dares to bomb civilians?"

He didn't bother hiding the disdain when he spoke of "that lot."

Mamó again tried to pull me away, but I shook her off and marched right up to him. "How dare you," I said, my voice low.

He took a step back, his eyes wide with surprise. "Excuse me?"

"How dare you come into my home and speak about Ian like that —about any of them like that." I jabbed my finger at his chest. "How can a good man turn? If ya really want an answer to that, you should look in the mirror. You soldiers think you're better than the rest of us because you wear a uniform and have the crown on your side. But it was *soldiers* who stood there and allowed us to be attacked over and over again. It was *soldiers* who broke into our homes, beat us, destroyed our property, stole from us, gassed us, and laughed as we suffered. And yet you dare to look down your nose at the men who stepped up to defend us?"

He opened his mouth to speak, but I wasn't finished yet.

"You criticize them for using bombs, but it was *soldiers* who went through our homes and took our weapons, leaving us without any other means of defense. How can a good man turn? Imagine being a man shoved to his knees and forced to watch as his home is ripped apart and his defenses are stripped away while his children choke on gas." My whole body shook with anger. "You, the man who killed my Ian, for what—lying to ya? Embarrassing you because you stuck up for him and were wrong? You dare to act like you're better than *him*?"

I slapped him across the face, feeling a thrill of pleasure at the sting on my palm. Annie gasped and looked at me with horror.

Lieutenant Montgomery stared at me wide-eyed, his mouth slack with shock.

I turned on my heel and walked out.

The next day, I returned to the cliffs, gazing at the sparkling sea below. There was no storm to rage into, just calm turquoise waters stretching to the horizon, a rare gift for a land where the sea and sky were veiled with gray mist all winter. It was beautiful.

I stared at the sea, wishing it could grant me its secrets. The storm I understood. But this—this calm tranquility, this dazzling beauty and unexpected color—was something that felt alien to me now. The sea and the sky had poured out all of their rage, but unlike me, they hadn't become hollow and lifeless after. They'd roared with violence only to become this: a beautiful, shimmery world of color, somehow more vibrant and alive than before.

I'd vented my anger to the one who truly deserved it, but instead of feeling better, I only felt empty again, a hollow, lifeless vessel trapped in a fog only I could see.

My hand reached to my belly, reminding me that the words I'd just thought weren't true. I wasn't lifeless at all. I carried within me a life Ian and I had created together, and no matter how hard things were, I owed it to this child to stay strong.

"I'm sorry," I whispered, holding my hand over the wee swell that marked where my babe grew. "I'll try harder. I'll find a way to be strong for you. We'll figure out how to make a shimmery, shiny life, won't we? We'll learn how to be like the sea and shine even brighter after this storm. I promise you, I'll find a way."

I didn't leave the cliffs any earlier that day. But instead of standing alone against the wind, I sat down on the grass and rested my weary feet, letting the earth hold me as I grieved. And the sea whispered a song to my soul, a gentle song about salty tears and the ocean that held them all. A song of moonlight and magic, of changing tides and sweeping waves. A song of letting go and letting the waves carry me home.

Annie was waiting for me in the kitchen when I returned. She was a picture of youth and beauty, her cheeks rosy with love and her eyes bright with hope that couldn't be dimmed by the worry she held for me. It brought a stab of pain to see her like that, making me think of a time not so long ago when I was starry-eyed and full of dreams for a life with the boy I loved.

Her hands were clasped together on the wooden table, but when I walked in the door, she pulled them to her, tucking them into the pockets of her thick cardigan. I gave her a quick nod, then looked away and walked past, heading straight for the blessed solitude of my bedroom.

"I need to talk to you, Fi." Her voice was low, hesitant.

I stopped, taking a slow breath as I bit my lip. I knew she and Mamó both expected me to apologize for my outburst, but I wouldn't.

"I'm very tired," I said, hoping to avoid talking at all.

"It's important. Please."

I turned slowly, facing her. Her youth and innocence filled me with joy and jealousy at the same time. I was so grateful my baby sister had never had to face the things I'd seen the past two years. That rang true no matter how badly I wanted to direct some of the rage eating me alive toward her for daring to date someone I considered an enemy.

But I longed for some of that life and color to return to me. Longed to look into the mirror and see something other than the gray, hollow shell I'd become. My sister shone like the sea had today, and I so desperately wanted just a sliver of that for myself.

"Sit down," she said, nodding toward the chair.

"I won't apologize for the things I said last night—or for slapping him," I warned as I took the wicker chair at the head of the table.

"I don't expect ya to. We all know we need to make allowances for ya, considering..." Her eyes dropped to the table.

Ah. "Then what do ya need to talk to me about?" At the downcast look on her face, my tone softened. "I suppose Mamó told ya the truth about how Lieutenant Montgomery is the one who shot Ian. I'm not angry with ya, Annie. You didn't know. I'm sorry that it has to end this way, but—"

She looked up, alarmed. "End? No, Fi, you misunderstand me."

My eyes narrowed. "You *are* going to end things, aren't ya? Now that ya know the truth of who he is?" My heart began to beat faster than it had in quite some time, a signal that danger might not be as far away here in the village as I'd once thought.

She took a deep breath, trembling. "No, I'm not. I'm to marry him in the summer. That's what I wanted to talk to you about." She withdrew her hands from her pockets and laid them on the table, allowing me to see the tiny ring that symbolized their engagement.

The room felt like it was spinning again. I gripped both sides of the table, holding on like it could stop the madness.

She reached across and put a hand over mine. "I know it's a shock, but—"

"How could you marry him?" I interrupted, yanking my hand away from hers. "He who killed my Ian. He who wears the uniform of the ones who tortured and terrorized us."

She winced at my words and pulled her hand back, twisting her thumbs.

"He shot Ian in the streets like a dog," I said, forcing her to hear the words again. "And you, my precious sister, agreed to *marry* him? How could ya? Are you a traitor, too, then? Have you no love for your family, for your very blood?"

She turned red, looking away. Her bottom lip—so full, so young still—trembled as a tear pricked the corner of her eye.

"Aye, Fiona," she said, her voice wavering though she tried to be strong. "Of course I love ya. But you're wrong about him. He's a good man. I thought you'd be able to see that, seeing as how he stood up for you and Ian both."

"How can you say that?" I wanted to shake some sense into her. "You've no idea what we went through in Belfast."

"Nor do you have any idea what *he* went through in Belfast or what we've gone through here," she snapped, showing a fire I'd never seen in her before. "What you and Ian went through is terrible, but you're not the only ones who have suffered these last two years."

I sat back, stunned.

She rose and smoothed down the front of her cardigan, a failed attempt to hide the trembling in her hands. When she looked at me again, she squared her shoulders and lifted her chin. "Lieutenant Montgomery is a good man. What happened to Ian isn't his fault. Ian made a choice to do what he did, knowing the consequences he might face for it. I hope that someday you'll find it in your heart to be happy for us. I hope someday you'll realize you're wrong about Edward—and I hope to God he's wrong about you."

She turned to walk away, but I grabbed the sleeve of her sweater, stopping her in her tracks.

"Wrong about me? What's that supposed to mean?" I asked, demanding answers.

Guilt swam across her face. She dropped her eyes again and placed a hand on the table as if to steady herself. "Ian was radicalized by violence. It's something Edward has seen time and time again, both in the people in Belfast and in his fellow soldiers. He's stood against it, always, even when it's his own men. You've seen that. We're both brokenhearted that Ian chose the path he did. Now, Edward's concerned the same thing is happening to you."

My eyebrows rose to the ceiling. "Lieutenant Montgomery thinks *I'm* radicalized? That I'm, what, going to start hiding bombs in the postal office?" The very idea was ludicrous.

Annie didn't flinch. "He doesn't know what you might do," she said quietly. "But he warned me that you might be a terrorist yourself now, like Ian. The things ya said, the way ya slapped him... He's asked me to keep an eye on ya."

She couldn't have made up something to stun me more if she'd tried.

"He's asked ya to turn tout against your own sister?"

"It's not like that—"

I stood, furious, and paced the room. "Do you honestly think me capable of something like that?" I faced her, needing her to see the devastation on my face.

"I don't know what you're capable of anymore!" She threw her arms up in the air. "You've cut me out completely since you've been home. You don't talk to me. You don't talk to Mamó. You're angry like I've never seen you before!"

"Of course I'm angry!" I yelled back. "They killed my husband!"

Something inside me broke. The anger that kept me propped up failed, falling like the rotten wood pilings of a decrepit pier, giving way to a flood of heartbreak so fierce I feared that it might kill me. I sank to my knees on the floor, sobbing as the waves of grief washed over me.

He was really gone. This wasn't a nightmare I'd wake up from; it wasn't a foggy dream. I would never feel his hand holding mine again, would never lie against his chest in the bed we shared. I'd never see his dimples flash as his face lit up in a grin or hear him tease me about my superstitions. He was gone, and I was alone, and I didn't know how I could bear it. I didn't even know who I *was* without him.

I wasn't sure I wanted to.

Annie let out a little cry and knelt beside me, wrapping her arms around my shoulders. "I'm so sorry," she said through her own sobs. "I'm so, so sorry."

The shadows had grown long by the time I could raise my head and speak. Annie had stayed with me the whole time, her face as wet with tears as mine.

I gripped her hand. "I'm sorry," I said fervently, though I couldn't put into words why I felt such sorrow in my heart. I still didn't regret the words I'd spoken to or about Lieutenant Montgomery. But I grieved for hurting Annie, and I mourned the distance between us that had risen beside my grief for Ian.

She clasped my hands in hers. "I love you. Please talk to me. Don't keep shutting me out."

I nodded and began to spill my heart—all of it, even the pieces I'd tried to hide from myself. I told her how only part of me was proud of Ian—and how the other part of me felt as if he'd chosen the fight over us, his new friends over me. How I knew that what the IRA was doing was wrong, but I'd closed my eyes to it because I didn't know what else to do. How terrifying it had been living there and how we'd all suffered. How I envied the respite Ian had at Queen's and how I regretted staying in the Falls and not forcing him to choose earlier.

And how I also couldn't fully regret it, because had I left, I feared he would have stayed anyway and we would have had even less time together. We wouldn't have made our sweet child, the only thing I had left to hold on to.

I spilled all of it, talking and crying until the sun sank below the earth and our bellies rumbled with hunger.

We were still sitting on the floor when Mamó came home. She paused in the doorway, a look of understanding on her face. I expected questions, but she was patient. She unwrapped her shawl, placed her basket of herbs on the table, and asked us to help her get dinner together.

After we'd eaten, we tucked in by the fire with hot cups of tea, and I repeated it all to her. It was easier the second time. Now that I'd let the words loose, they no longer felt like poison in my soul.

"Many things can be true at the same time," Mamó said quietly when I'd finished. She held her ceramic mug in both hands, close to her heart. "It's true that Ian was a good husband to you, and it's also true that his choices hurt you. It's true that you're proud of him for wanting to stand with the weak and defenseless, and it can also be true that you're ashamed of how he did it. One doesn't cancel out the other."

The truth of it felt like freedom.

Annie spoke slowly. "It's true that I love Edward. But it's also true that I-I don't know if I can marry the man who shot my brother." She glanced at me with a worried look on her face. "Because I think I love my sister more than I love him."

Fresh tears ran down my cheeks. I pulled my hand out from underneath the blanket that covered me and reached for hers.

None of us spoke again. There was nothing else to say. But we stayed there together, all three of us, while the fire danced and crackled. The winds picked up, howling against the windowpanes, but the cold air couldn't reach us in the warmth of the cottage.

A feeling of contentment spread through me, a once-familiar friend I'd almost forgotten. With it came another truth, the one the ocean had tried to sing to me before.

The anger I'd wielded had felt so real, but in truth, it was a defense against the things I'd been afraid to face, afraid to feel. When the rotten pillars had crumbled and the waves had washed over me, I'd finally surrendered to the grief that threatened to drown me. And while the rage I'd screamed into the ocean had only left me hollow until anger rose again, facing the truth had helped me start to release the weight of it all. My heart wasn't yet a shimmery turquoise sea. But where it had broken, I felt it slowly begin to mend, and the steady beat of it assured me that I would get through this, somehow.

I looked at Mamó and Annie with warmth in my heart, thinking of how grateful I was to have them both and how I knew they'd be by my side, helping me start over.

But I was wrong. Because though we felt safe and cozy together in the flickering firelight, danger still danced in the shadows outside.

I was a marked woman. The dangerous widow of IRA terrorist Ian Flanagan.

The man who had killed him couldn't let me go unpunished.

34
SACRIFICES

Fiona

March 1972

Glenarm

The porch door shut with a bang, drawing my attention from the row of dirt in front of me. I'd been tucking pea seeds into the earth, strangely conscious of how things had changed since the last time I'd helped Mamó plant her spring garden. I worked more slowly now, and my thoughts were far more serious. My dreams were smaller, more fragile than before. But they were real, and I held tightly to them, knowing how precious it was to begin to dream again.

"I hope you're not coming to help in *that* dress," I called out playfully as Annie made a beeline for me.

When she reached me, I saw she was far too pale and that her hands trembled.

"I need to talk to ya," she said, her voice shaky.

"What's wrong?" I asked, jumping to my feet. I wiped the dirt from my hands on the old kitchen towel I'd tucked into my apron.

"I've just come from seeing Edward." The look on her face was pure devastation.

I put my arm around her shoulder and led her over to the wooden bench that sat in the corner of Mamo's garden. The blue paint was chipped and peeling, and the wood sagged from age and wear, but none of us could bear to replace it. Too many important talks had been had on this bench. It was a monument, and it would stay in the garden until nature broke it back down into earth.

"Did he not take the news well?" I asked, feeling a pang of empathy for Annie. After the day I'd fallen apart, she'd decided that when Edward returned, she would tell him she wanted to delay their wedding. She wasn't sure she could marry the man who had killed Ian, even if it had been justified. Even if she could eventually make peace with it, she didn't want to do it when my grief was still fresh. It was important to her that her sister dance at her wedding, and she couldn't ask it of me now.

She nervously twisted the hem of her skirt in her fingers. "No, he didn't take it well. He's angry."

I sighed. "I'm sorry, Annie."

"Don't be." She bit her lip, looking down. "Fi, I hope you'll forgive me for this, but... I don't think I can delay the wedding after all."

Her words startled me. "What?"

She looked up, her eyes pleading as she clasped my hand in hers. "The wedding must go on as planned, and you must be there. You must accept Edward and smile and be happy. Most importantly, you mustn't say a word about Ian. Promise me."

I pulled my hand from hers, staring at her with my jaw dropped. "Annie, what is going on? I love you, and I want you to be happy, but surely ya know I'm not ready to even face Edward again, much less celebrate your union with him and call him my brother. I will try to accept it, in time, but—" My hands began to shake just thinking of it.

I wanted to forgive him, for Annie's sake, but I couldn't look at him without picturing Ian's death.

Her eyes darted from left to right, like she was afraid to be overheard. "What I'm asking is impossible, I know," she admitted, her voice low despite our solitude. "But, Fi, I'm begging you. Whatever you have to do to accept it, please. You don't know how important it is." Tears welled up and overflowed, dripping down her face faster than she could wipe them away with the sleeve of her yellow sweater.

"If ya know it's impossible, then why ask it of me?" My heart broke in two. I pulled her to me and patted her back as she cried on my shoulder. "Oh, dear one, what are you keeping from me?" A thought hit, stealing my breath. "You're not pregnant, are ya? Oh, Annie."

She shook her head quickly. "No."

"Then what is it?"

She spoke, but the words were muffled on my shoulder. They had to be—because if I'd heard her correctly, it would shatter me in two.

I pulled back, forcing her to look me in the eye. "Say it again."

She cast her eyes down. "Because he said he'll protect you."

"Protect me from what?" I demanded.

She could not look at me. "He said it's a crime for you to have known that Ian was in the IRA and not reported it. The speech you made the night you slapped him... He could not believe you defended Ian like that. He said you talk like a radical, and it makes him wonder if you might have even been involved."

"Involved?" I didn't think my jaw could drop any lower.

She nodded, looking up at me with tearful eyes. "Fi, they're going after families now too. Imprisoning women, even. Edward doesn't want that to happen to you, but he said it will if you keep going like this. And I love you, Fi. I cannot bear for you to be imprisoned. You have to let me protect you."

The knife stabbed deep.

My wee sister. It was my job to protect *her*, not hers to protect me. The world was upside down, and all I knew was that somehow I had to find a way to make it right.

"It sounds like he's threatening me to stop you from delaying the wedding." My voice shook with anger. All the hatred I'd felt for Edward since the day he shot my Ian came roaring back.

He would not take my sister too.

She shook her head quickly. "He didn't threaten you. Fi, he says he should have reported you right away, but he didn't because he'd like to think it was just grief talking. He said he knows my heart—and Mamó's—and that while Ian might have led you astray, he has to believe that you have a good soul deep down. You're in danger, though, whether he says anything or not. He said if Ian was shot by a British soldier, it's only a matter of time before the army comes to interrogate you, and they'll be looking for anything to make their case."

"*If* Ian was shot by a British soldier?" I asked, the rage building up inside me like a violent storm. "He's the one who shot him!"

"He swears he didn't," she said before biting her lip. The worry that clouded her eyes told me she was struggling with this as much as I was—a fact that only made me angrier. "He said he wasn't there that night."

"And you believe him?" I pushed off the bench and started pacing in front of her, desperate for an outlet for the rage coursing through me.

"I don't know," she admitted. "But I do believe that you're in danger of internment. He said you need to renounce what the IRA is doing and make it clear which side you're on. And if we marry as planned, he said it will look good to the others that he is in our family, that we are willing to forge an alliance. I will convert, and—"

"No," I cried. "You cannot give yourself away for my sake, nor can you abandon your faith, your heritage!"

The world hung silent. Even the sheep stopped bleating, and the wind stopped its whispers until she finally raised her eyes and looked at me. Bravery strengthened her features so that she looked years older.

"I must. Or else you're to be interned without trial come Monday.

There's a round-up scheduled already. I promised him I wouldn't tell you, but—"

"I'll run," I cried. "I'll hide. But you cannot marry him. You cannot marry someone who's forcing you into it when you asked him to wait, not even for me."

She jumped up and grabbed my hands. "You can't run." Her face was white. "Don't ya see? If you run, he'll know I told you and then I'll be the one who supported a member of the IRA. *I'll* be the one imprisoned."

I froze as the pieces fell into place.

He wasn't just threatening me. He was threatening my baby sister too. Forcing his hand so that he could have the bride he'd chosen, whether she liked it or not.

I fell to my knees and vomited, heaving until there was nothing left inside me.

When I finally finished and wiped my mouth, she took a deep breath and spoke as if it were all settled, her chin raised resolutely.

"I loved him once. It's hard to imagine loving him now, but maybe there will come a day when I do. I can protect you—protect *us*. I know it's hard, but I need you to be strong. We'll smile and pretend, and then they'll stop looking at you. It's the only way to make them stop."

I didn't answer her because I knew she was wrong.

I could never pretend to embrace my husband's killer, and I could never dance at my sister's wedding knowing that it wasn't her choice.

It wasn't her job to protect me.

It was my job to protect her.

35
THE PRICE OF FREEDOM

FIONA

March 1972
Belfast

I hugged my arms tightly around my body as my leather boots marched over the flagstone pavements of Central Belfast, heading toward the Catholic pub where Seamus had agreed to meet me. The city smells choked me and filled me with dread, as the nightmare of a life marked by bombs, bullets, and gas flooded my memories.

I despised this city. Someday, I'd leave it for good and never look back.

I slipped into the dark pub. Though it was still early afternoon, the bar was lined with men perched on barstools, slowly sipping pints as a way of filling the day since they couldn't find work. Their heads swiveled my way as I entered, and more than one of them shot me a disapproving look. A young woman alone in a pub in the middle of the day was a strange sight.

Two years ago, I would have shrank beneath their gazes. But the new me, the one who'd risen from the ashes when her life was burned to the ground, simply straightened her spine and glared at them.

They dropped their gazes before I did.

I unwrapped my scarf and made my way to the back of the pub, where Seamus had told me he'd be waiting, passing by more than a dozen men on the way. The atmosphere felt charged with pride and anger, and the voice in the back of my mind that still clung to reason told me it was a bad idea for me to be here. This was the kind of place that was often targeted for attack. The men who sat here did so knowing that, at any moment, a petrol bomb could fly through the window. It was a kind of defiance, I supposed, to sit calmly and drink stout instead of hiding away.

Seamus spotted me and raised his hand in welcome. My chest tightened when I saw he was joined by Kieran and a man I thought I'd never see again: Fergus.

I slid into the booth with them, ignoring the part of my brain that told me to run far away from these dangerous men. Seamus had helped me, I reminded myself—he'd given me a stack of money for me and the babe. Ian had died for their cause. I was safe with them.

My trembling body didn't get the memo.

Seamus shot me a sympathetic look. "How did it go at the barracks?"

I bit my lip and shook my head, trying not to cry. "They blew me off—again. Wouldn't even let me get past to talk to an officer about getting Ian's remains released. The soldier told me to try the RUC."

Fergus scoffed. "Ya can't go to the RUC. They'll not tell ya anything, and they'll harass ya for asking. They're worse than the Brits, as hard as that is to believe." A shadow passed over his face.

I studied him, sad to see he looked ten years older than he had before his arrest. Whatever he'd endured during internment had aged him quickly.

"How's the family?" I asked quietly.

He held my gaze. "They're good. I appreciate ya doing what ya could for them while I was in the cages. Ya've helped us a thousand times, and I'll not forget it."

I gave him a faint smile. "I know they're glad to have ya back. It's hard to—" I stopped myself, unable to get the words out over the gravel in my throat, because while I was glad they had Fergus, I'd never have Ian back.

I was on my own, and it felt so unfair.

I could feel Kieran's eyes on me. I glanced at him but turned away quickly. Those dark eyes seemed to see too much, and though I'd had the strength to glare at the men at the bar, I was still far too intimidated to glare at Kieran.

It didn't help that I didn't know where he stood or even how I felt about him. He was a tout—that much was certain. It was his fault Ian was dead as much as it was Lieutenant Montgomery's. But he'd cared enough to try to warn Ian away from the operation that night when doing so put him at great risk. He had to know that if I told Seamus and Fergus about the note, he'd face punishment. I couldn't understand him, and that made him even more terrifying somehow.

Seamus cleared his throat. "So, what're ya looking for from us, then? Are ya wanting us to try to find the lad's body for ya?"

"Yes, but..." I shook my head and took a breath, steeling myself. "That's not why I'm here. I'm in trouble, like."

The men exchanged glances.

"What kind of trouble?" Fergus asked, his brow furrowed.

"My sister, Annie. She's dating Lieutenant Montgomery, the soldier who shot Ian."

Fergus choked on his beer. "What's this about?"

Kieran's face darkened. He leaned forward, putting his elbows on the table. "That's a dangerous thing," he said, his voice low and deadly. "It was just last November that they shaved a girl's head for that in Derry. Tied her to a lamppost and tarred and feathered her."

My eyes widened. "Are ya serious?"

He nodded.

Seamus lowered his voice. "Are ya wanting us to punish your sister, then? Teach her a lesson for being a soldier lover?"

"No!" I straightened and shook my head quickly. "No, of course not. But we're in a bind." I explained how Lieutenant Montgomery was using the threat of internment to get her to convert and marry him.

Fergus leaned back and let out a noisy exhale. "Brit bastards."

"She only wants to protect me," I said tearfully. "We need to hide. I was hoping yous could help."

The men exchanged glances again.

"Give us a few hours," Seamus finally said. "We'll put it up the line. Meet us at Kieran's flat tonight at nine o'clock."

I took a sharp breath. It was terrifying enough going to Kieran's flat in the daytime. Walking there at night was unthinkable.

But I ignored my instincts yet again and nodded, agreeing to the plan.

Kieran's face was unreadable when he opened the door to his flat and silently welcomed me inside. Seamus and Fergus waited on the couch. Seamus lifted his whiskey in greeting when I took the same chair I'd taken before. My hands gripped the arms of it as the memory of hearing that Ian had been shot flashed back, so vivid it felt like I was reliving it all over again.

"You alright?" Kieran asked, his voice low.

I nodded, refusing to look at him.

"We think we can help ya," Seamus announced, ignoring my waves of grief. "Do ya have a passport?"

"Aye," I answered weakly.

"What about your sister?"

I shook my head. "No, she'd have no reason to. Ian and I got ours together because we were dreaming of traveling abroad, having a real honeymoon after he graduated from Queen's."

At the time, the dream had seemed so real. But it was one more thing we'd never get to do together.

"That complicates things," Seamus said. "But we'll see what we can do. We've a lad who's able to forge documents, like. He can get the both of yous to America, where ya'll never have to deal with the Troubles again."

I wanted to weep with relief. *America.* The land of the free. A land where there would be no internment without trial, where my sister wouldn't have to convert or marry against her will, and where there would be no reminders of Belfast or the IRA or any of this wretched nightmare.

"Thanks," I said, my heart swimming with gratitude.

He cocked his head. "Well, don't be thanking me yet. There's a price for your papers."

"I have all the money ya gave me," I said eagerly. "Will that be enough?"

"It's not that kind of price, I'm afraid."

A deep sense of dread filled my soul. Once again, my body cried out for me to run.

But once again, I shoved my instincts down and forged ahead.

"What kind of price?" I asked coldly, fearing what he'd say next.

Seamus gave me a regretful look. "Ya have to kill the bastard who shot Ian."

36
MARKED WOMAN

Fiona

March 1972

Belfast

I stared at Seamus, thinking I must have heard him wrong. Perhaps the strain of everything that had happened had made me lose my marbles for good.

"I-I need ya to say that again," I said shakily.

"Ya have to kill him," Seamus repeated. "That's the price."

Surely it was a joke. But his face stayed serious.

"But I can't. It's wr—" I stopped myself, realizing I should choose my words very carefully. I was sitting with three men who regularly killed for the IRA, and though I'd willfully ignored my instincts, I still had enough of a desire for survival to know that offending them would not be a smart move.

"We'll give ya what you need," Seamus said calmly. "We can teach ya how to plant a bomb or let ya borrow a pistol. It'll be up to you to make sure ya don't get caught. Our man will take care of the documents ya need to get across the border, but they won't work if you're a marked woman."

A marked woman. That was my excuse. "But I'm already a marked woman," I said quickly. "I'm to be interned on Monday."

Kieran shook his head. "He was likely saying that to put the pressure on your sister. It's true there's a roundup scheduled—we've a source who confirmed it. But if your name was already on the lists, there'd be no talk of you dancing at their wedding and him protecting you if you went along with it."

I stared at him, shocked both by his words and by how many of them he'd said. I wasn't sure I'd ever heard him say so much.

Seamus nodded in agreement. "Montgomery's a snake who'll turn ya in the first chance he gets, but if he's using ya as leverage to get your sister, then you'll not be on any lists yet. We have a short window of time for you to get the job done and get out of here."

"There has to be another way," I cried. "You're asking me to murder someone in cold blood!"

Fergus leaned forward, his face angry. "Don't ya want to get revenge for Ian's death? That man shot your husband, took him away from you and your baby. I thought you'd be jumping at the chance to see justice done."

I shrank from his anger.

Seamus jumped in, using the soothing tone he'd begun using anytime he spoke to me. "It's not cold blood, Fiona. This is a war. Casualties are part of it. God knows enough people have died on *our* side. You have a connection to an officer, a way to get close to him. That kind of thing doesn't come around often for us."

"But—"

"Our resources are slim," he said, his tone sharpening. "Belfast is full of innocent Catholics who'd like to get out of here and go somewhere safer. Did ya honestly think the IRA would go to such lengths to get you to safety without you doing something for them in return?"

My head swam. It seemed so stupid, now that he'd said it, but I supposed I had thought they would. After all, he'd given me the money before, and there hadn't been strings attached to that.

"I'm sorry," I whispered, rising. "I can't do it."

Kieran rose, too, blocking the doorway. "Ya have to," he said, those piercing eyes burning into me.

"But—"

"If ya want to live, ya don't have a choice," he said coldly.

I moved backward, bumping into the chair. "They won't kill me in the cages," I said, swallowing hard.

"It's not the cages you have to worry about." This time, the words came from Fergus.

I fell back into the chair, feeling boxed in. My heart thudded as my eyes darted around the room, looking for a means of escape.

"*We're* not going to hurt ya," Seamus said, holding his hands up. "That's not what the lads mean."

"Then what do ya mean?" I demanded, spitting the words out with a bravery I didn't actually feel.

Seamus sighed and kicked back, putting his hands behind his head. "Your sister is dating a British officer," he said slowly. "The same officer who killed our man Ian. Surely ya know how that looks, Fiona."

I shook my head.

"There was talk before Ian's death," he said carefully. "People were wondering why Ian was released so quickly when the others had to stay in the cages."

"Lieutenant Montgomery vouched for him," I said, confused.

"Exactly." He frowned. "That didn't look very good. To tell ya the truth, some of the men up the line were beginning to wonder if Ian was a tout."

I stiffened. "Ian would never."

"That's just what we told them," Seamus agreed. "And then Ian got shot by the very officer who freed him, clearing his name. Informants don't tend to get killed by the army. But it's still a curious thing, isn't it? That connection? Then we find out that the very same officer is dating Ian's sister-in-law."

"I don't understand…"

He leaned forward. "Very few people knew about the operation taking place that night. We were shocked when the army seemed to know exactly where we'd be. It raised a question. How did they find out? Now we circle back to all those connections."

I saw where he was going, and I thought I was going to be sick. My eyes darted to Kieran, but his face held a warning. I could tell them the truth, that Kieran was the tout. But would they believe me? Not likely.

Seamus's face held pity in it. "We like you, Fiona. But ya have to admit it looks bad. Maybe Annie's the tout."

"Annie didn't know," I whispered. "She couldn't have. She hadn't spoken to Ian in months."

"I believe ya," Seamus said gravely. "But *you* could have known. *You* could have gotten word to your sister—or directly to her boyfriend. You see what I mean?"

My hands went to my knees, thinking of what they did to informants. "I'm not a tout," I said, my voice breaking. "I promise you. I didn't even know what was happening that night. Ian never told me anything. And I would never have done something that would put him in danger."

Seamus raised his hands in defense. "*We* know that. Don't we, lads?"

Fergus and Kieran nodded in agreement.

"I told the men up the line how you helped my family," Fergus offered. "How ya saved my wife's life, and Michael's too. How I brought countless lads to ya and you took them in and tended their wounds. I pled your case."

"But they want proof of your loyalty," Seamus said. "Otherwise…"

"Otherwise, it's my kneecaps," I said, gulping.

Fergus shook his head. "The penalty is higher for a betrayal like this. The IRA can't allow traitors to threaten the mission. You know that."

I didn't want to cry in front of them, but I couldn't stop the tears that rolled down my cheeks. "So you're saying I have to kill him or the IRA is going to kill me?"

"Not just you," Kieran said. "You and your sister both."

"She's a soldier lover," Fergus added. "The IRA believes that kind of thing has to be punished. They won't spare her, even for your sake."

I was trapped with only one way out.

37
POISONED PLANS

Fiona

March 1972

Glenarm

I gathered my supplies and slipped out of the house while Annie and Mamó slept. The sky was dark, save for the sliver of moonlight overhead. A flashlight weighed down the pocket of my sweater, but I didn't need it yet. I knew where I was going.

I let the tears come, grieving for what I must do. Had Ian felt this way? Like the IRA had left him with no choice but to go against his conscience?

I hated myself for the choice I'd made, but I didn't see another way out. Even as angry as I was, I'd go to the cages to avoid killing Lieutenant Montgomery. I might have even considered letting the IRA kill *me* to avoid breaking one of the commandments, but I was carrying a child within me. It wasn't just my life—it was my child's.

They'd threatened Annie too. That meant there was only one choice. If it was Annie's life or the sorry soldier who'd killed my Ian,

I'd choose Annie every time. I'd pay whatever price I had to pay to keep her safe.

Then I'd flee to America and leave this island forever.

When I was well out of sight of the cottage, I finally clicked on the flashlight to light my path, making my way over grassy hills to the bog where I'd find the plant I needed.

There would be no pistols or petrol bombs for me. I'd refused it all, promising the lads that I knew what I was doing. That if I were going to kill, better for me to do it with poison. They'd seemed impressed by my plan and agreed to it.

But they would hold my escape papers until after I'd done it.

I crept through the saggy marsh until I spotted the basal rosette I was looking for: the early growth of fresh water hemlock, Ireland's most poisonous plant. My hands trembled as I slipped on leather gloves to protect myself from the dangerous toxins. I took a steadying breath, then stuck my trowel into the dark earth and began to dig.

The sun had risen by the time I made it back to the cottage.

Mamó worked in her garden, frowning when she saw me emerge from the hill behind the house. "Where have you been off to this morning?"

"I couldn't sleep," I said. It wasn't even a lie. "I went for a walk."

She nodded toward the basket in my hands. "What did ya find?"

I gripped the handle of the basket, keeping it turned toward me to block the contents from view. "Nothing. I suppose I was too distracted to do any foraging today."

She rose to her feet, groaning when her weight shifted to her bad knee. "Oh? Then why is your trowel covered in dirt? And why are your knees muddy, like you've been kneeling in wet earth?"

Mamó's sharp eyes never missed a thing.

"Please don't ask me questions I can't answer," I said quietly.

She gazed at me. "I suppose this is about your trip to Belfast yesterday."

I nodded, unable to look her in the eye.

"Fiona, if you're in trouble, you can talk to me," she said gently. "I'll help ya find a way out of it. Ya have my word."

"Ya can't help me out of this one," I said, my voice breaking. "And it's not just me that's in trouble. It's all of us. Ya have to trust me."

"So it's that bad, is it?"

I nodded again.

She leaned on her rake, letting out a heavy sigh. "I dreamed last night that you were bound for the Americas."

"We all can be," I said, feeling a prick of hope. "I'm working on arrangements."

She shook her head. "I'm an old woman, Fiona. I'll never leave the island. Ireland's in my blood. I don't want to die in a foreign land."

"Please," I begged. "Please come with me."

Her eyes softened. "I can't. No matter how much I want to watch you and that wee babe of yours grow, I can't do it."

My chest squeezed. "You're not asking me to stay though."

"No." She shook her head, sadness and grief washing over her face. "Trouble will always follow ya here if you stay. I can't wish that for ya, no matter how much I'll miss ya. It's your destiny to go." She brought her fist up to her heart. "Though I don't know how I'll bear it."

I dropped my basket and ran to her, grabbing her in an embrace. It didn't seem possible for there to be any tears left in me, as many as I'd shed the last few days, but they poured out of me again as we held each other in the garden.

"I'll miss ya so much," I sobbed.

"How soon do ya leave?"

"Tomorrow night."

She pulled back, gripping my face in her hands. "Whatever it is you're planning to do before then, ya don't have to. There's always another way, Fiona. Talk to me and I'll help ya find it."

I shook my head sadly. "There's no other choice this time."

"We'll—"

"No," I said, cutting her off. "There's only one way for me to save you and Annie."

I stepped out of her embrace and retrieved my basket.

It was time to finish what I'd started.

When my preparations were finished, I called my sister into my room, where we could speak without being overheard. Even so, my eyes continually darted from side to side, and my ears pricked as I kept a listen out. We were far from the flats in Belfast with their paper-thin walls, where the neighbors could hear every word. But the two worlds had merged so thoroughly that it was hard for me to remember that.

"I have a plan," I told Annie as I closed the door to my room.

She took a deep breath and sat on my bed, listening.

I gave her a timid smile. "We can go to America. The lads are working on forged papers for us."

"By the lads, you mean the IRA," she said slowly.

Guilt pricked at my association with them, but I nodded. "Yes."

She looked away, her shoulders slumping. "But I don't want to go to America."

I grabbed her and forced her to look at me. "Annie, you're in danger. If ya stay, either your boyfriend is going to have ya interned for telling me his plans or the IRA is going to kill ya!"

Her head jerked back. "Me? Why would the IRA kill me?"

I explained the situation to her, feeling my guilt creep higher as the look on her face turned to pure horror.

"This is so unfair!" She held her face in her hands.

"I know. Believe me, I know."

She was quiet for a few moments, then she looked up at me in agony. "I can't do it."

"Annie, you have to."

"I'm furious at him for threatening ya," she said shakily. "I'm angry that he's pushing me to get married when I told him I needed time. But he doesn't deserve to die for that."

"What about for killing Ian? Does he deserve to die for that? This is a war, Annie. Soldiers die in wars. It's either him or us. Do ya love him so much you're willing to die for him, and watch me die as well?"

She didn't have a reply for that one. When she dropped her gaze, I pushed forward.

"I've prepared a tea," I said, patting the pouch I carried in my pocket. "I'll serve it tonight when he calls."

Her features clouded with confusion. "Tea?"

"It is very important that he, and he only, drinks the tea. Do ya understand? And you must not let him kiss ya after he's had it. If it spills, do not touch it. "

Understanding began to dawn in her eyes. "Fiona—"

"I'll make the tea," I said, cutting her off. "But you'll have to serve it to him. It's a heavy burden I'm putting on ya, but I cannot do it myself. He knows what I am, and he'd never drink a tea I prepared for him. But he trusts ya enough to take ya into his home as his wife. Ya must act normal. Ya can't give him any reason to suspect. Do ya understand?"

Her eyes were wide with fear, but she nodded.

"How does he normally take his tea?"

"Sweet," she answered shakily.

"Perfect. We'll make it sweet with honey, and it will help mask the flavor. You'll need to have a cup of something else—something safe—for yourself. They have to look the same so that he doesn't get suspicious, but you absolutely cannot mix them up." I gripped her hand. "One sip could kill ya."

She nodded, biting her lip.

"The tea is strong," I said quietly. "It will only take one cup. When it is done, we'll pour out the tea and burn the leaves in the fire so that no one can examine them. Wash the pot and his cup thoroughly, and fill them with whatever you were drinking so that, if anyone looks, it appears that you were both drinking the same thing."

"What will happen to him?" Her whole body was shaking.

I hated that she'd asked. I didn't want to lie to her, but I knew she would have a hard time going through with it if she knew the truth. His death would be violent. Seizures, convulsions... It would be horrid.

So I lied. "He'll die quickly," I said, giving her a reassuring smile. "Like a heart attack."

"And what will happen to me?" Her voice was so small.

"Nothing." My voice was firm. "I promise ya. We'll flee to America and be safe."

She stared past me, out the window. "But if we do this, he'll no longer be a threat to us, and neither will the IRA. So we can stay, right? We won't have to leave."

"I don't know," I said slowly.

But her excitement was growing. "We can. If it looks like he had a heart attack, no one will suspect the truth. The IRA will know you're not a tout, and Ian's death will be avenged. Everything will be over, and we can stay here, safe and together."

"Aye, you're right," I said, pretending to go along with it.

One lie had led to another, and now I'd have to figure out how to handle things when my sister realized I'd betrayed her by not telling her the truth.

It would be obvious who poisoned Lieutenant Montgomery.

We'd never be safe in Northern Ireland.

38
THE HEART OF DANGER

FIONA

March 1972
Glenarm

I could only pack what I could carry. This made choosing what to take simple, though painful. Most of what I owned would have to be left behind.

I dressed in layers, wearing as many clothes as I could in order to save room in my bag. There were a few things I couldn't leave behind, like the precious photographs of me and Ian before Belfast, when life had been beautiful and full of promise, and the wedding quilt Mamó had made me, pieced together from remnants of our christening dresses, my mother's wedding dress, and other family memories. She'd waited until after the wedding to finish it so that she could include a square made of my own wedding dress too. The quilt would take up most of the room in my bag, but I couldn't bear to part with it. It was the most precious thing I owned.

There were no tears now, though I knew grief would come. But I needed strength to get through this. Otherwise, I'd never make it.

My packing was interrupted by a timid knock on the door. Mamó poked her head inside.

"Do ya have what ya need?" she asked, her eyes red from crying.

"I think so."

"I've some money—"

"No," I said, interrupting her. "My friend Seamus gave me some when he came before. It'll see us through until Annie and I get on our feet."

Mamó came over and sank down on my bed. "Annie's not coming with ya."

I dropped the shirt I was folding and looked at her in astonishment. "She has to. Ya know that."

"No," Mamó said, shaking her head. She placed her hand on mine. "I've accepted that this is your fate, child, but it's not Annie's. She doesn't want to go. She'll stay."

"It's not safe—"

"It is," she said, interrupting me this time. She sighed heavily. "I'll handle everything. Annie told me your plan. I want ya to give me the tea and let me take care of it. You can leave before he arrives and be gone before it's done. I'll make sure Annie's not involved."

My jaw dropped. "You'll... You'll take care of it?" I couldn't believe what I was hearing.

She nodded gravely. "I'm older than ya both. I've seen more death in my life than the two of yous combined. I can handle what needs to be done. Annie's angry at Edward, but she loved him once. She won't be able to go through with it."

The weight of it sank into me. "Aye, you're right. She won't. She's too gentle."

Mamó nodded in agreement. "She's young and hasn't had to witness the horrors of war up close yet, and she still feels something for him. I can see it. Even if she somehow managed to find the strength, you and I both know she'd have to witness him dying a terrible death. It'll scar her forever. Ya can't want that for her."

A tear dropped down my cheek. "Of course not. I just can't think of any other way. He'd never trust me while I'm angry, and I wear my feelings for him on my face. I can't pretend to be okay around him."

"Aye, I know," she said quietly. "That's why I'm telling ya to leave it to me. He trusts me. Annie will be innocent and won't have to witness his death or carry that burden on her, and you can escape before he's even counted as missing."

"But I thought you were against violence?"

"I am," she said gravely. "But it's my job to protect the family. If I have to choose between violence and protecting my girls, I'll do what has to be done."

"What if they suspect ya?" I trembled at the thought of it. Mamó didn't deserve to go to prison for the mess I'd gotten us in.

She smirked. "Child, surely ya know me well enough to know I can take care of myself. Ya forget, I worked as a spy for the IRA during the War of Independence. I've seen and done more than you'll ever know. There will be no body for them to find and no reason for them to suspect us."

I wavered. "Are ya sure?"

"Aye, I'm sure. Give me the tea." She held out her hand.

I slipped the bundle of hemlock into her palm, knowing a great burden had been taken off of me and Annie both.

Mamó had always taken care of us. I hoped I could do the same for someone else someday.

She looked at the stack of things I was packing. "I see you're taking your quilt with ya."

"I can't bear to leave it behind."

She shook her head. "It'll take up an awful lot of room in your bag."

"It's worth it." Tears pricked my eyes.

"Aye," she said softly, stroking her hand over the patches. "Some things are worth the sacrifice." Her hand stopped, and she frowned. "It has a tear in it, so it does. I'll mend it before ya leave."

"You don't have to," I said. "I can do it after I'm settled."

She cracked a grin. "If I thought you could stitch decently enough to do it yourself, I'd let ya, but I can't have ya ruining my prized work now." She reached for the quilt and pulled it into her lap. "I'll have it fixed up in a jiffy."

"You're too good to me," I said, fighting back tears.

She squeezed my hand, giving me a sad smile. "I have something else for ya," she said, reaching into her pocket. "Something easier to carry on your journey." She pulled out her silver locket and handed it to me.

"Oh, Mamó." I ran my fingers over the intricate Celtic knotwork. The necklace was one of Mamó's favorites. She'd been wearing it my whole life.

"I put a pinch of mugwort inside," she said, looking at the necklace fondly. "It's for protection. You know, St. John wore a girdle of mugwort in the wilderness."

"I know," I said, smiling. She'd mentioned it, along with countless other pieces of herbal lore, probably a hundred times.

"It will help keep ya safe." Worry crossed her face. "Oh, Fiona. I know ya have to leave, but it's hard to let ya."

"Ya felt that way about Belfast," I said quietly.

She nodded. "I still wish you and Ian had never gone."

"I do too," I admitted.

I said goodbye to Annie, to Mamó, to everything I'd ever known. It felt like a strange dream. Then I began my final journal to Belfast, knowing I'd never return to Glenarm again.

Either I'd make it to America or the IRA would kill me before I had a chance.

I made it to the city just before nightfall. My bag drew the attention of the soldiers, and I was searched at the first checkpoint. My heart railed against my chest even though I knew they'd find nothing in the bag to concern them. Catholics moved all the time in Belfast—they had to.

It was already too dark when I reached the outskirts of Kieran's harsh neighborhood. My feet had swollen, and my tight leather boots felt unsteady on the flagstone pavements of the dark alley. The reality of what I had done set in, and panic rose within me.

A glance at Ian's pocket watch confirmed that the time had come. With me safely in Belfast, and Annie eating dinner with the friends who would be her alibi, Mamó would be serving tea to Lieutenant Montgomery, telling him that Annie was running late and would be there shortly.

He would be dead within minutes—if he wasn't already. Killed by the poison I'd dug and prepared.

Mamó might have served the tea, but I was the real murderer.

I'd traded his life for mine and Annie's. I only hoped it wasn't all for nothing. Because here, in the dark alleys of Belfast, I remembered exactly how dangerous the IRA was.

My hands gripped the straps of the heavy bag slung over my shoulder, pulling it tighter to my body as if it could somehow keep me safe here in the heart of danger. No matter how many deep breaths I took, my heart pounded in fear, even as it throbbed with grief. How can a heart keep beating after it's been shattered a thousand times?

I should be dead.

Maybe I am. Maybe this is purgatory. Maybe that's why everything is so dark, so empty.

Gunshots rang out in the distance, but I barely noticed them. Living in Belfast, they'd become so much a part of the tapestry of my life that I'd become numb to them.

I wasn't used to the darkness, though, even though it was my second time to walk these streets after sundown. It was dangerous to walk them during the day. At night?

It was a death wish.

A woman like me shouldn't have been in these dark alleyways where the air felt heavy with rage and paranoia. Where it was impossible to tell friend from foe. Where even your friends might turn out to be your worst nightmare.

Except I'm someone's worst nightmare now. So maybe this is exactly where I belong.

A door creaked open and my heart nearly stopped. The woman stared at me with malice on her face.

I wondered if she was as afraid of me as I was of her.

I gave her a feeble smile, then diverted my eyes, trying to show her I was no threat. But I continued to watch her in my peripheral vision. She closed the door slowly, and I let out a breath, my shoulders sagging in relief.

But my belly cramped with fear when I reached my destination —the door I had to knock on in order to leave behind the danger surrounding me on all sides.

Out of the frying pan and into the fire.

I have no choice. Not really. There's only one shot at safety now.

No choice, I told myself over and over as I stood with a clenched fist held frozen in midair, refusing to obey my order to knock.

No choice, my mind said. But my soul knew the truth.

There's always a choice. And the one I made will cost me everything.

My head hung low, and a single tear fell down my cheek as I finally brought my fist to the heavy door. And then I knew I wasn't dead—yet—because my broken heart shattered all over again.

39
FLEEING

Fiona

March 1972

Belfast

The heavy wooden door opened just an inch, with one suspicious eye peering through the crack before opening it the rest of the way.

Peggy pulled me inside. "Fiona, we've all been banjaxed about Ian and worried sick for ya."

I swallowed over the lump that had formed in my throat. "Aye. It's been a difficult time. Where are the lads?"

Kieran rounded the corner, followed by the other two. "We're here. Has it been done?"

I nodded. "Ian has been avenged," I whispered, surprised by the tears that followed.

Seamus's face broke out into a grin. He grabbed a bottle of whiskey. "Then I salute ya, Fiona, and I'll raise a toast to ya. Where's your sister?"

"She's not coming," I said quietly.

The men exchanged glances. The wariness on Fergus's face was enough to make my heart thud in warning.

"She's grateful to have her problem taken care of," I said, choosing my words carefully. "She was so angry at Lieutenant Montgomery that she was willing to hand him the poisoned tea herself. But with him no longer a threat, and with us having proven that we're loyal to the cause, she sees no reason to leave the land she loves so dearly."

"And you?" Kieran's gaze pierced me. "Do you still see a reason to leave this land?"

"Aye." I swallowed hard. "I cannot risk internment. Not with a child growing inside me."

They exchanged glances again.

Fergus cleared his throat. "We'll need to confirm that it's been done. I'm sure ya understand."

My heart skipped a beat. "What proof can I offer? It's not like ya told me in advance I needed to cut off a finger or something to bring as evidence of what I'd done."

"I have someone on the inside," Fergus said easily, as if my whole life weren't hanging in the balance. "If Lieutenant Montgomery doesn't report in the morning, we'll know. If he does, well…"

"You'll shoot me," I said wryly. I was so tired I wasn't sure I even cared anymore.

"You don't seem worried," Seamus said, grinning.

"Aye, I'm not. It's done. But I'm exhausted, and I've no place to stay. What am I supposed to do while ya wait around for your confirmation?" My grief had turned to irritation—and fear. I leaned on the first, knowing that it would mask the other.

"That's why I'm here," Peggy announced. "A chaperone for ya. You'll sleep here. If all goes well, we'll see ya off in the morning."

"Seems like it would be better for me to get out of the country before my known enemy goes missing," I pointed out.

"Aye, better for you," Fergus said. "But more dangerous for us."

"Fine," I said, sighing.

I had at least twelve more hours to live, but I had to spend them at the worst place possible.

I was starting to think I'd prefer the cages.

The men were out most of the night. I caught brief periods of sleep underneath Peggy's watchful eye, but despite my exhaustion, I never felt safe enough to sleep deeply.

When morning came, the men returned. Seamus led the way with his obnoxious grin.

"Looks like you really did it," he said, grabbing the whiskey again. "Lieutenant Montgomery didn't report for duty this morning. Never made it home last night. No one has seen him for hours. They've already questioned your sister, who said he never arrived for their date, so she had dinner with friends instead. Nicely done, Fiona Ó Flannagáin."

"Thanks," I said, sitting up wearily. "Does this mean I can leave now?"

"Are ya sure ya don't want to stay and work for us? We could use someone in poisons." Seamus grinned, sloshing whiskey as he did.

My muscles tensed. Surely they wouldn't go back on what they'd told me, would they? "No," I said firmly. "I want to leave. I *need* to leave."

"Wouldn't hurt to get her to do a few more before we hand over the papers," Fergus added, sparking fresh fear.

"A deal is a deal," Kieran said, scowling. "She did her part. Now give her the documents. We're supposed to be men of our word, aren't we?"

"Alright, alright," Seamus said, rolling his eyes. "I'm only teasing. But let a man finish his whiskey first."

Kieran shoved Seamus out of the way, went to a cabinet in the corner, and pulled out a manila envelope. He glanced at me. "You've got your passport?"

"Aye."

"And money? Enough for travel?" He took the chair in front of me and opened the envelope.

"I think so."

He nodded. "Good. Here's your visa. It's forged, but it will pass. There's also the name of a man in here. He's one of ours. Look him up when you arrive. He can help you settle."

"Alright."

"We've a network over there," he said. "Even men who are American citizens. One will marry ya, if ya like, so you can get your green card."

The idea shocked me. "What? I don't... I mean, I can't. I just lost my Ian. I don't want another husband." I shook my head quickly, feeling more afraid by the minute.

He shrugged. "It's your choice. But you're on your own if ya don't hook up with the network."

"Understood," I said, swallowing hard.

"Are ya ready, then?" he asked, casting a doubtful glance at me.

"Aye, I'm ready."

"You've two options. I can take you to the airport here in Belfast. If you fly from here to Heathrow, you can take the Pan Am to New York. It's not a bad flight, from what I'm told—seven hours or so. Or you can take a ferry to Liverpool, then take the train to Southhampton. The QE2 makes the trip to New York about once weekly. The crossing takes about five days."

Five days versus seven hours. Of the two, I preferred the idea of taking five days. Longer if I had to wait for a crossing. Anything to lengthen the time it took before arriving in New York and starting a life I'd never wanted.

But Ian's voice seemed to whisper in my ear. *If there's a chance the law will be after ya, the faster ya get out of here, the better, my love.*

"Take me to the airport," I said.

Lieutenant Montgomery hadn't reported to work. There was no time to waste.

40

ANGELS IN LONDON

FIONA

March 1972
Belfast to London

Leaving wasn't easy, even after Kieran insisted the lads keep their deal with me. It was dangerous for them to be spotted in Belfast and even more dangerous for me if I was caught with them. Dread settled in my belly as I faced the very real possibility that I could be stuck here, despite what I'd done.

It felt like I was holding my breath the whole day as the lads argued about the best way to get me past the checkpoints and to the airport. I tried to say I'd walk by myself, but all three of them seemed against it, like they were half afraid that I might turn against them and give up their location in order to save myself.

It hit me that they might want me gone as badly as I wanted to leave, which gave me another obstacle to face. The truth was that if they wanted me gone, the easiest way to do it would be to shoot me. I didn't deserve it, not after I'd helped them. But the poor girl in

Derry hadn't deserved to be tarred and feathered for dating a soldier, either. The rules in Northern Ireland weren't fair, no matter who was making them. If nothing else, I'd learned that over the last few months.

In the end, it was Peggy who had to escort me. The lads knew she wouldn't be looked at with the same suspicion they would be.

When she and I left the flat, heading on foot toward the safest route to the airport, I told myself that I could finally breathe, that I was past the worst of it.

But I think I knew even then that she was as dangerous as they were. That she'd kill me just as quickly as one of them would if she thought I was a threat to her family.

I didn't know that I could blame her for that. After all, I was now a killer too. I knew what it was like to be willing to do things you never thought you'd do to protect the ones you loved.

Peggy barely spoke to me as we walked. She seemed angry, though I didn't know why. I tried asking her about her children and telling her how happy I was about Fergus coming home. But she only gave short answers and was as cold to me as she had been since the day Ian got released.

When we finally made it to the airport, far later in the day than I would have preferred, she gave me a cold smile.

"I suppose you're happy about leaving, then? Getting away from all the troubles the rest of us have to live with, whether we like it or not."

It stung. "Not as happy as ya might think," I said quietly. "I never wanted any of this. Never wanted to have to leave my country, my family, my home. I certainly never wanted to lose my husband. Aye, I'm grateful to be safe. But I wish we all were. I'm not your enemy, Peggy."

She cocked her head. "Aye, well, you've convinced Kieran of that right enough. Why else do ya think he worked so hard to get this chance for ya? It's not fair to the rest of us who sacrifice everything for the cause only to go hungry and do without."

My jaw dropped. "Sacrificed everything? Ya have your family—your husband, your children. I'm sorry for what you've been through, but I think *I'm* the one who sacrificed everything. Nothing about this is fair. If it was fair, I wouldn't have been forced to go against everything I believe and give up everything I hold dear, just to keep myself and my family alive."

My words didn't seem to move her. She rolled her eyes. "You keep telling yourself that. But it's your husband's fault you're in the spot you're in, love. He's the one ya should be angry at."

I stared at her, speechless, as she turned on her heel and walked away without another word.

I was finally alone. I knew I wasn't yet safe, but I felt safer than I had since I'd left the village. Safe enough to maintain an outwardly calm appearance as I bought a ticket to Heathrow and found my way to the boarding gate for my flight. I had hours to kill and nothing to do.

So I sat there with nothing but my thoughts, and the weight of what I'd done began to sink in.

I'd committed a grave sin. The thought grieved me deeply, but I couldn't exactly feel sorry about it.

When I went to the ladies' room to tidy up, I stared at myself in the mirror, barely recognizing the woman who stared back at me.

What had I done?

Worse, what had I become, that I'd taken a life and didn't feel sorry for it?

I threw up three times before I was able to get on the plane.

My flight was the final one between Belfast and London that day, and Heathrow Airport had already become quiet when we disembarked. I forced myself to chat with a few people who seemed like regular travelers and discovered that, although the flights were finished for the day, the terminal stayed open all night. I decided I'd try to find a quiet place to sleep at the airport to save money. I was so weary that the thought of trying to get a taxi and find some place else to stay overnight made me want to cry.

It was pure exhaustion and grief, I knew, draining the last bits of energy from my body. If I were home, I'd go to the hawthorn tree and make a medicine to soothe my aching heart. But home didn't exist for me anymore, and after what I'd done, I wasn't sure the plants would even give me their medicine. I'd used a plant to kill instead of heal. My life as a healer might well have been over. I'd broken my vows and grieved the very heart of God.

Though I couldn't help but think God's heart had already been grieved by the sins of the British army long before I'd gotten involved. Perhaps Ian was right and there was such a thing as a just war. If there was, then maybe there would be forgiveness for me.

Whether or not forgiveness was to be mine, a quiet place to sleep was not. Just as I settled down on one of the hard benches in a dark corner, making a pillow of my bag, a staff member came to shake me and ask me to leave. He wasn't rude—his eyes even had a bit of sympathy in them. But I didn't bother to beg. I repacked my bag and headed out into the cold night air, raising my tired arm to flag a taxi.

The first car to approach was an older vehicle. A man hopped out and promised me a cheaper ride than the London black cabs, but the glint in his eye made me shrink back and I shook my head, heading instead for the hackney carriage that had pulled up behind him.

The professional driver hopped out and took my bag. "Where to, Miss?"

"I-I don't know. I need a place to stay the night. Somewhere close and cheap."

He eyed me. "From Ulster, are ya? Belfast perhaps?" He let his own Irish accent slip through, as if he were dropping a mask. He'd hidden it so well I hadn't even caught it when he first spoke.

"Aye."

His eyes shone with sympathy. "The village of Hounslow is close by. I can take ya to a guest house there. It's clean and safe. The ride will cost ya about two pounds. The room, five pounds, seeing as you're a Belfast girl."

I raised an eyebrow. "Is that more or less than it would cost me being from somewhere else?"

He grinned. "Less. She charges ten if you're American."

I relaxed. "Alright. That will be fine. Thanks a mill."

He opened the door for me and loaded my luggage before hopping back in front. I sank into the seat and closed my eyes. The cab smelled of leather and petrol, and another wave of nausea hit. I clenched my fingers, hoping I wouldn't embarrass myself by vomiting again.

He started up the cab and began making his way through dark streets, lit only by the yellow glow of the London streetlights. The road was bumpy, and I bounced straight out of my seat when he hit a large pothole. My mouth began to sweat, and I prayed the ride would be short.

I was his only passenger, and I was grateful for it. All I wanted was to sink into the darkness and be alone.

But he wanted to talk through the partition. "Are ya here to visit London?"

"No." I wasn't going to divulge more, but then I realized I might be in need of information. "I'm actually heading to America. If I want to fly out tomorrow morning, what time do I need to be back here?"

He whistled. "Last minute, are ya? I'd get there bright and early, I would, and prepare to pay dearly for a last-minute ticket. If you've time to spare, you could book in advance through an agent and stay a few days in London. Might save ya a few bob."

My heart sank. Now that I'd made the decision to fly, I just wanted to get it over with. Plus, there was the added danger of every day I stayed here. I'd plotted the death of a British soldier. I had to get out of London as quickly as possible.

"I need to try tomorrow, thanks."

He eyed me in the rearview mirror. "Like I said, you'll need to get there early. If ya like, I can pick ya up before the sun rises. You'll have to skip out on the breakfast Mrs. Davies makes for her guests, and that's a heartbreak for sure. But it can't be helped if you're determined to fly tomorrow."

"I'll be ready first thing," I said, grasping on to the little bit of hope.

"Alright then. Here we are."

The cab pulled up to a plain brick house. The porch light was on, and a small wooden sign by the door read "*Rooms Available.*"

"It's alright now," he said gently, perhaps seeing my fear. "Mrs. Davies is nice enough. You'll be safe here, and I'll be back for ya in the wee hours of the morning. We'll get ya to America, far away from the Troubles."

I jerked my head, feeling sudden fear that I'd been found out. But that was silly. I was a young woman leaving Belfast in the middle of the night. Of course he'd connect it to the Troubles. That's why we all left.

"Thank ya for your kindness," I said.

He gave me a smile and a nod before hopping out of the cab. I counted the money I owed him while he came around and opened my door. He carried my satchel up to the front steps and knocked, then waited with me. I was grateful for his presence. Though this neighborhood was a sanctuary compared to where I'd spent last night, I was feeling particularly fragile, and every friend on the journey felt like an angel sent to watch over me.

I chided myself for that thought though. I was a murderer. I'd given up my right to angels.

When Mrs. Davies answered the door in her dressing gown, I shrank back again. She was a large woman with a heavy scowl, who seemed to resent the fact that we'd interrupted her sleep. But her eyes softened when she saw my driver there.

"Well, Pat, what have you brought me tonight?" She turned her gaze to me and looked me up and down.

"A fellow Belfast girl. She needs a room for the night—longer if she can't get a flight to America tomorrow. I'll be back in the morning to take her to the airport."

They exchanged looks, and she gave him a quick nod. "I'll have tea and toast waiting for you."

"Oh, but it will be before dawn," he protested.

She held her hand up, stopping him. "Everyone needs a bit of tea and toast before a journey. Come on in, then," she said to me, grabbing my bag out of his hands. "Let's get ya settled. You can still have a few hours of sleep, anyway. It's five pounds, and you pay in advance here. If you need another night, you can pay me tomorrow."

"Yes, of course," I murmured, fishing five precious pounds out of my envelope and handing it to her.

She took it and stuffed it down the front of her dressing gown. Pat made his escape, and she locked the door behind her, then led me through the living room to a long hallway. At the end of the hall, she opened a door and flicked on the light, revealing a sparsely decorated room with a twin bed. The walls had faded floral wallpaper, and the bed had a single pillow and a thin quilt. There was a small dresser and a wash basin in the corner.

It was sparse, but it looked like heaven to my weary soul.

"The washroom is right across the hall here," she said, pointing to another door. "It's shared with all the guests. You can turn on the electric heater if you get a chill, but mind you don't run it all night. The check-in counter at Heathrow opens early, so Pat will likely be back by five in the morning." She gave a little shudder. "There's an alarm clock there on the dresser. I'll be up at four thirty with your tea and toast."

"That's really not necessary," I said, though my stomach growled loudly, betraying me.

She gazed down at my waist and gave me a look of sympathy. "You paid for breakfast and you'll have it, though I can't manage the full meal that early. But perhaps you could also do with some cheese and bread tonight, and a cup of tea?"

I opened my mouth to say no, but truthfully, I was very hungry.

I'd barely had a bite to eat since leaving the village. Tears pricked my eyes and I nodded. "I'd be grateful."

"Say nothing of it. I can spot a soul in need of tending, and there's nothing like a cup of tea to soothe a weary heart. I'll be back with it in a jiffy."

She turned and headed out of the room. I sank onto the bed, letting a mix of tears I didn't fully understand fall.

I was still crying when she returned. She gave me a kind smile as she set the tea tray on the bed. Then she gave me a handkerchief from her pocket.

"Here you go, love. Is it all that bad now?"

I nodded, even though I knew I couldn't possibly tell her how bad it was.

She didn't ask questions. But she sat with me until my tears dried up. Then she made sure I drank every bit of the tea and ate every bite of the food.

"There, now, that's a bit better, isn't it?"

"Aye," I said softly. "Though it doesn't seem right that a bit of food and a cup of tea should soothe my soul. I don't deserve it."

"Ah, but you're wrong there," she said, shaking her head. "Every human soul deserves a bit of kindness when they're down."

"Thank you," I said, not trusting myself to say anything else. I was so close to spilling everything, even knowing that doing so might lead to my arrest.

She patted me on the hand. "You're safe here, love. Whatever's happened, whatever you've done. Whether you're Catholic or Protestant—doesn't matter, not under this roof. You'll find nothing but kindness in this home."

My eyes widened with surprise.

"There's hard times in Belfast," she said quietly. "I know that. Plenty of evil things being done against both sides. But we're all God's children. I've always believed the good Lord cares more about how we treat each other than about the rest of it, don't you?"

I nodded, swallowing hard. "Most people say it's more complicated than that."

She shrugged. "I suppose I don't care so much what those people say."

"You're a kind woman."

Her face wrinkled up in a smile. "Someone was kind to me once, when I needed it. Now I try to keep my eyes open for others who need the same." She rose, taking the empty tray with her. When she reached the doorway, she turned back. "You're safe here. We'll get you to America. That's a promise."

She disappeared with a final smile, closing the door gently behind her.

I slid underneath the covers, pulling the quilt all the way up to my nose, and made myself a promise that, someday, I'd show someone the same kindness Mrs. Davies had shown me.

Someday, when I met someone who was in a bit of trouble, I'd give them something to eat and a cup of tea and sit with them. I'd tell them they were safe with me, no matter who they were or what they'd done.

And I'd do it in honor of the woman who'd sat with me on the darkest night of my life.

41
PUNISHMENT

Fiona

March 1972

London

When Mrs. Davies left me, I fell asleep in the little twin bed without so much as washing my face. The exhaustion completely took over, and I slept like the dead until she woke me the next morning, shaking my arm to let me know that Pat would be there any moment, and that if I wanted to grab a bite to eat, I needed to do it quickly.

With bleary eyes, I scrambled out of bed and dragged my bag into the bathroom so I could make a quick job of washing up. When I went downstairs, I found a larger breakfast than I'd even hoped for waiting for me.

"Ya need to fatten up, child," Mrs. Davies scolded. "You're thin as a rail."

"Stressful times," I answered.

"Well, starvin' yourself won't make them any less stressful, now, will it? Eat up."

I gave her a grateful smile and ate until I couldn't eat another bite. The moment I finished, Pat popped up, like he'd been waiting for a signal from Mrs. Davies. Based on the look they exchanged, I wouldn't doubt that he really had been.

I gave Mrs. Davies a tight hug goodbye and told her I was grateful for her kindness. Her thin lips pressed tight, and she gave me a sharp nod, but the tears in her eyes reminded me that she was a softer soul than she let on.

Pat carried my bag with a whistle and opened the door for me like I was a fine lady instead of a runaway from Belfast.

"Feels like a good day to start a journey," he announced cheerfully when he got into the driver's seat.

"Too bad I started it yesterday," I quipped.

He roared with laughter. "Aye, but you're right. May it be a good day to finish your journey, then."

"Aye," I answered with a smile.

A thousand fears tried to play inside my head, but I shut them all out. Things might have gone poorly for me in Belfast, but I'd had nothing but luck since landing on these shores. I'd found kind friends, a safe place to rest, and a full belly. I began to have hope that things might be okay after all.

I said goodbye to Pat with as much gratitude as I had for Mrs. Davies, then bought my ticket for America. When the plane began to lift into the air, I felt a thrill of excitement I hadn't felt on my flight the night before.

Everything that had brought me here was terrible. I'd take all of it back if I could, starting at the very beginning when Ian told me he wanted to apply to Queen's—though, truth be told, that might have had a different kind of sad ending. Telling my husband that I wasn't willing to support his greatest dreams would have likely driven a wedge between us. We'd have avoided the nightmare we went through, but maybe I'd have lost his heart anyway. And who knows?

He might have still joined the IRA, like the lads in the village that we saw sneaking off each week to do things we never asked about. Even in Glenarm, he would have wanted to stand up and help protect our people.

A deep truth settled into me. I couldn't change the past, no matter how much I wished for it. But this was a great opportunity to change my future. To start a new life, me and my wee babe. I put my hand on my belly and made my child a promise that I'd make better choices in America. I'd find us a safe place to live, and I'd be ever so careful about what friends we brought into our lives. I'd dedicate myself to healing work again, and we'd put Belfast behind us forever.

I really believed it too.

The cramps started a few hours into our flight. I did my best to hide my pain, gripping the arms of my seat until my knuckles turned white, biting the inside of my cheek until it bled.

I made my way to the bathroom on board, and a new truth overcame me, one I didn't want to face.

I was losing my child too.

There was another angel on that flight, one who saw the distress I couldn't hide. She switched seats to sit beside me and spoke in a quiet voice, telling me everything would be alright. She held my hand and didn't leave my side. When the plane landed in New York, she had her husband carry my bag while she helped me off the plane.

They were from New York, returning home after a visit. But she didn't go home as planned. She took me straight to the hospital, where I heard the words that confirmed my fears and made me wail with agony. My heart, whatever was left of it, ached with a pain so fierce I was certain I'd die that night. And I didn't even care. I think I half hoped the pain would kill me.

I didn't have anything left to live for.

42
GHOSTS FROM THE PAST

FIONA

August 1973
New York City

I hid my smirk as I listened to the women on the bench beside me talk about the crime in New York City. They were terrified of how dangerous the city had become.

Sure, there was crime enough. The city was always dirty, and the air was polluted.

But I still felt a thousand times safer than I had in Belfast.

I'd been in America for over a year, as hard as it was to believe. Kimberly, the woman who had gotten me to the hospital, had given me a job and a place to stay while I got on my feet. She said that she and her husband had decided on the trip that they should hire a nanny to help with their children and meeting me had been fate. That they needed me as much as I needed them.

I knew that wasn't true. They could have had their pick of nannies, and they'd have been far better off with one who wasn't a complete and utter wreck like I was. But Kimberly was a kind woman who was always looking for ways to do good in the world. I later found out that her younger sister had died from an ectopic pregnancy when she was about the same age I was. When Kimberly had seen me clutching my abdomen on the plane, she'd felt like her sister had whispered to her that I needed help.

I was grateful. I also didn't know how to reconcile it all. I'd committed a grave sin. I'd taken a life, and it felt like my baby had been taken from me as punishment for it. But Mrs. Davies, Pat, and Kimberly all felt like angels sent to me when I'd needed them the most. How could I reconcile that?

I couldn't talk to just anyone about what I'd done. But eventually, I confessed everything to my new priest. He was a wise, gentle man who told me God hadn't taken my baby as punishment at all. He said these things just happen sometimes, that I should know that, having been a midwife in training in Ireland. That the stress and trauma my body went through was just too much.

He said that God knew why I did what I did and that, even though it was wrong, I was forgiven. But I still wasn't able to forgive myself. And when the priest asked if I would volunteer as a midwife and herbalist for the poor families in their church, I told him I couldn't. Not because I didn't want to help, but because I was terrified that my medicine would be cursed and I would bring harm instead of healing.

He told me I was too superstitious, but that I'd be forgiven for that, too, since I was from Ireland. After all, he said, the Irish couldn't really help it.

So time went on, and I kept working for Kimberly's family. I saved nearly all the money she paid me because I didn't know what to do with it. I tried writing to Mamó and Annie, but the letters got returned.

Then one night, I dreamed of Mamó, and I knew she'd passed on. The dream made me brave enough to call someone else in the village to ask about them. He told me they were gone, taken by the Troubles. Then he called me a tout and hung up on me.

So I grieved for them, like I'd grieved for Ian and for our babe.

I'd lost everything. *Everyone.* Yet here I was in New York, living in a beautiful townhouse for free, stashing away money from an easy job. I'd survived when none of my family had. It wasn't right, especially when it was my fault Annie and Mamó had gotten caught up in it.

Sometimes, it felt like the guilt was going to eat me alive. All I could do was shove it down and keep going. It was that or let it break me completely.

Sometimes I thought about letting it.

But I'd made it to August in 1973, a full year and a half since I'd left. At Kimberly's urging, I'd gone down to Central Park to a music festival where some new band called The Eagles was playing. The band was good. But I felt strangely listless. I kept wandering around the outskirts of the lawn like some invisible magnet was pulling me around, keeping me from sitting still or even dancing to the music.

Then I bumped into someone's broad shoulders, and when he turned around, I knew exactly why my nervous system wouldn't settle.

"Fiona?" Kieran's dark eyes went wide. "Is it really you?"

The nightmare of Belfast rushed back in an instant. I took a step backward, my hands shaking.

He put his hands up in surrender, glancing around like he didn't want anyone to notice him. "You're in no danger from me," he said quietly. "But I can't believe I ran into ya here. Can we talk?"

I was tempted to turn and run away. But I remembered that he was the one who had helped me escape, so I swallowed hard and nodded.

Relief flashed in his eyes. He shoved his hands into his pockets and turned, walking away from the edge of the crowd. When we were as alone as you can be in the city, he turned to me and spoke in a low voice.

"Are ya doing okay?"

"Not really," I said weakly. "It's been hard, like."

He nodded. "I know what ya mean."

"What are ya doing here?"

He sat down on a bench, sighing. "Same as you. I had to leave, or else they were going to kill me."

I took the seat next to him. "The soldiers?"

"No." He shook his head. "The IRA."

My breath caught. "Why would they kill *you*?"

His dark eyes looked straight into mine. "You already know why. I'm a tout, Fiona. If they'd caught me, they would have put a bullet in the back of my head. It got too dangerous, and they were on the verge of figuring out it was me. The army decided I was too valuable to let get killed, so they made a deal with the Americans, and here I am."

"So ya really were the tout," I said slowly. "I thought so at first, but then you were still working with them months later and I wondered if I'd been wrong. But I wasn't. You were the one who told the soldiers about the operation. You're the reason Ian was killed."

He nodded solemnly. "Yes, I was. I suppose that makes *you* want to kill me now too? I wouldn't blame ya for it."

I took a deep breath, searching for all the anger I'd once had, but it was gone. I still grieved Ian, but I'd already taken revenge once and it had made things worse, not better.

So I shook my head. "No. Not exactly."

"Good." He took a deep breath. "But there's something I have to tell ya, and when I do, you might change your mind."

"What is it?" My heart leapt with fear. Was he going to tell me that they'd shot Annie and Mamó after all? I already knew as much. But hearing it from the man who'd done it was another thing.

Kieran shifted toward me. His dark eyes looked straight into mine. Deep regret etched itself onto his face. "Ian wasn't killed by a British soldier. He was shot by the IRA."

I gasped. "*You* killed Ian? Not just by giving away his location, but actually—" I stood, putting my hands over my mouth to cover my sob.

Kieran jumped up, grabbing my arm so that I wouldn't run off. He turned me and made me look at him.

"No, not me," he said gently. His hands gripped my arms firmly, holding me upright when my knees threatened to give out underneath me. "I would never... I tried to warn him. That's why I gave ya that note."

"I don't understand." Agony ripped through me. "You said he was at an operation. That Lieutenant Montgomery killed him."

"We lied, Fiona. We lied the whole time."

"But why?" I cried. "Why would you say that if it wasn't true?"

Kieran's face was pure misery. "It's my fault. I didn't pull the trigger, but it's still my fault."

He let go of me and buried his face in his hands. "They knew someone was leaking information to the Brits, but they didn't suspect me. They thought it was Ian. They started wondering about him when he got released so quickly after internment. They started watching him, but he didn't give them a single reason to doubt him, so they backed off."

"If they didn't doubt him anymore, why did they kill him?" My head swam. I sat back down on the bench, afraid I would pass out if I didn't.

Kieran sat too. "The IRA has eyes and ears everywhere. One of the lads in Glenarm got word to Seamus that your sister was dating a British soldier. Seamus wanted to know the soldier's name. He found out it was Lieutenant Montgomery—the man who'd vouched for Ian to be released—the same week Ian told us he wanted to leave and take you back to the village."

"So they assumed they'd been right the first time," I whispered.

"Exactly. When they told him they needed help with an operation, it was just to get him there so they could execute him."

It felt like all the blood drained out of me at once as the pieces began to fall into place. "You *knew* they were going to kill him?" I cried.

He shook his head again. "No, Fiona, I swear to you. I tried to warn him off with that note, but only because I knew that operation was going to be taken down by the soldiers. He wanted out and you were expecting a baby—I was trying to save him from being arrested. I had no idea what they were planning."

I swallowed hard. "But the paper said he was shot by a soldier. I still don't understand."

"Don't you see? Ian wasn't even there."

"What?"

He shook his head in frustration. "That's what I'm trying to tell ya. Ian wasn't even at that operation. He knew there was one planned for that night, but he wasn't part of it. Nor was I. Seamus sent word to me and Ian that they needed help, but it was a ruse. Two men picked us up in a car. I thought we were all going to help with the operation, but they drove us down south instead." He looked sick.

"South?"

"Over the border." He looked down. "They have farmhouses out there. Places they can go. I didn't realize what was happening at first. I thought maybe they were going to interrogate us both, since they'd kept me in the dark. When Seamus shot him in the head..." He looked like he was going to be sick.

"Seamus?" I took a sharp breath, but it didn't reach my lungs. The world was spinning out of control. I couldn't breathe. I couldn't think.

"Aye," he said slowly. "Seamus was there waiting for us. He was in charge of our little crew, so he was. The boys up the line wanted to send a message to traitors. They'd decided kneecapping wasn't enough."

Seamus killed Ian.

Anger and shame flooded me. My face burned with heat as I realized how Seamus had played me like a fool. "He told me it was Lieutenant Montgomery. He convinced me to *kill* over it. Are you telling me, honest like, that it was a lie the whole time? That I killed an innocent man?" I held my fist to my stomach, wishing it were a knife.

"I'm sorry." Kieran hung his head.

"Why didn't you stop me?" I cried.

He looked me dead in the eye. "For the same reason you did it. Because I knew they'd kill ya if you didn't, and I didn't want an innocent woman paying for my mistakes. Ya didn't deserve to die, Fiona. I'll not apologize for that."

I sank back, unable to say anything.

"I did what I could to make things better," he said, like he was trying to convince himself as much as he was me. "I know you may scorn me for being a tout. But I believed in the fight and wanted to help protect our people. I joined the IRA because what they were doing to us Catholics was wrong, and I wasn't going to stand by and do nothing while women and children were terrorized."

I looked at him, realizing he was as tortured as I was. That he wasn't just telling me about Ian—he was making his own confessions. I saw the pain in his eyes and recognized it as a mirror to my own.

Any hatred I might have held toward him over what had happened to Ian disappeared.

I squeezed his hand. "It's a noble thing to want to defend the oppressed," I said softly.

"Aye. But not so noble to be a tout."

"So why'd you turn?"

His jaw tightened. "Because what started as self-defense quickly changed to something I couldn't defend. I was against the bombings from the very beginning. So was Ian."

"He was?" My heart lifted in hope.

Kieran gave me a sad look. "Aye, he was. He said so, too. Said he didn't want to be part of anything that harmed the innocent, that if we did that, we'd be no better than the other side. He was brave, saying so in a room full of angry men who hungered for revenge."

My shoulders sagged, both with sadness and with gratitude for this one bit of knowledge that helped put the picture of the husband I'd loved back together, at least a little.

"I'm glad to know that," I said over the lump in my throat.

"He was a good man," Kieran said gently. "Better than most of them. But he also realized, faster than I did, how dangerous of a situation he and I had gotten ourselves into. He shut up and went along with things, trying to convince himself it was justified. Seamus and Fergus believed in fanning the flames of anger as much as they could, and they were the ones in charge."

"I always thought you were," I admitted. "You seemed so foreboding."

"Nah," he said, a hint of a grin slipping through. "I was just always listening. Now you know why. I made a contact in the army and created a system for alerting him to events where civilians might be in danger. I helped stop as many civilian casualties as I could, while still trying to do my part to keep our neighborhoods safe. I played both sides—more than the British will ever know, thankfully. If they did, they would have left me to be shot instead of getting me here."

"Was Ian a tout too?" I honestly wasn't sure if I hoped he was or wasn't anymore. Everything was so confusing that I didn't know what to think.

"No, he wasn't." Kieran swallowed hard. "I'm sorry for what they made you do. They thought they were being merciful, like, giving you a chance to prove that you wouldn't betray the cause like they thought Ian had. I knew they were wrong, but I didn't know how to save ya from it."

I sighed again, feeling the utter horror of it all. We'd been fighting two armies all along: the official one and the one made up of our own people who were so paranoid and angry they were willing to kill their own to make a point. It was just like Mamó had feared, history repeating itself.

"I wish we never would have gone to Belfast," I said, voicing the regret I could never seem to shake from my soul.

He stuck his hands into the pockets of his jacket and stared at the tree ahead. We were both quiet for a long time before Kieran spoke again.

"How's the city treating ya here?"

I shrugged. "Alright. I have a good job and a nice place to live."

"Did ya hook up with the network?"

I shook my head. "No. I wanted to leave all of that behind."

"Do ya have friends here?" He glanced over at me.

My soul felt too weary to fake a smile. "Not really. I'm not very good company these days."

He gave me an understanding look, and I knew I wasn't the only one still trying to put myself back together after what we'd endured.

His eyes brightened. "How's the baby?"

When I dropped my head, unable to answer, his face fell.

"I'm so sorry," he said quietly.

I nodded in acknowledgement, wiping away the tear that slipped down my cheek.

Kieran put his arm around me. I put my head on his shoulder and we sat in silence again, both grieving the last few years of our lives as we listened to the distant strains of The Eagles playing their set. It wasn't romantic, although we might have looked like a couple to people walking by. It felt more like a funeral, one we both needed desperately.

We needed to say a final goodbye to our old lives.

When the music stopped, Kieran turned to me.

"I'm not staying in New York," he said. "It's not safe for me here. Too many people connected to the IRA. Besides, I've had enough of cities to last me a lifetime. I want to disappear into the forest and live a quiet life somewhere."

I gave him a half smile. "That sounds lovely, actually."

"The place I'm going is called Rosemary Mountain. It's a small mountain town in Tennessee. Land there is cheap."

"Rosemary Mountain," I said, repeating the words slowly. I'd never heard of the place before, but the name sang to my soul like it was calling me home.

"You should come, too," he said. "You'd have a friend there at least. I've heard it's a lot like the hills back home, minus the sea. Misty mountains, all blue and green, land as far as you can see. Fresh, clean air. Room to have a garden and some chickens. And I could look out for ya, make sure you're safe. I owe Ian that."

His voice broke when he said Ian's name. I realized what a good man Kieran really was. He'd tried to save Ian.

He'd tried to save everyone.

"A garden and chickens sound nice," I admitted, allowing myself to contemplate one more move to save my life.

I thought of blue hills covered in mist, of fog-filled mornings, towering trees, and starry skies. I thought of how nice it might feel to put my hands in the dirt again, to plant seeds and grow things, and to live a simple life in a quiet place.

Then I thought of the growing pile of money hidden underneath the mattress in my room.

"Tell me, Kieran," I said, feeling a spark of hope I hadn't felt in so very long. "Just how cheap is this land?"

43
HEALING

FIONA

Spring 1975
Rosemary Mountain

I grinned, looking at the little stone cottage Kieran had built for me. It reminded me of a miniature version of the one I'd left behind in Ireland. *Very* miniature. But it was more than enough for me.

"So? Do ya like it?" Kieran asked proudly, his muscled arms crossed in front of him.

The man who stood beside me was barely recognizable as the lad I'd met in Belfast. He'd grown stocky and strong from manual labor. His hair went uncut, and his beard had grown long.

We spoke little of it, but I knew that it was only partly because of his mountain man lifestyle. He'd changed his looks primarily because he was a dead man if the IRA ever found him—and after what he'd witnessed, they would haunt his nightmares forever. He'd changed his looks, his name—everything—and come to Rosemary Mountain to spend his life off the grid.

I was the one soul who knew his true identity. The one person who could turn him in to the people who wanted him dead. He'd trusted me with the truth anyway. His faith in me had been a healing balm to my heart.

I turned my gaze from him back to the cottage. "Aye, I love it. Ya do good work. I can't believe ya built the whole thing by hand."

He shrugged. "It's nothing."

"It's *something*," I said. "You've a real talent there."

He was silent for a moment. "It feels good to build something. To make something lasting. Feels even better to repair something that's been broken."

"Better than destroying something," I murmured softly.

"Exactly." He slung his arm around my shoulder.

"Well, ya did a fine job. My new home is the prettiest one on the lane." My face broke out into a grin again. "I can't believe I own my own home. And land! Real land of my own, where I can have a garden."

"Aye, ya do." He shot me another grin. "What are ya going to do now?"

"I-I don't know." It hit me that I hadn't thought that far.

So much planning and preparing had gone into this. I'd worked for Kimberly, saving every dollar she gave me, for another year and a half after my first conversation with Kieran. He'd moved to Rosemary Mountain and found a piece of land for himself, then called me from a payphone in town when he thought he'd found one that was right for me.

I'd bought it sight unseen.

Kieran built his home first, then started mine that fall. He had to put it on hold over the winter, but he started up again in early spring. When he called to tell me that it was nearly finished, I bought myself an old truck, said goodbye to Kimberly and her family, and hit the road.

Everyone in New York thought I was crazy for moving somewhere I'd never even been, but I just laughed. After all, I'd done it before—twice.

"The third time's the charm," I muttered under my breath.

"What's that now?"

"Nothing," I said, shaking my head and reminding myself not to be so superstitious.

But as the priest had said, it would be forgiven. After all, I was Irish. I couldn't really help it.

I paid Kieran the rest of what I owed him and sent him on his way. It was nice to have a friend here, and I knew he hoped we'd be more. I saw the love in his eyes for me. I'd be lying if I said I didn't feel the same way. The more I got to know him, the more I admired his strength, his conviction, and his heart. He hadn't joined the IRA to be a rebel or to get revenge—he'd done it because he was willing to sacrifice himself to protect others. When the IRA crossed a line that went against what he believed to be just, he'd done everything he could to make it right.

He was loyal, brave, and strong. His quiet presence made me feel safe and protected. Every time I was around him, I felt myself growing to love him even more.

But it didn't feel right to let myself have that happiness. Not after the things we'd done. I carried too much guilt to even consider it. I couldn't imagine waking up every morning next to someone who reminded me of my worst mistake just because of who he was.

I'd come to Rosemary Mountain hoping to somehow forget.

I unpacked my things, full of gratitude for this little house of my own, a solid place for me to put down roots. Then I put on my boots and went for a walk on the land I hadn't had a chance to fully explore. The mountain was beautiful, and Kieran had picked out a prime spot for my wee cottage. The land felt like pure peace. Happiness.

But the more I explored, the heavier my footsteps became.

I didn't deserve a wonderful life like this.

This house, this land... How was it that I got to have all of this when everyone I'd loved had paid the ultimate price? How could I possibly enjoy it knowing that I'd survived and they hadn't?

Kieran deserved peace. He'd put himself in harm's way a thousand times trying to protect people on both sides. But I'd done nothing like that. I'd killed a man to save my family, only for them all to die in the end anyway. The only person I'd saved was myself, and I was the one who deserved it least.

It felt like the only way to honor the ones I'd lost was to be miserable my whole life.

With my heart heavy, I turned to go home, taking a slightly different path back. A hundred yards down the hill, I stopped in my tracks, awed by the sight in front of me. The fading sunlight hit a tree that stood alone in a little clearing: a hawthorn tree covered in white blooms and glowing in warm sunlight.

It was pure magic—the kind that sent warning chills down my spine. A tree like this, alone on a mountaintop, surely had to belong to the faeries. If I went near it this late, they might sweep me away to their world, forced to serve them for all time and never to be seen again.

The threat propelled me forward instead of away.

I fell onto my knees in front of the hawthorn tree, closing my eyes as I inhaled the familiar fragrance of its blooms. I was swept away by memories of Mamó and Annie and Ian. I began to truly weep, for the first time since I'd lost my child.

I watered the earth with my tears until the sun slipped far below the trees and the forest grew dark. But no faeries came to steal me away.

Instead, I felt a sense of peace come over me that I hadn't felt in so very long, and for the first time since I'd left Ireland, I heard the whispers of a plant speaking to my heart.

I am medicine, and I am for you. Take my flowers, my leaves, and my berries and make a tea to heal your heart. All I ask in return is that you remember the truth of who you are.

"But I don't know who I am anymore," I cried. "Who am I without the ones I love? I am no longer a granddaughter, a sister, a wife, a mother. I am nothing."

The words came to my heart so clearly that I couldn't deny them. *You are a bean feasa.*

I lifted my head in shock. "But I used a plant to kill. I am not worthy to make plant medicine anymore."

The leaves of the tree seemed to ripple with laughter. *Who are you, young one, to decide who is worthy of carrying medicine to those who need it? Only those who know what it is to be wounded can truly know what it is to be healed.*

The leaves rippled again, and a breeze blew through, caressing my face gently. I closed my eyes, but they sprang open again at the hoot of an owl.

Do not fear. This owl brings a gift, not an omen.

A feather fluttered down, landing beside me. I picked it up.

A reminder of your medicine, bean feasa. Use your gifts well.

I rose from the ground and picked blossoms in the moonlight. Then I made my way back to my wee cottage and started the teakettle.

I hadn't known what I was going to do, but it seemed I'd been given a job after all.

44
THE REASON

Daphne

Rosemary Mountain

Present

Fiona wiped her eyes as she finished her story. "So there you have it," she said. "I'm a poisoner. It's time I've paid for my crimes. I should have paid long ago."

I couldn't say anything at first. I was overwhelmed with grief for what she'd suffered and admiration for the way she'd rebuilt her life and dedicated it to serving others, despite loss and hardship I couldn't fathom.

Emerson spoke first, his own voice raw with emotion. "Fiona, no one could blame you for what you did. You were manipulated and put into a terrible position by a terrorist organization that threatened your family."

"*I* blame myself," she said. "I've had many years to think over things, to wonder if there was vengeance in my heart that I didn't want to admit to myself. At the time, I convinced myself that the only option was to do what they wanted. But if I've learned anything over the years, it's that there's always another choice."

I grasped her hand. "I can't imagine the guilt and pain you've borne all these years. But, Fiona, that doesn't change the fact that you didn't kill Alva. Or did you? Is there something I'm missing?"

"Of course I didn't," she scoffed. "Alva was one of my dearest friends."

"Then why did you confess?" I asked, frustrated and confused.

She stared at me as if the answer was obvious. "Because when Greg told me that poor Alva had died of poisoning and that I'd been named as a suspect, I knew I'd been granted a chance to pay for what I did. I'm ready to do it."

"You can't," I cried. "Fiona, don't you see? If you take the fall for this, Alva's real killer will get away. How is that justice?"

Fiona gave me a sly smile. "Oh, Daphne. You don't actually think Alva was poisoned, do you?"

"Um... Yes."

She brushed off the idea like it was ludicrous. "Her heart and lungs have always been weak, poor thing. She had barely recovered from pneumonia, an infection that always gives her trouble, and was already packing up to go on another trip instead of taking the rest she needed. I hate it, but her heart was bound to give out on her at some point, the way she was carrying on—working all hours of the night, traveling all the time, and trying to act like a teenager." Fiona shook her head sadly.

"But—"

Fiona ignored me. "I'm betting Erick found out that Alva was leaving her money to me, so he decided to point the finger my way, hoping he'd get to keep it instead. He can have it for all I care. I never wanted her money anyway."

"But the water hemlock—"

She rolled her eyes. "Yeah, yeah. They won't find water hemlock on their tox screen, but it doesn't matter. It degrades so quickly that we don't always find it in cows we know for a fact died after eating it.

That's why I waited so long to tell Greg about it. I knew by the time they did the autopsy, they could just say it degraded before they ran their tests. With a confession, who's going to care that there's no proof?"

My jaw dropped. "You... You framed yourself for murder, even though you believed Alva died of natural causes?"

She nodded, looking almost proud. "I told you. I saw a chance to pay for what I'd done. The past has been weighing heavy on me lately. I guess that's what happens when you get older."

I glanced at Emerson, biting my lip. I was under strict orders not to disclose information about the case, but... This might be the difference in catching Alva's real killer or not. I had to believe that Greg would approve.

Emerson gave me a small nod, like he could read my mind. It was all the encouragement I needed.

"Fiona, I'm not supposed to tell you this, but they found dried water hemlock in the jar of tea you took to Alva."

Her face changed to horror. "What?"

I nodded slowly. "Alva really *was* poisoned—by the very poison you told them to look for."

Tears sprang to her eyes. "No. Oh, that's a terrible way to die." She rocked back and forth, pain etched into her face. "I can't believe it."

My mind raced, trying to put the pieces of the puzzle together. The only way any of this made sense was if Alva had been killed by someone who knew what Fiona had done—someone who knew how guilty she felt and how unlikely it was that she'd fight the charges.

I grabbed Fiona's hand again. "Fiona. Does Kieran still live here?"

Her head rose quickly. "He wouldn't."

"This had to have been done by someone who knew what you did," I explained. "He's the only one. He has to be Alva's killer."

She shook her head, her lips pressed firmly together. "No. You don't know him. He wouldn't hurt a fly, and he certainly wouldn't hurt me that way."

"We at least need to talk to him about it."

The stubborn look I knew so well settled onto her face. "I'll take the blame before I turn him in. I'm telling you, Daphne, he didn't do this."

"Then who did?" I asked, frustrated. I stood up and paced, biting my thumbnail.

Emerson's calm voice entered the conversation. "Did you tell anyone else here about your past?"

"Thank you for finally asking a smart question," Fiona said sharply, throwing a glare at me. "But no. I never told a soul until today. Kieran's the only one I've ever spoken to about it—except the priest I confessed to in New York, and he'd be long dead by now."

"You have to at least consider that he—"

"No," she interrupted. Her voice was angry. "You've heard my side of the story, but you haven't heard his. That man suffered and lost as much as I did, and he hates violence as much as me, too. I know him. I'm as sure that he didn't do it as you were about me."

She stood. "Look, I hope you find who killed my friend. It changes things, knowing someone really did poison her. But it wasn't him, so don't go there. And you should know that this doesn't change the fact that I'm ready to face the punishment for what I did. So even if I don't go away for this, I'm going to turn myself in and tell the truth about what I did in Ireland."

Her declaration took the breath out of me. She turned and marched to bed with a stubborn lift of her chin. Emerson's arms wrapped around me, and I sank into him and sobbed.

Even if I solved this case, I was still going to lose Fiona.

45
THE TRUTH

Daphne

Rosemary Mountain

Present

I couldn't sleep. Emerson sat up with me, holding me while I grieved. Fiona's story had ripped my heart out, but knowing she was determined to spend the rest of her life in prison was even worse.

She'd been so young, and she'd been manipulated by an evil, heartless man who hadn't cared who suffered as long as he'd achieved his objectives.

Not that he even had. Fifty years later, Northern Ireland was still part of the UK instead of unified with the Republic of Ireland, and while the laws had improved, violence between Catholics and Protestants had never fully ended. Many neighborhoods were still segregated, divided by "peace walls." There were still paramilitary groups that rejected the peace agreement and engaged in violence. I'd seen news reports of a petrol bomb being thrown into a parade just last April.

The violence had solved nothing—but it had cost Fiona everything.

Emerson pressed a kiss to the top of my head. "You okay?"

"No."

"I'm sorry." He stroked my hair. "How can I help?"

"I don't know." I pulled the ends of my sleeves over my fingers and tucked my hands underneath my chin. "I just… I'm not ready to give up. On any of it."

"I'd be surprised if you were," he said, a trace of humor in his voice. "Any ideas on who Kieran is? Maybe I could go talk to him."

"I really don't," I admitted. "John O'Malley has an Irish heritage, but he was born here, and I don't think his father is still alive. Other than that, I can't think of anyone it might be."

"We'll figure it out. I'll think of a way to ask my contacts without raising suspicion."

I pulled out of his arms and kissed him, caressing his cheek with my hand.

"What's that for?" he asked, grinning.

"For being the most supportive man on the planet." I smiled. "Listen, I'm going to be up late. You can go to bed if you need. I know you must be exhausted."

"Not at all," he said, stifling a yawn.

I gave him a look. Emerson worked twenty-four-hour shifts and had probably been up for thirty-six hours straight by this point.

"Go to bed," I said before kissing him again.

"What are you going to do?"

I shrugged. "Research. We have Kieran's name and the names of his associates in Ireland. There are tons of historical archives on the internet. Maybe I'll get lucky and find a lead."

"Good luck." He stood, squeezing my shoulder.

"Thanks." I blew out a breath.

I needed more than luck. I needed a miracle.

With a steaming-hot cup of coffee in hand, I curled up on the couch with my laptop. Thor settled in beside me, laying his head over my ankle.

"We've got this, right?" I asked.

The mournful look in his eyes wasn't exactly reassuring.

But I felt optimistic as I typed in the first name and started scrolling results, taking tiny sips of the hot coffee. When that one didn't get me anywhere, I typed in another. Then another.

After a few dead ends, I found something that stopped me in my tracks.

I traded my coffee for a notebook and began scribbling down information as quickly as I could. One lead turned into another, and soon I was following a trail that led me somewhere I'd never expected.

Hours later, I gasped as I realized the truth.

I stared at my notes, certain I knew what had happened but unable to prove it. Not without confirming it ... which meant calling one of the ghosts from Fiona's past.

The number was right in front of me.

I glanced at the clock, then looked up the time difference between Tennessee and Ireland. We were five hours behind them, which made it nine a.m. there, a perfectly reasonable time to call. I bit my lip, nervous. If I was wrong, I could be hastening Fiona's imprisonment. No one else knew what she'd done. She might change her mind about turning herself in.

If I made this call, her identity and her location would no longer be secret. I would be opening up a can of worms that had been sealed for over fifty years. It was a huge risk, and I wasn't at all sure it was my decision to make.

A thousand warnings rattled off in my head about how I should ask Fiona first, or at least run my theory by Greg. But I couldn't tell him Fiona's secret, and the thought of telling Fiona what I believed without definitive proof made me feel queasy.

So I picked up the phone and dialed the number, praying it wouldn't blow up in our faces.

A pleasant female voice with a soft Irish brogue answered.

"Hello," I said, swallowing back my reservations. "Is this Annie McNeal?"

The woman laughed. "I haven't been a McNeal in many years, but I once was, yes."

"The same Annie McNeal who had a sister named Fiona?"

Time froze. The woman finally answered, her voice shaky. "Do you... Do you have word of my sister?"

I let out a breath and smiled. "I think I might. I have a friend named Fiona Flanagan. She recently told me she had a sister named Annie that she'd lost touch with when she moved to America. Do you have a few minutes to talk?"

Annie let out a sob. "Yes. Yes, of course I do. Oh my goodness. I can't believe it." I could hear her smile right through the phone. "Is Fiona okay?"

I didn't want to waste time mincing words. "Yes—for now. But she's in trouble, and I think you might be able to help."

"Tell me what you need," Annie said, her tone switching to pure business.

I took a deep breath, then began to weave a story of my own.

46

WHAT REALLY HAPPENED

Mamó

March 1972

Glenarm

I waited for Lieutenant Montgomery to show, flipping the packet of water hemlock in my hands. I wasn't sorry for what I'd done or what I was about to do. Taking care of my girls was the most important thing, and if it meant breaking one of the commandments, then I'd ask forgiveness later. I was certain God would understand, given the circumstances.

It was my job to protect Fiona. So help me, I'd do it.

When Lieutenant Montgomery arrived, I invited him in and told him to sit.

He gave me a strange look. "Where's Annie?"

"Annie's not coming," I said, pouring him a cup of tea. "It's me you need to talk to tonight."

"Alright," he said, accepting the teacup with a pleasant nod. He took a sip, making a sound of appreciation. "What would you like to talk about?"

"Your future," I said, taking the seat across from him.

"I suppose you mean marrying Annie."

"No." I shook my head. "That's not what I mean at all. You won't be marrying Annie now."

His brow furrowed. "She's already said yes."

"Aye. That was before you threatened her sister. You can't expect her to want to be your bride now, can ya? Surely you're not a complete eejit."

"I wasn't threatening Fiona," he said, his expression concerned. He took another sip of the tea. "I was only trying to warn Annie so she could talk some sense into her sister. Fiona's name has been mentioned by my superiors. She's shown up at the barracks over and over again, asking about Ian's body, even though they told her they didn't have it. She insists that her husband was killed by a British soldier, even though there's no evidence of it. Between that and the people she's been seen associating with in Belfast, she's marking herself as a problem, and I can't protect her if she won't stop."

"Well, regardless of how you meant it, Annie took it as a threat. That's no way to start a marriage, now, is it? I'd hardly be a proper guardian to her if I let her marry a man who forced her into it by making her think it was the only way to protect the sister she loves."

He set the empty cup down. "I assure you that was not my intention. I'd never force Annie to do anything. I love her. I only tried to point out that it would work in Fiona's favor to support our marriage as planned. It seems there's been a big misunderstanding." His face was grave.

I cocked my head. "I think there may have been quite a few misunderstandings. I'm going to ask you a question and I expect you to tell me the truth."

"I will," he said with a nod. "I've nothing to hide."

I leaned forward. "Did you kill Ian?"

His expression was solemn. "I give you my word that I didn't. If that's not enough for you, I can prove that I wasn't even in Belfast that night. I'd already been restationed, and I have the papers to show it. I've never understood why Fiona thought it was me in the first place."

I took a deep breath. I was a good judge of character and an even better judge of when someone was lying. Lieutenant Montgomery was telling the truth.

"She believed that, Edward, because the IRA told her so. Just like they told her to kill you."

His head jerked back. "I beg your pardon?"

I leaned forward, pouring myself a cup of tea. "I rather suspect that the lad who told her all this is actually the one who pulled the trigger and shot our poor Ian. It wouldn't be the first time the IRA has punished one of their own for some sort of perceived betrayal."

His jaw dropped. "That's terrible. But what makes you think Ian betrayed them?"

"It's not anything that Ian did," I said calmly. "I'm afraid the fault lies solely with you."

He blanched. "I don't know what you mean."

I waved him off. "It's not your fault, really. You're a kind man, and you were trying to be fair. But Fiona told us how Ian got cut loose so quickly from internment. It put a target on his back, you see. I know how these lads are. I've been dealing with the IRA since longer than you've been alive. They're a suspicious, paranoid bunch. What you did would have been enough for them to start thinking he'd betrayed them."

Lieutenant Montgomery didn't say anything for a moment. When he spoke, there was true sadness in his voice. "I didn't even think about that. I was only trying to help out someone I considered to be a friend—or a friend of my brother's, anyway. I tried hard to stay neutral, to look for the best in people instead of assuming the worst, the way some of my company does."

"Aye, that's why we're having this conversation, because I've seen that in ya. I know you're a good man. What I need you to know is that Ian was, too. Whatever happened, whatever mistakes he made, he was still a good man who was trying to defend the innocent. And Fiona, my granddaughter, is a good woman."

"A good woman that the IRA asked to kill me," he said, a trace of humor marking his words.

"They did." I took another sip of my tea. "But you're alive, aren't ya?"

"I suppose you're telling me I have Fiona to thank for that?"

"Aye. Ya do. And I'm hoping you'll do us a favor."

He took a deep breath. "I suppose I owe you both my life, so of course. I'm at your service."

I gave him a hard look. "You give me your word?"

"I do. You have my word, whatever you need."

"Alright, then. Fiona is leaving the island. There's too much pain for her here. Besides that, the IRA is going to be quite angry when they discover that you're still breathing."

Understanding dawned in his eyes. "They'll think she's a traitor as well."

"Exactly. They've already threatened her—threatened all of us. And if we were lesser people, I'd have killed ya myself just to save our hides. But I'm not like that, ya see? I don't believe in it."

"I'm grateful," he said, chuckling. "But you still haven't told me what you need."

"I need ya to die."

His head jerked back again.

"Just for a few days," I said, laughing. "I need you to give Fiona time to get to America before the IRA starts trying to hunt her down, and I need you to give me and Annie time to pack our things and leave."

"You're both leaving, too?" The sadness that crossed his face convinced me that his feelings for Annie were real.

"Aye. It's not safe for us here anymore. I only moved here to help my girls, and now that we're on the IRA's radar, we can't stay. I'm taking Annie back to County Cork with me. It's my home and I've missed it so."

He looked down. "I suppose that's best."

"If ya love her, then yes, it is best for her to get out of here. But—"

He looked up, hopeful.

"If you give us the time we need to get to safety before you go after the men who wanted you dead, you'll be welcome to write to her and, eventually, to call on her there. With some time and space, I think she might come to see that you weren't the enemy Fiona told her you were."

"I hope so."

"I hope so too. And I hope you'll forgive Fiona for believing the worst about you. It's hard to see clearly when you're walking through grief."

"I think I can understand that—and forgive it," he said, offering me a smile.

"Good. Now let's plan your death."

47
THE KILLER

Daphne

Rosemary Mountain
Present

When I hung up the phone with Annie, I blew out a breath, then grinned. Fiona's sister was *alive*—and so was her husband, Edward Montgomery.

For all these years, Fiona had beaten herself up over something that had never even happened.

I couldn't wait to tell her. I threw on my jacket and headed down the trail, leaving Emerson sleeping even though I wanted to tell him the news too. I'd tell Fiona first; then we could celebrate tonight. Fiona hadn't killed Alva *or* Edward. She was an innocent woman who had nothing to confess or pay for.

Smoke rose from Fiona's chimney, bringing a smile to my face. We were one step closer to returning to normal. I jogged down the path through her garden and stepped onto her sun porch, tugging off my boots while I called her name.

She yanked the door open. "What on earth are you doing here at this time of day?"

"I have news." A sudden wave of nerves hit me. This was *big*. It was going to change Fiona's life—and her future.

"Well, come on in, then," she said, shrugging as she turned to walk into her kitchen. "Though I can't imagine all that much has happened since you left my house a few hours ago. Coffee?"

"Yes, *please.*" The aroma was heavenly. Fiona always made the best coffee.

She poured me a cup while I took a seat at her tiny kitchen table. When she placed the mug in front of me with a thud, she put a hand on her hip and gave me a suspicious look. "Why are you grinning like you just took first prize at the county fair?"

I shook my head, beaming. "Listen, there's probably a better way to tell you this, but I'm too happy to think it through right now. Fiona, you didn't kill Lieutenant Montgomery."

She rolled her eyes. "Just cause Mamó made the tea doesn't mean I'm not responsible."

"No, you don't understand. Mamó didn't kill him, either. She lied to you. She had no intention of poisoning him."

"Now I *know* you're crazy, because Mamó never told a lie in her life," she said, grabbing her mug to refill.

"She did that time. Mamó suspected the truth about Seamus all along. She told Lieutenant Montgomery what was going on, and he disappeared long enough for her and Annie to pack up and move to County Cork. By the time Seamus realized he wasn't dead after all, you were all safely settled, and the IRA had no idea where any of you were."

"How do I know you're not just telling me all this to convince me not to turn myself in?" She was clearly skeptical.

"Because I have proof."

"What proof?"

I took a deep breath, knowing that it was going to be a shock. "Well, for one thing, I spoke with your sister this morning. She's alive and well—and happily married to Edward. They're celebrating their fiftieth wedding anniversary next spring."

Fiona sank into her chair, as white as a ghost. "Annie's not … dead?"

"No." I shook my head, beaming. "She's not."

"But I had that dream about Mamó, and when I called the village, they said they were gone—taken by the Troubles…"

"They *were* gone. Gone, not dead. I'm sorry the person you spoke with misled you. You said he called you a tout—I'm guessing he was loyal to the cause and hated all of you for sympathizing with a British soldier."

She was still in shock. "Annie really married Lieutenant Montgomery."

"Yes," I said, hoping she didn't take that as a negative. "They knew he didn't kill Ian, and he proved himself by keeping them safe. They slowed down their engagement and waited until Annie was sure she wanted to marry a soldier, but yes. They're married."

Her eyes filled with tears. "I can't believe it," she whispered. "Annie's alive. And … happy? Truly?"

"Very happy," I said, smiling. "And even happier now that she knows you're alive too. She missed you so much."

Fiona clasped her hands together in front of her mouth and let out a sob. "I can't believe we wasted so much time. All those years I thought she was dead… She was alive. You found her in one night."

My heart broke for her all over again. The man in Glenarm had done a cruel, heartless thing. "I know. You lost fifty years. We can't change that, but you don't have to lose any more."

I pulled my cell phone out of my pocket and showed her the picture Annie had emailed me while we spoke. It was Annie, Edward, their six children, and seventeen grandchildren.

Fiona covered her mouth with her hand as she looked at it. Tears began to pour down her cheeks. "Oh, she's so beautiful," she said, her grief turning to joy. "She looks just the same. And look at Lieutenant Montgomery, still handsome and proud." She looked up at me in wonder. "I didn't ruin Annie's chance at happiness or kill an innocent man."

"No, you didn't," I said, smiling.

"I would have, though, if Mamò hadn't taken matters into her own hands." Her face fell. "That alone is still a sin."

"You don't know that," I said gently. "You might have changed your mind when it came down to it. You were barely more than a child, and you'd been lied to and put into a terrible position. Mamó knew you weren't thinking clearly and that you were desperate to protect Annie. So she protected you from the IRA—and from yourself."

Grief shuttered her face. "But she let me live with a lie all those years."

"She didn't mean to. That's the other proof I have. She wrote you a letter, thinking you'd find it before long."

"A letter?" Fiona looked confused.

I nodded. "It's hidden in the quilt. It's underneath the patch from Mamó's tablecloth. She sewed it in before you left, using different stitches than she had on the rest of the quilt, thinking you'd realize it was a message when you were thinking clearly again."

Fiona looked at me in astonishment. "The quilt? I never—" She cut off and rose from the table to get the quilt that had hung on her wall since the day she'd moved into the cottage. It had stayed there as a prized art piece Willa and I had made over countless times.

I'd never noticed a difference in stitches, either, and if Willa had, she'd never said anything—likely to avoid criticizing such a prized work. Mamò's clue hadn't been nearly as obvious as she'd thought, a sad flaw in her plan.

Fiona returned with it in her arms. She gently laid the antique quilt out on her kitchen table, then used a tiny pair of scissors to cut the stitches that held one side of Mamó's patch so she could stick her fingers inside. She looked up at me with surprise, then pulled out a thin plastic bag that held a folded piece of paper.

"All this time," she said in wonder. "That tablecloth fabric was thick enough to mask it, but I'm still embarrassed to admit I never noticed anything different."

She unfolded the paper with trembling hands and read it with tears streaming down her cheeks. When she finished, she held it to her heart, then gave it to me.

"You should read it, too," she said. "After all, I have you to thank for all of this."

Dearest Fiona,

I have something to confess. I told you a lie. You're blind with rage and grief right now, and you think there's only one choice. But that's not true —there's always another way, only it's hard to see sometimes.

Seamus told you Edward is your enemy, but I think he's lying to you. We may never know for sure, but I suspect that Seamus is the one who really killed Ian. The IRA doesn't look kindly on people who betray them, and I imagine they've created a whole story in their minds about Ian being a traitor, thanks to Lt. Montgomery looking after yous both and now being engaged to Annie.

I know from experience how hard it can be to see clearly when we're grieving a great loss. I can't let you make a mistake that will haunt you for the rest of your life. That's why I told you I would do it, so that you'd leave and get to safety. But I won't kill him. Not only because I believe he's innocent, but because even if he isn't, killing him would make me no better than him. It would solve nothing.

I'm an old woman. I've watched this battle play out for longer than you've been alive. Violence begets violence. Or, as the scriptures say, you reap what you sow.

I don't want war. I don't want more killing. So I'll not sow those seeds, in my life or yours.

Annie and I are going back to my home in County Cork. You might think it's unfair that we have to move, but the truth is that I've missed it there. I've friends and connections that will keep us safe. I want to spend the last years of my life somewhere filled with magic, love, music, and dancing. Not somewhere filled with soldiers and fighting. I've already lived through that once, and that was one time too many.

Besides, I think it will do Annie and Edward good to be forced to slow down their courtship. If Annie chooses to marry a British soldier, she will be in for a hard life. She needs to be sure. And since it won't be easy for him to visit her there, he'll have to prove himself to her—and to me.

If there's one final lesson I can give you, it's to remember that love is never the wrong choice. I've told you often that it's the most powerful force on earth, and I mean it. Love is what helps us see the worth of every soul, even the ones who go to a different church or fly a different flag. It's what reminds us that we were all created in the very image of God. We're all connected that way.

Love is more powerful than anything the IRA can do with their bullets and bombs, or anything the British government can do with gas and rubber bullets. Love is the only thing that matters in the end, child.

I know how often you cuddle up with this quilt, so I'm hoping you find this letter soon—but not too soon. I don't want you to turn around. I meant it when I said your fate is in America. Annie and I will be safe in County Cork, but I fear you wouldn't be. The IRA will take it too personally when they find out that Lieutenant Montgomery isn't dead, and the people of my old village might be wary of protecting someone whose husband was so involved in the violence. I think you, too, will do better far away from all of this, safe in America, where it will be easier for you to start over and let go of your anger.

But when you've settled, give us a call. You'll find me in my old village. Until then, I'll think of you every day and pray for you every night. I love you dearly, and I wish I could have spared you all of this.

Kiss that sweet baby for me when it arrives. Mamó loves you both so much.

By the time I finished reading Mamó's words, I was weeping.

"She was an amazing woman," I said, the words coming out strangled over the lump in my throat.

"Aye," Fiona said, smiling and crying at the same time. "Oh, but I've missed her so much. I'd give anything if I had found that in time to know she was safe and alive, and to talk to her again."

"Life has been very unfair to you," I said. My heart squeezed with the injustice of it all.

Fiona gave me a sad look. "I suppose it has in some ways. But it's also been very good to me. I've had a long life, and most of it's been happy. Not everyone can say the same. I'm glad to know that Annie had a long life too, and it seems hers was happy, which brings me more joy than I can say. But so many lives, like Ian's, were cut short. Seems like I got the lucky end of the straw."

"You constantly amaze me, you know that?" I shook my head. "And after reading this, I'm betting you get your inner strength and wisdom from the woman who wrote it."

I reached for the letter again, wanting to reread Mamó's words. But when I touched it, I got a hazy flash of another world. I jerked my hand away in shock.

"What is it?" Fiona asked, concerned.

"I-I saw something," I said, biting my lip. I stretched my fingers toward the letter again, preparing myself so I wouldn't jerk right out of it.

The flashes came back. "I'm in a kitchen, I think," I said, saying it all out loud so Fiona could follow along. "Pretending to cook, but I'm actually listening... I hear a familiar voice—yours, I think, but younger and with a much stronger accent. You're talking to a man."

"Ian?" Fiona asked, her tone hopeful.

I shook my head. "No... I'm pushing the door open so I can see. I'm worried about you. I don't trust him. I see your hands... He's giving you money—OH." I opened my eyes in shock. "The man who gave you money. That was Seamus, wasn't it?"

She nodded. "Yeah, that's right."

I couldn't believe it. "His voice, that smile—Fiona, your Seamus is Alva's boyfriend, Mr. Anderson."

"No." She paled. "If Seamus is here, I'm not the only one in trouble. We have to warn Kieran." She jumped up and grabbed her jacket, then pulled a shotgun out of the pantry.

"We'll call Greg," I said. "It's too dangerous for us to face Seamus alone."

"Do what you want, but I'm leaving now." Her face was dead serious. "It's early, and Greg lives down in the valley, too far away to get there quickly. If Seamus knows where Kieran is, we can't waste a minute. He saved my life. You can stay here and call for help, but I'm not waiting around for the cavalry."

I made a split decision and grabbed my phone. "You're not going alone. I'll call Greg on the way—and Emerson too. Maybe even Jackson and Cole. Anyone who can help."

She gave me a sharp nod and headed toward her truck.

I ran behind her, dialing Greg's number.

48
THE FIGHT

Daphne

Rosemary Mountain

Present

As Fiona sped around the twisty curves of a desolate road, panic began to grip me. I recognized this drive—it led to where I'd faced the darkest night of my life.

I swallowed hard. "Fiona, why are we heading toward Dead Man's Cave?"

"Not the cave," she said. "We're turning off before that."

Her answer only helped a little. When she'd given me the address I'd rattled off to Greg and Emerson both, I hadn't realized that it was on this side of the mountain. I hadn't been here since that night. It felt like a bad omen that Fiona and I were back here again.

Fiona turned her truck onto a gravel road so hidden that I would have driven right past it. The forest encroached so closely on the narrow lane that I was surprised we didn't have branches hitting our windows. I gripped the handle of my door and held on for dear life as Fiona flew around the curves, sending gravel spraying and causing a giant cloud of dust to rise behind us.

If we were anywhere close to our destination and Seamus was there, he'd know that someone was coming. Fiona's approach was the opposite of stealthy.

I gritted my teeth, knowing there was also no way Emerson and Greg were going to catch up with us quickly. Greg was driving from his home in the valley—he was at least half an hour away. Jackson was closer but not close enough.

Thank God Ellie had spent the night with Mom. Emerson had woken on the second ring and jumped into his truck, trying to catch us before I even hung up the phone. He'd only been a few minutes behind us, but he wouldn't match Fiona's speed on these gravel switchbacks. Only a maniac would drive like this.

Only Fiona Flanagan would do it with the kind of skill that gave me a *tiny* amount of hope we wouldn't fly over the edge of the mountain in the process.

She finally slowed down, turning onto yet another nearly hidden road marked by a tin mailbox. This time, she crept down the gravel driveway. Apparently, stealth mattered to her now, though I suspected that it was too late for that.

There was a small stone cottage at the end of the drive that looked remarkably like Fiona's except for the setting. While Fiona's home was tucked into a cozy lot with flower beds and tidy spaces, this one was surrounded by equipment: tractors, construction supplies, and what could only be called junk. There were multiple outbuildings, including a large barn. Chickens ran loose, pecking the ground, scattering as we drew close. Goats peered at us from behind a fence. A cow and her calf mooed in greeting. A scary-looking farm dog ran out from behind the barn, but his tail wagged as he barked at us, so I hoped that meant he was friendly.

"I guess this is Kieran's place?" I asked.

Fiona nodded. "Yes, but you can never reveal that name. The people here know him as Murphy."

"Murphy..." The name triggered a memory, and I smacked my face. "You mean *Old Man Murphy* is Kieran?"

I'd heard some of Greg's stories about the crazy man who lived off-grid in the mountains on an old-fashioned homestead. Murphy kept his hair and his beard long and had a ghillie suit he wore, pretending to be Bigfoot in order to scare trespassers on his land. Most of the deputies were terrified of him, but Greg insisted he was harmless.

"Yep. One and the same."

"I ... did not see that one coming," I muttered. Then I cheered, thinking of the implications. "But no one would have. Murphy lives totally off-grid and under a different name. I'm starting to think we freaked out about nothing, at least as far as he's concerned."

"How do you figure?"

"Even if Seamus found *you,* that doesn't mean he knows Kieran is here. You're still using your old name, and you came here on a legit passport. It makes sense that Seamus was able to find you. It took me one night on the internet to find Annie. Kieran though? He disappeared without a trace. Who would ever have connected him to Old Man Murphy?"

But Fiona wasn't paying any attention to me. "Something's not right," she said, scanning the area.

All of my worry had faded though. "Mr. Anderson's Range Rover isn't here," I pointed out. "Plus, the dog seems pretty chill. He's wagging his tail and looks happy. I think we're okay."

Fiona didn't agree. "*That* dog is always chill," she said flatly. "Worst guard dog in the whole world. But where's Princess?"

I frowned. "Who's Princess?"

She smirked. "The actual guard dog. She's a rescue Murphy saved from a dog-fighting ring. Total baby for him, but he was never able to fully rehabilitate her. She's mean. She'll take your face off just for looking at Murphy wrong."

Great. Just great.

"Come on," Fiona said, grabbing her shotgun. "There's a canister of bear spray underneath your seat if you want to grab it."

"For Seamus?"

"For Princess." She chuckled.

I groaned. "Look, Emerson will be here any minute. Why don't we—"

But Fiona had already hopped out of her truck and was moving toward the closest outbuilding.

I gritted my teeth, muttering about my stubborn Irish godmother, and called Emerson. "How close are you?"

"Close," he half shouted above the noise of his truck flying over gravel. "Are you guys okay?"

"Yes. Everything looks fine to me. No sign of Seamus's vehicle, no sign of disturbance, and the animals are acting normal as far as I can tell. But Fiona's worried because one of the dogs didn't run out, so she just jumped out of the truck with her shotgun and seems to be" —I smacked my forehead—"clearing the outbuildings one by one like she's a police officer."

Emerson laughed. "GPS says I'll be there in ten minutes. How did you guys get there so fast?"

"Fiona drove like a speed demon." I laughed, watching her clear another building while the "chill" dog stared at her with his head cocked like he thought she was crazy. "Get this. Kieran is Old Man Murphy."

"You're kidding," Emerson said, laughing.

"Nope. But he's, like, *way* off-grid. I don't think there's any way Seamus would know he's out here."

"Probably not," Emerson agreed. "Even if Seamus did show up, based on what I've heard about Murphy, I'm pretty sure he can handle it himself."

"Absolutely. I wouldn't be surprised if Murphy is watching Fiona from a window, laughing. She's putting on quite the show, ducking behind doors and crouching as she moves across the ground, acting like she's a soldier—a soldier wearing overalls, a hot-pink cardigan, and green muck boots."

Emerson snorted. "That's hilarious. I'll be there soon. I'll help Fiona satisfy herself that everything's okay. Then we can head home together."

"Sounds good. Love you."

"Love you too."

I hung up with Emerson and switched my phone to camera mode so I could take a video of Fiona's antics. I was giggling so hard as I watched her that I didn't even notice the shadow creeping over my window.

Until Seamus rapped his pistol on the glass.

I froze.

He motioned for me to stay quiet as he used his other hand to open the door.

"Daphne." His voice was so low I knew that it would never reach Fiona, who had just entered the barn. "I didn't know I'd have the pleasure of seeing you again so soon. Interesting that a police consultant is hanging out with a murder suspect, but I suppose they do things differently here in the States."

"Hello, Seamus," I said coldly.

His eyes flickered with amusement. "I see Fiona's told you who I am. I was starting to give up hope that she'd figure it out." He motioned for me to get out of the truck. "Hands in the air, lass."

I obeyed, mentally calculating how long I'd been on the phone with Emerson. He was seven minutes away at most. I could keep Seamus talking for that long.

"You *wanted* her to figure it out?" I asked.

"Of course." He chuckled. "Why else would I go to such lengths to remind her of what she promised to do back in Belfast? Walk toward the barn." He used the pistol to motion for me to take the lead.

"I assumed you wanted to punish her," I said, slowly doing what he'd asked.

He jabbed the pistol into my spine. "If that's all I wanted, I would have killed *her*, not the lovely Alva."

"I don't understand."

"Of course you don't. Faster." He jabbed me again. "You weren't supposed to be here, and I don't appreciate being kept out in the open like this." There was an edge of nervousness to his voice.

"You don't want Kieran seeing you before you sneak up on him," I said, realizing the source of his fear.

"Be quiet," he warned.

I glanced toward the house. Fiona's truck was parked in such a way that it blocked us from view when we were by it. But out here in the open, all it would take was Murphy walking by a window to see us.

I couldn't risk deliberately making noise with a pistol touching the base of my spine, but I slowed my steps, creating more chances for Murphy to see us.

Seamus leaned down, whispering in my ear. "I know what you're doing. Pick up the pace, lass, or I'll break your neck right here."

I had no doubt he was telling the truth.

"That's better," he whispered as I resumed a normal pace. We were almost to the barn. Fiona was inside with her shotgun, but she'd never fire at him while he used me as a shield. I needed to distract him.

"I understand now," I whispered.

"Oh, you think you do, do you?"

"Yeah. You didn't just want to punish Fiona—you wanted her to lead you to Kieran."

"Bingo." I could practically hear the smile in his voice. "Seems you're more clever than your friend. I hate that you know who I am."

The threat underneath the words chilled me.

"So you killed Fiona's friend in a way you knew would remind her of what she failed to do in Ireland, thinking it would scare her into running to Kieran."

"Exactly. It was a clever threat, wasn't it? Remind her of the debt she owed me and get her to lead me to the other traitor I needed to punish."

"Well, it would have been—except that, until this morning, she had no idea Lieutenant Montgomery was still alive. She genuinely thought she'd killed him."

There was a falter in his steps. "Did she really?" His voice was contemplative.

"Yes. She was shocked when I told her that her plan had failed."

"Well, I admit I feel a little bad now," he said, dropping his voice even more as he ushered me into the barn. He pushed me behind a heavy stall door, where we were hidden but he could watch for Fiona and Kieran both.

"Bad enough to spare her life?" I asked, looking up at him with hope.

"I'm not an eejit," he said, chuckling quietly. Then he put a finger to his mouth, warning me not to make a sound.

He moved behind me and cocked his pistol, putting it to my temple. My heart thundered, knowing that one squeeze of that trigger would end me.

"Please," I said weakly. "I have a daughter."

"Shut up," he whispered fiercely.

I heard Fiona laugh out loud from the other end of the barn. "Well, there you are! When I didn't see Princess, I was mighty worried. Didn't know she was expecting pups."

A raspy male voice answered her, his Belfast accent still thick from years of isolation. "Nor did I until a fortnight ago. She had them last night, so she did. One of the wee ones was struggling, so I didn't want to leave them."

"Don't tell me you slept in the barn all night to keep watch over a wee pup," Fiona said, her own Irish brogue coming through stronger in response to his. Her voice was so full of warmth and affection that I smiled, despite the gun held to my head.

"Of course I did," Murphy answered. "Miracle of life and all, don't ya know."

"You're a softy, so ya are." Their voices grew louder as their footsteps began to walk toward us. "Scare any kids lately?"

Murphy laughed. "I'm afraid not. Seems they've all learned to stay away from my part of the mountain. It gets a little borin' without having anyone to scare off, I'll tell ya. Lonely, too. 'Tis been a bit since you've visited, Fiona. I've missed ya."

Fiona sighed. "I'm sorry for it. We've a lot to catch up on, you and I."

"Sounds like trouble." Murphy's voice grew concerned—and close.

I could barely breathe. They were right in front of us. If the door hadn't been there, I could have reached out and touched them.

"Aye," Fiona said. She sighed again. "I don't know how to tell ya this, but Seamus has found us."

"*What?*" Shock rippled through Murphy's voice.

"He killed my friend. Poisoned her. I came to warn ya."

"Fiona, if Seamus knows where we are, we have to leave. *Now.* We'll never be safe."

Seamus pushed me out from behind the door, keeping me in front of him like a shield. "Aye," he said, chuckling. "You're right. You'll never be safe. But it's too late to leave. I'm afraid it's time you both pay for your sins."

Murphy's eyes went wide. He moved in front of Fiona, shoving her behind him.

The steel jerked away from my temple.

Boom.

Excruciating pain made me grab my ears. The deafening ringing in them was so disorienting that I thought I'd been shot.

But it was Murphy who crumpled to the ground.

Seamus's eyes gleamed with hatred as he watched his former friend groan with pain.

Blood oozed from Murphy's thigh, the deep-red color spreading across the faded denim of his jeans. He tried to stand but couldn't.

Seamus shifted his focus to Fiona and began to raise his gun again.

I grabbed the bear spray from my pocket and screamed for her to run.

49
THE DECISION

Daphne

Rosemary Mountain

Present

The stream of capsaicin hit Seamus square in the eyes. He screamed, grabbing his face with his free hand, and fired a shot in Fiona's direction. The wild shot hit the rafter above her.

She lunged forward, using the end of her shotgun to knock the pistol from his hands. It hit the ground, and I dove for it, my fingers reaching the cold metal just as Seamus tackled me, knocking the pistol out of reach.

He yanked me up, hauling me to his chest as a human shield against the gun Fiona had pointed straight at him. He held one hand to my throat and the other to the top of my head.

The ringing in my ears was so deafening I couldn't hear what he said, but I saw Fiona freeze. I shook my head no, but she nodded at Seamus and slowly lowered her shotgun, raising her hands in surrender.

She mouthed, *It's okay—I love you,* then closed her eyes and bowed her head.

I screamed, "No!" as Seamus let go of my throat, drew a second pistol, and pointed it at her. He put his thumb on the hammer.

Then I fell to the ground, crushed by the weight of his body. Hot, sticky blood dripped down the side of my face.

I clawed out from underneath him and scrambled to my feet.

Murphy stood above Seamus, holding a shovel in his hand. His white face dripped with sweat as he stared down at the unconscious man at his feet.

Fiona ran to him, throwing her support underneath his shoulder as she buried her face in his chest. He wrapped his arm around her and spoke words into her ear that I couldn't have heard even if my ears weren't still ringing. But I didn't have to hear them to know that he was telling her what he should have told her years ago—what had been clear since the moment I saw him jump in front of her.

Old Man Murphy was still in love with Fiona, all this time later. I had a feeling he'd never stopped.

I only hoped Fiona would allow herself to admit that she loved him, too, and that they both deserved happiness in whatever years they had left.

She lifted her head and looked up at him with tears in her eyes. He gazed down at her with a look of utter devotion. Her chest heaved, then she stretched onto her tiptoes and kissed him gently.

Emerson, Jackson, and Greg stood with their arms crossed, looking at the man Fiona and I had hog-tied on Murphy's barn floor. Seamus had regained consciousness and was glaring at us both, but he hadn't said a word.

That was one thing about the Irish. They knew how to keep their mouths shut.

"So let me get this straight," Greg said like he didn't quite believe us. "You're saying that Alva's boyfriend is actually a man named

Seamus Doyle from Belfast and that he poisoned Alva to get Fiona's attention so that she would lead him to a former IRA member named Kieran?"

"Correct," I said, grateful that my hearing had returned. My ears were still ringing and things sounded ... oddly garbled. But at least I could decipher what was being said.

Greg closed his eyes. I knew he was silently counting to ten. He had to do that a lot when I was around, it seemed.

"He told me there's a tracker on Fiona's truck," I explained. "He was waiting for her to go somewhere out of the norm, thinking it would be to this Kieran guy he thought was here in Rosemary Mountain."

Greg opened his eyes and gave Fiona a hard look. "But you're saying he was mistaken. That you lost track of Kieran years ago."

She shrugged. "Haven't seen Kieran O'Connor since I ran into him at a concert in New York back in the '70s. I'm guessing that, since he was an informant for the British Army, they probably helped him disappear a long time ago. That or the IRA already killed him for being a tout."

Greg shot me an annoyed look. I knew that his sense of justice was battling his obligation as a member of law enforcement.

"So, it's just a big coincidence that Mr. Anderson—Seamus—followed you to the home of a man of similar age who also happens to be from Ireland." Greg turned his gaze to Murphy, staring him down.

Murphy didn't flinch. He'd worked alongside some of the most dangerous members of the IRA. There was nothing Greg Morrison could do to intimidate him.

Fiona spoke up, giving Greg her most innocent look. "Well, of course it's a coincidence. I'm a midwife, aren't I? It's my job to help deliver babies. Right there in the back of the barn, you'll find a new mama with a full litter born last night. My timing was off, but what are you going to do?" She shrugged. "Murphy doesn't keep a phone like any regular person, so he couldn't call me to come early."

Greg pinched the bridge between his eyes. "Right. That makes total sense. You and Daphne called me, Emerson, and Jackson to come out here this morning because you were helping deliver puppies."

"No, because we knew Seamus was following us, you eejit," Fiona said, putting her hands on her hips. "We knew we were in danger and that you wouldn't want us handling it ourselves."

Greg looked back at Fiona and held up a finger like he was going to chew her out. But then his lips twitched and I knew she had won him over.

His face quickly turned serious again, though. He motioned for me and Jackson to step outside the barn with him so that he could speak with us privately.

When we were out of hearing, he sighed. "I believe you—about Seamus, that is. I can charge him for everything that happened today. But it's going to be a hell of a lot harder building a case for Alva's murder, especially since it's his word against a suspect who had the means, motive, and opportunity—and who already confessed. Besides, he has an alibi for the day Alva was murdered. His assistant confirmed it."

"Then the assistant is lying," I said flatly.

"I'm sure she is. He probably paid her off. But we'll have to prove it. We'll get a search warrant for his house and his vehicle. Maybe we'll get lucky. But right now, there's no evidence that he killed Alva."

"I'm not sure," I said, not wanting to get anyone's hopes up. "I think we might have some evidence after all."

"Oh yeah?" Greg cocked his head. "What's that?"

I glanced at Jackson. "Remember when we interviewed him?"

Jackson nodded, puzzled. "Yeah. What about it?"

"I reached over and put my hand on his arm in sympathy. He winced. At the time, I didn't think anything of it—I thought it was an emotional reaction. But when we were tying him up, I saw the skin on his forearm. It looks like it has chemical burns on it."

Jackson's face slowly spread into a grin. "You mean the kind you'd get if you dug up water hemlock and the oils from it touched your skin?"

"Exactly." I grinned back at him. "It looks just like the photos I saw on the internet. I'm guessing he wore gloves, but when he carried it, some of the oil seeped through his sleeve onto his arm."

"It might not be enough for a conviction," Greg warned. "But it's a step toward building a case."

"And it might be enough to make him talk," Jackson pointed out.

"I don't think so," I said, frowning. "I get the feeling he's been trained not to talk to law enforcement. But I'm not sure it matters." An idea was forming.

Jackson gave me a curious look. "What do you mean?"

"We need enough to get Fiona off the hook. Reasonable doubt, right? But what if we don't have to put him away for murder? What if we let the UK prosecute him for Ian's murder instead?"

"If he's not talking to us, he's sure not going to talk to them," Greg pointed out.

"Probably not. But if there was an eyewitness willing to testify... Someone who had a documented history of working with the British Army to stop terrorist attacks on civilians... Would that be enough for immunity for whatever that witness had done, including living under a false identity?"

Greg scratched his head. "Hypothetically, if that person existed... Immunity from being prosecuted for working with the IRA? Almost certainly. Amnesty for coming here on a forged passport? Not in this climate." He leveled a look at me. "The man could probably get a deal to live free and happy in Ireland, but I don't think there's any scenario in which he'd be able to stay in America."

My heart sank.

But the barn door flew open and a raspy voice spoke up, startling us all. "I'll testify and be glad to do it," Murphy said.

Greg crossed his arms. "Eavesdropping, are ya?"

"You're on my property, aren't ya now?" Murphy retorted.

"Fair enough."

"And you'll not have to worry," Murphy continued, leaning heavily on the garden hoe he was using as a makeshift cane. "I didn't come in on a forged passport. The army sorted it all. It was that or leave me to get shot in Belfast, and they knew they might need more information from me in the future. Safer for everyone to make a deal with the Americans to get me out. I've got clean documents—papers, visa, all of it. Murphy's not a false name. It's the new one they gave me."

"You sure?" Greg asked.

"Yeah, I'm sure. I was able to get my green card and then become a naturalized citizen. It's all real."

"No," Greg said, shaking his head. "I mean, are you sure you want to open up this part of your past? Even if you have immunity and citizenship, you're someone who has lived off the grid and alone for a long time. This will require you to step into the spotlight and deal with your past in a way you haven't. It won't be easy."

Murphy looked back into his barn, his eyes landing on Fiona. He smiled and turned back to us. "I think I've lived alone in the dark long enough, yeah?"

I nodded. "I think you both have."

He gave me a serious look. "There was a time when giving her safety was the best thing I could do for her. Then, it seemed like the best thing was to give her space so she could build a new life that didn't remind her so much of everything she'd been through. Now, I think maybe the best thing I could do would be to help her get real justice for Ian."

Greg clapped him on the shoulder. "You're a good man. One of these days, I'd like to hear your whole story."

"Aye." Murphy grinned. "When this is all over, we'll have a pint or three and I'll tell ya the whole thing. As long as you're buyin'."

Greg laughed. "Deal."

50
THE FUTURE

DAPHNE

Rosemary Mountain
Two Weeks Later

Fiona and I sat in her front porch rockers, enjoying a cup of her apple spice tea blend. The fall weather was crisp and beautiful but with enough warm sunshine to feel comfortable outside. Ellie was sitting up in Fiona's lap, jabbering a story in a language only Fiona understood. I was content to simply rock and watch golden leaves flutter down from the trees as I sipped a tea that tasted like Fiona had somehow captured the magic of autumn in a cup.

Ellie finally finished her story by saying, "The end!" as dramatically as possible, then falling back into Fiona's arms as if telling the story had exhausted her.

Fiona chuckled and clapped. "Very good! I loved the part about the princess riding off on the dragon."

Ellie smiled, then sat up again. "Chocolate?" Her eyes were bright and innocent.

"Great idea," Fiona said, helping her slide down to the ground. "You know where it is. Help yourself."

"Let me guess," I said, smirking. "You're the benefactress behind Ellie's secret chocolate stash?"

Fiona looked guilty. "I can't help it. The girl loves her chocolate."

"Says the woman who lectures me on nutrition because I buy granola bars instead of cooking a hot breakfast every morning." I raised my eyebrows and gave her an annoyed look.

"Hey now," Fiona said, pointing her finger at me. "It's one thing to eat a little junk as a treat, but it's another thing altogether to eat it as the most important meal of the day."

"Alright, alright," I said, laughing. "I'm not going to argue with you."

"Good," Fiona said. A sly smile crept onto her face. "You wouldn't want to argue with the woman who's about to invite you on the trip of a lifetime, would you? All expenses paid?"

"Oh really?" I shot her an impressed look. "All expenses paid, huh?"

"That's right. You, Emerson, Ellie—all three of you. I'd like to take you to Ireland with me."

I stopped rocking. "You mean you've decided to go home?"

She took a deep breath. "Well, I can't say it's really home, now, can I? I've lived here far longer than I ever lived there. And Annie isn't in Glenarm, where I grew up, anyway. I'm not certain I want to go back there—I think it might make me too sad. But I want to go to County Cork and visit Annie and Edward and meet their kids and grandkids. And I'd like for you all to go with me."

"That's incredibly generous. But have you considered how much that might cost? I don't—"

She waved me off. "I'm a rich woman now, aren't I? And what else am I going to do with all that money? I have everything I need right here. There's nothing I'd like more than to visit Annie."

"That doesn't mean you have to take us too," I said.

She began putting on her feeble act. "Oh, but Daphne, you

wouldn't send an old woman off by herself like that, would you?" She raised a shaky hand to her forehead. "I don't know that I can even carry my suitcase through the airport by myself. I'm liable to get lost and confused just trying to find my gate, much less navigating a whole different country."

"Oh, stop it," I said, rolling my eyes. "We would be *honored* to go with you. I just feel guilty about you paying."

She snorted. "Well, it's not like *you* can afford it. I imagine a part-time police consultant doesn't make more than a few pennies." She winked at me.

"Yeah, yeah. That's the thanks I get for saving your skin."

She laughed, then gave me that sly smile again. "Murphy sure thanks you for that. He's enjoyed my skin every night this week."

"Fiona!" I gave her a playful smack on the arm. "I don't need to hear that."

"You might," she said, grinning. "Maybe we know some things you don't. Have you ever taken a mustache ri—"

"Stop," I said, drawing out the o. "For the love of God, don't tell me any more. But speaking of Murphy, is he going with us to Ireland?"

"He is, though I've had to hear him gripe entirely too much about leaving his animals behind." She rolled her eyes. "You'd think the man never went anywhere."

"Well, it's been, like, fifty years since he has," I pointed out.

"True," she admitted. "But he'll have to get used to it if he ends up having to testify."

"Yeah, he will," I agreed. Although it didn't look like that was going to be necessary. "If he doesn't, are you okay with Seamus not being tried for Ian's murder?"

"I am," she said. "I've made my peace with it. The past is in the past—I'm ready to move forward."

I squeezed her hand in agreement. We *were* moving forward— and Seamus was going to pay for his crimes one way or another.

Greg and Jackson had found evidence of water hemlock having

been in the back of Seamus's Range Rover, on top of the chemical burns on his arm. They had also broken his alibi and had been able to use geofencing to place him at Alva's house at eleven on the day she died.

Seamus was stubborn and didn't want to talk. But Jackson had done some digging on why Seamus had left Northern Ireland and found some real leverage.

Seamus had worked for the IRA for another ten years before realizing they weren't actually getting anywhere and his luck was going to run out if he kept going. So he created an exit plan and a new identity: Neal Anderson from New Zealand, a country with an accent that people frequently confused with accents from the UK, Scotland, and Ireland. He stole a significant amount of money from the IRA and fled to the south, then robbed a bank in Dublin before flying to America on forged documents. With his money and charm, he'd lived successfully in America for decades—and used his former skills to work off the books for some very bad people.

So Greg showed him the evidence and gave him a choice: confess, plead guilty, and serve out his time in a federal prison or keep his mouth shut and force a trial, risking potential extradition to the UK, where he'd almost certainly end up in prison with the men he'd stolen from and betrayed.

In the end, it wasn't much of a choice. In my opinion, that was another form of justice. He'd made Fiona feel like she only had one option. I thought it fitting that he had been put in the same position.

So he confessed and explained everything.

His affair with Alva had been real. It was fate, in his mind, that on his first trip to his new lover's home, he had seen a framed photograph of a girl he immediately recognized: Fiona Ó Flannagáin, the woman who he believed had outsmarted him.

He was smooth and managed to ask Alva about her without raising suspicion, confirming he was right about her identity. With champagne flowing freely, Alva had happily chattered about her friend, telling him about how Fiona was from Ireland and had moved to Rosemary Mountain in the '70s.

His original plan was to find out enough to locate Fiona and kill her. But Alva kept talking, enjoying his attention, and happened to mention that Fiona had moved here with another chap from Ireland —a real quiet fellow who had built her stone cottage by hand.

Seamus knew that it couldn't be a coincidence. Kieran, a stonemason in Northern Ireland, had disappeared just days after Fiona had. He was the one who'd insisted they uphold the bargain and let her go, and everyone around them knew he was half in love with her.

Seamus thought he must have been in on the whole thing and killing Fiona was no longer enough. He wanted Kieran too. But there was a problem—there was absolutely no trace of a Kieran O'Connor in Rosemary Mountain, and even Alva said she had no idea where "the mountain man" lived. He was a crazy loner, she said. She'd met him a few times in the late '70s and early '80s but hadn't spoken to him in decades. She only remembered that he had long hair and a full beard. But he was still around here somewhere. He'd built Fiona a new stone garden bed just that spring.

Seamus became obsessed with his desire for revenge. He considered interrogating Fiona for Kieran's location but quickly discarded the idea. After all, she hadn't flinched when she'd lied to him about Lieutenant Montgomery. She was as stone cold as if she'd been in the IRA herself. She'd never give Kieran up.

Instead, he started watching her house and following her, hoping she'd lead him to Kieran. He rented one of the hunting cabins on the lane using a false name, a disguise, and a beater truck, so that if anyone noticed him, they wouldn't connect him to Alva's boyfriend.

Meanwhile, he pretended to be madly in love with Alva to keep plying her for information. Most of their relationship was over the phone. He only had to be available in person one week a month to keep up the ruse.

When he finally realized following Fiona would get him

nowhere, he decided to take drastic measures and draw her out with the one thing that would terrify her: her own plan for killing Lieutenant Montgomery.

He waited until a day Alva had told him Fiona was visiting, then ditched his disguise and surprised Alva with an unexpected visit. He brewed the tea that killed her, then put some of the dried hemlock in the jar Fiona had brought, knowing that Alva's greedy nephew would leap at the opportunity to throw Fiona under the bus. He needed the police to question Fiona and tell her what was going on, but he knew that the evidence was weak enough that the odds of Fiona actually being arrested and held without bond were almost nothing. After all, he needed her free to lead him to Kieran.

The flaw in his plan was that he had no idea Fiona believed she'd killed Lieutenant Montgomery. He never could have predicted that decades of guilt would cause her to confess to a murder she hadn't committed—or that she wouldn't realize someone had actually murdered Alva, much less that Seamus had done it.

He'd meant to scare her into a trap. But in the end? He'd started an investigation that cleared up decades of misunderstanding and opened up Fiona's entire future. And while she and I *had* walked into his trap, we'd also walked right back out of it.

He'd underestimated Fiona Flanagan—again.

Now, he had another choice to make, although I couldn't tell Fiona about it yet.

Greg had asked the DA to offer Seamus a reduced sentence of just five years, in exchange for the location of Ian's remains so that Fiona could finally bury her husband properly. The DA had agreed that morning and was scheduled to present the deal to him that afternoon.

Greg and Jackson were both confident he would take it.

But what Seamus didn't realize was that we'd set a trap of our own. Yes, he'd serve just five years for Alva's murder—but the Feds had already started an investigation into his business dealings and planned on charging him with a long list of other crimes committed on U.S. soil. The deal didn't cover those.

We knew he'd try to wiggle his way out of those charges, but it didn't really matter. We were fine with him only getting five years. Because as soon as he finished serving time in America, the UK would request his extradition and try him for his crimes in Northern Ireland—and by giving up the location of Ian's remains, they'd have a slam-dunk case there too.

He'd never be a free man again.

51
THE MOST POWERFUL MEDICINE

FIONA

Rosemary Mountain
Three weeks later

I buttoned a thick cardigan over my housedress, slipped my feet into my green wellies, then gathered the supplies I kept on my back porch. My round wicker basket, stained with a hundred harvests. My Hori Hori gardening knife with the serrated edge and a shape that doubled as a digger. My small pruners, the perfect size for taking cuttings. I smiled at the sight of all of them. They were the tools of an herbalist, the tools of a *bean feasa*.

The tools of a calling that had been the greatest honor of my life.

I pushed the screened porch door open and stepped down into my garden, pausing at the bottom of the steps to close my eyes and take a deep breath. Even though I'd experienced it a thousand times, I still found myself surprised and grateful by the beauty of dawn on a late autumn day. The trees and the rocks seemed to sing a different tune every season, but this one was my favorite.

Slow down, they seemed to whisper. *The hard work of summer is over. The harvest is gathered, and it's time to gather close with loved ones. The slow season is coming. It's time to rest. Isn't it lovely to let go?*

"Yes," I spoke aloud, smiling at the trees who wore dresses of gold, rubies, and citrine—dresses they worked so hard to produce but never tried to hold. Every autumn, they let their most beautiful creation fall to the ground and slowly transform into the nutrients that would feed the trees in a future season.

I'd bet that half our human problems came from trying to hold too tightly to what we were never meant to keep. We humans held the knowledge, but the rest of creation seemed to have us beat when it came to wisdom.

"Hello, my friend," I sang, greeting the garden spider who'd made her web on one of my trellises. "And hello, little one," I sang to the toad who'd buried himself in one of my pots to keep warm, with just his wee head poking out of the soil. They were all my friends, these other tiny souls who shared this space. No one could ever be lonely in a garden. There was a wealth of friendship to be found there.

I'd been given a wealth of good human friends these past few years as well, and I was so grateful for each and every one of them that sometimes it felt like my heart would burst.

I climbed the hill behind my garden, one step at a time, annoyed at the ache in my knees that seemed to get a little worse every year. But my destination was worth it, so I'd deal with the achy joints and make a cup of meadowsweet tea when I got home to soothe them.

The sky grew lighter with every step, and when I finally reached the hawthorn I'd come to visit, the clearing was lit up with a beautiful early morning glow.

"Hello, old friend," I said, putting my basket on the ground and walking up to stroke the leaves of the beautiful tree. "I've come to ask for some of your berries."

Once again, all these years later, it felt like the tree somehow spoke directly to my heart. *You're always welcome to them.*

"I know," I whispered. "But they're not for someone else this time. I've come to ask for myself."

Is your heart broken, bean feasa?

I smiled. "No. Not anymore."

You're welcome to the berries just the same. But if your heart isn't broken, why do you need them?

I took a deep breath. "My heart was shattered a long time ago. I put it back together slowly. It took a long time, but it healed. But even though it healed, I kept it closed—at least partly."

I looked down, trying to figure out how to explain it. "I thought I had done something horribly wrong. I thought I had to be punished for it. Maybe I still do—I intended to do wrong. That's sin enough."

You do love to beat yourself up. The leaves of the tree rippled with the wry humor I often sensed from this particular one.

"Yes, well... I'm trying to let go of that," I said, smirking. "And I'm trying to open up my heart to things I never thought I'd have again. Love. Family. Forgiveness for my enemies."

Will you include yourself on that list? Will you forgive yourself for intending harm so many years ago?

Tears pricked my eyes. "I'm trying."

You've always been able to see the value in everything around you—human, plant, and animal alike. Yet you've never believed you were worthy of the same grace. You healed from sadness, but you never healed from that.

You are loved. You have always been loved, even in your darkest moments. You have never needed to earn it.

Take my berries and make your tea, and may they open your heart to every good gift that is waiting for you. Forgive yourself, bean feasa. Love and be loved. Love is the most powerful healer of all, more powerful than all the plant medicine combined.

Tears streamed down my cheeks from the truth of the words—and from the pure love I felt radiating all around me.

I lifted my face to the sky and breathed a prayer of gratitude from the depths of my soul. Then I picked up my basket and began to fill it with dark, tender berries.

While I did, I thought of Mamó, and Annie, and even Ian ... and of a little village in Northern Ireland, where the sea raged and then turned to emeralds.

I thought of Murphy and how beautiful it was to be loved by someone who knew the worst things you'd done and loved you anyway.

I thought of Daphne's sweet mother, how she'd once been like a daughter to me, and how grateful I was that Daphne had come back to Rosemary Mountain and given me the gift of family again.

I marveled over how unbelievable it was that she'd found Annie alive and well, and that I would soon reunite with my sister on the island that still sang to my soul. That I'd soon meet nieces and nephews and have a whole new family to love.

I thought of how Christmas would soon be here and how beautiful it would be this year, spending it surrounded by my chosen family—a family that continued expanding and growing in ways I never would have imagined.

I thought of spiders and toads and falling leaves and the snow that would soon come ... and of how we'd soon shift out of the dark of winter into days that kept growing longer and brighter, leading us to beautiful springtime and summer's sunshine.

I thought of all this, and more, and I smiled.

Thank you for reading Fiona's story!
Adore Fiona? Me too! Sign up for my mailing list and receive a free BONUS scene plus a recipe for Fiona's Hawthorn Tea.

Can't get enough Rosemary Mountain? Read Greg and Janet's story in *Mountain Shadows*, the first book in the Rosemary Mountain Romantic Suspense series!

If you enjoyed this book, I would so appreciate you taking the time to leave a review at your preferred vendor. It truly means the world.

AUTHOR'S NOTE

Ireland is in my soul. Many of my ancestors hailed from there. Long before I knew that, I saw video footage of Ireland and nearly wept, overcome with the feeling of *home*. But to this day, I've never set foot on Irish soil. Every time I've made travel plans to go, something has happened that has forced me to cancel (hello, pandemic and travel restrictions!). I think that's why I wrote Fiona's character as an exile from Ireland from the very beginning. She always represented a part of me who loved Ireland and considered it home, but didn't live there. And, for reasons you now know, she couldn't go back—no matter how much she longed for it.

I hinted at Fiona's past in the original Rosemary Mountain books, but I wasn't sure if I would ever write her story. It felt too tragic, too heartbreaking for the series. After all, her story didn't have a happy ending. But it wouldn't let me go, and eventually I knew not only did I have to write it, but that it would be the most important book I'd written thus far. You may not feel that way, and that's okay —I know this is a book that will resonate deeply with some and not at all with others. I needed to write it anyway.

Nearly everything Fiona and Ian went through really happened during that time period. I used historical events to dictate the course of their time in Belfast. The rioting, the bombings, Falls Curfew, internment without trial, tarring and feathering, kneecapping, killing suspected informants—all of these things were based on very real history.

Republican paramilitaries are known to have killed at least 68 informants during the Troubles, 17 of whom are known as "The Disappeared." These individuals were executed and secretly buried. Four of them have never been found. (Williams and Leahy 2022) (Press Association 2024)

I did a significant amount of research for this book; however, I think it's important to note that it is, in the end, a work of fiction and should not be read as a historical account. The Troubles were real, but the characters in *Poison in the Tea* are not. I tried to ensure that the names I chose were not associated with any big names from that time, but I'm also aware that I wasn't able to cover every single news article or book written. Please know that any coincidence with any real person or situation is unintentional. The characters and the murder plot(s) in this story were created from my imagination.

The other reason why this story should not be taken as a historical account is because writers cannot help but write from their own lens, just as readers will read the book through theirs. I wasn't even alive when the events of this book took place; I certainly didn't go through them myself. I wrote a story about the troubles in Belfast, but I wasn't writing through the lens of someone who actually went through them—I was writing through the lens of someone living in America in 2025. Make of that what you will.

This was a sad, heavy book to write, and I know that, for many of you, it will have been a sad, heavy book to read. But I hope, at the end, that you are left feeling hopeful—and loved.

As Fiona once said in *Murder on the Mountain*, "Love is never stupid, and it's never wasted. It's the most powerful force on earth. Your love will make a difference. You may never know or see it, but it will, because that's what love does."

For further reading about the Troubles, I highly recommend:

- "Only Wounded" by Patrick Taylor
- "Say Nothing: A True Story of Murder and Memory in Northern Ireland" by Patrick Radden Keefe (recently made into a gripping drama series for Hulu)

REFERENCES

2025. CAIN: Key Events of the Northern Ireland Conflict. https://cain.ulster.ac.uk/events/index.html.

Keefe, Patrick R. 2019. *Say Nothing: A True Story of Murder and Memory in Northern Ireland*. N.p.: Knopf Doubleday Publishing Group.

McGreevy, Ronan. 2019. "How the Troubles began: a timeline – The Irish Times." The Irish Times. https://www.irishtimes.com/news/ireland/irish-news/how-the-troubles-began-a-timeline-1.3987076.

Press Association. 2024. "Families of the Disappeared victims of the Troubles appeal for help to end their pain." *The Journal* (Belfast), November 2, 2024. https://www.thejournal.ie/disappeared-victims-of-the-troubles-families-appeal-6530997-Nov2024/.

Williams, Eleanor Leah, and Thomas Leahy. 2022. "The 'Unforgivable'?: Irish Republican Army (IRA) informers and dealing with Northern Ireland conflict legacy, 1969-2021." *Intelligence and National Security* 38, no. 3 (August): 470-90. 10.1080/02684527.2022.2104000.

ACKNOWLEDGMENTS

I'm incredibly grateful for the team that supports me as I write every book.

Thanks to Camille for your encouragement and valuable feedback—and for being a safe place for authentic conversation about the toughest issues. You are amazing.

Thanks to Abbey for encouraging me to write this one even though it meant pausing another series, for always being there when I needed a sounding board, and for making me laugh on the heaviest writing days. I just adore you.

Thanks to Mickey, my editor, for your hard work and dedication. This novel came at the worst time for you, yet you made it happen and finished ahead of schedule—I am amazed by you!

Thanks to Jessica, my lovely beta reader, for your enthusiasm, support, and helpful feedback. Knowing that I can always count on you is such a gift.

As we wrap up 2025, I'd like to express my thanks to Juniper Tree Meadery and Weber's Book House for their support. These NEA businesses have been so kind and encouraging, and have shared my books with so many local readers. My heart aches to see Weber's close this fall. Support and shop local, my friends.

Acknowledgements for a book featuring Fiona would not be complete without thanking the herbal mentors and teachers I've had over the years: Juliet Blankespore, founder of The Chestnut School of Herbal Medicine; the entire Chestnut team, the Herbal Academy of New England (now known simply as Herbal academy); Asia Suler;

jim mcdonald; the late John Gallagher; Rosalee de la Forêt; and the legendary Rosemary Gladstar, for whom Rosemary Mountain is named. And while I didn't have the privilege of learning herbalism from her, I'd like to acknowledge the legacy left by my Nonnie, the woman who could cure just about anything with a poultice.

Thank you to my children, Aiden and Will, for being amazing cheerleaders and for helping me in a thousand ways this year.

Finally, thanks always to my husband, Brandon. You are an incredible partner, and I fall more in love with you every year. You're the gold standard—better than any MMC I've ever written.

ABOUT THE AUTHOR

Nicole Gardner lives in NE Arkansas with her husband, their two sons, and their two crazy dogs. If she's not at her desk, you'll likely find her either in the garden, or creating teas and tinctures in the kitchen.

Nicole's background is in psychology. This fascination with human behavior and relationship dynamics plays a significant role in her writing and the way she shapes her characters.

www.nicolegardnerbooks.com